KU-591-162

The ANGEL'S COMMAND

Other books by Brian Jacques

Redwall

Mossflower

Mattimeo

Mariel of Redwall

Salamandastron

Martin the Warrior

The Bellmaker

Outcast of Redwall

Pearls of Lutra

The Long Patrol

Marlfox

The Legend of Luke

Lord Brocktree

Triss

The Great Redwall Feast

The Redwall Map and Riddler

Redwall Friend and Foe

Build Your Own Redwall Abbey

Castaways of the Flying Dutchman

Seven Strange and Ghostly Tales

BRIAN JACQUES

The ANGEL'S COMMAND

A Tale from the
CASTAWAYS *of the*
FLYING DUTCHMAN

Illustrated by DAVID ELLIOT

PUFFIN

PUFFIN BOOKS

Published by the Penguin Group
Penguin Books Ltd, 80 Strand, London WC2R 0RL, England
Penguin Putnam Inc., 375 Hudson Street, New York, New York 10014, USA
Penguin Books Australia Ltd, 250 Camberwell Road, Camberwell, Victoria 3124, Australia
Penguin Books Canada Ltd, 10 Alcorn Avenue, Toronto, Ontario, Canada M4V 3B2
Penguin Books India (P) Ltd, 11 Community Centre, Panchsheel Park,
New Delhi – 110 017, India
Penguin Books (NZ) Ltd, Cnr Rosedale and Airborne Roads, Albany, Auckland,
New Zealand
Penguin Books (South Africa) (Pty) Ltd, 24 Sturdee Avenue, Rosebank 2196, South Africa

Penguin Books Ltd, Registered Offices: 80 Strand, London WC2R 0RL, England

www.penguin.com

First published in the USA by Philomel Books, a division of Penguin Putnam Books for
Young Readers 2003
First published in Great Britain in hardback in Puffin Books 2003
2

Set in Dutch 766 BT

Made and printed in England by Clays Ltd, St Ives plc

British Library Cataloguing in Publication Data
A CIP catalogue record for this book is available from the British Library

ISBN 0-670-91323-5

HE LEGEND OF THE *FLYING DUTCHMAN* is known to all men who follow the seafaring trade. Captain Vanderdecken and his ghostly crew, bound by heaven's curse to sail the world's vast oceans and seas, for eternity! The curse was delivered by the angel of the Lord, who descended from the firmament to the very deck of the doomed vessel. Vanderdecken and his evil crew were bound, both living and dead, to an endless voyage. Only two were to escape the *Flying Dutchman* – a mute, ragged orphan boy, Ben, and his faithful dog, Ned. They were the only two aboard who were pure of heart, innocent of all wickedness.

The angel had washed them both overboard in a storm off Cape Horn – castaways of the *Flying Dutchman*! Barely alive, they came ashore at Tierra del Fuego, the tip of South America. Unfortunately, they, too, were casualties of the angel's curse, destined to live endlessly, without growing older by a single day. However, heaven, being merciful, decreed that Ben was granted the power of speech in any language. Additionally he could communicate with the dog by process of thought. Thus began a friendship that was to last through many centuries. Given refuge by an old shepherd who lived on Tierra del Fuego, the two remained with the old man until his death, three years later. It was then that the angel commanded them to travel on – their mission, to do good and help others wherever the need arose.

And so they went forth, this strange blue-eyed lad and his faithful black Labrador, orphans of the mighty waters, travelling the world together. Never stopping too long in one place, where folk they befriended would grow older and die, for Ben and Ned were eternally young. Wandering endlessly, commanded by an angel. Haunted by Vanderdecken's spectre, they went north, up into the wild and untamed jungles, mountains and savannahs of South America's wild continent. What adventures, untold sights and perils awaited our friends! This narrative follows their rov-ings after several years. Fate landed Ben and Ned back again near the sea, the Caribbean, whose coasts were home to lawless men. The buccaneers!

I take up my pen to tell you the tale.

Book One

LA PETITE MARIE

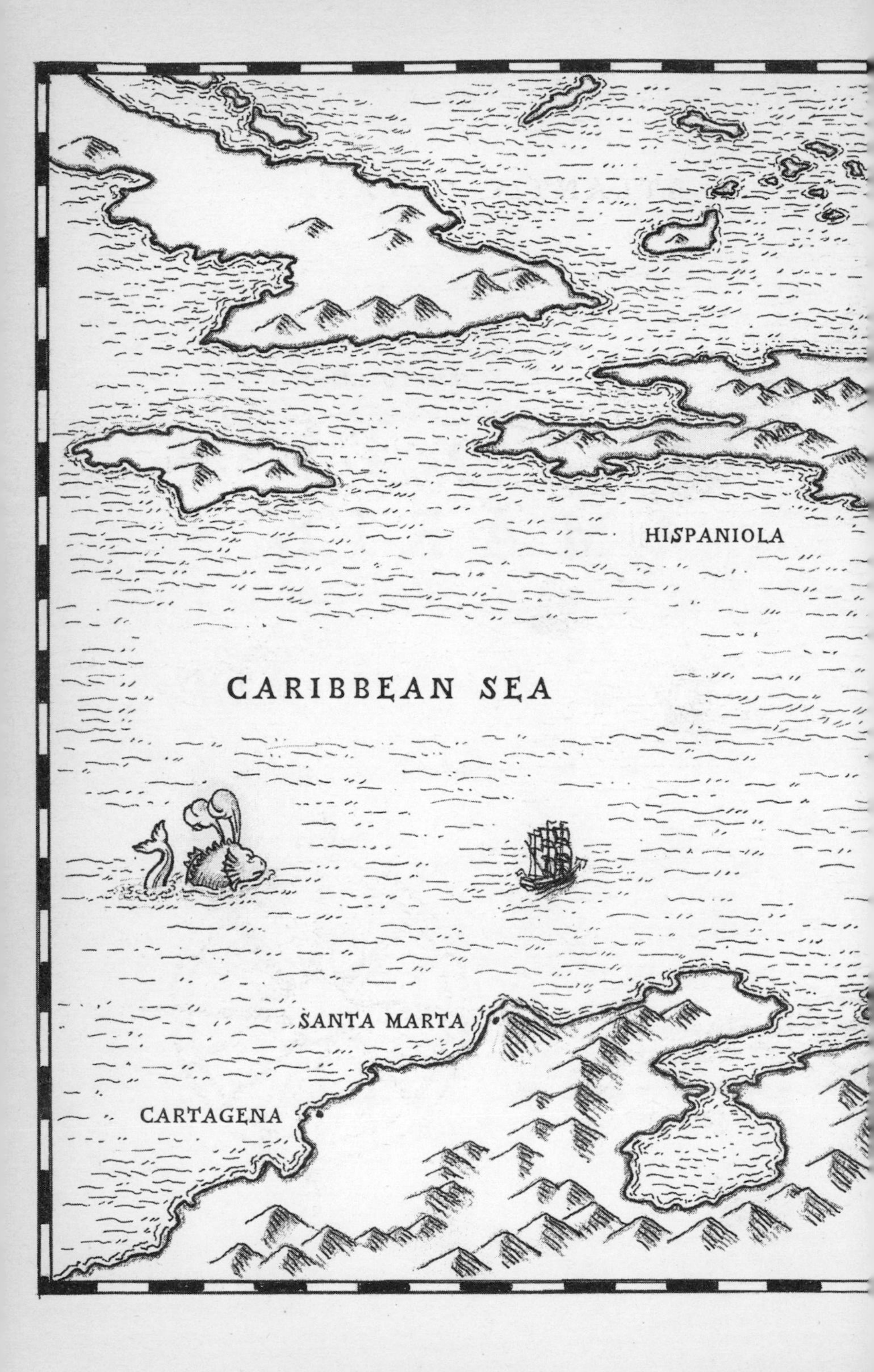
HISPANIOLA
CARIBBEAN SEA
SANTA MARTA
CARTAGENA

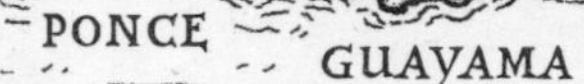
ATLANTIC OCEAN
MONA PASSAGE
PUERTO RICO
PONCE
GUAYAMA

CARTAGENA, 1628

GREAT AND GOLDEN, like an enormous, newly minted doubloon, the Caribbean sun

presided over the waterfront. Ships of all nations, from salt-crusted skiffs to stately galleons, bobbed on their moorings, each craft facing bow onto the harbour wall. Children clambered and played upon the bronze cannons fronting the jade and aquamarine waters of the wide Caribbean Sea. Along the dusty quayfront fishing boats unloaded their catches straight to the stalls. Noise and bustle were everywhere. Women sold plantains, melons, coconuts and an amazing variety of exotic fruits and vegetables. Parrots squawked and monkeys chattered from their cages of split bamboo. Men squatted in the shade, bargaining for spices, rum, snuff and tobacco. Young girls danced and sang to the music of guitars and drums, cajoling coins from passers-by.

High in its ornate tower, the bell of Santa Magdalena clanged dully over the red-tiled and palm-thatched dwellings, which ranged from austere Spanish architecture to bedraggled local hovels. Taverns, bodegas and inns were packed to the doors with laughing, brawling, arguing and drunken seafarers, pirates, free-booters, corsairs and buccaneers, known collectively in Cartagena as The Brotherhood – those beyond the law of honest men.

Ben and Ned sat among the trees, where it was relatively peaceful and free from trampling feet. After travelling alone in sparsely populated regions of South America for so long, they had been watching the teeming life of the quayside for fully an hour, both rather taken aback by this sudden surge of noisy humanity. The big black Labrador passed a single thought to his tow-headed young companion.

"Well, are you hungry enough to go and explore yet?"

The boy smiled into his friend's moist, dark eyes. "It would be a nice change to eat something cooked by somebody else besides myself. Come on, Ned, let's take a look."

The dog pondered his companion's thought for a moment, then rose gracefully and returned the mental comment. "Hmph! If I had hands instead of paws I'd make a wonderful cook. I can't help being a dog, you know."

Ben patted Ned's head affectionately, answering the thought. "I'll wager you'd be the world's best cook, just as you're the nicest dog on earth!"

The black Labrador's tail wagged. "Oh, you're just saying that because it's true. Follow me. I'll sniff out the place where the food smells good."

People did not pay much attention to the pair as they strolled along the harbour street, a tow-haired lad of about fourteen years, dressed in an old blue shirt that lacked buttons and a pair of once-white canvas trousers, tattered and frayed at the hems, walking barefoot alongside a big black dog. Ned threaded his way between crates of live, clucking chickens and barrels of still-slithering, silver-scaled fish. They skirted a crowd who was watching an entertainer wrap live snakes about his body. Ben stopped to watch the performance, but Ned tugged at his shirt-tail. "What d'you want to do, watch street shows or eat? Come on!"

Ben obediently followed the dog, his eyes drinking in the colourful spectacle of crowded humanity as he went.

Ned halted at the front doors of Cartagena's biggest water-front tavern and winked one eye at Ben. "Someone's roasting beef in there, my mouth's watering!"

Ben's strange, clouded blue eyes stared up at the swinging sign. Crude artwork depicted a grinning jaguar taking a bath in a barrel of rum. Below this in scrolled lettering was the name Rhum Tigre. The whole aspect of the tavern was that it might once have been the home of some prosperous Spanish merchant, now converted into a drinking den with upstairs accommodation for paying guests. Ben hesitated, doubtful as to whether he should enter. Sounds of a fiddle and hoarse voices discordantly singing rowdy ditties emanated over the babble of gossiping seamen within. Ned sat scratching behind his ear with a blunt-clawed back leg, communicating mentally.

"Enter, callow youth, if thou art not afeared!"

Ben shifted from one foot to the other, and he shrugged. "Easy for you to say, mate, but I'm the one who'll get thrown out if they find we have no money."

Ned was still in a playfully encouraging mood as he replied, "Tut tut, m'boy, leave this to your trusty hound!"

He rose and trotted inside, with Ben sending urgent thoughts after him. "Ned! Come back here . . . wait!"

The dog's mental answer floated back to him. "Money's never stopped us so far, Ben. Faint heart never won roast beef. Woof! Just look at that carcass on the spit!"

Ben shouldered his way in through a gang of departing men. The moment he stepped inside, he froze. Faces were all around him, faces like those he had encountered aboard the *Flying Dutchman,* unwashed, unshaven, gap-toothed, tattooed and brass-earringed. Scowling, grinning wickedly, slit-eyed, broken-nosed, knife-scarred ruffians – faces like those which returned sometimes to haunt his dreams. Ben stood rooted to the spot, seemingly unable to move, until Ned tugged at his shirtsleeve, growling as he mentally reassured his friend. "Step lively, mate, they won't harm us. I felt the same as you when I came in here, but my stomach got the better of me. Look over there!"

The object of Ned's desire was a cavernous old fireplace where, over a bed of glowing charcoal, two cooks were slowly turning a spit on which was transfixed an entire side of beef. Juices and fat from the roasting meat popped and sizzled as they dripped onto the flames. Every now and then, the cooks would stop turning the spit. Using long, sharp knives they would slice off a chunk of beef for a customer, pocketing the coins they were given. Ben felt his stomach grumble aloud at the sight. He was very hungry.

Ned chuckled mentally at him. "Ho ho, I hear a gurgling gut, a sure remedy for any fears."

Ben stroked the Labrador's silky ears. "So you do, but a gurgling gut with empty pockets isn't much use. What d'you suggest?"

The fireplace was constructed in the centre of the room. Through the flames could be seen a bar area and some tables. Something was going on at the largest table, where onlookers were gathered round to watch whatever it was.

Ned began tugging Ben towards the table, passing a message. "Let's see if we can't pick up a coin or two over yonder."

The crews of two pirate ships, the *Diablo Del Mar* and *La Petite Marie*, were watching their captains gambling. Rocco Madrid, master of the *Diablo*, was winning, and Raphael Thuron, master of *La Petite Marie*, was losing, heavily. Rocco's sword, a fine blade of Toledo steel with a silver basketed handle, lay on the table. Behind it was an ever-growing pile of gold coins from many nations. The Spanish captain played idly with his long, grey-streaked black curls, smiling thinly as he watched Thuron. "Make your choice, amigo, where is the pea?"

Thuron, the French captain, stroked his rough brown beard with heavy, club-nailed fingers, his eyes roving over the three down-turned walnut shells lying on the table between them. He flicked Rocco a hate-laden glance, growling, "Don't hurry me, Madrid!"

Sighing heavily, Thuron looked at the dwindling pile of coins, which were stacked behind the blade of his cutlass on the opposite side of the table. He bit his lip and concentrated his gaze on the three walnut shells, while Rocco Madrid drummed his fingers on the tabletop.

"I am not hurrying you, amigo. Shall I take my siesta while you try to find our little friend the pea, eh?"

The *Diablo*'s crew chuckled appreciatively at their captain's witty observation. The more gold Thuron lost, the slower and more deliberate he became.

The French captain spoke without looking up from the three nutshells. "Huh, the little pea might be your friend, but she's no friend o' mine, not after ten losses in a row!"

Rocco twirled his waxed moustache, enjoying his opponent's

discomfiture. "Who knows, the little pea, she might change her mind and fall in love with you. Choose, amigo."

Thuron made a snap decision. He turned up the shell that lay in the centre of the three. It was empty, no pea lay under it. A cheer went up from the *Diablo*'s crew, and groans from the men of *La Petite Marie*. Thuron separated five stacks of gold coins from his meagre pile, swiping them towards the Spaniard with the back of his hand.

One of the coins fell from the table and clinked upon the floor. Ned was on to it like a hawk on a dove. Diving beneath the table, he took the coin in his mouth. Madrid held out his open hand to the dog, rapping out sharply, "Here! Give!"

Ned ignored the Spaniard, turning his big dark eyes towards Thuron. The Frenchman liked the dog immediately. He, too, held out his hand, speaking in a friendly voice. "Who owns this good fellow?"

Ben moved up alongside Thuron. "I do, sir. His name's Ned."

Communicating mentally with the Labrador, Ben sent him a message. "Give him the coin. I like him better than that other one."

Ned wagged his tail. "So do I. Here you are, sir!" He dropped the coin into the French captain's palm.

The Spaniard snarled as he reached for his sword. "That's mine, give it here!"

Thuron grinned and winked at Ben. Taking a fresh gold piece from the small pile, he flicked it to Rocco Madrid. "Take this one. The boy's dog earned that gold piece. You, lad, what's your name? Speak up."

The boy tipped a finger to his forehead. "Ben, sir!"

Thuron took the coin and spun it in the air. Ben caught it

deftly and awaited orders. The Frenchman nodded approvingly. "Get me some of that meat and some ale, too. Keep the change. Get something for yourself and the dog."

Ben thanked Thuron and passed a message to Ned. "Come on, pal, let's sample the beef!"

Ned replied as he stood on his hind legs, placing both front paws on the table alongside the French captain. "You go, Ben, I'll stay here and watch. That Spaniard is too lucky for my liking. See if you can get me a bone, with plenty of meat and fat on it."

Captain Thuron stroked the black Labrador's silky ears. "Leave Ned here with me, Ben. I've got a feeling he's lucky."

Ben elbowed his way through the tavern customers and went to get the food. The cook gave him two healthy slices of roast beef, laying each one on a crusty slice of bread. He added two large ribs dripping with hot fat and thick with meat. Ben purchased the ale and pocketed the small coins that made up the change. When he returned to the table he noticed that the Frenchman's pile of gold had grown even smaller. Ned's thought informed him, "He's lost again. That Spaniard's cheating."

Madrid eyed the food and stood up. "Excuse me, amigo, that meat looks good. Let's take a break while I get some."

Rocco's bosun, a thickset Portuguese, interrupted. "I'll get it for you, Cap'n."

The Spaniard picked up his sword. "No, I'll get it myself. I like to select my own meat. You keep an eye on my gold."

Members of the two crews went along, tempted by the sight of the beef. There was a lull in the game. Ned explained to Ben about Rocco Madrid's dishonesty. "My eyes are quicker than most – I saw him palm the pea. After he's shuffled the shells about, there's nothing under any of them. Then when he has to pick up his own shell, he palms the pea back onto the table, as if it had been lying under the shell. That Spaniard is quick and clever."

Thuron had been watching the boy and the dog looking silently at each other. He finished chewing and spoke. "I was hoping your Ned would change my luck, Ben, but it seems I'm bound to lose. Blast his eyes, Madrid has all the luck today! Hey, boy, are you listening to me?"

Moving slightly closer, Ben murmured out of the corner of his mouth so that the remaining crew members of the *Diablo Del Mar,* at the other side of the table, could not hear. "Don't look at me, sir, keep your eyes straight ahead and listen to what I say . . ."

Rocco Madrid had carved the beef with his own sword. He ate it at the bar and drank a glass of red wine. Fastidiously wiping his lips on a silk kerchief, he returned to the gaming table, where Thuron sat waiting. Placing his sword back on the table, Madrid smiled affably. "So then, my good amigo, you wish to continue playing. Bueno. Maybe the little pea will come your way this time."

Madrid placed the pea upon the table and covered it with the centre one of the three down-turned walnut shells. Ben watched closely as the Spaniard's long fingers began deftly moving the shells, right to left, left to right, centre to side, side to centre. Then he saw the trick. The shells were moving so fast that he almost missed it. Rocco shifted the shells so skilfully that at one point the shell with the pea beneath it went slightly over the lip of the table. The pea was flicked out into his lap, almost faster than the eye could follow.

Ned's thought cut into Ben's mind. "See, I told you! Now all he has to do is drop his hand and jam the pea between his fingers, while our friend is sitting there deciding which shell to choose. When he makes his pick, there'll be nothing beneath it. The Spaniard will make his choice then, skilfully dropping in the pea as he overturns the shell, and there he has it, a winner again, eh?"

Ben patted the black Labrador's head. "Not this time though."

Rocco sat back, the same thin smile on his lips as he announced confidently, "Make your play, Capitano Thuron. How much this time?"

Thuron's first mate and his bosun had edged their way around the table until they were standing on either side of Rocco Madrid. Thuron leaned forward, eyeing the sly Spaniard levelly. "That gold there, your side o' the table. How much d'ye reckon you've got there, my friend?"

Rocco shrugged. "Who knows, amigo, it would take quite a time to count it all up. So, are you going to play?"

Thuron smiled then. "Aye, I'm going to play. There's more gold aboard my ship, you know that. So let's stop messing about with small wagers. I'm going to bet all I've got against what lies on this table. One chance, winner takes all!"

Rocco Madrid could not resist the invitation. "You are a real gambler, amigo. I accept your wager, eh!" He looked up to his crew for approval, immediately sensing all was not well as he saw the bosun and first mate of *La Petite Marie* hemming him in.

Thuron had one hand beneath the table. He smiled roguishly at his adversary. "There's a dagger either side of you and a loaded musket pointed at your belly from my side. I'm betting there's no pea under any of those three shells. Don't move a muscle, Cap'n Madrid! Ben, lad, turn the shells over!" The boy swiftly did as he was bid. There was, of course, no pea. Sweat ran in rivulets down the Spaniard's sallow face.

The entire tavern had grown silent. All that could be heard was the crackle of beef drippings spilling onto the fire. There was death in Thuron's voice. "Sit still, Madrid. You don't want to get that pea lying in your lap covered with blood. You, *Diablo* crew, don't be foolish. There's no sense in dying because your captain's a cheat. Stay still and you won't come to any harm. The game's over, I win! Anaconda, pick up that gold!"

Captain Thuron's steersman, Anaconda, was a black giant with a huge shaven head. He shrugged off a linen shirt, displaying awesome muscles. With a few swift moves he swept the gold coins inside his shirt and knotted it into an impromptu carrier.

Rocco Madrid's lips scarcely moved as he sneered at Raphael Thuron. "You will not get away with this, my friend!"

Thuron stood, his musket still pointed at the Spaniard. "Oh yes I will . . . my friend. Right, lads, back out, stern first. Anybody makes a move, take no notice of them. Just kill their capitano. Ben, you'd best come with me, for the good of your health. Bring my lucky dog too!"

Ben felt Ned's thought penetrate his mind. "Do as he says, mate. This place isn't safe any more!"

Once they were out on the quayside, the entire crew of *La Petite Marie* took to their heels and ran for it. Ben and Ned found themselves up front, with Thuron and his giant steersman. A cart of oranges was overturned, and some chickens broke loose from their cages as the mass of fleeing pirates dashed through the crowd. The singing girls began screaming, and the snake performer dropped his reptiles.

Thuron bawled towards a trim three-masted vessel lying bow onto the harbour. "Make sail! Make sail! We're coming aboard! Make sail there!"

As he clattered up the steep gangplank, Ben could see the crew members on watch clambering into the rigging, whilst others loosed the ship's headropes. There was a small culverin in the bows. The captain roared out orders for it to be loaded. He knelt by the little swivel cannon, beckoning Ben to his side. "We'll blow them off the quay if they try to follow. Hand me that tow!"

Ben saw the thick, smouldering rope end and passed it over to Thuron.

Ned sent a thought to Ben. "I hadn't figured on going to sea again, ever!"

The boy replied mentally to his dog, "We've no choice. It's either that or stay in Cartagena and get killed." He turned to Thuron. "D'you think they'll follow us, Cap'n?"

The Frenchman held the burning tow near the culverin's touch hole, nodding. "Maybe not right away, boy, but he'll be coming after us. Rocco Madrid lost a lot of face today. By the way, how did you know he was cheating? I just thought I was extra unlucky today."

Ben knew it would be futile trying to explain about Ned, so he lied. "I've seen that game played before. As soon as I came to your table, I saw Captain Madrid palming the pea. Where are we bound, sir?"

Raphael Thuron threw an arm around the boy's shoulder. "Home to la belle France, thanks to you. I'm finally set for good. This pirating life is too dangerous, my friend!"

ONCE *LA PETITE MARIE* HAD BEEN POLED AWAY from the harbour wall, Anaconda swung her about to face the freshening breeze, taking the ship out into the Caribbean. The

all too familiar memory of a swaying deck beneath his feet brought back dreadful memories of the *Flying Dutchman* to Ben. He lay flat on the deck face down, pictures of Vanderdecken and his villainous crew flashing before his mind.

Ned lay down beside him, flashing urgent thoughts. "Don't let it get the better of you, Ben. Vanderdecken's a bad thing to think of. Cap'n Thuron's our friend, a good man."

One of the passing crew put a hand to Ben's back and shook him. "What ails ye, lad? Come on now, up on yer feet!"

Ned stood over Ben, the dog's hackles bristling as he growled viciously. Thuron pushed the man aside.

"Leave the boy alone. Maybe he's seasick already. Ben, are you feeling ill?"

Wiping cold sweat from his brow, Ben lifted his head. "I'll be all right, Cap'n. I was frightened back there."

The Frenchman nodded. "I was too, boy. Rocco Madrid has a formidable reputation. He's also got almost twice as many crew. Only a fool wouldn't have been afraid. You'll be all right.

Go aft, take Ned with you, lie down in my cabin. I won't let anything happen to you, Ben, you're my luck. Both of you."

The big cabin at the ship's stern was cool and comfortable. Ben lay down on the broad, velvet-quilted bed and fell into a dreamless slumber. Ned jumped up beside him and laid his head across the boy's feet. "Hmm, I wonder how far away France is. A good distance, probably."

La Petite Marie was now under full sail, ploughing the blue-green waters of the mighty Caribbean Sea.

Evening rolls of purple cloud were striping the crimson sky as the sound of an opening cabin door roused Ben. Ned nuzzled his leg. "Wake up! Here's food!" The crewman who followed Thuron into the cabin placed a bowl of fresh water down alongside a plate of stew. He loaded the rest onto the bedside table before leaving.

Thuron sat by the table. "Ben, here boy, eat up, I made the stew myself."

Ben sat on the edge of the bed alongside the table. There was a bowl of stew, some fresh fruit, and water to drink, and he tucked in heartily.

Thuron watched him eat. The Frenchman chuckled and ruffled the boy's hair. "Not feeling ill any more, eh? 'Tis hard to tell who has the better appetite, you or old Ned there."

The dog, who was licking a plate clean, shot Ben a thought. "Huh, who's he calling old? I'm naught but a pup yet."

Ben replied mentally, "Aye, a fat hungry pup!"

Ned growled. "Fat yourself, tubby youth!"

The captain's stubby finger turned Ben's chin until their

gazes met. There was sea in the boy's clouded blue eyes – ancient deeps and far horizons lurked in them. Raphael Thuron stared into the young fellow's calm face. "You're a strange lad, Ben, where are ye from?"

Ben averted his eyes and picked up a slice of pineapple. "From the Tierra del Fuego, sir."

The Frenchman raised his eyebrows in surprise. "The land of fire down at the tip of this big country! That's a great distance from Cartagena, lad. How came ye to travel so far?"

Ben did not like lying to the captain, but necessity had forced him to be untruthful with anyone who wanted to know of his mysterious life. "I was a shepherd boy helping an old shepherd down there. He told me that he had found me on the shores, after a shipwreck. I worked with him . . . Ned was his dog. Early one spring the shepherd died in an accident, so I wandered off with Ned. We've been travelling over four years. We visited many places before reaching Cartagena."

Thuron shook his head in wonderment. "You must have been little more than a babe when the shepherd found you on the shore. What was the name of the ship you came from?"

Ben shrugged. "The shepherd never told me. He said that the vessel must have sunk in a storm. I don't remember anything, apart from living in his hut, rounding up sheep with Ned and enduring the awful weather down there. Have you always been a seaman, Cap'n?"

Ned's thought flashed through Ben's mind. "I liked the way you changed the subject there, mate. That was a clever touch, too, saying I belonged to the old shepherd. What our friend doesn't know can't hurt him."

Ben kept his eyes on Thuron, who began telling of himself. "Aye, I've been seafaring since I was younger than you, Ben.

I was born in a place called Arcachon, on the French coast. I didn't want to be a poor peasant like my father, so I ran off one day and joined the crew of a merchant ship. On our voyage to Cadiz we were attacked by Spanish pirates. They slew most of our crew but kept me as galley boy. Since then, I've spent most of my life aboard one vessel or another. If I'd been weak, I'd be dead by now. But here you see me, Raphael Thuron, master of my own ship, *La Petite Marie*, a French buccaneer!"

Ben looked up at the captain. "You must be very proud of yourself, sir."

The Frenchman poured himself a glass of water, swirled it about reflectively, then shook his head. "Proud, d'ye say? I'll tell ye something now, Ben, that I've never told any living soul. I'm ashamed of what I've made of my life. Ashamed!" He kept swirling the water, his eyes fixed on its motion. "Me, the older son of an honest, religious family. Oh, I was a wild one, not like my younger brother Mattieu. It was my parents' hope that one day I would reform and make them proud by becoming a priest. My younger brother Mattieu was more suited to that sort of thing. He was a good boy, though I often got him into trouble. Being a farmworker like my father was a gloomy alternative. So I ran off to sea, and here I am all these years later, a man living outside of the law, buccaneering. But no more. This wicked trade has seen the last of Raphael Thuron. I'm done with it all, boy. Finished, d'ye hear!"

This came as a shock to Ben. "What made you decide that, sir?"

The Frenchman quaffed his water, slamming the glass down so hard that it cracked. "I saw ye today, Ben, standing there with Ned. You reminded me of what I was once, a cheery lad with a trusty hound at his heels. 'Twas you spotted Madrid's cheatin' ways. I knew then my life had to change. You're my lucky boy, you and Ned. I've been storing wealth away. Now, with what I took from Rocco Madrid, I'm a rich man. I'll make up for my buccaneering ways, Ben, you'll see. I'll return to Arcachon and help my family. We'll build a château, Ben, and buy a big vineyard. I'll give money to the church and the poor. Folk will speak of me like . . . like –"

Ben interrupted the captain. "Like a saint?"

A huge smile spread across Thuron's heavy face. "Aye, lad, that's it, lad, like a saint. Saint Raphael Thuron!"

He burst out laughing, Ben joined in, and Ned set up a howl. The Frenchman wiped tears of merriment from his eyes onto his brocaded sleeve. "And you two will share in it. Young Saint Ben and good Saint Ned. How does that sound to ye, eh?"

Convulsed with mirth, the black Labrador chortled away. "Hohoho, good Saint Ned? I like that, I'll wear a collar of gold, like a halo that's slipped down round my neck!"

Ben returned his thought. "And I'll wear a long, flowing shirt and a pointed hat, like a bishop. Hahahaha!"

Thuron remarked through his laughter. "Oohahaha, look at you two, anyone'd swear you were gossiping together. Hahaha!"

Ben slapped the Frenchman's back so hard that it stung his hand. "Heeheehee, that's a good 'un, gossiping with a dog, heehee!"

The proceedings were interrupted by the bosun, Pierre, bellowing from the sternmast lookout point. "Vessel astern, showin' over the horizon in our wake!"

The captain dashed out onto the deck, with Ben and Ned hard on his heels. Crewmen with worried faces clattered up from the mess deck, carrying weapons and priming muskets as they made their way to the stern rail. Thuron pulled a telescope from his coat lining and sighted on the dark smudge to the rear, which was all they could see of Cartagena. He swung the glass to and fro, halting as he caught sight of sail.

"Rocco Madrid and the *Diablo Del Mar*! Well, he didn't waste much time, did he? Stand by all hands, we're in for a sea chase. Load those cannon, Anaconda, I'll take the wheel. Come on, Ben, bring Ned too – I'm going to need all the luck ye can bring me!"

Captain Rocco Madrid called up to his lookout. "Have they sighted us yet, Pepe?"

Loud and clear, the lookout bellowed back, "Sí, Capitano, they are piling on sail to escape us!"

Rocco's bosun, Portugee, handed the wheel over to his captain. "Shall I roll out all the cannon an' give 'em a full salute? Capitano, we can outgun the *Marie* easily."

Madrid narrowed his eyes until they were wicked slits. "No, no, Thuron has the gold. He is of no use to me on the bottom of the sea with his ship. *Diablo* will outrun them, we'll take the *Marie* an' her crew alive. I want to sail into Cartagena with everyone aboard that ship hanging from their own yardarms. Our Brotherhood on shore will know then: no man takes gold from Rocco Madrid and lives to tell the tale!"

Rocco's first mate, a fat Hollander called Boelee, spoke up. "Even the brat an' his dog?"

The Spaniard drew out his telescope and scanned the distant ship. "Especially the brat an' his dog, amigo. Lessons must be taught by making hard examples."

Aboard *La Petite Marie*, Thuron was roaring orders. "Pile on every stitch of canvas there! Up the rigging, every man jack of ye! Pierre, Ludon, climb out onto the bows an' chop away those rope fenders. She'll cut the waves cleaner with a sharp prow!"

Pierre, the bosun, and Ludon, the mate, scrambled over the bows with cutlasses held in their teeth.

Ben looked anxiously at the Frenchman, voicing his thoughts aloud. "Are you sure we can outrun them, Cap'n?"

Thuron smiled grimly. "We've got to, or we're all dead men. Don't worry, boy, my ship may be smaller, but she's faster, I'm sure of it. With me at the helm, Madrid will get a run for his gold. That big, awkward tub of his was never built for sea chases. Our *Marie* will show him a clean pair of heels, providing he doesn't use his cannon. 'Tis my job to keep us out of his range until he tires of the chase, though I'm certain that Spaniard doesn't want to sink us. If Madrid does get us within distance, he'll try to snap off our masts."

Ned was struck by an idea, which he imparted to Ben. "It'll be dark in an hour or two, so why don't we make sure the ship isn't showing any lights to give away our position?"

Ben immediately passed on the suggestion to Thuron. The Frenchman was wholly in agreement. "A good thought, lad. Go and cover the ports and douse any lanterns you can find. I can probably lose him in the dark. Anaconda, take the wheel. Let's go below and study the charts, Ben. Then maybe we can be like the fox – stop running and hide!"

After dousing every available lantern and curtaining the galley ports so that the glow from the stove would not betray their position, Ben and Ned went to the captain's cabin. Thuron had a chart spread out on the bed. He tapped the point of a dagger against a spot on the coast. "There, Santa Marta, that's where we'll hide."

Ben studied the chart: Santa Marta was just north up the coastline from Cartagena. He turned to the Frenchman. "But, sir, that's back the way we came."

Ned put his paws on the bed and scanned the map, thinking, "So it is!"

But the captain explained his strategy. "Madrid doesn't know we're bound across the ocean to France. He thinks we're on a sea chase, north across the Caribbean. So I'll take a sweep east and turn south just after twilight."

Ben caught on to the plan quickly. "Clever! Madrid will be searching ahead and we'll side-slip him. He'll go sailing off into the sea while we head back to land – a good idea, sir!"

Ned sent out a sobering thought. "Pretty risky though!"

The boy was taken slightly aback when Thuron replied as if he had heard the dog, though it was pure coincidence. " 'Tis risky, I grant you. If Madrid or his crew spots us, we're done for. But I'm willing to take the chance. There's a high, rocky point that sticks out into the waters around Santa Marta. If we can get by the *Diablo* unnoticed, we'll lie in the lee of it and be well hidden."

• • •

Rocco Madrid stared into the reddening horizon, watching day fade into night. He called up to Pepe. "Have you still got them in sight, amigo?"

Pepe scrambled down, grunting with the exertion. "Only just, Capitano. I will want your seeing glass to keep track properly. I only need a lantern or galley stove glint to tell me where *La Petite Marie* lies."

The Spaniard handed over his telescope. "Be careful with it."

Pepe began his laborious ascent of the mast, grumbling. "I'll miss something to eat, being stuck up there."

Rocco heard him and replied humourlessly, "You'll eat when I say. Move from that crow's nest and you'll have to eat supper through a slit in your neck!"

Pepe reached his lookout post and swept the seas ahead through the telescope. "I see them, Capitano, their galley fire is shining out like a beacon!"

Ben watched the wooden spar bob away on the waves to the port side of the ship. A heap of old sailcloth, soaked in lamp oil, blazed merrily on the spar's topside. He patted Ned's head fondly. "If I was wearing a hat, I'd take it off to you, mate. That lighted spar is a stroke of genius!"

The Labrador stood with his front paws against the port rail, sniffing as he returned the thought. "If I was human I'd be an admiral now. Suppose you'll tell our cap'n that it was your idea, eh?"

Ben shook his head. "I won't even mention it."

Ned dropped his ears comically. "Oh, go on, tell him and get all the glory for yourself. I know what it's like to lead a dog's life, all work and no praise."

Ben lightly kissed the top of his dog's head. "There, you're getting my praise now. I don't know what I'd do without you, Ned. The world's smartest dog, that's you!"

Thuron emerged from his cabin and pointed to the decoy light. "Hah! That's a great trick. Was it your idea, Ben?"

The boy answered, speaking the truth. "No, sir, it was good Saint Ned who thought of it!"

The Frenchman cuffed Ben playfully. "Don't make me laugh. Sound carries far on open waters, you know."

Moonless dark fell over the softly soughing waves, and clouds cloaked most of the stars. Rocco Madrid handed the wheel over to Boelee and went to the foot of the mast. He called up in a hoarse whisper, "Where is the *Marie* now, Pepe?"

Pepe's nervous whisper reached his ears. "I cannot see her any more, Capitano. I had your glass on the galley light and poof! It went out. Someone must have closed the galley door."

Madrid's teeth grinding together made an audible noise. "Idiot, you mean you've lost her. She must have put on even more sail. We'll keep a straight course. I think we're right in Thuron's wake. He's heading for Jamaica and Port Royal, I'm sure he is. Boelee, set your course due north. Portugee, keep her under full sail. We'll sight him by daylight tomorrow, there's nowhere to hide on the open sea. I'll be in my cabin. Wake me an hour before dawn."

The Spaniard stalked off to his cabin, leaving the three crewmen searching the night-dark horizon. Rocco Madrid would not be a pleasant captain to sail with if they lost *La Petite Marie*.

Ben helped Captain Thuron's crew to slacken sail as the dark, humped cliffs of Santa Marta hove into view. Ned watched as the giant steersman, Anaconda, took the vessel carefully into the western lee side of the towering rocks. Thuron gave orders for the anchor to be dropped. He chuckled softly as the boy joined him on deck. "Our *Marie* is safe here for the night. I'll wager that the *Diablo* is bound at full speed for Kingston or Port Royal – where else would a Brotherhood vessel head for in the Caribbean? First thing tomorrow we'll slip round the headland and make a straight run east, out of this sea and into the Atlantic Ocean. Then 'tis France and home, eh, boy?"

Ben threw the captain a smart salute. "Aye aye, sir!"

AROUND ON THE eastern side of the Santa Marta cliffs, little more than two miles from where the *Marie* was anchored, lay another ship, the *Devon Belle*. She was a privateer, carrying a letter of marque from the king of England, Charles the First. Little more than pirates themselves, privateers preyed upon other pirates and ships that were hostile to the privateer's own homeland. They were common to many countries – France, Spain, Portugal and the Netherlands. *Devon Belle* was a British privateer. King Charles had signed a licence for her captain to raid and plunder any foreign ship he chose, on the pretext that a vessel not flying a British flag was either a pirate or an enemy. Carrying his letter of marque, the privateer captain would attack and conquer all before him, taking charge of all treasures and booty he captured. Very profitable ventures for the English Crown, which took a large share of the spoils. Privateer captains usually posed as officers of the British Navy, pretending that they were clearing the seas of pirates and keeping the world's shipping lanes free for honest seafarers.

Captain Jonathan Ormsby Teal was such a man. Elegant, suave and well educated, the ambitious eldest son of an impoverished noble family, he had chosen to make his living on the high seas and had taken to the trade like a duck to water. His ship, though small, bristled with armament, cannon barrels poking from every port, for'ard, aft and amidships. At present he was playing his favourite game, lying in wait for any craft sailing out of Barranquilla or Cartagena and ready to leap out on them from his hiding place on the east side of the Santa Marta cliffs. Captain Teal was rapidly becoming the scourge of the Caribbean Sea. He affected to wear a square-tailed foxhunting jacket of red and revelled in the nickname his crew had given him, Cap'n Redjack. All he was waiting for was the coming of daylight and some unsuspecting ship to pass the headland in range of his guns. Now he sat in his tiny stateroom, sipping Madeira wine and toying with an assortment of gold coins, mainly doubloons. The clink of pure, bright gold was music to the ears of Cap'n Redjack Teal!

Ned and Ben slept out on the deck, as it was warm and humid in the shelter of the high rocks. The boy and his dog stretched out amid rope coils piled on the forecastle, hoping to catch a passing breeze.

Ben had barely sunk into a slumber when he was awakened by Ned. The black Labrador was whimpering in his sleep, paws and ears twitching fitfully. The boy sat up and smiled. What dreams was the dog dreaming? First he would make a moaning sound, then give a little yip, his nose would wrinkle and his flanks would quiver. Dreams, what strange visitations they were.

Ben got up and went to stand in the prow, looking out past the cliffs at the dark sea. Then he saw something that he knew was no dream.

The *Flying Dutchman*!

Standing out in the moonless night, surrounded by an eerie green radiance, there was the accursed ship, storm-torn sails fluttering on some nameless wind, ice bedecking the rigging, its hull thick with barnacles and marine debris. It turned slowly, broadside on, allowing phantom waves to wash it nearer to shore. Closer it drifted, closer.

The boy stood riveted with horror, unable to run, fear jamming his eyes wide open. He longed to scream, shout, anything to break the dread spell. His mouth opened, but no sound came forth. Now the ghostly vessel was so near it was almost upon him. He could see the awful form of Captain Vanderdecken lashed to the wheel, his long, salt-crusted hair flowing out behind him, his tombstone-like amber teeth bared by bloodless lips in the deathly pallor of an ashen face. Vanderdecken stared through mad, blood-flecked eyes at the lad and his dog, who had been cast away long years ago from his ship by an angel from heaven. The fearsome apparition glared balefully at Ben, getting closer by the moment.

Then Ned rose to his feet and began barking and baying out long, anguished howls, which echoed off the cliffs.

A voice rang out from the crew's accommodation. "Shut that dog up, someone. Where's the boy?"

There was the slap of bare feet upon the deck as Ludon, the mate, ran up onto the forepeak. He saw Ben standing out on the bow, rigid, with Ned alongside him still barking madly. Ludon grabbed Ben's arm. "What's the matter with ye, boy, can't ye control that animal –"

At the sight of someone seizing his friend, Ned hurled himself on the mate, knocking him flat. Suddenly Thuron was among them. Ben shuddered and collapsed to the deck. The

Frenchman picked him up like a baby, aiming a kick at Ludon as he did. "Ben, lad, are you all right? What did you do to the boy, Ludon?"

Scrambling away from Ned, the mate protested, "I never did anything, Cap'n, on my oath. I heard the dog making a noise and came to see –"

Thuron roared at the hapless Ludon, "Don't ever touch this boy, and keep away from the dog. These two are my luck. Leave them both alone. Understood?"

Hurt and bewildered by the anger of his normally affable captain, Ludon slunk off, back to his bunk.

Ben regained consciousness on the bed in the captain's cabin, with Ned licking his face. He sat up, rapidly communicating with him. "Did you see it? Vanderdecken was there, I saw him, he was coming after us, I'm sure of it. Did you see the ship, Ned?"

The dog thrust his front paws into Ben's chest, knocking him back on the bed. "I saw it in my dreams, but I couldn't break the spell of the nightmare. I couldn't wake myself, Ben. I could feel the Dutchman getting closer, nearer than he had ever been since we were on his ship all those years ago. I knew you were in danger, I wanted to help you. Then suddenly I started to bark for the angel to come and save us both. That must have done the trick. Though for an angel, Ludon has bad breath and dirty feet!"

Ben remained flat on the bed and gave Ned a slight smile. "Thanks, mate, you're a true friend. Where's the captain?"

The dog allowed the boy to get up as he nodded towards the door. "Oh, him, he's in the crew's mess, giving them a severe talking-to. Old Thuron doesn't like anyone messing with his two lucky friends – we're to be left alone by all hands."

Ben shook his head regretfully. "I wish he hadn't done that. I like the crew of the *Marie.* They may be pirates, but they aren't as bad as the crew of the *Dutchman.* They were wicked."

Ned licked Ben's hand. "Well, you're a lucky lad, and I'm a lucky dog. We'll just have to put up with it. Get some rest now. Our cap'n said he'd stay out on deck. Go on, mate, sleep. I'll stay here and keep watch for both of us."

The boy scratched behind his faithful dog's ear. "I know you will, Ned. You're a good, trusty hound."

Ned winked at Ben. "Don't go to sleep right away. Keep scratching my ear, just there. Ooh, that feels wonderful!"

Eventually they both fell into a deep and peaceful sleep. Ben dreamt he was drifting amidst golden clouds in a glorious dawn, high over a calm sea blue as a cornflower. Softly, like distant bells across a meadow, the angel's voice floated into the corridors of his mind.

> "Beware the walking dead by night,
> Banished by our Saviour's sight,
> And when all faces turn away,
> Leave the sea upon that day,
> But shun the gold, thou honest heart,
> Watch not a friend you loved depart!"

The next thing Ben knew was the sound of Ned, growling softly at a knock on the cabin door. Anaconda's giant frame almost blocked out the pale dawn light as he stooped and entered, bearing a tray. Placing the contents on the bedside table, he indicated two bowls of oatmeal, some fruit, and water for Ben and Ned.

"We sail now. Cap'n say you eat this." The big man turned and padded silently out.

Ned heard a dull bump against the ship's side and nodded to Ben. "Sounds like the anchor being hauled."

Ben began eating hurriedly. "I'll go and lend the crew a hand to make sail!"

Thuron watched as Ben swung nimbly from the rigging and landed lightly on deck next to his black Labrador. The Frenchman admired the boy's agility. "A monkey couldn't have done that better than you, lad. Well now, my lucky messmates, are ye ready to sail for France?"

The boy threw a salute. "Aye aye, sir!"

Ned wuffed and wagged his tail. Captain Thuron smiled happily. He turned and called orders to Pierre, who was at the wheel. "Take her out steady beyond the cliffs, Bosun. Then set your course nor'east through the Caribbean, out 'twixt Hispaniola and Puerto Rico into the Atlantic deeps!"

Ben felt a thrill of anticipation. Certainly there would be unknown perils out on the wide ocean – hardships, too. But this was a voyage to another continent. His sense of adventure was stirred. He felt a kinship with the crewmen of *La Petite Marie* as they struck up a farewell shanty. Ben felt like a true seafarer, out on his second voyage, halfway across the world. Captain Thuron sang along with the rest as Ben hummed, not knowing the words, and Ned wagged his tail in time with the music.

"Fare thee well, ye fair Susannah,
And to all the friends I know.
Adieu to the shore I might see no more,
I am sailing so far from you.
The seabirds are wheeling and crying,
And we're bound to cross thc great main,
I must follow the sea, so think kindly of me,
Maybe one day I'll see thee again."

Percival Mounsey, the cook aboard the *Devon Belle,* was fastidious in his duty to Cap'n Redjack. The master of an English privateer was always served breakfast first, so the cook had risen at dawn and hauled in a yellow-scaled flatfish from a baited line he had hung off the stern rail on the previous night. Having cooked the fish to perfection on his galley grill, he arranged it fussily on a silver platter with thin slices of lemon, a sprinkle of red pepper and a dash of rock salt. He placed it on a tray, along with half a decanter of Madeira wine and two of the special thin malt biscuits from Redjack's personal tin. Folding a serviette neatly, he put it in the captain's pewter goblet. Carrying the tray aloft on the flat of his left palm, the plump little cook set off along the starboard deck for the captain's cabin. About halfway along the deck, he stopped to admire the sun rising through a pink and pearl misted cloud. Mounsey sighed. He loved the Caribbean and its exotic climate. That was when he saw the ship rounding the tip of the headland beyond the cliffs. The cook dashed for'ard, still balancing the tray. He kicked at the two crewmen who were sleeping away their watch.

"Charlie! Bertie! Look, a ship!"

Captain Redjack Teal was seated at his dining table, clad in a silk dressing gown and a tasselled hat, awaiting his breakfast. However, this morning proved a little different from others. Instead of the cook's gentle tap to warn him of the meal's arrival, the cabin door burst open and the cook was pushed to one side as the two watchmen hurtled into the room shouting, "Cap'n! Cap'n, sir –!"

Teal sprang up in a fury, his finger pointing at the doorway. "Out! Out of my cabin, confound your eyes, or I'll have the hides flogged from your oafish backs. Out I say!"

Bertie spoke up hesitantly. "But, but, Cap'n, beggin' your –"

The captain fixed him with an eye that would have frozen Jamaican rum on a warm day. "Outside . . . now!" Both crewmen knew better than to argue and stumbled out. Still standing outside balancing his tray, Mounsey gave them a knowing look, then tapped gently on the door, which he had just shut behind them. Teal's voice called out languidly, "Come."

The cook glided in smoothly, setting the tray carefully on Teal's table and rearranging a lemon slice as he spoke. "A very good mornin' t'ye, sir. H'I wish to report two h'of the crew's watch, waitin' outside to see ye, sir."

The privateer captain poured himself some Madeira, moderating his voice to its usual aristocratic drawl. "Really, two of the watch, y'say. Send the fellows in, please."

Mounsey called to Charlie and Bertie, both standing outside. "H'enter, an' close the door be'ind yew!"

Teal glanced over the rim of his goblet at the pair, standing awkwardly in his presence. Before either of them could speak, he held up a hand for silence and began lecturing them. "Never taught to knock politely, were we? Now, repeat after me: Bumpkins should always knock before entering the cabin of a captain and a gentleman of breeding. Repeat!"

Charlie and Bertie stumbled over some of the words, but they managed, after a fashion. Teal wiped his lips by dabbing at them with the serviette.

"Politeness is the first rule to one's captain. Now, you there." He picked up his fork and pointed at Charlie. "What exactly was it you wanted to report, eh? Speak up, man."

"Ship off the starboard bow, Cap'n, passin' the 'eadland. Looks like a French buccaneer, sir!"

Teal's fork dropped, clattering upon his plate. "Demn ye man, why didn't you say?"

Bertie piped up. "We was goin' to, sir, but you said –"

The gimlet eye froze him to silence as Teal reprimanded him. "Excuse me, but did I address you?"

Bertie shuffled his bare feet and stared hard at them. "No, sir."

The captain nodded. "Then hold y'tongue, sirrah!" Teal made it a point never to know the names of his crew. Such things were beneath him. He stared at Charlie. "A demned froggy, eh? Buccaneer, y'say? Still in range, is he?"

Charlie kept his eyes front and centre. "Aye, sir!"

Redjack Teal rose from his chair. "Well, I'll teach the scoundrel to cross my bows. Cook, send in me dresser. You two, report to the master gunner and tell him to turn out his crew on the double and await me orders."

Rocco Madrid had been wakened and called up on deck at first light. His three top crewmen, Pepe, Portugee and Boelee, were grouped sheepishly on the afterdeck, avoiding their captain's disgusted looks.

Madrid drew his sword and prodded the long spar, which

still smelled of oil and burnt canvas. He pointed the sword at Portugee. "When was this thing found, and where exactly was it?"

The bosun tried to sound efficient. "Capitano, it was found less than a quarter hour ago. We pulled it from the water, Boelee and I. Pepe knows exactly where it was."

Pepe cleared his throat nervously. "Sí, Capitano, the spar was drifting in our wake, I was lucky to spot it."

Turning on his heel, the Spaniard strode to the rail. He sheathed his sword and stared pensively at the water. The trio watched him apprehensively, trying to gauge his mood. Much to their relief, he was smiling when he turned to face them. "A decoy, eh, very clever. That spar tells me two things. One, the *Marie* is not headed for Jamaica and Port Royal. Two, they were sending us the wrong way. So, what does this tell you, amigos?"

The three stared dumbly at him as his smile grew wider.

"Donkeys, you have not the brains among you to make a capitano. Thuron would not be fool enough to turn and sail back to Cartagena. No, I think he's taken off at an angle, east, out to the sea. So, he will head for one of two places, Hispaniola or Puerto Rico. Here's what I plan on doing. We will sail east also, right through the strait between the two islands and out into the Atlantic. It doesn't matter which island he's chosen – when Thuron puts out to sea again, we'll be waiting for him. Boelee, bring me my sea charts. Portugee, take the wheel and head *Diablo* due east. The French fox will not escape me this time!"

Pepe stood by Portugee at the wheel, speaking in a low voice as the captain walked away. "How do we know Thuron won't sail for the Leeward or the Windward Isles, or maybe for La Guira, Trinidad, even Curaçao, or right out to Barbados?"

Portugee turned the wheel steadily, blinking as the sun caught his eyes. "We don't know, Pepe. Didn't you hear him? We're donkeys with no brains, he's the capitano. So whatever he decides must be right. Unless you'd like to go tell him you know better!"

Pepe shook his head vigorously. "I have no desire to be a dead man, amigo. The capitano knows best, this donkey will obey his orders without question."

4

BEN HAD NEVER BEEN ABOARD A SHIP AT SEA that had been fired on. The first thing he heard was a distant boom. Both he and Ned looked up to the sky, the dog sending him a puzzled thought. "That sounds like thunder, but there's hardly a cloud anywhere in the sky."

Anaconda's deep voice rang out. "All hands down, we bein' fired on, Cap'n!"

Thuron was opening his telescope as he hurried to the stern rail when there was a tremendous splash in the water about fifty yards astern. The Frenchman sighted his glass, shouting orders as he did so. "British privateer sailing out of Santa Marta's east coast! Carrying enough cannon for a man-o'-war, curse him! Pierre, tighten the braces and run out staysails port and starboard! He hasn't got our range yet. We'll need every stitch of canvas if the *Marie*'s to outrun him!"

A second cannon boom exploded. This time Ben heard the iron ball cleave the air with a whistling noise. Both he and Ned were drenched with spray as the shot hit the waves, less than twenty yards from the stern.

Then the chase was on. A good stiff breeze took up any slack in the sails of *La Petite Marie* as she shot off like a startled deer. A small, agile crewman named Gascon climbed to the stern lookout point with the captain's spyglass rammed into his belt. Ben and Ned stood anxiously at Thuron's side, staring up at Gascon as he sighted the glass on their attacker and yelled down, "They're comin' on fast, Cap'n, 'tis a twenty-two gunner, with four culverins in the bows. I can just see the crew standing to with muskets!"

Despite the peril of their predicament, Thuron smiled grimly. "Hah! Typical privateer, overgunned and overmanned. Our *Marie* sports only half their number of cannon, and we cut off our fenders yesterday. We'll outsail the fat-bottomed Englander. He won't get any king's bounty out of Raphael Thuron, you can bet your boots on that, boy!"

Ned shot Ben a hasty observation. "Well, at least our cap'n isn't short of confidence. I like his style!"

Ben wiped salt spray from his eyes and addressed the captain. "I think we'll have to sail a lot faster than the privateer to stay out of gun range, sir."

Thuron threw an arm around the boy's shoulders. "Aye, lad, but our *Marie*'s a fast little lady, and I've got my lucky Ben and Ned with me. Don't worry, as long as we can keep those cannonballs from shooting our rudder away and any chain shot from ripping off our masts, all he'll hit is our wake. I've outrun privateers before. Get down!"

Ben, Thuron and the dog flung themselves flat to the deck. There was a harsh, whirring noise and a resounding crack. The captain lifted his head at the same time as Ben. Thuron nodded toward the stern rail. Hanging wrapped around the ornate gallery rail, the wood of which was splintered and split, was a chain attached to a cannonball about the size of a man's fist.

The Frenchman whistled soundlessly. "That was close. Here, lad, come and take a look at some chain shot!"

Keeping low, they crawled to the rail. Thuron reached up and unwound the object, hauling it aboard. It was like a bolas – three lengths of chain joined at the centre to form a letter Y, with a small iron ball attached to the end of each chain.

The captain weighed it in his big round hands. "British Royal Navy issue. Poor buccaneers like me cannot afford such murderous, expensive toys. Look, here comes another! Stay on your feet, boy, it won't hit us. We're stretching our lead on the sluggard!" Ben heard the deadly whirr and saw the second chain shot plough harmlessly into the sea two ship lengths behind them.

Captain Redjack finally appeared on deck after breakfasting and having his dresser's attention. He flipped a lace kerchief from his red velvet sleeve and flicked a spot of black powder from his oyster-silk knee breeches. Turning to the master gunner, whose name had slipped his mind, he held out a well-manicured hand and spoke. "Confound ye, man. Don't stand there gogglin', make y'report!"

Captain Redjack focused the telescope, which the gunner handed him, on his quarry, studying the vessel as the gunner reported. "She's a French buccaneer all right, Cap'n, sir. I tested 'er speed with a couple o' cannon shots. She's fast. Though I managed to wrap a chain shot round 'er stern galley, sir."

Redjack took the glass from his eye and tapped it in his palm. "Faith, did ye now? Cowardly froggy, look at him, runnin' like a spring hare. Mistah, er, steersman, I want ye to take us right within the gun range of yon fellow. Can y'do that, eh?"

The steersman, a lanky, gloom-faced man, tugged his forelock. "She's 'igher out the water than us, sir. By 'er lines I'd say the Frenchie was built fer speed. But I'll do me best, Cap'n."

The privateer captain stared down his nose at the steersman. "Don't do y'best, sirrah. Do a lot better'n that, eh? Three golden guineas for the man who sets first foot on the pirates' deck. Three stripes from a rope's end for all hands if we lose the villain. Demme, but if that isn't a fair offer, eh?"

The crew knew Redjack to be a man of his word. A hard-faced mate began bellowing orders. "Pile on extra spritsails an' bowsails, take cutlasses an' loose those fenders. Jump to it, ye layabouts!"

Redjack smiled benevolently at the mate and held his arms wide to give him the benefit of his outfit: oyster-silk breeches, white stockings and silver-buckled high shoes, his cuffs and throat frothing with cream silk lace beneath a freshly pressed and laundered red hunting jacket. "Oddsfish, that's the style, dress t'suit the occasion, I always say!"

Not daring to venture back up the mast again, Gascon crouched on the afterdeck viewing the *Devon Belle* through Thuron's telescope. "The Britisher's pilin' on canvas, y'can see he's pickin' up more speed right away, Cap'n!"

Thuron nodded. "Just keep us running with the wind on an even keel, Ludon. We'll lose him before we're halfway to Hispaniola and Puerto Rico."

The steersman, Ludon, called back to his captain. "Can't keep 'er runnin' due east, wind's freshenin' to the south. We'll have to tack, Cap'n!"

Thuron gestured to Ned and Ben. "Watch me, I'll show you how to tack and skim." Thuron took the wheel from Ludon and spun it expertly, explaining his tactics to Ben. "If we can't sail dead east, the next best thing is to tack. First into the wind, then away from it, so the ship heels over a touch and skims sideways. That way our *Marie* keeps up her speed. Sailing due east in a south wind would slow us down. Gascon, what's the privateer doing now?"

From behind the captain's back the lookout answered, "The Britisher's doin' the same as us, Cap'n, tackin' an' skimmin' like a pondfly."

Beneath his foppish posturing, Captain Redjack Teal was no fool. At that moment, he was watching the French ship keenly. He, too, had ordered the *Devon Belle* into a tacking manoeuvre while alerting his gunnery master to attend the portside cannonry. Teal reckoned he had gained a small distance on the other vessel. He waited until the moment was right, ready to take a gamble. The opportunity presented itself suddenly when he saw that the two vessels, whilst tacking, were broadside on to each other. Standing alongside his master gunner, the privateer captain rapped out swift orders: "Right, sharpish now, give her a full broadside, quick as y'like, man. Now!"

Ten cannon rocked back on their carriages as they went off with one frightening explosion!

• • •

All hands aboard the *Marie* threw themselves flat as they heard the roar of approaching cannonballs. Ben gasped as Ned hurled himself on his master's back, protecting him. Next moment there was horrendous crashing, smoke, flames and the sound of screaming men.

Thuron was on his feet instantly, shouting, "Run south, run south with the wind. Leave off tacking!" He hauled the dog off Ben. "Are you all right, boy?"

With the noise still ringing in his ears, Ben jumped up. "I'm fine, Cap'n, see to your ship!"

Ben and Ned were hard on the Frenchman's heels as he hastened about, checking the damage. Luckily no masts had been chopped down by the cannonade, the rudder was intact and the *Marie* had not been holed. But the entire galley had been blown to pieces, clear off the deck. Pierre, ashen-faced, staggered up clutching a wounded arm. "Three crew dead, Cap'n. Galley an' everythin' in it, cook included, all gone. 'Tween decks is burnin', though not badly."

Thuron ripped a swathc of lining from his frock coat and bandaged Pierre's arm as he issued orders. "Get those flames put out! Check all the rigging! Ludon, keep her hard south. Take us out of range!"

Ben saw the captain's brow crease and his eyes narrow. "Can we still outrun them, sir?"

Thuron stroked his beard and stared back at the *Devon Belle*. "Aye, at a pinch, lad, at a pinch. But I've thought of a better way than running from the enemy. I'm going to stop him chasing us. Anaconda, remember Puerto Cortes?"

The giant's face lit up in a huge grin. "Aye, Cap'n, that's where we captured little Gerda from that Hollander. Shall I have her brought aft?"

The Frenchman drew his cutlass. "Rig a block and tackle!"

Ned sent a puzzled thought to Ben. "Gerda can't be that little, not if they need a block and tackle to raise her. Ask him who little Gerda is, Ben."

The boy asked, and Ned was all ears as Thuron explained. "Little Gerda is a strange gun we captured from a Hollander merchant ship bound for a garrison at the tip of Yucatan. It has a long barrel, not wide enough to fit a full cannonball but built to fire further than a cannon. You'll see."

Little Gerda was indeed a strange weapon. Ben helped to swing it onto the stern deck and set it up on a pivot, which was intended for the bow culverin.

The captain stroked its long barrel approvingly. "I knew this would prove useful one day. See the barrel? It is meant for long-range firing. Gerda's magazine will take twice the normal amount of gunpowder – her barrel has seven layers of thick copper wire bound onto it, so it won't split under pressure. The vent is too small for a proper cannonball, so can you guess what I'm going to use, Ben?"

The boy caught on instantly. He picked up the chain shot that Thuron had left lying by the cracked rail. "This would fit into little Gerda's mouth, I think."

The Frenchman winked broadly at him. "Right, my lucky Ben! Let's give the Britisher his chain shot back as a returned compliment. Anaconda, Gascon, set the gun up. We'll get it ready while we're still on the run!"

Ned and Ben scampered below on the captain's orders, where they collected any old soft lengths of cloth to act as wadding and some palm oil to soak it in. On the way back they took the rammer from the for'ard culverin to tamp little Gerda's shot down tight.

Between them, Thuron and Anaconda were raising the gun's trajectory and sighting it right.

A crewman aboard the *Devon Belle* stood dutifully by with tray, decanter and goblet. Captain Redjack Teal took his morning measure of Madeira wine, asking a seaman who was relaying observations from another stationed in the crow's nest, "You fellow, what's the froggy doin' now, eh?"

The seaman shouted up to the lookout, "Cap'n wants to know what the French vessel's doin'!"

The lookout yelled back down, "Runnin' due south with the wind, clearin' up the mess we made o' their midship decks!"

The seaman reported back to Teal, who had already heard the lookout's reply. "She's runnin' due south, sir, makin' runnin' repairs as she goes."

Sipping Madeira, Teal dabbed his lips and smiled. "Stap me, that's a good 'un, eh? Makin' runnin' repairs whilst runnin' away. Very droll indeed!"

The lookout called down again, "I think they're riggin' a cannon up at the stern, can't make it out properly though, sir!"

The seaman turned to his captain. "He says, he thinks . . ."

Redjack dismissed him with a haughty glance. "Go away, sirrah, y'sound like an echo in a cave. I heard him. Gunner, get up an' see what that oaf's blitherin' about, will you?"

The master gunner climbed obediently up the mast into the crow's nest with the lookout. Shading his eyes, he peered at the *Marie*.

Teal called up testily, "Give him the demned glass!"

The gunner took a sighting through the telescope lens.

"Looks like a long-nosed culverin, sir. We're well outta range. 'Twon't shoot half this distance, Cap'n, sir!"

Teal held out his goblet for more wine. "Well, let the silly Frenchies amuse themselves by tryin', eh? Haw haw haw!"

There was a distant echo of a sharp crack, followed seconds later by a whirring scream, ending in a loud crash!

Shorn off by chain shot, the *Devon Belle*'s foremast swayed crazily for a moment, then fell.

Aboard the *Marie,* a loud cheer went up from the crew. Ben and Ned danced jubilantly around the French captain, the dog barking and the boy shouting joyfully, "You did it, Cap'n, what a shot! Chopped off their foremast!"

The captain stood nonchalantly, a stick with burning tow at its end still held in his hand. He flourished it and bowed. "Raphael Thuron was once a gunner aboard the *Star of Sudan,* a corsair that was the terror of the Red Sea!"

Ned passed Ben a thought. "There's old Pierre coming up from amidships. Look at the face on him, you'd think it was the *Marie* that'd had her mast shot off!"

Pierre's misgivings became clear when he spoke to his captain. "When the galley got hit, most of the supplies went with it."

Thuron's face fell. "Is there anything left?"

Pierre shrugged. "Half a leakin' cask of water an' one sack of flour, that's all I salvaged."

Captain Thuron's happy mood evaporated promptly. "We'll last out until we make Hispaniola or Puerto Rico. Take the wheel, Pierre. Back on the eastern course. Anaconda, you and I will work out a ration of water and flour for each man until we can get more provisions."

Ned sent a sideways glance and a thought to Ben. "Maybe we're not so lucky for the cap'n. Tighten your belt, mate, there's hard days lying ahead of us."

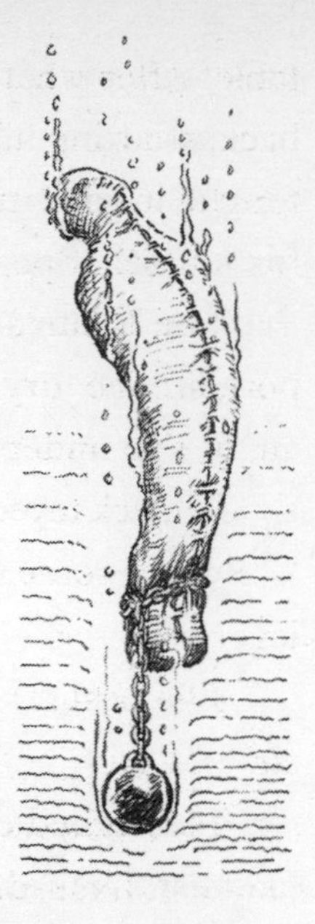

5

CAPTAIN REDJACK TEAL WAS not a happy man. He was, in fact, rather unhappy and, as such, made sure the entire crew of the *Devon Belle* shared his feelings wholeheartedly. It was noon of the second day since Teal had lost a foremast to his own chain shot. The French buccaneer vessel was now more than a day and a night ahead, off into the wide blue Caribbean Sea. The British privateer had continued sailing in pursuit, but like a gull with an injured wing, she had soon dropped far behind, sloughing awkwardly along whilst running repairs were carried out on the broken mast. After severely chastising all hands as he had vowed he would, Redjack had taken to his cabin. There was not a man aboard who had avoided six strokes of a tarred and knotted rope's end, three strokes for losing the quarry and an added three for what their captain termed "lack of discipline and a sullen demeanour".

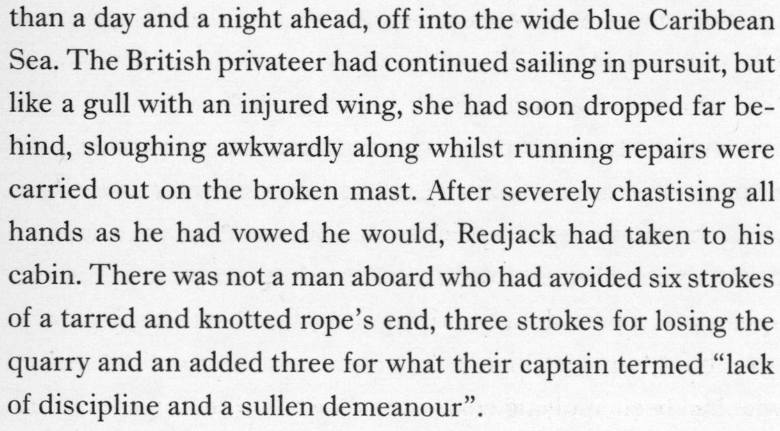

At a timid tap on the cabin door, Teal glanced up from his noonday goblet of Madeira. He snapped out briskly, "Come!"

The bosun stumped in, wooden splints bound either side of a fractured leg. Tugging his forelock respectfully, he stood wincing. Teal pretended to study a chart that was spread across the table. After what he judged a suitable period, the captain sat back, studying his bosun disdainfully. "Struth, man, have ye no tongue in your mouth, eh? Don't just stand there lookin' sorry for yourself. Speak!"

The bosun's Adam's apple bobbed nervously. "Beg to report, sir, the jury mast is now rigged an' in place, all shipshape an' fit t'go under full sail again, Cap'n."

Redjack toyed with his goblet, staring at the bosun's injury. " 'Twill be some time before you can go under full sail with that leg, eh?"

The bosun kept his eyes straight ahead and replied, "Aye, sir."

Teal sighed despairingly. "Lettin' a mast spar fall on y'leg like that. Lackaday dee, you're a foolish fellow. What are ye?"

Still staring ahead, the man was forced to repeat, "A foolish fellow, sir!"

Rising in a world-weary fashion, Teal refilled his goblet to take out on deck with him. "Stir your stumps, then, let's go an' take a look at what sort of a job's been made."

A shrill blast on the bosun's whistle sent the crew hurrying into four lines on the main deck. Without a second glance, Teal swept by and went to inspect the new foremast. It was a section of common ash tree from the ship's lumber stores, held by spikes and rope lashings to the original foremast stump, which was about four feet high. The ship's carpenter and his mate, who had been applying coats of melted tar to the rope binding, stood respectfully to one side.

The captain circled the jury-rigged mast twice, peering closely at the work. "Hmm, not half bad. Will it hold sail without crackin', eh?"

The carpenter saluted. "Aye, sir, I reckon she'll take a blow!"

Teal, assuming the new mast was wood that they had picked up along the South American coast, smiled briefly at the grizzled workman. "Good man! Though I wager ye'd sooner be usin' stout English timber, a trunk of ash from back home, eh?"

Knowing what to do, the carpenter nodded cheerily. "Aye, sir!" He watched Teal strut off, wondering how a man could become ship's captain without being able to identify a plain piece of English ash from the ship's stores, which was what he had used.

Captain Redjack Teal went to stand on the afterdeck to give a speech to his crew waiting at rigid attention below on the main deck. Now he was a stern father, berating his wayward children. "As captain of this, His Majesty's ship, and as the bearer of the king's own letter of marque, I am bound by me duty t'keep the high seas free of pirates an' their ilk. But my crew are failin' me! An' a demned sloppy lot ye are! Lettin' a confounded Frenchie get away like that, eh? Call y'self gunners? I had him broadside on, an' all ye could do was wreck his worthless galley! Call y'selves marksmen? There wasn't a single musket shot from us, no enterprisin' fellow tried to take out their steersman or captain! Then, if y'please, we had a fool at the wheel who couldn't take us out o' the way of a single chain shot! He crippled us!"

All hands stared at the deck, as if the answer lay there. Teal continued working himself up into a fine old temper. "Call y'selves English privateers, hah! Ploughfield donkeys an' cabbage-furrow bumpkins, that's what y'are! But things are goin' to change, I'm goin' t'make marines of ye, fightin' sailors that'd make the wives of England proud! No more rope's end, 'tis the cat-o'-nine-tails for any man who doesn't jump to it. We're goin' to capture the Frenchman, or we're goin' to send him'n his whole demned froggy crew to perdition an' a watery grave! Do ye hear me?"

All hands shouted as one man, "Aye, sir!"

He turned to the mate who was holding the Madeira goblet in waiting. Teal took several sips and mopped lightly at his cheek with a kerchief. Berating a crew was tiring work. He was about to leave the deck when the mate reminded him, "Permission to carry out burial at sea, Cap'n?"

The captain tried to look as if he had not forgotten. "Oh yes, quite. Chappie the mast fell on, wasn't it? Well, fetch him out an' let's get on with it."

The corpse was borne to the amidships rail, wrapped tightly in sail canvas, weighted at the feet with holystones – chunks of sandstone used for scouring the decks. The canvas was rough-stitched up the centre with twine, the last stitch being put through the dead man's nose: a traditional seafaring way of making sure the man was really dead. Six crewmen held the bundle, balanced on a greased plank, over the rail. Teal took the Bible and skimmed swiftly through the regulation prayer for the dead, ending with a swift amen, which was echoed by the crew.

Then the six bearers began tipping the board up, reciting as they did:

> "Let's hope Father Neptune
> Has saved him a fine fortune,
> An' all the pretty mermaids
> Will sing a sweet 'n' slow tune.
> For here goes some mother's son,
> Now all the prayers are said,

With holystones round both heels,
Tip him overboard, mates, he's dead!"

There was a dull splash as the canvas parcel hit the waves and vanished down into the sea.

Captain Redjack straightened his cravat. "Put on all sail, Mr Mate. Take her due east in pursuit. Let me know when the Frenchman's sighted. Er, by the way, what was that fellow we just put down, eh?"

"That was Percival, Cap'n," the mate replied.

Teal looked faintly mystified. "Percival who?"

"Mounsey, your cook, sir."

The captain shook his head sadly. "Cook, y'say! Hmm, rather inconvenient. See if y'can find a good man to replace him."

Three days had passed aboard *La Petite Marie.* The weather had stayed fair and the winds steady. Ben stood in line, carrying two bamboo drinking cups. Beneath the makeshift canvas galley awning, Ludon and a crewman named Grest were serving the water ration out to all hands. Ben held out the first cup, and Grest filled the ladle two-thirds and tipped it into the tow-headed boy's cup. Then Ben held out the second cup.

Grest eyed it, glaring at Ben. "One man, one measure, that's all anybody gets!"

Ludon whispered something to Grest, who wordlessly dipped the ladle and gave Ben a second measure.

Captain Thuron strode up. "Are you having any trouble, lad?"

Ben shook his head. "No trouble, Cap'n, just getting

the water for me and Ned." The boy walked off, followed by his dog.

The captain poked a thick finger in Grest's shoulder, making the man flinch. "That dog gets water, the same as any man aboard. Make sure you serve him the proper measure, d'you hear?"

As Thuron strode off, Grest muttered, "Water for a dog? There's hardly enough to go round for ourselves!"

Thuron turned, having heard the remark. He smiled at Grest. "Hand me that ladle, friend."

Grest did as he was ordered. Thuron bent the metal ladle handle easily in his powerful hands. Still smiling, he placed the bent ladle round Grest's neck and twisted both ends together. It was like an iron collar round the man's neck. Thuron allowed the smile to slip from his face.

"The day you want to be captain, just let me know!"

Ned licked his bamboo cup dry. "Funny how you take a simple thing like a drink of water for granted, until there's not much to be had."

Ben smiled into his dog's dark eyes, returning the message. "No sign of rain either, or we could've collected some by spreading a sail and catching it. I wonder how far off Hispaniola and Puerto Rico are."

The black Labrador picked up the cup in his jaws. "I don't know. Let's go and ask the cap'n."

Thuron was standing in the bow with the glass to his eye. Ben and Ned went around by the starboard side, avoiding those still in line for their water. Ned stopped at the back of the canvas-sheet galley, alerting Ben with a swift thought. "Don't make any noise, mate. Come and listen to this."

Ludon and Grest were whispering to a man named Ricaud as they served him water. "When we were moored at Santa Marta, Thuron kicked me, just because I tried to stop that cur from barking!" Ben overheard Ludon complaining. He also heard Ned's indignant mental reply.

"Cur? Huh! Listen to that scurvy mongrel!"

Grest was in agreement with Ludon. "Aye, if that lad an' his dog are so lucky, then why are we runnin' from a privateer, with hardly a bite to eat nor a drop to drink? Call that lucky?"

Ricaud was a whiner, Ben could tell by his voice. "A drop is right. How can a man survive on only this lousy dribble of water? How much is left in that barrel, Grest?"

They heard Grest swish the water as he tipped the barrel. "Not enough to get us through tomorrow. We might be sightin' land about then. I'll tell ye one thing, though, Thuron's out to cause trouble for me. I'm not staying aboard this ship. Once I'm ashore I'll be off. There's plenty more vessels lookin' for crew round those two islands."

Ludon's voice answered him. "Let me know when ye jump ship. I'm not stayin' aboard to be kicked around. How about you, Ricaud?"

There was a chuckle from Ricaud. "The great Cap'n Thuron wouldn't be so high'n'mighty without a crew. I'm with ye, an' I'll put the word round. I wager there's more'n a few among us who'd be wanted by the authorities back in France."

Ludon sounded cautious. "You're right, mate, but don't let Pierre or the Anaconda know, they're loyal to Thuron. Just ask around, easy-like, but make sure you talk to the right men."

Ned stared at Ben, transmitting his thoughts. "You go and

see the cap'n. I'll keep my ears and eyes open around here. Tell him what you've heard, Ben."

Thuron was scanning the horizon through his telescope and had his back to Ben. On hearing the boy's footsteps behind him, the Frenchman turned. Ben felt embarrassed at having to tell his friend what he had heard. "Cap'n . . . I . . . er . . ."

The buccaneer stared into his companion's mysterious blue eyes: he saw ageless honesty mingled with storm-clouded distant seas. He smiled to ease the boy's discomfort. "Speak up, lad. What's troubling you?"

Ben tried again. "It's the crew. They're . . ."

The Frenchman nodded knowingly. "Planning to desert the *Marie* when we make landfall. Don't look so surprised, Ben – it doesn't pay for a captain to be ignorant of his crew's feelings. No doubt you've heard the muttering and spotted the hard glances. I've watched them, too, for a while. Ah, they aren't bad men, really, but they get like that from time to time. Well, look at it their way. We've run from Rocco Madrid, been attacked by the privateers and now we're about to run out of rations. What right-thinking seaman wouldn't want to leave such a vessel? The Caribbean isles are friendly and sunny, and there's other ships in their harbours for a man to make his berth in. Besides, some of this crew are wanted men in France, most in the pirating trade are." He laughed. "I probably am myself, but I'm rich and willing to take my chance."

Ben could not help but admire his friend's wisdom and easygoing outlook. Even so, he felt bound to ask the question, "What do you plan on doing about it, sir?"

Thuron faced the sea and put the glass back to his eye. "Oh, I've made my plans, lad. The first is to sight land and get all hands ashore in a place where I can keep my eye on them. Not some waterfront town full of taverns, but a nice quiet cove with running water and a native village close by where we can trade for most of what we need. Trouble is that I haven't spotted land yet. I know we've run a bit off course in the last day or two, but the islands can't be too far off. Here, you take a peek. You're my lucky boy – mayhap you'll spy something."

Ben took the telescope, focused it and searched the horizon bit by bit.

Thuron chuckled. "That's the way, use those lucky blue eyes of yours. I'll go and find Ned. Hope he hasn't signed up with the deserters."

Ben kept his eye to the glass. "Shame on you for thinking such a thing, Cap'n. There's none more faithful than my Ned!"

A distant speck on the horizon caught Ben's attention. He felt as though ice water were trickling down his back. Some sixth sense told him that it was the *Flying Dutchman*. Swiftly he angled the lens away southward. A dark-purplish smudge on the far skyline dispelled his fears. The boy's spirits soared. "Cap'n, I can see land! There, over to the southeast!"

Thuron took the telescope and clapped it to his eye. "Where, Ben, where? I can't see a thing."

He returned the instrument to the boy, who immediately found the far-off smudge. "Crouch down, Cap'n, I'll keep the glass steady. See it way over there?"

The Frenchman screwed his eye hard to the brass aperture. "Your eyes must be a lot better than mine, Ben, I don't see a thing. No, wait . . . Aha, there 'tis! Tell Anaconda to alter our course two points south, then dead ahead. Ben, Ben, my lucky shipmate, you've done it again. Land ho!"

• • •

The black Labrador sat stoically, listening to most of the crew grumbling and disputing over the stern rail. Suddenly they heard the captain's joyful shout, and it worked like a charm. Everything became hustle and bustle as the crew broke off to attend to their duties. Anaconda began singing in a deep, melodious voice.

> "Haul away for the islands, mates,
> That's the place to be.
> Way haul away!
> There's fish swim in the bay, me boys,
> An' fruit on every tree.
> Way haul away!
> The livin's good an' easy there,
> So sunny an' so free.
> A shady place to rest your head,
> We'll anchor in the lee.
> To me way, haul away!
> Oh haul away, do,
> All hands turn out an' hear me shout . . .
> Away boat's crew!"

Ned, standing alongside the giant steersman, threw back his head and bayed. Ben laughed as he exchanged a thought with the Labrador. "You'll have to learn the words, Ned!"

The dog sniffed and gave him a dignified glance. "Does a fiddler, a drummer or a guitar player have to know the words? Ignorant boy, can't you see I'm providing a wonderful accompaniment to our friend here!"

• • •

With the westering sun crimsoning her sails from astern, *La Petite Marie* nosed into Guayama, a cove on the southeastern coast of Puerto Rico. They dropped anchor outside the shallows, where she would not be left high and dry on sandbanks by an ebbing tide. Captain Thuron ordered Pierre to lower the ship's jolly boat. It was a small craft and would have to make the journey to shore four times.

Knowing that the bosun was loyal to him, the captain chose him to make the first trip. "Pierre, you and Anaconda will take the first lot. Ben, you and Ned, go second; Ludon, you're third. I'll make the last trip ashore. Anaconda, stay aboard the jolly boat and make the return journey each time. Leave your muskets aboard, everybody, cutlasses too. Take only your knives. We don't want to show weapons – folk on the island might take it as an unfriendly gesture. Give the order, Anaconda!"

Any protests about leaving guns and swords aboard were forgotten. The men felt their spirits rise as the giant black steersman roared through cupped hands, "Away boat's crew!"

When Ben's turn came to go ashore, he seated himself in the prow of the little boat and sent a plea to Ned, who was standing next to him. "Keep that tail still or you'll beat me to death before I can put a foot on firm ground!"

Ned flopped his head from side to side, answering, "Sorry but it's impossible, we dogs have naturally wagging tails. I'd feel miserable keeping my beautiful tail still."

Pierre was waiting on shore with the first group, who had already gathered wood and lit a fire on the palm-fringed beach. The loyal bosun called Ned and Ben to his side, where they stood slightly out of hearing of the other crewmen.

Pierre kept his voice low. "Our fire can be seen from the *Marie*. 'Twill be night shortly, the men won't go wandering off in the dark."

Sounds of the tropical forest rang out behind them, strange noises of unidentifiable birds, beasts and reptiles, either hunting or being hunted.

Ben drew closer to the firelight. "Have you found water yet?"

Pierre shook his head. "Tomorrow maybe. Here, have a coconut. There's plenty about under the palms." He cut through the thick, fibrous husk, revealing a good-sized nut. Piercing it with his knife, the bosun gave it to the boy. Ben sucked the clear, sweet milk down. It tasted delicious.

Ned's paw tapped him on the leg. "D'you fancy sharing that?"

Ben hugged the Labrador briefly. "Sorry, Ned, I'll get you one of your own right away."

By the time Captain Thuron came ashore, all hands were dozing around the fire. He joined Pierre, Ned and Ben, who were drinking coconut milk and munching away at the white nut, and explained his plans in a low voice: "I've noticed that already three hands have deserted since we made landfall here. Ludon, Grest and Ricaud. They're hiding out somewhere inland by now. Anaconda has taken the jolly boat back to the *Marie* for the night – that way they won't get any ideas about taking over the ship. He'll row back to shore in the morning. Pierre, you'll take the boat back then and stand guard aboard the *Marie* during the day. We'll relieve you from time to time. I've smuggled some muskets and cutlasses ashore in a sack. If it comes to a mutiny, we'll be ready, though I hope it won't. Ben, you and Ned take first watch; I'll take over from you. Pierre, you relieve me for the last watch. I'm not sure what will happen tomorrow. I'll just have to plan things as they come. Now I must get some rest. Stay awake, my lucky Ben, you and Ned keep a weather eye on all hands."

Ben sat by the fire, tossing odd pieces of driftwood on the flames to keep it going as he stared into the dark mass of trees and foliage skirting the beach. He wondered what the morning would bring. Ned lay next to him with a broken coconut clutched between his forepaws, growling softly as he chewed away the soft white inner part from its hard wooden shell. Ben listened to his comments.

"Gurr, this is good. Why didn't I try coconut before today? Like a soft bone, but sweet and juicy. Gurr, nice and crunchy!"

The blue-eyed boy chuckled. "A coconut-eating dog – now I've seen it all! Do you think you could tear yourself away from that nut for a moment? We're getting low on driftwood. There's plenty along the tide line. I'll stay here and keep watch."

The black Labrador stood and stretched himself. "When I'm captain of my own ship, I'll make you go and get driftwood. It's not an easy life, you know, fetching this and searching for that, while you sit by the fire."

Ben passed his friend a mock serious thought. "Right, mate. We'll call your ship the *Black Dog,* and you can order me about day and night!"

Ned trotted off to the left along the beach, still grumbling. "Huh, don't think I won't. There'll be no idle boys aboard my vessel. Oh, and another thing, she'll be called the *Handsome Hound.* I don't like the sound of the *Black Dog*!"

Ben watched him go. He knew why Ned had gone to the

left. Ever since they had landed, both had avoided looking out to the waters that lay on their right. Ben knew it was because both he and Ned could feel the presence of Vanderdecken and the *Flying Dutchman*, hovering somewhere out in the seas. Feeling the hairs prickle on the back of his neck, Ben looked at the fire, then at the snoring ship's company of *La Petite Marie.* They were no trouble at the moment. Carefully avoiding a chance peek at the ebbing tide, he turned his attention to the dark, tangled forest.

Suddenly he felt sorry that the dog was not at his side. Something had moved in the gloom-cast undergrowth. He sat quite still, hoping the captain or one of the crew would awaken to break the spell, which kept his eyes riveted on the bushes fronting the tree line. There was the movement again, slow, silent and stealthy. Was it some wild jungle predator, a jaguar perhaps, or a giant python stalking him? The shape partially materialized as it moved out of shelter onto the pale, moonwashed sand. Ben wished it were a wild animal – that he could cope with. But this was the shape of a man, sinister, dark and phantomlike, clad in a long black gown with a pointed hood that hid his features. It was like looking at somebody with just a black hole for a face.

Fear numbed Ben's limbs and constricted his throat. He sat there, staring in horrified fascination as the eerie apparition glided soundlessly towards him, hands outstretched. It drew nearer and nearer . . .

EARLIER THAT SAME EVENING, THE *DIABLO Del Mar* had sailed into the straits that lay between Hispaniola and Puerto Rico, the waters known as the Mona Passage. Rocco Madrid had made a slight change to his plans. He called the mate, Boelee, and explained the scheme. "Why run straight out into the Atlantic, amigo? Would it not be more sensible to take a look at the harbours of each island on either side of these straits first?"

Boelee knew better than to disagree with Madrid, so he agreed. "A good plan, Capitano. We may even see the Frenchman's ship tied up in port. That would make things a lot easier than standing out in the ocean, awaiting a sea battle!"

Stroking his moustache, the Spaniard looked critically across the expanse, from left to right. "Which island would you visit first, Boelee? Hispaniola or Puerto Rico? Where's Thuron likely to make landfall, eh?"

The mate wanted to visit Hispaniola first. He knew of a few good taverns there. So he chose the opposite, certain that Rocco Madrid would disagree. "If 'twere up to me, Capitano, I'd take a look at Puerto Rico."

Madrid stared down his long, aristocratic nose at Boelee. "But it isn't up to you, amigo. I'm the one whose word counts aboard this ship. I say we go to Hispaniola first, to the Isle of Saona. It's the first likely landfall for any ship sailing this way."

Boelee nodded deferentially. "As you wish, Capitano!"

He said it too glibly, and Madrid eyed him suspiciously, then on a whim changed his mind again. "Maybe your choice was a clever one, Boelee. Let's double-guess Thuron. We'll put about for Mayagüez, a Puerto Rican harbour I know well. He'll probably think that we'd head for Saona. What are you looking so down in the mouth for, amigo? You wanted to go to Puerto Rico. I heard you say so not a moment ago. Am I not a kind master, to have granted your wish so readily?"

Boelee took the wheel from Portugee and turned the *Diablo* toward Mayagüez. Though Rocco Madrid was still smiling from the little joke he had played on the mate, and though he swaggered confidently about the foredeck, his mind was not easy. The Spaniard was torn by doubts as to the location of *La Petite Marie* – he seethed with resentment towards Thuron. At all costs the gold must be retrieved. Rocco did not take into account that it was he who had cheated the gold from the Frenchman in the first place. No! It was his gold, and he could not lose face in front of his crew by letting it, and Thuron, slip through his fingers. Besides, some of the gold had really belonged to him – it had been his stake in the game. Raphael Thuron and his crew had to pay for their boldness. He would punish them, yea, even unto death!

The spectral figure halted in front of Ben and sat down. Enormous relief flooded the boy: this was no evil ghost, it was only an old man. But what an old man!

Firelight reflected off his face as he pushed back his hood, revealing weather-lined features of immense serenity and kindness. A thousand wrinkles creased his brown-gold skin as he smiled through dark Latin eyes set in deep cream-coloured whites. Ben could see, without the least doubt, that this was a good and honest old fellow. His hair was wispy, pure silver; the robe he wore was that of some religious order, and a wooden cross of polished coconut shell hung from his neck on a cord. He spoke in Spanish, which the boy could readily understand.

"Peace be with you, my son. I am Padre Esteban. I hope that you and your friends mean no harm to me or my people."

Ben returned his smile. "No, Padre, we only need food and fresh water, so we can continue our voyage."

A thought from Ned flashed into Ben's mind as he saw Ned returning, dragging a large dead tree branch along the sand: "I felt your fear. Who is the man? Where's he from?"

Ben replied mentally to the Labrador. "Come here and take a look at his face, Ned – he's a friend, Padre Esteban."

Ned released the branch and came to sit by Ben. "Padre Esteban, eh? He's more like a statue of a saint than a man. I like him!"

The padre reached out a hand that was the colour of antique parchment. Stroking Ned's offered paw, he was silent for a while. Then, staring at Ben, he shook his head in wonder. "Who taught you to speak to an animal?"

Somehow, the boy was not surprised that the charismatic old man had the wisdom to read his mind. He decided to tell him the truth. "Nobody taught me. It was a gift from an angel. Could you really tell I was talking to my dog, Padre?"

The old priest never once took his eyes off Ben. "Oh yes, my son, you are called Ben, and this fine dog is Ned. But I see by your eyes that you have not been a young boy for many, many years – yours has been a hard and difficult life."

Ben was shocked by Padre Esteban's perception. He felt as if he wanted to pour out his story to the wonderful old man.

The padre merely reached out and took Ben's hand in his. "I know, Ben, I know, but there is no need to burden an old man with your history. I see great honesty in you. The evil of this world has not tainted your heart. I must go now, but I will return at dawn. My people will see to the needs of your ship. Tell the captain we mean no harm to you." He paused. "I must ask you to do something for me, Ben."

Squeezing the padre's hand lightly, the boy nodded. "Anything for you, Padre Esteban. What is it?"

The old man took the cross and its cord off and placed it about Ben's neck, tucking it inside his shirt. "Wear this. It will protect both you and your dog from the one who pursues you. Remember it when you are in danger."

Ben took the cross in his hand. It glistened in the firelight. The depiction of the figure upon it had been carved carefully into the wood and outlined with dark plant dye. When the boy looked up again, the old man had gone.

Ben told Thuron of his encounter with Padre Esteban, but he did not tell him of the cross or what the old man had seen in his eyes. The Frenchman warmed his hands by the fire. "See, I knew that you two were lucky to me. Don't worry, I'll pay the padre for anything he can give to us in the way of supplies. Well done, lad. You and Ned get some sleep now. There's lots to do once day breaks!"

• • •

Dawn's first pale light was streaking the skies over a smooth and tranquil sea, and the *Diablo Del Mar* was little more than three miles off the coast of Mayagüez. Rocco Madrid was roused from his cabin by a shout from Pepe, the lookout. "Sail off the stern to starboard!"

The Spanish pirate captain hurried out on deck and clapped the telescope to his eye. "A fishing vessel! Portugee, come about to meet it. I'll have words with the skipper."

Fear was the first reaction shown by the thin, tombstone-toothed Carib who skippered the small schooner-rigged fishing craft. He knew he was facing a pirate vessel whose guns he could not outrun. The man had dealt with those of The Brotherhood before. Hiding his terror behind a huge grin, he held up two large fish, shouting, "A good day to you, friends. My fish are fresh caught during the night, the finest in all these waters. Will you buy some and help to feed my poor wife and ten children, amigos?"

The *Diablo* loomed up alongside the small craft, dwarfing it. Rocco Madrid leaned over the midship rail and looked down at the skipper. Producing a gold coin, he spun it towards the fisherman, who caught it with great alacrity and waited in respectful silence to hear what the dangerous-looking pirate had to say.

Madrid held up another gold coin meaningfully. "Keep your fish, amigo. Where have ye been trawling? I mean you no harm – all I want is information."

The skipper swept off his battered straw hat and bowed, testing the gold coin between his teeth as he did so. "What can

I tell you, señor? We are bound for Santo Domingo on Hispaniola after three days and nights fishing the waters round the Isle of St Croix. Ah, it is a hard life, yes?"

Madrid nodded. "Never mind your life story. If you want to earn that gold piece, and the one I have here, tell me: did you see any other ships since you've been out? I'm looking for a French buccaneer named *La Petite Marie.*"

Holding the hat flat against his chest, the skipper bowed again. "I cannot read the letters, señor, but we sighted a vessel. Not as grand and large as your ship, but round in the bow and very fast-looking. She flew the skull and blades, just as you do. A Brethren vessel, eh?"

Rocco's eyes lit up. "That's her! Where was she when you saw her, amigo? Tell me!"

The skipper waved his hat back over his shoulder. "Sailing toward the southeast coast, I think, maybe to Ponce, Guayama or Arroyo, who knows?"

The Spaniard stroked his moustache, slightly puzzled. "What would Thuron want around there? Hmm, maybe he has a secret hiding place. I'll soon find out, though!" He pocketed the gold coin and drew his sword, pointing it at the hapless fishing-boat skipper. "I know Hispaniola well. If you've lied to me, I'll find you. Ten children is a lot for a widow to support, remember that."

Dismissing the fishing boat, he turned to Pepe. "Get my charts, I'll take charge of this operation!"

Pepe hurried off to the captain's cabin, where he gathered up charts, muttering to himself, "When did he never take charge? But who am I to mention this, nothing but a donkey."

• • •

Aboard the *Devon Belle*, Captain Redjack Teal was also studying his charts whilst taking breakfast. His new cook, an undersized seaman named Moore, stood nervously by, watching as Teal forked a minute portion of fish into his mouth. The privateer captain pulled a face of disgust and spat the food onto the floor, then glared balefully at Moore. "Curse your liver'n'lights, man, do ye call this cooked, eh?"

Moore tried to stand his ground and look respectful at the same time. He saluted and spoke with a thick Irish accent. " 'Twas boiled t'the best of me ability, Yer Honour!"

"Boiled!" Teal remarked, as though the word were an obscenity. "Boiled? Who the devil ever told ye I take boiled fish t'break me fast, eh? Not another word, sirrah. Stand to attention! Clean this mess up. Take that demned fish out o' me sight! Report t'the gunner for six strokes of a rope's end and thank your ignorant stars 'tain't the cat across your back. If ye ever bring me boiled fish again, I'll have ye boiled alive in your own galley. Get out of me sight!"

After the unfortunate Moore had left the cabin, Teal quaffed several goblets of Madeira and stalked out on deck in high bad humour. He called the mate to attend him. "You there, has land been sighted yet?"

The man tugged his forelock. "Nary a sightin' yet, Cap'n, but we should spot somethin' by midmorn, sir."

Teal could think of nothing to say except, "Well . . . well, make sure ye do! An' report t'me, straight off, d'ye hear?" He thrust his telescope viciously at the mate. "Take this up t'the crow's nest, tell that lookout to keep his confounded eyes skinned for land. Move y'self, man!"

He stalked off, exclaiming aloud, "Boiled fish? Can't abide the foul stuff. Worse than boiled mutton, if y'ask me, far worse!"

By midmorning the entire crew of the *Devon Belle* were fervently hoping their captain would stay in his cabin until his temper had calmed. Gillis, the captain's dresser, sat in Cook Moore's galley, sharing some boiled fish with his shipmate and complaining bitterly, "Cap'n, is it? I've seen better cap'ns in charge of a saltfish barrow. Kicked me, he did, aye, kicked me, an' for what? 'Cos one of his buttons was loose. Ain't nothin' in regulations says a man has t'get kicked for a loose button, is there, cookie?"

Moore rubbed his rear end, still smarting from the gunner's knotted rope. "Only a kick? Sure now, weren't you the lucky one. How does that boiled fish taste to ye?"

Gillis was about to reply when the call came loud and clear. "Land ho! East off the for'ard bow. Land hoooooo!"

The feeling of relief that swept over the *Devon Belle* was almost tangible in the air. Smiling faces were seen as crewmen lined the bows to catch a sight of the headland when it became visible on the horizon. Shortly thereafter, Redjack Teal strutted out onto the deck, freshly attired by Gillis in his favourite red hunting jacket and pristine linen accessories. A naval officer's sword, complete with brass scabbard, clanked at his side.

Before all hands could busy themselves at their chores, Teal caught them with their backs to him, scanning the horizon for land. He gave his crew a brisk lecture, like a schoolmaster censuring a class. "Nobody got any work t'do, eh? Stand still there when I'm addressing ye, face me, straighten y'selves up!"

All hands braced themselves stiffly on the swaying deck, chins tucked in, staring straight ahead. Teal looked them over contemptuously, speaking in his affected nasal drawl. "Right, listen t'me, gentlemen, an' I use the term loosely. From me chart calculations I have brought this ship in sight of Puerto Rico, where we will engage the enemy. It will be approximately early evenin' before we reach the coast. I fully intend to sail in like one of His Majesty's ships o' the line, smart as paint, an' with guns bristlin'!"

Every man knew what was coming next as the captain let a moment's silence pass, then stamped his foot down hard. "This vessel is a pigsty, a demned pigsty, d'ye hear me? First mate an' bosun, put all hands to holystonin' decks, swabbin' out scuppers, coilin' lines an' polishin' brasses!"

Springing forward, the mate and bosun saluted. "Aye aye, sir!"

Wheeling sharply, Redjack turned his back on them and continued. "I'm goin' t'me cabin now, but I'll be back out at midday. All hands will be ready for inspection, cleaned up an' lookin' like British sailors an' not like some farmyard rabble. This afternoon, you sloppy men will take exercise, dancin' hornpipes an' singin' shanties. Any man not doin' so with a cheerful demeanour will be punished. Is that understood?"

Without waiting to hear the crew's dutiful chant of "Aye aye, sir!" Teal strode purposefully off to his cabin, feeling the collective glare of hatred from his crew directed at his back.

Handing the bosun a length of tarred and knotted rope, the mate selected a wooden belaying pin. Veins stood out on his neck as he bellowed at the crew, "Don't stand there gawpin', get about it! You 'eard the cap'n!"

As all hands went about their tasks, the bosun and mate walked the deck, conversing in undertones. No love was lost between either of the men and Teal – the bosun's voice was hoarse with indignation. "Playin' at bein' Royal Navy again, are we?

Blast his eyes, Teal wouldn't recognize a real privateer if one fell on him from the yardarm. How'd he ever get to be a cap'n?"

The mate chuckled drily. "Aye, I've wrung more salt water out of me socks than he's ever sailed on. Did ye hear him tellin' as how his calculations've brought us this far? He's done nothin' night'n'day but ask me where we are."

The bosun flicked his rope end at a slacking deck scrubber. "I tell ye, mate, 'twill be funny if there ain't a sign o' that Frenchie when we gets to Puerto Rico. Haha, what'll Teal do then, make the crew sing an' dance more 'ornpipes an' shanties to conjure the buccaneer up? D'ye think the Frenchman will be at Puerto Rico?"

Spitting neatly over the side, the mate shook his head. "If he is, there'll be none more surprised than me. That ole Frenchie's long gone, prob'ly off into the Atlantic Ocean. Cap'n my eye. I was told Teal ran off from England 'cos of gamblin' debts. The eldest son of a noble family, eh?"

Entirely in agreement with his companion, the bosun winked. "An' not a ha'penny piece 'twixt the lot of 'em. I tell ye, this ship's run by a pauper who knows more about the back an' front end of a horse than the bow an' stern of a ship!"

The mate tapped the belaying pin in his cupped hand. "Aye, an' 'tis poor seamen like us who have t'put up with the likes o' Teal. Come on, we'd best see the men get this craft shipshape afore Redjack comes back on deck."

Running fair with a sprightly morning breeze, the *Devon Belle* edged closer to the island of Puerto Rico.

Padre Esteban was as good as his word. He entered the buccaneers' camp at daybreak, bringing with him two dozen of his people. These were silent, dark-eyed, coffee-skinned locals carrying fearsome-looking machetes.

Ned sent a swift thought to Ben: "They look peaceful enough, but I wouldn't like to get on the wrong side of those lads!"

Ben nodded. "Look at the supplies they've brought with them."

Besides a roasted goat, a pig and some chickens, the men brought smoked fish, a full honeycomb and an amazing range of fruit and vegetables, plus a large sack of rough home-ground corn flour.

Pointing to a pile of empty gourds, the old padre explained, "For water, there are plenty of pools and streams about to fill these vessels with. How are you this morning, my son?"

Ben smiled as he shook the old man's hand. "I am well, Padre. Thank you for your help. This is wonderful!"

Padre Esteban allowed Ned to stand with his front paws against his chest. He stroked the dog fondly. "The Lord has always smiled on us. There is food aplenty for all on this bounteous isle. Ah, here comes your captain."

The Frenchman and the padre kissed cheeks in the Continental manner, on each side. It was obvious that the captain had taken to the old fellow at first glance.

"I am Raphael Thuron, master of *La Petite Marie.* My friend, how can I thank you for all of this? Here, take these gold coins I have with me, there're twenty of them – is that enough?"

Shaking his head, the old man pressed the gold back into Thuron's hand. "Gold brings trouble and death with it. The food costs nothing to grow, it is given freely to friends with good hearts. Take and enjoy it, in the name of our Lord."

Ned licked Padre Esteban's hand as he communicated with Ben. "See, I told you last night, this old man is a saint!"

As if he had intercepted the message, the padre chuckled. "There are good men and bad men. All my life I have tried to be good, but I am no saint. Just a man who likes to help others."

Ben had never seen a pirate weep, but he noticed that Thuron sniffed loudly and brushed a sleeve across his eyes. "Well, you've certainly helped us, my friend. Pierre, signal the ship, we need to get all of this back aboard. Padre, are you certain that there is nothing we can give you in return for all this good food? Anything?"

Padre Esteban had a quiet word with one of his men, a big fellow who looked like some type of village headman. He shrugged and turned back to the Frenchman. "Perhaps if you have a bit of canvas and some iron nails to spare. They are hard to come by, away from towns and ports."

Captain Thuron agreed happily to the simple request. "Ben, when you get back aboard the *Marie*, I want you and Anaconda to load up any casks of nails we have and half of our spare canvas. Anaconda will row you and Ned back here so you can present them to the padre."

All that day the jolly boat plied back and forth between the ship and shore. The entire crew of the *Marie* were sorry to leave Guayama and the gentle old priest. Ben and Ned were the last to leave; Anaconda sat in the boat whilst they made their farewells to Padre Esteban. The boy carried a message from his captain to the padre: "Cap'n Thuron says that he hopes the nails and canvas will be useful to you. He also told me to tell you to watch out for three men who have deserted the ship. They are called Ludon, Grest and Ricaud. Though what you will do if you find them I don't know, Padre."

Ned passed a brief angry thought. "I know what I'd do with the rats. Deserters, huh!"

The old man shrugged. "They will be gone by now, to some large port on the island, where they will meet others of their kind. Thank your captain for me, Ben. He is a good and honest man, a rare quality in a buccaneer. My son, I wish you could stay, but I feel in my heart that you are not destined to abide here with me. Keep the cross by you and remember what I said. It will protect you. Now go – I wish both you and your faithful Ned a happy life. I cannot wish you long life, because I know you already possess that. But think of me now and then. I will pray for you both. Go now, and the Lord be with you."

Ben would forget many things in the years to come, but he would never forget that sunny afternoon saying goodbye to the old padre. Turquoise surf crested white as it boomed to break upon the golden sands of the beautiful island of Puerto Rico. The tears from the old man's face were salty as the sea as he kissed the foreheads of the blue-eyed boy and his dog. Bobbing up and down on the swell, the jolly boat drew away, with Anaconda plying the oars strongly. Ben and Ned stared through the unashamed mist of sorrow-dewed eyes at the lone figure standing on the beach, signing the air open-handed with a cross to speed them on their way.

7

THE SHIP'S CARPENTER OF THE *DEVON BELLE* practised a few chords on his fiddle and sat atop the capstan, ready for the ordeal to come. Even more than the hardest chore, the crew hated and detested regulation shanty singing and hornpipe dancing. None of them were skilled at dancing, and most of them had voices totally unsuited to singing. But it was mandatory in the British Royal Navy that a captain could order his crew to sing and dance as an exercise. Redjack Teal ignored the fact that they were privateers; he preferred Royal Navy customs and discipline.

Highly relieved that they were not part of the exercise, the mate and bosun stood by, ready with the rope end and belaying pin to deal with reluctant singers and lackadaisical dancers. Suppressing a snigger, the bosun cast an eye over the waiting crew. "Look at 'em, did ye ever see such a blushin' pack o' bearded beauties? They're enough to give any maiden nightmares!"

Trying hard to keep a straight face, the mate replied, "I'll wager

Teal tells the carpenter to play 'The Jolly Captain'. I think 'tis the only shanty he knows."

The carpenter, who had overheard the conversation, spat over the side in disgust as he repeated the name of the tune. " 'Jolly Cap'n'? We're on the wrong ship t'be singin' about a jolly cap'n, mate. Stow it, here he comes!"

Teal appeared on deck. Drawing in a deep breath, he tapped his chest. "Wonderful day, eh? Sea air, nothin' quite like it! Bracing. Makes a man want to sing an' dance! You there, er, Carpenter, give us a rousing tune. Hmm, let me see. Ah, 'The Jolly Captain', I like that one. All hands look lively now, no slackers or mumblers. Carry on, player. One, two . . ."

Teal tapped his foot in time to the music as the carpenter played. The crew were forced to dance awkwardly, imitating the tasks of rope hauling and capstan turning as they bellowed the lyrics discordantly.

"Ho the wind is blowin' fair, lads,
An' the sun shines on the sea,
Adieu to all our sweethearts,
An' old England on the lee.
We'll sail the oceans over,
In a good ship tight'n'free,
We've got a jolly cap'n,
An' right happy men are we!

Hurrah hurrah hurrah, me boys,
For the king's royal family,
An' for the jolly cap'n,
Who takes good care o' me!

There's skilly in the galley, lads,
An' good ale in the cask,
From far Cathay to Greenland,
What more could sailors ask.
Through storm an' tropic weather,
We'll sing away each mile,
For merry men are we to see
Our jolly cap'n smile!"

Teal made a rolling motion with his hand and called to the carpenter, "That's the stuff, keep goin', man, play it again!" He pointed at the mate and the bosun officiously. "You two there, see they all step lively. Any man not singin', give 'im somethin' to sing about, hot an' heavy!"

Further west along the coast from Guayama, the little settlement of Ponce basked in the noon heat with hardly a breeze to ripple the tall palms. Captain Rocco Madrid had anchored the *Diablo Del Mar* just behind a small headland and taken his crew ashore. In the village, he interrupted the locals at their siesta. To show them he was a man not to be trifled with, he drew his sword and whipped off the head of a fighting cock that had pecked at him. The good folk of Ponce did not scream or panic, they merely sat in the shade of their palmetto-thatched huts, staring at the pirates silently.

Madrid glared back at them awhile, then turned and gave orders to Portugee and Boelee. "Take half a dozen crew and search the other side of the headland for signs of the Frenchman. I'll deal with these villagers. Don't waste time. If Thuron hasn't been here, we'll need to move on to Guayama swiftly."

When the men had left, Madrid pointed to an old fellow with calm, dignified features, who looked likely to be some type of village patriarch. "Have any ships been here? Speak."

The man shrugged. "Not for a long time, señor."

Touching the man's throat with his sword point, the Spaniard loaded his voice with menace. "If you lie, I will kill you!"

The old man did not seem impressed. He sounded matter-of-fact. "What reason would I have to lie? No ship has been here of late."

Rocco Madrid had encountered Caribs like this before. He knew the old man was speaking the truth. However, he felt the need to assert his authority before he lost face to the patriarch's impassive stare.

Rocco sniffed the air and nodded towards a fire, which was tended by two women. "What are you cooking there?"

One of the women looked up from a cauldron she was stirring. "Stew, with goat meat, plantains and maize."

Rocco pricked the old man's throat with his blade. "Get me some, and my men, too!"

The patriarch's eyes looked sideways at the woman. "Give them the stew."

The woman moved to start serving, but Madrid flicked the sword tip beneath the old man's chin. "You will serve us!"

With a neat movement, the man slid away from the sword and stood erect gracefully. "I will serve you."

Pepe, the lookout, sat alongside Rocco, guzzling stew from an earthenware bowl. Smiling happily, he wiped grease from his lips with the back of his hand. "Capitano, this is good stew, yes?"

The Spaniard looked disdainfully at the bowl, from which he had only taken a single small taste. "Good stew, no!"

The sudden explosion of a musket shot set parakeets to squawking in the trees. This was followed by a scream. Rocco Madrid leapt up, sword at the ready, knocking the bowl from Pepe's hands. "Go and see what that is, quick!"

He signalled to three other crewmen. "Go with him!" Pulling a loaded musket from his broad belt, the Spaniard looked at the old man, who was standing by the fire. "Who is out there?"

The old fellow licked stew from his fingers. "How would I know that, señor? I cannot be in two places at once."

Turning to the two women, the Carib said something in a completely strange tongue. The women smiled and nodded.

Rocco guessed it was some kind of insult, or fun they were poking at him. He pointed the pistol towards the old man's head. "Speak again without my permission and I will kill you!"

The old man did not appear frightened by threats. "Death comes to us all sooner or later. We cannot escape it."

The pirate captain was about to pull the trigger, when Pepe came hurrying out of the thickets behind the huts. "Capitano, look who we've found. Bring him out, Portugee!"

With his own belt knotted about his neck, Ludon, the former mate of the *Marie*, was dragged out of the bushes by Portugee and the search party. Boelee gave Ludon a kick in the back that sent him sprawling at the Spaniard's feet.

Ludon let out a terror-stricken whimper. "Don't kill me . . . please!"

Portugee yanked on the belt. "Shut your face, worm!"

Boelee put a booted foot on his prisoner's body. "Three of 'em, Capitano, they bumped right into us out there. They tried to run away, but Maroosh shot one an' Rillo chopped the other one down with his cutlass. We saved this piece of scum for you. Remember, this was the one who put a blade to your neck in the tavern at Cartagena."

Madrid grabbed Ludon by the hair and smiled into his face. "Of course! Welcome to our camp, amigo."

Tears cut dirty patterns through the dust on Ludon's cheeks. "I wouldn't have harmed ye, Cap'n. I ran away from that accursed Thuron. I never wanted to be one of his crew, I swear on my life I didn't. Don't kill me, I beg ye!"

Madrid's smile grew even wider. "I won't kill you, amigo . . . not yet. Put more wood on that fire, Pepe. This one is going to tell me where Thuron and his ship are."

Ludon screamed and sobbed. "Oh don't, Cap'n, please don't! I'll tell ye where they are, ye don't have t'do that to me!"

Madrid turned away and spoke conversationally to his bosun. "They always lie, but the flames bring out the real truth. Haul him over to the fire while I continue our little talk."

The old Carib man's voice cut across Ludon's moaning and pleading. "Señor, you will not do this in my village. You will leave now, all of you. Go to your ship, or die here!"

Madrid gave the old man an insolent smile as he repeated, "Die? You dare to say that to me? Maroosh, blow that old fool's brainpan out with your musket!"

Before Maroosh could raise the gun, he gasped and pulled a brightly feathered object from the side of his neck. It was a dart, made from a long, sharp thorn. He stared stupidly at it and dropped the musket. His legs began to tremble, and he sat down in the dust.

The Carib patriarch glanced at the treetops surrounding the village. His voice became flat and stern. "We saw your ship long before you came here. Only fools do not take precautions. My hunters are hidden all about our village – they never miss with their blowpipes. You, señor, I have suffered enough of your bad manners. Take your men and go. Leave that one behind, he is already dead. Just as you will be if you choose to stay."

The pirates stared in horrified fascination at Maroosh, who was still sitting on the ground, trembling fitfully.

Rocco Madrid put up his sword and musket and began walking backwards out of the village. "Boelee, get the crew back to the *Diablo*. We can't stand against invisible Caribs with poison darts."

Dragging Ludon with them, all hands from the *Diablo* backed out of the village. What galled Rocco Madrid most was the way the patriarch and his people carried on with their work, completely ignoring the Spaniard and his retreating men. Rocco was inwardly seething, for the blood of Spanish grandees ran in his veins. Keeping face and demanding respect, repaying insults and avenging slights were ingrained into his character.

Boelee watched his captain's face the moment they were back aboard ship. From the way a tic started up in Madrid's left eyelid and his teeth began making a grinding sound, the mate knew Rocco Madrid had vengeance on his mind.

Scowling dangerously, Rocco strove to keep his voice normal. "Weigh the anchor and put on sail, load all portside cannons. Portugee, take her round the headland, but don't set course for Guayama straight away. We're going to settle accounts with those heathens and blast their village to splinters!

Cannonballs are the best answer to poison darts. I'll teach those savages a lesson in manners!"

There was thunder in the afternoon as the cannons of the *Diablo Del Mar* pounded the pitiful little settlement. Huts disintegrated, palm trees snapped like matchsticks, and destruction, flames and smoke were everywhere. The Spaniard laughed at the sight of high-flung debris still falling on the flattened ruins.

"Stand off and take us down the coast, Portugee. Bring our prisoner to my cabin, Boelee. Now I'll have words with him!"

The patriarch and his people had deserted their village the moment they had first sighted the *Diablo Del Mar* rounding the headland. Now they wandered out and stood onshore watching the stern of the departing pirate ship. It was not the first time Brotherhood vessels had wrecked their huts. Nobody was harmed, for it was easy to hide from big, clumsy cannons. Palmetto and bamboo grew in profusion, so it was a minor inconvenience to build more huts. The patriarch put his arm around a sobbing woman. "Why do you weep? Are you hurt?"

She shook her head. "I forgot to take my goat – a tree fell on him and killed him."

The old man's face remained impassive. "You can have my goat. Yours will do for tonight's meal."

Ben was up in the rigging of the *Marie*, helping to trim the sails. Glancing down he could see the anchor appearing through the clear waters as it was weighed. Ned stood wagging his tail, looking up at Ben and sending him thoughts. "What's it like up there, mate? I'll bet you can see for miles."

The boy replied mentally. "You wouldn't like it, Ned. The masts sway a lot, and when I look down, the ship seems to be quite still. But you do get a great view from up here. I can see the water change colour from green to blue over towards the horizon, and I can see . . ."

The remainder of the words were shouted out loud by Ben. "A ship! Ship ahoy, Cap'n!"

Thuron hurried to the forepeak, pulling his telescope out as he followed the direction that Ben was pointing. It took only a moment to confirm the Frenchman's fears.

"Well spotted, lad. 'Tis the privateer! Get that anchor aboard, Anaconda. Take us west, but hug the coast. The Englishman mightn't have seen us yet, and there's a chance we can give him the slip. Come out of that rigging, Ben! All hands on deck!"

Thuron took the wheel from the giant steersman. "That breeze is blowing onshore, we'll have to tack a bit. What's that? Sounds like thunder, did ye hear it, mate?"

Anaconda scanned the sky. "Ain't no thunder, Cap'n. Not a cloud anywhere. Not the privateer, neither. That Englishman's not goin' to fire guns from so far off, no point in it."

Thuron had to agree. "Aye, we'd have seen the splashes of cannonballs falling short in the sea. Well, whatever it is, we're getting out of here and heading for the Mona Passage 'twixt Hispaniola and this island, bound into the Atlantic."

Early evening shades were starting to tinge the eastern horizon cream and pink. Aboard the *Devon Belle* all hands sat about, catching their breath and mopping away the sweat of their afternoon exercise, which had been hard and long. Captain Redjack Teal had decided they were slacking and had doubled the time they spent at singing shanties and dancing hornpipes. Finally Teal went to his cabin, having had enough of watching the ridiculous prancing and off-key singing. Besides, he had missed his midnoon ration of Madeira.

Putting aside the fiddle, the carpenter blew on his numbed fingertips. "If I have to play 'The Jolly Cap'n' one more time, I'll throw meself overboard!"

Loosing the splints on either side of his injured leg, the bosun massaged his limb gently. "Hmm, the old leg's feelin' better today."

The cook laughed bitterly. "Hah! That's all the dancin' ye never had to do!"

The bosun replied scornfully. "Dancin', did ye call that dancin'? I've seen a duck on a hot plate dancin' better than you lot –"

"I agree with ye, sirrah, demned sloppy lot, ain't they?" The captain had sneaked from his cabin and was standing close by. He liked surprising his crew – it kept them alert. Now he took a sip from his goblet and remarked languidly, "Lackaday, tired are we, lying about like a lot of half-paid skivvies. No meals to make, Cook, not a soul on watch, no lookout, ship takin' care of itself, eh?"

The crew leapt up and tried to look busy. Everyone knew that Captain Redjack could always find work for idle hands. Teal was thinking up a few more sarcastic remarks when a shout came from the topmast.

"Ship ahoy, 'tis the Frenchman, sir!"

Sprinting smartly up into the bows, Teal swept his glass over the coast until he caught sight of *La Petite Marie*. "Hah, so 'tis! Skulkin' west an' huggin' the shore. A pound to an ounce o' China tea the Frenchie's makin' for the passage out into the ocean, eh!"

He slammed the telescope shut decisively. "Well, he ain't goin' t'make it! We'll take a point west an' cut the impudent whelp off with a straight run for the headland at the channel mouth. Meet him almost bow on!"

Teal hurried the length of the ship, cuffing anyone who was not fast enough to move out of his path, then seized the wheel from the steersman and spun it to alter course. "Leave this to a qualified captain, the froggy won't escape me this time!"

The steersman protested, "But Cap'n, the wind's runnin' onshore, we'd have to tack to make your course!"

Teal looked at the man as if he had lost his mind. "So, d'ye think I know so little of navigatin' that I can't tack, eh? Stand aside, sirrah, an' watch me!"

Trying to keep his voice reasonable and respectful, the steersman explained, "Beggin' y'pardon, sir, 'tis all right running with the wind on a jury-rigged foremast. But if ye try tackin' her, the mast won't take it. 'Twill either snap or flop over, whichever way the wind takes it, sir."

Redjack Teal's face turned the colour of his hunting jacket. He lashed out and slapped the steersman's face, hard. "Demn your insolence, fellow! Who d'ye think you're talkin' to, eh, eh? Tellin' me how to steer me own vessel? Go below an' polish the anchor chain. Mr Mate, put a gag on this man, that'll curb his impudent tongue!"

Shoving a belaying pin sideways into the steersman's open mouth, the mate tied it there with a length of cord that went tightly around the back of the man's neck. He led him off to the anchor-chain locker, whispering to him, "Sorry, matey, I've never had t'do a gaggin' before, but orders is orders. Thank y'stars Redjack never had ye flogged."

The steersman looked dumbly at the mate, tears running from his eyes at the injustice of the punishment.

Teal watched the foremast start to sway as he ran the ship side on to the wind. He called out, "Carpenter, attend me quickly! Move, man!"

The ship's carpenter ambled up and tugged his forelock. "Sir?"

Teal nodded towards the awkwardly swaying foremast. "Can ye not do something t'stop that confounded thing wobblin' about?"

The carpenter scratched behind his ear. "What d'ye want me to do, Cap'n? I did all I could to it in the first place."

Teal's knuckles showed white as he grasped the wheel. "Do anything t'keep it still. I know, take another man with ye an' coils of rope. He'll climb the mainmast, you'll climb the foremast. Get as much rope 'twixt both masts as ye can, then stick a boat oar through the ropes an' twist until they get good an' tight. That'll steady our foremast."

The carpenter had never heard such a stupid idea. Squinting his eyes, he scratched behind his ear again. "Beggin' y'pardon, sir, but are ye sure 'twill work?"

Redjack looked from the anchor-chain locker to the carpenter. "D'ye wish to argue with your captain, sirrah?"

The man came to rigid attention. "No, sir!"

Teal nodded. "Good. Then get on with it. I know 'twill work, I've heard of it done before. Jump to it!"

• • •

Joby, the carpenter's assistant, draped two coils of rope across his shoulders as he held a whispered conversation with the carpenter. "What's goin' on? What're we supposed to be doin'?"

Adjusting the ropes on his own shoulders, the carpenter picked up a jolly-boat oar. "Redjack's orders! You've got to climb the mainmast, an' I've got to climb the foremast. Cap'n says our job is to wind ropes between both masts. Then he wants me to stick an oar through the ropes an' twist it round an' round 'til it gets tight. He reckons it'll brace the foremast break so that the ship can tack properly. Up y'go, Joby!"

Shaking his head, Joby began climbing. "It won't work!"

The carpenter shrugged. "You an' me both know that, but who are we to argue with Redjack?"

Aboard the *Diablo Del Mar,* the lookout scrambled down from his watch point in the crow's nest. Dashing to Rocco Madrid's cabin, he burst in, shouting, "Capitano, I've found the Frenchman, he's running up the coast, sailing straight in our direction. Come an' look!"

Madrid grinned like a hungry wolf. Sheathing his sword, he winked at Ludon, who was bound, spread-eagled, to the table. "A lucky day for you, amigo. We'll talk later."

The *Marie* was still a good distance off as the Spaniard watched her through his telescope. He spoke his thoughts aloud to the lookout. "Has Thuron gone blind? Does he not see us, Pepe?"

Pepe picked at his yellowed teeth with a grubby fingernail. "Who knows? What do we do now, Capitano?"

Madrid's mind was racing, and now he formed a swift plan. "Portugee, steer us in closer to land. No use standing out here in full view. Thuron looks as if he has all sail piled on, maybe he's fleeing from something. Who cares? We'll lie in close to shore and spring out on him once he gets close enough. Boelee, get a boarding party ready, hooks and grappling irons. If we're quick enough, we can take Thuron's vessel without firing a cannon. Pepe, make sure we're showing no lights. 'Twill be dark soon. We'll sail out of the night an' pounce on him!"

Ben and Ned were on the stern deck with Captain Thuron, watching the privateer. Thuron pointed. "See, Ben, they've changed course. I wager the Englishman is trying to cut us off before we reach the Mona Passage."

Ben looked anxiously at the Frenchman. "And will he, sir?"

Thuron chuckled. "Nay, lad, not with a jury-rigged foremast wobbling about – he could never outsail our *Marie*. Even so, I could still give him the slip once 'tis dark."

Ned's paw scratched against Ben's leg, and he caught the dog's agitated thought. "Ben, I can feel the *Dutchman* up ahead, can you?"

The boy patted his friend's back. "You must have sharper instincts than me. I can't feel a thing. Are you sure?"

Panting anxiously, the black Labrador pulled him along the deck towards the prow. "I'm not certain whether 'tis the *Dutchman* or not. But I've got a very bad feeling that there's something waiting for us up yonder."

Ben trusted the dog's instincts. Letting go of Ned, he went back astern and spoke to Captain Thuron. "Sir, I feel there's something not right with our course. Wouldn't it be better if we stood out to sea a bit more?"

Thuron stared into the lad's strangely clouded eyes. "You look worried, Ben, what is it?"

The boy shook his head. "I don't know, sir, maybe there's hidden reefs along the coastline. I know I'd feel a lot safer out in deep water. It's just a feeling I've got."

Thuron gazed at Ben a moment longer, then made a decision. "So be it, you're my lucky lad. Anaconda, take her out a point. Mayhap we will be safer out there, and we'll still be out of range of the privateer's guns – he's trying to run ahead of us and block the passage."

The giant Anaconda spun the wheel a half turn. "Aye aye, Cap'n, but we'll have to tack harder. That onshore wind is startin' to blow heavy. A squall might be comin' up."

Pierre the bosun slapped Ben's back. "Better out at sea in rough weather where we can't be driven ashore. You'll make a cap'n one day, boy!"

Ben smiled. "Oh, I'll leave that to Ned, he's always wanted to be master of his own ship. I'll be the cabin lad."

Pierre, Anaconda and Thuron roared with laughter at this remark.

Pepe called down from the crow's nest, "Capitano, the Frenchman is putting out to sea!" Madrid cursed under his breath. Less than a mile off and his quarry was deserting the coastline.

He rapped out orders. "We can still cut him off, amigos. Portugee, take the *Diablo* out quickly. We should be able to run alongside of Thuron. I'm certain he hasn't seen us yet. Take her out!"

Portugee tugged at the big steering wheel, but it moved only fractionally. He called out, "Boelee, bring some help, lend a hand here, the wind's catchin' us side on! We're goin' landward!"

Madrid tapped his foot anxiously, berating the men as they fought to turn the stubborn wheel. "Fools! Didn't you feel the wind getting up? Put your backs into it!"

There was a bump, and the Spaniard did a little sidestep to keep himself from falling when he heard Boelee groan. "We're in the shallows, the hull's scraped bottom!"

Rocco Madrid drew his sword and slashed uselessly at the air. "Then get oars, pikes, poles, anything! Push her off before Thuron escapes! You, you and you, get to the first bow cannon! Load with chain shot, I'll chip her mast off as she comes by!"

Rain started to spatter the *Diablo*'s decks as Madrid knelt at the cannon holding a glowing piece of towrope. He squinted along the cannon barrel, sighting on the spot where the *Marie* would pass offshore in a moment. "We'll see how fast our little French bird can fly with a broken wing. Hah! Here she comes now . . ."

Portugee and Boelee managed to get the *Diablo* off the sandbank at that precise moment. They wrestled with the wheel as she turned slightly and her stern bumped off the underwater hazard. Rocco Madrid was knocked backwards as he fired the cannon.

8

AS HE GLIMPSED THE GUN flash from the corner of one eye, Ben heard the familiar shrieking whirr cut the night air. He hurled himself flat. Ned bulled into the back of Thuron's knees, knocking him down beside Ben. *Whump!* The noise was followed by a loud ripping sound.

Thuron leapt to his feet, roaring at his steersman. "Take her out! We're being fired upon!" Heeling out into the rainswept Caribbean, the *Marie* sailed on a zigzag course, tacking to get out of danger.

Ned shook rain from his coat, thinking, "It couldn't have been the *Flying Dutchman,* Ben – ghosts can't fire cannonballs."

Ben answered his friend's thought. "That wasn't a cannonball, it was chain shot. I remember the sound from when the privateer fired on us."

Thuron's strong hands hauled Ben upright. "Up ye come, lucky lad. Look at that!"

Ben saw the foresail directly overhead, now nothing but a mass of canvas tatters flapping wetly in the wind. Anaconda, who had given the wheel over to Pierre, ambled along. He whistled softly at the sight of the wrecked sail.

"Someone tryin' to chop our mast, Cap'n. Who was it?"

Wiping raindrops from his telescope lens, Thuron swept the coast. "The *Diablo*. I'd forgotten about her. That fox Madrid must have found our trail. Hah! His aim hasn't improved much. All he did was blow a hole in a foresail. If that chain shot had hit its target, we'd have been without a foremast!"

Anaconda made a sobering observation. "Aye, Cap'n, an' if we'd been on an upswell instead of a downswell, you an' your lucky mates would've been mashed to ribbons!"

The Frenchman, who could still retain his sense of humour even in the midst of a crisis, remarked drily, "Aye, an' then Ned would have never been made captain of his own ship!"

Ned sent Ben an indignant thought through the ensuing laughter. "I fail to see the humour in that remark!"

The Frenchman grew serious as he took another sighting through his glass. "We've got trouble enough for any vessel now, an English privateer to one side an' a Spanish pirate to t'other. Well, Mr Anaconda, what would you do in a case like this?"

The giant steersman gave a deep bass chuckle. "Cap'n, I'd be doin' the old Trinidad Shuffle."

Ben looked from one to the other. "What's the old Trinidad Shuffle?"

Thuron winked at him. "I'm going to take the wheel. You tell him, mate."

Anaconda explained. " 'Tis dangerous, but clever if we can pull it off, Ben. We let Madrid chase us, but we sail dead ahead, straight for the privateer. Madrid's sailing close behind us, see. We take in sail and let him. All he can see is our stern, so in the dark he'll think he scored a hit an' chopped our mast, because we're travellin' slow. The Englander should put about, not wanting to present his ship broadside to the *Marie*. At the last moment, we fire on both ships, give Madrid a shot from our stern and one for the privateer from our bows. Then we hoist every stitch of sail and run off west into the night. The Englander knows he's got no chance of catching the *Marie*, 'cos he's got a broken foremast. But any privateer has more than enough cannon to outgun a pirate. The *Diablo* is a bigger, much richer-lookin' prize than us – and now he's dead ahead. So, what would you do if you were the privateer, Ben?"

The boy replied promptly. "I'd attack the Spaniard!"

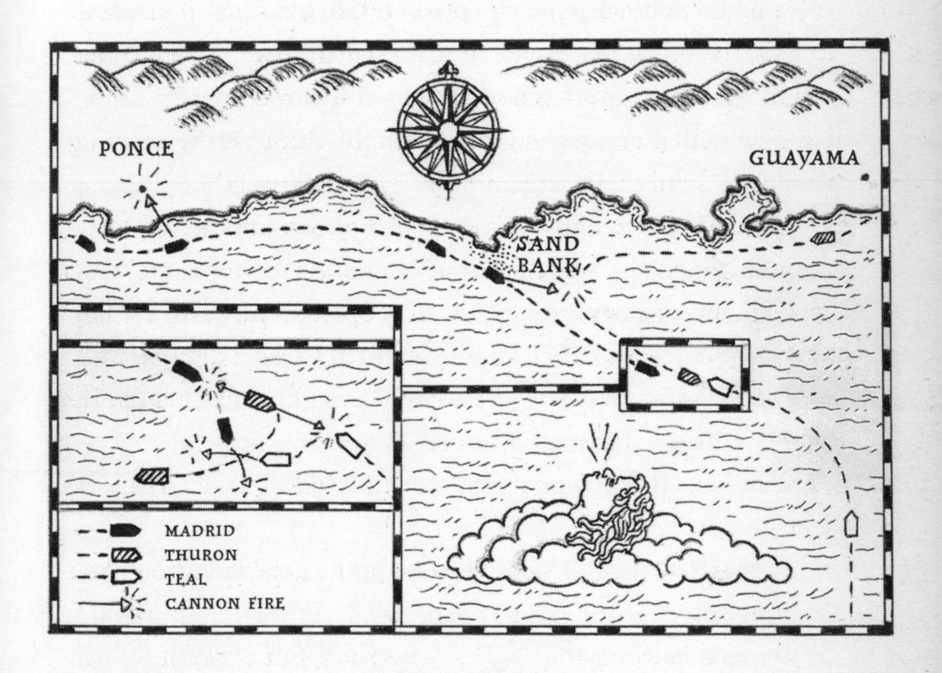

• • •

The lookout aboard the *Devon Belle* wiped rainwater from his eyes and called out to Captain Redjack Teal, who was holding the wheel manfully. "The Frenchman, sir, she's 'eaded on a course straight for us! Cap'n, sir, there's another ship sailin' in the Frenchie's wake! On me oath, sir, another ship!"

Teal's voice grew squeaky with excitement as he spun the wheel. "We're comin' about, can't sit broadside on to 'em both!"

Joby and the carpenter were still aloft. They had rigged the ropes around both masts. From the top of the foremast to three parts of the way up the mainmast the rope formed a coil six strands deep. The carpenter had thrust the oar through the ropes and twisted it, taking up the slack until the thick hemp was almost as taut as a fiddle string. Suddenly the *Devon Belle* came about quite sharply, the prow dipping deep and sending up a huge bow wave. Letting go of the oar to steady himself, the unfortunate carpenter signed his own death warrant. Spinning like a propeller, the oar smashed into the man's face, sending him flying from the foremast top. His body struck the rail and bounced off into the night-dark depths of the Caribbean Sea.

Joby screeched, "Man overboard!"

Captain Teal gritted his teeth. Men who were foolish enough to fall overboard in the midst of action on a stormy sea were of little concern to him. Teal winced and ducked low at the boom and flare of gunfire from the *Marie*'s for'ard end.

Rocco Madrid, from his vantage point at the *Diablo*'s stern, was highly puzzled by the noise. "Pepe, what's the Frenchman up to? Where's he firing?"

Pepe, who had been concentrating his attention on the *Marie*, shouted and gesticulated wildly from his high perch. "Capitano! I can see a vessel dead ahead of the Frenchman, now – he's firing on it!"

It was at that moment that Anaconda fired off his stern cannon at the Spaniard, close in the *Marie*'s wake. The *Diablo*'s bowsprit and ornate gallery rails exploded in a cascade of rope, iron and wood splinters. At the same time, a shot from the *Marie*'s for'ard end chopped the *Devon Belle*'s foremast off at the stump, and it hung crazily in the mess of ropes holding it to the mainmast.

All was confusion, smoke and flame aboard both the Spaniard and the privateer. Thuron took advantage of the chaos to perform his Trinidad Shuffle. Along with a new sail to replace the one damaged by the chain shot, every other stitch of canvas aboard the *Marie* was brought into play for the daring manoeuvre. Thuron spun the wheel hard about as full sail blossomed overhead. *La Petite Marie* heeled sharply over, her lower sailtips brushing the waves. Ben could feel Ned huddling against him as he crouched under a stairway, holding on tightly. The *Marie*'s prow dipped deep against the rollers, sending up a roaring bow wave. For a brief moment she teetered in the stormy sea, broadside on between both the other two vessels. Then Thuron turned the wheel hard right and gave his *Marie* her head. Like an arrow from a bow, the speedy ship shot off shoreward, with the gale ballooning her sails. Two cannon roared out, one from the privateer, the other from the Spaniard. The cannonballs crossed each other's path in the Frenchman's wake and whizzed off to splash into the dark Caribbean waters. Thuron laughed like a madman as his ship sped into the night.

Once out of range, he began tacking west to avoid the shore. With Ned howling at his heels, Ben ran out of hiding to join in with the cheering crew.

Pierre took the wheel from his captain, shaking Thuron's hand heartily. "You did it, Cap'n! You did it!"

Falling on both knees, the Frenchman hugged Ned and Ben, still laughing as he replied to the bosun, "Nobody can dance the old Trinidad Shuffle like Raphael Thuron!"

The *Devon Belle*'s master gunner hurried to his captain's side, pointing at the *Diablo* dead ahead. "If ye bring us broadside, sir, we can blow 'er out the water!"

Redjack Teal roared at the unfortunate man, "Blow a prize like that out of the water? Look at her, sirrah, are ye mad? With our guns mounted at her ports an' my colours flyin' from her masthead, she'd be the finest vessel in any sea! I intend capturin' that ship for me own use. Let the Frenchie go, an' bad cess to him. We'll attend to that fellow as soon as yon galleon's mine."

He beckoned to the mate. "Attend me closely. That ship's already turnin' to run off – 'tis your duty to stop it gettin' away. Take this wheel an' stick to her wake like treacle to bread, keep her close. Gunner, see if you can rig cannon to fire either side of her, port'n'starboard. We'll chase her in to the shore an' pin her down. Then I'll take her. Demned fine ship she is, eh!"

Rocco Madrid's normally sallow face paled further at the realization that he was facing an English privateer. He watched the *Diablo* trying to turn sluggishly as Boelee and Portugee wrestled with the wheel. Having no for'ard sheets and bowsprit hampered the operation greatly. Boelee chanced a frightened glance as the ship began turning. "I've heard tell o' that hellshark, 'tis an English privateer. See the coat 'er master wears? He's Capitano Redjack!"

Portugee almost let the wheel slip from his faltering grasp. "Redjack! They say he's worse than a Barbary corsair!"

Madrid's hand slid to his sword hilt as he hissed a warning. "Shut your mouths, I know who he is. Listen, this Redjack has lost his foremast. Maybe he doesn't want to fight. Boelee, easy now, take us a point to starboard."

No sooner had the *Diablo* nosed a foot out of place than Teal's cannon boomed a warning shot to starboard, accompanied by a crackle of musket fire peppering the Spaniard's stern.

Boelee brought her back on course smartly. "Capitano, that bad man has many, many more guns than us. If we try to run, he will send the *Diablo* to the bottom."

Portugee was in full agreement with the mate. "How can we run without any bowsails? He will murder us all!"

Madrid focused his telescope on the privateer less than a quarter of a mile behind. He saw the cannon bristling from every port, the crew lining the rails with primed muskets, and the red-jacketed figure watching the for'ard culverins being loaded with grapeshot, a deadly combination of musket balls, scrap iron and broken chain. Grapeshot could sweep a deck with murderous effect. Two more culverins had been brought up from the stern. Four culverins loaded with grapeshot at short range!

Madrid felt icy sweat trickle down his brow. This Redjack was a cold-blooded assassin! The Spaniard's mind was in a racing turmoil as he turned to his men. "Keep a straight course. I'll talk to this Redjack in the morning. Mayhap he'll listen to a proposition. I'm going to my cabin. Keep dead ahead. Don't upset him."

• • •

With the onset of dawn the rain ceased. Mist floated across the soft, lapping sea, the sun rising like a great blood orange in the east, setting a wondrous hue of pale cerise over the Caribbean waters. Captain Thuron joined Ben and Ned, who were breakfasting off fruit and coconut milk on the forecastle deck. He sat with them, watching a backing breeze dissolve the light fog.

"A pretty sight, eh, Ben? I will miss these waters. Do you know where we are?"

The boy nodded. "Almost into the Mona Passage. We should sight the Isle of Mona off the port bow before midday, sir."

Thuron's bushy eyebrows raised. "Very good, how did you know?"

Ned looked up from the coconut he was gnawing at. "Tell the good captain that it was your faithful hound who informed you of our position. Go on!"

Ben smiled at his friend's message as he addressed the captain. "Ned told me that he heard Anaconda saying it to Pierre when he relieved him at the wheel."

Thuron ruffled Ned's ears. "Do you really talk with this dog?"

Ben kept a straight face as he answered. "Oh, all the time, sir!"

The Frenchman chuckled. "I believe you, how could I not? You have such honest faces, both of you."

Ned passed his friend another thought. "I'm the one with the honest face, really. You've grown to look quite furtive over the last few decades. But I've grown more innocent. Look: truth and honesty are stamped all over my noble features!" Ned panted. Letting his tongue loll, he waggled his ears.

Ben could not help laughing aloud. Thuron laughed with him. "Tell me, what is Ned saying to you now, lad?"

The boy stroked his dog's back. "Ned says he wants you to

teach him the Trinidad Shuffle so he can use it sometime."

Ned left off chewing his coconut to reprimand Ben. "Ooh, you dreadful fibber. I said no such thing!"

Thuron interrupted the mental conversation. "Tell him I'll teach you both to catch flying fish – they come through these waters on their way to the Gulf of Mexico. Flying fish taste good, grilled with butter and oatmeal."

Ned went back to tackling his coconut. "Flying fish! Huh, who does he think he's fooling?"

Thuron pointed a stubby finger at the bows. "Look!" A flying fish was clearly visible, soaring level with the ship.

Ben leapt up. "There's another! Ned, did you see that?"

The black Labrador stood on his back legs, with his front paws on the rail. He pulled back sharply as another fish flew briefly by and skimmed over the bow wave. "Whoops! Seems a shame to catch them. Do they really taste good? Ask the cap'n to teach us to catch a few, Ben!"

Most of the morning was spent leaning over the prow, watching the flying fish trapping themselves in a net that Thuron had spread from the peak to the bowsprit. Anaconda sang cheerily in his rich deep bass as he supervised the cook in the galley. Ben listened as he pulled a fish from the net and marvelled at the huge spreading fins it used to soar over the waters.

> "Come on, come on, you flyin' fish,
> Fly up here into my dish.
> Birds is birds, that's how they act,
> Fish is fish, an' that's a fact.
> Foolish thing, I bet you wish
> You knew if you was bird or fish!

Fly fly o'er the sea,
Spread your fins an' come to me.

You flyin' fish, come on, come on,
I'm a sailor an' a hungry one.
In the air you sure look great,
But you taste much nicer on a plate.
Cook in the galley, warm that dish,
Here comes another little flyin' fish!

Fly fly o'er the sea,
Spread those fins an' come to me."

They had passed the Isle of Mona and Mayagüez when the cook hammered his ladle against a stove lid and shouted to all hands, "Fish is done, all cooked to a turn. If ye don't come quick, the Anaconda will eat 'em all!"

Ned raced ahead of Ben, sending a thought back to him. "Move yourself, youth. I believe every word the good cook says. Hope Anaconda saves a few for me!"

Thuron and the boy raced side by side, following Ned to the galley. All hands were jostling one another in line. Still relieved to have escaped both their foes, the men laughed and joked with one another.

Ben exchanged a thought with Ned. "What a difference between this and our first trip together with Vanderdecken aboard the *Flying Dutchman*."

The black Labrador bristled. "Don't even mention that hell-ship or mad Cap'n Vanderdecken and his crew of bullies. I'd sooner be aboard a good honest pirate ship like the *Marie* any day!"

Bowing to the dog's wisdom, Ben washed all thoughts of the accursed *Dutchman* from his mind. Instead, he concentrated on the bright sunlit Caribbean day, his friend Raphael Thuron, the merry bustle of crewmen and the anticipation of tasting his first cooked flying fish.

Rocco Madrid was in deep trouble. The privateer had chased the *Diablo Del Mar* straight into the shallows of Puerto Rico's palm-fringed shores. The Spaniard paced his cabin, wondering what the Englishman's next move would be. Cowering in a corner with a rope around his neck that was secured to a deck ring, Ludon, former mate of the *Marie*, watched him with wide, frightened eyes. Both men knew they were in a fearful situation.

Through his cabin window Madrid could see the *Devon Belle,* not three ship lengths away. She was broadside on to the *Diablo,* cannon bristling, almost daring the Spaniard to take the first shot. Rocco Madrid had more sense than to try. He felt like a rat in a trap – it would be plain suicide to attempt any show of aggression. Redjack Teal had an awesome reputation for slaughter.

Portugee and Boelee came skulking into the cabin like a pair of naughty schoolboys about to be punished for some misdemeanour.

Boelee looked sheepishly from the privateer in the bay to his captain. "What are we going to do, Capitano?"

Madrid answered with a lot more confidence than he felt. "Do, amigos? We do nothing for the moment. The first hand is up to the Englishman to play."

Portugee remarked with a scowl, "The only cards Redjack

deals us will be wrapped around cannonballs. Unless you plan on makin' a move, Capitano, we are all dead men!"

There was a rasp of steel leaving scabbard, and Portugee was suddenly backed against a bulkhead with the Spaniard's sword at his throat. Madrid hissed venomously at him, "You'll be a dead man sooner than you think if you let your tongue flap foolishly, amigo. I do the thinking aboard this ship without the advice of idiots. Leave this to me, I have a plan. Meanwhile, both of you get out on deck and close all the cannon ports. Boelee, run up a white flag of truce. Portugee, lock up all the muskets and swords. Keep all hands below deck, tell them to make no noise. Now go!"

The Spaniard aimed a kick at Ludon. "You! Keep your mouth shut until I tell you to talk. I have plans for you."

Rocco Madrid came smartly out on deck the moment he saw a white flag fluttering from the *Devon Belle*'s masthead. Captain Redjack was standing amidships with a long, trumpet-ended megaphone to his lips. His voice carried clearly across the space between the vessels. Crewmen stood by with cocked muskets, ugly cannon snouts poked menacingly at the *Diablo* as Teal called out, "One false move an' I open fire. *Comprende?*"

The Spaniard cupped both hands round his mouth and shouted back, "I understand English, señor. What do you want?"

Teal's reply was sharp and officious. "I am Captain Jonathan Ormsby Teal of His Majesty's ship *Devon Belle.* I carry letters of marque an' reprisal as a privateer. I require your complete an' unconditional surrender. Immediately!"

Madrid kept his voice normal, though he was inwardly fuming at the foppish Englander's high-handed manner. "Capitano, you have my word as a Spanish grandee that the first shot will not come from my vessel!"

Teal snorted contemptuously as he raised the hailer to his mouth. "Fire at your peril, sirrah! I'll blast your lungs'n'lights to perdition an' dye this bay red with your foul blood! Answer me! Do ye surrender now . . . eh?"

The Spaniard spread his arms placatingly. "I surrender, Capitano – only a fool would refuse your offer. But first I would talk with you. I have a proposition, amigo. One that could make you a very rich man – will you listen, señor?"

Teal took a moment, whispering orders to his bosun, mate and master gunner, before making a reply. "A rich man, y'say? Stand fast, I'm comin' over. Blink an eye an' a dozen musketeers'll blow it out!"

Rocco Madrid bowed elaborately. "No tricks, I promise! Let us talk like civilized men. I will await your arrival in my cabin with some fine wine for both of us. With your permission, Capitano, I will retire now."

Twenty crew, armed with muskets and rifles, packed into the *Devon Belle*'s jolly boat. Teal sat in the stern, behind them. In his cabin, Madrid held tight to the scruff of Ludon's neck as he loosed the rope. Thrusting Ludon to the window, the Spaniard pointed to Teal as he instructed his captive. "Hearken to me carefully. See the red-jacketed one? He can save both our lives. When I tell you to speak, you will lie to him, lie as you've never lied before, amigo. Tell the Englishman that *La Petite Marie* is carrying a vast fortune in gold. Ten, twenty times more than he took from me at Cartagena. You saw it yourself, with your own two eyes. Do this and you may live to be a rich fellow. Understand?"

Sighing with relief, Ludon nodded furiously. "Aye aye, Cap'n, ye can rely on me. I swear it on my mother's grave!"

The *Diablo*'s decks were empty as Redjack Teal and his men came aboard. Teal murmured to his bosun, "Perfect! Take y'men an' batten down the hatches, seal all doors except the cap'n's cabin. Kill any pirate that shows his face on deck. Send two fellows back to the *Devon Belle* with our jolly boat an' the Spaniard's. Bring back every available hand who ain't mannin' a cannon. Cut along now, quick an' quiet as y'like!"

Teal strutted into the Spaniard's cabin, hand on sword hilt. Rocco Madrid bowed courteously. "Welcome to my humble accommodation, Capitano. Some wine?"

Ignoring the decanter of port and goblets, the privateer drew a fancy silver-chased pistol and pointed it. "I'll take your surrender first!"

Madrid drew his sword carefully and offered it over his forearm, hilt first. The privateer tested the blade's balance nonchalantly and thrust it into his own belt. Still aiming the pistol, he sat at the cabin table, his eyes never leaving the Spaniard.

Ludon crept forward and filled the goblets. Crossing his legs and leaning back, Redjack took a sip and nodded towards Ludon. "An' who, pray, is this fellow, eh?"

The Spaniard smiled slyly as he played his ace card. "This is the man who can make us our fortunes, señor. He was first mate aboard the French buccaneer. Tell the English capitano what you saw, amigo."

By evening the deal had been hammered out, more to Teal's satisfaction than to the Spaniard's. But Rocco Madrid accepted all terms, telling himself that he could always alter the balance at a later date. Unarmed, the entire crew of the *Diablo Del Mar* were marched up on deck in fours and made to wade ashore in the ebbing tide. Surrounded as they were by a fully armed and very hostile English crew, they were forced to comply sullenly.

Boelee and Portugee led the first lot. Chest high they waded towards the sandy beach. Portugee looked warily about. "I don't like this, there's sharks in these waters!"

Boelee gritted his teeth. "The real sharks are aboard our ship, but we don't get any say in the matter. If Madrid's playin' us false, I'll track him to the ends of the earth!"

Just then, Rocco Madrid appeared on deck alongside Teal. The Spaniard exchanged words with his lookout, Pepe. Before he went over the side, Pepe nodded and shook hands with both Madrid and Teal.

Boelee and Portugee were waiting as Pepe splashed ashore. They ran to meet him.

"What did the capitano have to say to you?"

"Redjack, did he have anything to say? Tell us, Pepe!"

The *Diablo* crewmen gathered around as the lookout explained. "Redjack, he said nothing, but the capitano told me to tell you all: we are joining forces with the privateer and sailing out into the ocean to capture Thuron's ship!"

Boelee shook his head in disbelief. "Are you sure?"

Pepe sat down on the warm sands. "Sí, amigos! Here is what will happen. We will crew the privateer ship; Capitano Redjack will take us in tow. He will command the *Diablo* after he has moved his own cannon aboard her and repaired the bowsprit. After we have taken Thuron's vessel, Redjack will cut the *Diablo* loose to sail back to the Caribbean."

Portugee gnawed thoughtfully at his lip. "But why do both ships need to sail about chasin' Thuron, did he say?"

Pepe grinned as he related what his captain had told him. "That prisoner from the *Marie,* you know what he said? I will tell you. Thuron is quitting these waters, going back to his home in France. That is why he put in to Guayama. For years he has been burying all his booty there, and he went to dig it up before he crosses the ocean. The man saw it, a real treasure, chests an' barrels of plunder. Our capitano made him talk – now he has made a bargain with Redjack. Good, no?"

All eyes were on Boelee. He was the most astute member of the *Diablo*'s crew, having served longest with Madrid. Sitting down, he pursed his lips and squinted one eye. Then he laughed. "Good, yes! Two ships can find Thuron out there a lot easier'n one could. Ho ho, that Rocco, he's craftier than a sack o' monkeys. I'll wager he's got a plan formed already. You mark my words, mates, Rocco Madrid'll end up with all that booty, or my name ain't Boelee!"

The crew set about building a driftwood fire on the shore as night set in. The *Devon Belle*'s crew towed the *Diablo* out and secured her alongside the privateer. Teal commanded the entire operation, striding about and giving orders as blocks and tackles hauled cannon between the two ships. Rocco Madrid sat in Teal's cabin aboard the *Devon Belle,* sampling the Madeira while he formed bloodthirsty schemes for future days. Joby, who had now been promoted to carpenter, had a party at work replacing the bowsprit with timbers from the *Devon Belle*'s broken foremast as others laboured at rigging new foresails and bowlines.

One of the men nodded towards the pirates onshore. " 'Tain't fair! Lookit that lot, layin' about on the sand while we're sloggin' our guts out aboard this tub!"

"You were sayin'?"

The man turned to see Teal standing there. He bent his back to the task, apologizing humbly. "Nothin', Cap'n, never said a word, sir!"

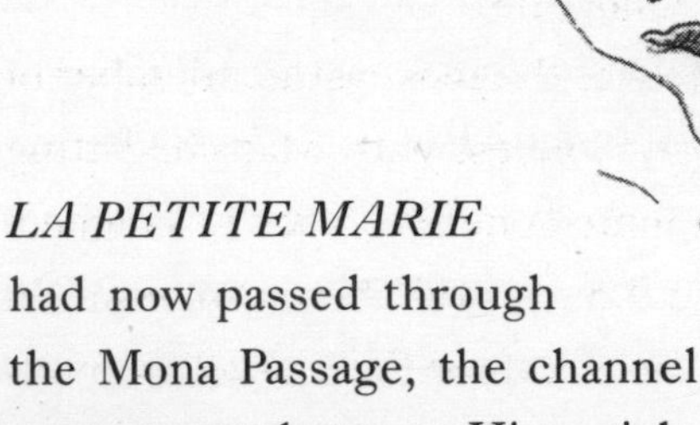

9

LA PETITE MARIE had now passed through the Mona Passage, the channel between Hispaniola and Puerto Rico. Ben and Ned were in the captain's cabin, getting a lesson in navigation from the Frenchman. A large, untidy chart was spread out on the bed, with books and a sextant holding down its scrolled corners.

Thuron indicated a spot on the map. "This is a simple old chart, rough but reliable. We are about here by my reckoning, see, Ben?"

The boy studied where Thuron was pointing. "We're actually out in the Atlantic Ocean. Where do we go from here, Cap'n?"

Thuron stroked his beard. "Right across this chart and on to a second one which I have. This ocean is a strange place, boy, not much is known about it. Many ships have been lost and never heard from again. No one knows how deep the seas and oceans of this world are. When you sail the high seas on a vessel, I wager that you don't think of what lies beneath its keel. Have you ever thought of that, Ben?"

Ned interjected his opinion into Ben's thoughts. "Personally,

I try hard not to. Why frighten yourself? Leave the underneath of the sea to the fishes, I say!"

Ben stroked the black Labrador's ears to silence him. "Hush, Ned, don't interrupt. Listen to the cap'n!"

Thuron tapped at the deck with his foot. "Underneath our pitiful little ship lies a whole world. Valleys, hills, deserts and huge mountains!" He smiled into Ben's startled blue eyes. "Never thought of that, have you, lad? But 'tis a fact. One day men may go there to explore it. Hundreds of thousands of leagues, clear and visible near the surface, where daylight and the sun can penetrate, descending to shaded blues and greens, then on to where it is dark as a moonless night with no stars. But down, ever down to complete blackness, fathomless and silent as the grave, a realm of fish that are all sizes. Some no bigger than a babe's fingernail, others massive, monsters of the deep who have lurked there since the earth was young!"

Ned lay on the bed, covering both ears with his paws and whining as he transmitted his thoughts to Ben. "Wait'll I get my paws on land again. I'll never go near any water, not even a duck pond!"

Ben stroked his dog soothingly as the captain continued. "Aye, and here are we, no more than a tiny splinter in the scale of things, bobbing up and down over the great deeps where the Bible says leviathans and behemoths dwell. We're a tiny, bold species, Ben, no doubt about it!"

The boy nodded agreement. "I suppose we are, sir, but could you stop frightening Ned and tell me which way we're bound?"

Thuron looked from the dog to the boy and chuckled. "I think 'tis you and not Ned who is afeared. Where are we bound? Straight northeast. The only land 'twixt here and France is some little islands they call the Azores. Come on, my lucky mates, we'll go and tell Pierre to alter the course from due east."

They followed the captain out on deck, where he gave orders to Pierre, who was at the helm. Obeying his captain's command, the trusty Pierre turned the wheel. He frowned and turned it again, then turned it a bit more. "Cap'n, she's not coming about, look!" Thuron watched his steersman turn the wheel once more.

Pierre shook his head in bewilderment. "I've turned this wheel so much that we should be heading south by now. Something's wrong, Cap'n!"

Thuron took the wheel. "Here, let me try." There was no resistance in the ship's wheel; it spun freely. The Frenchman held it still and rested his forehead against one of the carved mahogany spokes, pondering the problem.

Ben could not help asking, "What's wrong, sir?"

Thuron straightened up, shaking his head. "If I knew, I'd be able to tell ye, lad. But I have an idea what caused it. The Trinidad Shuffle. It couldn't have been anything else. Our *Marie* isn't a young girl any more, she's getting on to be an old lady – things start to wear and tear. That was a wild and stormy night, and we were caught 'twixt two vessels. When I did the shuffle, it was a hard an' punishing manoeuvre. I think that something broke, or cracked, or came loose. Between then and now, with all the steering we've had to do, a part of the rudder has been damaged. I'll wager that's what it is. Ben, go and fetch Anaconda."

The giant black man was off duty, napping in his hammock, when Ben shook him gently. "Cap'n wants to see you, sir."

Anaconda swung gracefully to the deck. Flashing a brief smile at the boy, he ducked neatly out of the cabin. Thuron was not a small man, but he had to lift his chin to meet the big fellow's eyes.

"Our *Marie* had an accident while dancing the Trinidad Shuffle, my friend."

Anaconda picked up a coil of rope as though it were a piece of string. "This old lady's prob'ly hurt her rudder, Cap'n. I better take a look."

He lashed the rope to the *Marie*'s stern bollard and dropped it into the sea. Going hand over hand, he lowered himself into the water, taking a deep breath before he submerged. They lost sight of Anaconda once he went under the curving after end.

Ned poked his head between the gallery rails. "Good job he hasn't been listening to the cap'n talking about leviathans an' behemoths, and all sorts of sea monsters lurking about down there!"

Ben returned his dog's observation. "Oh, I think Anaconda could hold his own – have you seen the size of that knife he wears in the back of his belt? I've seen smaller swords. He's been under quite a while now, though. I hope nothing's happened to him, Ned."

Pierre's voice interrupted the thought. "He's coming up!"

The handsome giant's head showed through the smooth wake water, then broke the surface. Anaconda blinked, snorted and hauled himself neatly back aboard. "Need copper strip, hammer an' nails, Cap'n – her rudder's come adrift. It's flapping about down there like a tavern sign."

Thuron smiled with relief. "Thank the Lord for that, my friend. We've got strip an' nails aplenty. Will it take ye long to repair?"

Anaconda shrugged his powerfully muscled shoulders. "Might take a few dives, but I can't do it alone. My fingers are too thick for threading the strip between the break and the helm spindle. 'Tis a narrow gap. Now if I had somebody down there with me, I could hold the rudder flap together. They could pass the copper strip through the narrow part. We'd start by nailing one side to the flap. I'd hold the rudder together, then when the other end of the strip was passed through, I'd secure it with another nail. One or two more nails through the strip either side, and she'd be good as new!"

Thuron began shedding his coat, giving orders to some crew members who had come to see what was wrong. "Bring another rope, a hammer, some copper strip and a handful of brass nails."

Anaconda took hold of his captain's hand. "Cap'n, your hand ain't as big as mine, but look at those fingers. They're stubby, an' far too thick."

Suddenly the crew began to disperse, as if they all had urgent duties to attend. Thuron watched them scurry off. "Ask a seaman to sail a ship, he'll do it without question. But ask him to put a toe into the ocean, eh, Pierre?"

The mate scoffed. "Most of 'em can't swim – they're a-feared o' deep water, Cap'n. I'll do it."

Anaconda shook his head. "Last time I saw fingers like yours, Pierre, they were selling them as pork sausages on the quay at Cartagena. Let's see your hand, Ben."

One glance at the boy's slender fingers was enough. Anaconda winked at him. "You'll do!"

Thuron threw an arm about Ben's shoulders. "Hold on there, he's not going under the ocean. This lad's my lucky boy!"

Ben slipped from under the captain's arm. "Lucky enough to be the right one for the job, and lucky that I'm aboard the *Marie* when I'm needed. I'll do it, Cap'n!"

Ned sprang up, placing his paws on Ben's chest, communicating, "No, Ben, don't do it, please!"

Ben took the dog's head in both hands, staring into his friend's dark, pleading eyes. "Someone has to help Anaconda or we'll be rolling about the Atlantic this time next year. I know if you were me, you'd offer, Ned, but paws aren't much use. Hands like mine are needed. Now don't you fret, I'll be careful, I promise!"

Thuron took Anaconda to one side. "My friend, keep your eye on the boy while you're down there. I don't want any harm coming to my lucky lad!"

The big steersman saluted. "Nor do I, Cap'n. He'll be safe with me. Ben, mate, are ye ready to get wet?"

Throwing aside his shirt and kicking off both shoes, Ben coiled the extra rope over his shoulder. "Aye aye, ready!"

The sweet, cloying taste of port wine was not to Redjack Teal's liking, so he sipped at a goblet of the paler, more subtle Madeira. He was highly pleased with himself: as a ship, the *Diablo Del Mar* was an enviable prize. Rocco Madrid's former cabin, which was more like a stateroom, had been thoroughly cleaned out and furnished with Teal's own possessions. It was, he felt, more fitting to an English gentleman's taste. Again he tested Madrid's sword, a classic Toledo blade far more elegant than his own Royal Navy-issue sword. Freshly laundered and attired, he struck several poses with his new weapon whilst watching himself in a long cheval mirror, probably plundered from some prosperous merchant craft by the Spaniard. Laying the sword aside, Teal picked up a scroll and strutted regally out on deck.

Rocco Madrid was aboard the *Devon Belle* when he spotted

Teal. Negotiating the plank that had been fixed between the two vessels, he made straight for the Englishman.

Redjack permitted himself an affable smile. "Ah, there you are, a splendid afternoon, Cap'n Madrid, eh?"

Controlling his indignation, the Spaniard made a small formal bow. "Your *Devon Bella,* Capitano Teal, it is stripped bare. Why aren't my crew allowed aboard to repair the mast, make everything ready for our voyage, provision her with victuals and water? Where is the French prisoner Ludon? My mate and bosun, the *Diablo*'s crew – why are they still left idling onshore? Why do you not send the ship's boat for them? They are needed to help out here."

Still smiling cheerily, Teal tapped the Spaniard's chest lightly with the scroll he carried. "Faith, sirrah, one thing at a time! What an excitable fellow ye are, t'be sure. The French chappie, I have him under guard in the chain locker. Can't let him escape, can we, eh? As for the rest, all in good time, my friend, all in good time."

Rocco Madrid glared suspiciously at Teal. "When, señor? When?"

Teal adopted a look of mild surprise. "Why, now, Cap'n, within the hour if y'like. All ye had t'do was ask."

Madrid felt he had gained a point with his confrontation. He decided to push his advantage with the foppish little peacock of an Englander. "We need to have our arms back. What use will we be, chasing a pirate ship without arms? Thuron is a formidable fighter."

The smile left Captain Redjack's face. "Your weapons will be returned when I feel it appropriate. As for cannon, this ship has enough for both of us. Don't want to sink the Frenchie, do we, eh? Leave all that treasure on the ocean bed?"

Madrid heaved a frustrated sigh. "We will not catch Thurlon by sitting here. He gets further away by the hour, señor. Have I your permission to bring my crew aboard their ship?"

Teal nodded. "By all means, m'dear fellow. You there, bosun, lower the *Devon Belle*'s jolly boat for Cap'n Madrid to go ashore."

Rocco Madrid climbed into the jolly boat. Seating himself, he looked quizzically up at Teal, who was leaning over the *Diablo*'s ornate midship rail. "Capitano, do I have to row this boat ashore by myself?"

The Englishman shrugged. "Of course, Cap'n. Leaves more room for crew on the return journey, don't it!"

The Spaniard fitted the oars into the oarlocks and began paddling clumsily away. He had not got more than two boat lengths when Teal hailed him.

"You there, listen to this!" Teal unrolled the scroll and began reading aloud. "'Under the authority granted to me by our Sovereign King, Charles the First, I take possession of this vessel by Letter of Marque and Reprisal. God save the King and protect England and confound her enemies!'"

The jolly boat wobbled as the Spaniard let go the oars and stood up, shouting, "English pig, you are playing me false!"

Three rifle shots rang out, and Madrid fell backwards in panic. Totally surprised that the shots had missed him, he knelt up cautiously to see Teal pointing at him.

"Count y'self lucky to be alive, ye Spanish dog! I don't make bargains with scurvy pirates, nor do I trust 'em! 'Twould take too long to hang ye an' all that filthy crew. I'm maroonin' ye, sirrah, an' ye best row for shore before that boat sinks. Bad cess to ye an' all your ilk!"

Rocco Madrid gave vent to his spleen, roaring and cursing as the jolly boat began filling with water from the three musket balls that had pierced it below the waterline. "Redjack turncoat! Scum of the seas! I curse you to the fires of hell! May sharks tear out your lying tongue and fish feed on your misbegotten bones!"

Captain Redjack Teal gave his bosun a languid glance. "Rather excitable – Latin temperament, I shouldn't wonder. Can't lay at anchor here all day, listenin' to pirates usin' language like that, eh? One thing he did say was true, we're losin' time hangin' round here. Take the *Devon Belle* in abaft of us, weigh anchor an' make full sail!"

Rocco Madrid and his crew stood on the tide line in the late afternoon sun, watching the wind fill the sails of their former ship as she ploughed off with Teal's old craft in tow.

Pepe turned his anguished gaze on Madrid. "What are we going to do, Capitano?"

The Spaniard sat down on the sand and began dragging off his long boots. They were sloppy with seawater from his walk ashore from the jolly boat, which lay submerged a hundred yards off, where the shallows started. Madrid pointed out to it. "Boelee, Portugee, take some men and see if you can drag the boat up on dry land."

Boelee remained motionless. Then he spat at Madrid's back. "You don't give Boelee orders any more. A capitano without a ship, that's what ye are. Go an' get the boat yourself!"

Madrid scrambled upright and ran at Boelee, fist clenched. A mate aboard any pirate ship has to be hard and tough, and Boelee was one such man. Sidestepping the charge, he tripped

Madrid, dealing him a hefty punch to the back of the neck as he went down.

The mate stood over him. "You ain't no capitano, you're a fool. Got yourself tricked by Redjack with your lies about Thuron carryin' dug-up treasure. Now we're all marooned high'n'dry without a proper weapon between us, save for our belt knives. Well, are ye gettin' up to fight me, Madrid?"

Rocco Madrid's hand flashed to his scabbard, but it was empty. He flinched as Boelee aimed a scornful kick at him.

The mate's voice dripped contempt. "Stay down there where ye belong. Because if ye get up, I'll kill ye with me bare hands!"

Rocco Madrid sat alone as evening fell, deserted by his crew, who had chosen Boelee as their new leader. All hands sat around the fire, which they had kept going since arriving ashore. Portugee, who was looked upon as second-in-command, gnawed on a broken coconut. He looked automatically to Boelee. "Well, what are we goin' to do now?"

The mate pinched out a spark that had settled on his arm. "That Redjack is as big a fool as Madrid. Don't he know ye can't maroon a pirate on an isle as big as Puerto Rico? Brotherhood vessels put in to all the ports here. Mayagüez, Aguadilla, Arecibo, San Juan. I'll wager we're not far from Ponce. A couple o' days' march an' we can sign up with the first ship we see there. Marooned? Huh, we ain't marooned!"

This seemed to cheer most of the pirates – the prospect of a port with ships and taverns aplenty was far better than facing the misery of being marooned. Pepe nodded towards the figure of Rocco Madrid, sitting alone in the darkness about fifty yards from the company around the fire. "Will we take him along with us?"

Portugee was not in favour of the idea. "He can go to the teeth of hell in a handcart for all I care, eh, Boelee!"

Boelee spat into the fire. "Madrid's bad luck to all of us now, mates. We can't have him taggin' along. He was a powerful man among The Brotherhood leaders. If 'n I know Madrid, he'll blame the loss o' the *Diablo* on us, an' I'm the first one he'll come after. He'll get me strung up for mutiny. There's only one thing t'do with Capitano Rocco Madrid. Bury him here!"

A pall of silence fell over the crew. Portugee was overawed at the suggestion, his face showing pale in the firelight as he addressed Boelee. "Kill Madrid? Who would dare do such a thing?"

Boelee pulled the broad-bladed dagger from his belt and twirled it expertly. "Well, seein' as how you're all so chicken-hearted, I'll do the job! But when we get to a port, every man jack of ye better keep his mouth shut about it. I'll say that Madrid was slain by the privateers when we lost the *Diablo*. Anyone says different an' I'll gut him! So, turn your backs or close your eyes if ye don't want to see the deed done. Madrid's only a treacherous worm, we're better off without him!"

Flat on his stomach, Boelee crawled away from the fire with the knife clenched in his teeth. Away from the firelight, his path described a wide half circle. All that could be heard was the surf pounding up onto the shore and the odd crackle of blazing driftwood from the fire. Ahead of him, Boelee could see the Spaniard's back – he was sitting drooped over, as though he had dozed off. Boelee wriggled noiselessly forward, transferring the knife from mouth to hand. He held it tight, ready for a hard upward thrust between the former captain's ribs. Closer he edged, closer, until Madrid's back was within striking distance. Coming up on his knees, Boelee locked his free arm around the Spaniard's neck.

Rocco Madrid's head lolled to one side just as Boelee felt the light tickle of coloured feathers against his forearm. With a horrified gurgle he released his quarry and stumbled backwards.

Four poisoned darts had ended the life of Rocco Madrid: one behind his ear and three in his cheek. The Spaniard lay huddled grotesquely on the sand, his body still warm. Panting and sobbing raggedly, Boelee stumbled across the beach to the fire.

Portugee grabbed hold of him as Boelee, too, fell, both legs still kicking convulsively as he tried to clutch at the sharp bamboo sliver sticking from his throat.

The ancient, bearded patriarch whose village they had destroyed appeared at the edge of the firelight. His gaze swept the petrified crew. "You are back. Only fools would want to return after what you did here!"

He strode off into the dark as the drums started up. *Thonk thonk thonk thonk!* A hollow ceaseless rattling sound. Silent as moon shadows, the Carib hunters, their bodies striped with dark plant dyes, closed in on what had once been the crew of the *Diablo Del Mar.*

16

CAPTAIN THURON HAD BEEN RIGHT: IT WAS another world beneath the surface of the sea. Golden sun rays turned to faint curtains of pastel blues and greens as they lanced down into the depths and small bubbles rose in silvery cascades from the barnacle-crusted hull of the *Marie*. A few tiny, fat, jewel-coloured fish that were travelling beneath the ship nosed harmlessly against Ben's cheek. Pulling themselves down the line tied to the stern, Ben and Anaconda descended to the rudder.

Owing to the shadow cast upon the water by the ship and the curve of the hull, it was rather gloomy, though the broken rudder was fairly visible. Ben's long tow-coloured hair swayed softly around in a shifting halo as he secured his rope to the end of the spindle that stuck out below the rudder. Anaconda secured the neck of the bag that held their equipment to the rope, leaving their hands free to work. Still grasping the stern line, they inspected the damage.

The big man waggled his hand at Ben, who produced some copper strip and the hammer from the sack. Anaconda signalled with one finger. Ben rummaged a nail out and passed it to him while holding the end of the strip against one side of the big oblong rudder. Gripping the rope with his legs, Anaconda half knocked the nail through the copper strip and into the rudder timber, then dropped the hammer back into the sack and pointed upwards. Ben transmitted a thought to Ned up on deck. "We're coming up for air!"

The dog's reply flashed though his mind. "Thank goodness for that, I thought you'd both decided to be fishes!"

The two broke the surface, blinking and gasping for air. Thuron sat on the deck with his legs between the gallery rails and called over the side, "Are you both all right? What's it like down there?"

Ben called up to him. "It will take a couple of dives, but we've got one end of the strip fixed with a nail."

The Frenchman made as if to rise. "Well done! D'you need more help? I'll come down an' lend ye a hand!"

Anaconda shook his head. "There's only room for me an' the boy, Cap'n. You'd be in the way."

Ben was in agreement. "Aye, you stay up there, sir. Stop Ned from taking over the ship. He's keen to be a cap'n, you know."

The black Labrador glared at Ben from between the rails. "Aye, and I won't stand impudence from my crew, young feller!"

They submerged again, this time for Ben to thread the copper strip between the back of the rudder and the spindle. However, there was a build-up of barnacles and green, hairlike seaweed. The boy used Anaconda's knife to clear it, then began poking the strip through, fraction by fraction. It was difficult, the soft copper bending every time it hit a snag. Twice more the pair had to go up for air, but on the fourth descent, Ben's fingers, now cold and slippery from the green weeds, managed to thread the strip through. Anaconda half fixed it from the other side with a nail, then they were up again for more air.

Ben waved to Thuron. "We've got it, sir. Now we only have to stretch the strip tight and get more nails in it on both sides!"

Thuron smiled gratefully. "Pierre, tell the cook to make these lads a good hot bowl o' soup apiece. It must be cold down there, working as long as those two have." He waved as they submerged once more.

This time Anaconda took six nails in his mouth. He began to work swiftly, though it was extremely difficult. Ben held tight to the rudder, trying to prevent it from moving, his body shaking as each hammer blow struck. Suddenly the hammer slipped from Anaconda's grasp, and his hand hit the nail head hard: blood gouted out like a red ribbon into the sea. Ben gestured through the shadowed water that they should go up, but the giant grinned and shook his head, signalling that there was only one more nail to go. Gamely, he spat the last nail into his hand and began nailing the last bit of strip to the rudder. It went home with four hefty whacks. Anaconda pointed upwards – then everything happened at once.

Up on deck, the ship's wheel, which was unmanned to allow the rudder repairs, took the bite of the newly repaired rudder. The wheel spun half a turn, sending the rudder crashing into Ben's head. Through a pain-filled mist of semiconsciousness, he let go of the rope and floated up. Looking back, he saw the big steersman reach a hand up towards him, when a massive, dark shape struck Anaconda. For a moment the water was a seething mass of bubbling crimson, and then something lashed sharply, stinging the back of Ben's leg. He lost all his senses, whirling upside down in red-streaked blackness as Ned's wild baying and calling echoed inside his brain. "Ben! Howoooooh! Beeeeeen!"

Thuron saw the blood and bubbles rising. Clamping a knife in his mouth, he dodged around the howling dog and dived over the rail without a backward glance. Ben was dangling upside down underwater, the broken rope wrapped about his leg. A crimson trail plunged down into the misty depths. There was no sign of Anaconda. The Frenchman grabbed the boy and the rope, tugging furiously as he saw other massive, dark shapes homing in on them both.

They were dragged from the sea by a crew hauling frenziedly on the rope. Thuron never once let go of Ben or the rope; his whole body wrapped around both. As the pair were manhandled over the stern rail, a huge head, its razor-toothed mouth agape, cleared the surface a handsbreadth away from the Frenchman's foot.

Pierre flung a boat hook after it, shouting, "Sharks! Sharks!"

Several of the crewmen, who were armed with loaded pistols, fired at the sinister fins, which had begun circling the *Marie.* A musket exploded in the air as Pierre knocked one man's arm up. "No, don't fire! You'll hit Anaconda, you fool!"

Thuron was thumping Ben's back as seawater poured from the senseless boy's mouth. The Frenchman looked up, his face a picture of tragedy and shock, and screamed, "Anaconda is gone, Pierre, he's gone!"

The firing ceased, and all hands stared at one another in disbelief. Anaconda gone?

• • •

Ben lay on the bed in Captain Thuron's cabin with Ned alongside him, trying to reach his friend. However, the dog's thoughts could not penetrate the boy's fevered mind. Disjointed images of storming seas and large waves crashing upon rockbound shores, the *Flying Dutchman,* with Vanderdecken at the helm and lit all about with the eerie green light of St Elmo's Fire wreathing its rigging. Ned tried to interpose calming thoughts into Ben's delirium, licking the boy's hands and whining softly, "Ben, Ben, it's me, Ned. You're safe now, mate. Lie still, rest now!"

Thuron brought a little brandy mixed with sugar and warm water. Ned watched as he poured a few drops between Ben's lips. The Frenchman spoke his thoughts aloud to the dog as he ministered to the boy. "There now, that'll help him, I think. He's had a bad time, Ned. I'll stay here with you until he looks better. Thank the Lord he wasn't taken by those hellfish. Poor Anaconda, we'll never see him again. Apart from you and Ben, he was the best friend I ever had, rest his soul!"

Thuron settled down in a chair and put his feet up on the end of the bed, assuring the Labrador in a weary voice, "At least our Ben's safe, eh, boy? Don't you fret now, he'll be fresh as a coat o' paint by tomorrow."

With her rudder back in working order, *La Petite Marie* sailed northeast, out into the night-time vastness of the mighty Atlantic Ocean. Raphael Thuron was asleep, one elbow on the table, his cheek resting in an open palm. Ned, too, stretched on the bed with his head lolling across the boy's feet. Ben drifted in and out of slumber, quiet and still for the most part. Then strange spectres began haunting his mind. Were his eyes open or not? The boy was not sure, but he could see through the ornate, oblong stern window. The sea was moon-flecked and smooth, yet far out it appeared stormy. Cold sweat poured from Ben's brow. There in the distance, riding the gale, the *Flying Dutchman* was coming towards the *Marie*. Ben lay there, robbed of all power of speech or movement, watching the ghost ship getting larger and closer. He could not even pass a thought to his dog. Vanderdecken's wild, despairing face banished everything from his mind. Ben could see him standing at the *Dutchman*'s wheel. Lifting a corpselike finger, he beckoned the boy to come to him, staring at Ben with eyes like chips of tombstone marble that pierced his entire being. Now the *Flying Dutchman* was sailing level with the *Marie*. *Tap! Tap!* The accursed captain's finger rapped upon the windowpane, calling, signalling Ben to come aboard his vessel. The petrified boy suddenly realized he had no grip on reality, no control of his limbs. Was he still lying on the bed, or was he sitting up, getting out of bed and walking trancelike towards the apparition outside the window? Vanderdecken smiled triumphantly, exposing long yellow teeth as his black lips curled back, his beckoning finger, like a swaying serpent, calling his victim to him.

The feeling seeped slowly into Ned's mind as his eyes opened blearily. Then he felt his hackles rise, and he came wide awake. He leapt up with a sharp bark, and Vanderdecken turned his attention upon the dog, glaring and hissing viciously. In that moment, Thuron was wakened by the bark. He saw Ben, momentarily free of the spell, snap the thong that held a carved coconut-wood cross around his neck. Thuron dropped to the cabin floor as Ben threw the cross at the thing hovering outside; then the Frenchman grabbed the chair by a leg and flung it with all his might from flat on his back.

11

AMID THE RENDING CRASH OF GLASS AND WOOD, a high-pitched, keening screech ensued. Ned was standing with his paws up on the sill, barking out at a calm night sea. Shakily, Thuron pulled himself over to where Ben was sitting on the cabin floor.

He grabbed the boy and hugged him tight. "Ben, are you all right? What in the name of heaven and hell was that thing at the window? Was it a man or a fiend?"

Before Ned could think out a warning, Ben had spoken. "It was Captain Vanderdecken of the *Flying Dutchman*!"

Thuron ran to the smashed window. Regardless of the broken glass and splintered frame, he leaned out and scanned the empty ocean.

Turning slowly, he looked from the dog to the boy. "I think you've got something to tell me, lad!"

Ned sent a swift thought to Ben. "Well, you've already told him who it was – are you going to let him know the rest?"

Still facing the captain, Ben answered his dog's question. "He saved my life, we can trust him. I'd best tell him everything. He'll understand, I know he will."

The black Labrador closed his eyes resignedly. "I hope he will!"

The crewman Gascon, who had not gone with the other three deserters, was taking his turn at the wheel. He had heard Ned's bark and the window breaking. Looking astern, he saw the captain's chair, with the cross on its thong tangled about it, floating off into the night. Tying the ship's wheel on course with the helm line, Gascon hurried to the captain's cabin door. He was about to knock when he heard voices clearly from within. Carefully he pressed an ear to the door and listened. Ben was speaking to Thuron. What Gascon heard that night chilled his very soul into a terror-stricken silence.

Captain Redjack Teal had found some good old ripe cheese in the cupboard. Along with a goblet of Madeira and a few of his special biscuits, it provided an excellent midday snack. There was a respectful tap at the door. Dabbing his lips fastidiously with a silken kerchief, he called, "Come!"

The bosun stumped in, dragging the prisoner Ludon behind him. He threw the man to the floor and saluted by touching a many-thonged whip to his temple. "Gave 'im two strokes, sir, just as ye ordered."

Teal stood, adjusting Rocco Madrid's sword about his waist. "Hmm, good man. Carry on!"

The bosun saluted again. "Aye aye, Cap'n!" He left the cabin, closing the door carefully behind him.

Ludon cowered on the floor, sobbing and hugging himself.

Teal sounded bored as he poured himself another drink. "Oh, stop that blubberin', sirrah, y'sound like a pig with the colic. Don't look so demned sorry for yourself, man!"

Ludon turned a tear-stained face up to Teal, whining piteously, "You had me whipped, sir, for no reason at all!"

Redjack wrinkled his nose. It was hard to understand the rough English that Ludon had picked up in Caribbean ports. "Lackaday, fellow, I never do things without any reason. I never had ye really flogged, just two strokes o' the cat. So now ye know what it tastes like, eh? I did it to show ye I mean business. I want the truth, an' no lies. Of course ye can lie away an' think you're foolin' me, but that'd mean ten strokes for every little fib. Hmm, imagine that!"

Ludon shivered and sat up straight to stop the weight of his shirt from touching the wounds on his back. "I'll tell ye the truth, sir, on me oath I will. Just ask the questions an' I'll do me best to answer ye!"

Teal sat down again and studied the prisoner closely. "Of course ye will. Now, tell me, where exactly is your captain Thuron bound for?"

Ludon answered promptly. "He is sailing back to the place of his birth in France, somewhere called Arcachon, sir. Thuron was always talking of giving up the buccaneering life. Now that he has enough gold, he plans to live like a true gentleman there, with land and a château, sir."

Teal tapped his chair arm pensively. "How much gold does he possess, and don't give me any hoary old tales of buried treasure. How much exactly, eh?"

Ludon swallowed hard. "I cannot say exact, but about fully the weight of a man the size of your bosun, sir."

Teal drew his sword and tapped the prisoner's back lightly. Ludon grimaced and arched his back. Teal chuckled. "That'd be a good fortune for any man, if 'twere in coins. Nice solid gold coins can be spent anywhere. All these fabulous stones, strings o' pearls an' fancy rings usually turn out t'be fakes, or highly identifiable. Give me gold coins anytime, eh!"

Rooting out a chart, he spread it across the table and studied it. "France y'say, let me see. Ah, here 'tis, Arcachon, just off the Bay of Biscay. D'ye know, methinks I'll give your buccaneer captain a run for his money."

Ludon ignored his aching back for a moment. "Sir, you mean you'd chase Thuron clear across the Atlantic Ocean to the French coast?"

Teal warmed to his new idea. "But of course! I've got a handsome new ship, plenty of supplies an' the promise of a fortune. I'll overtake the rascal long before he ever enters French waters, an' hang him from his own yardarm! Then I'll put about for England, imagine that, eh! Captain Jonathan Ormsby Teal, comin' home with three ships an' a fine selection of gold coin. I'll rename this vessel the *Royal Champion* an' take the other two in tow. Stap me liver, I'll make a pretty picture, sailin' up the River Thames with the men cheerin' an' the ladies flutterin' their fans an' kerchiefs. Hah, confound me breeches if I ain't promoted to admiral within the very year!"

Ludon kept silent, hoping that the *Marie* could outrun Teal, at least until they were both in French waters. With France and England always at war with each other, there was a chance things could work out well for him. It was likely that they could all be captured by the French Navy. Thuron and his crew would be hanged as pirates, Teal and his men would either end up on the gallows beside them or be held in prison for ransom by the English. If he could lay hands on the gold, it would be a simple matter to bribe a French naval captain to accept a fabricated story. He could pose as a Caribbean merchant, taken captive by the English privateer and robbed of his gold. Once ashore in France he planned on vanishing over the border into Spain. Rich men can live happily anywhere.

Teal was right – plenty of gold coin was the answer to everything.

Once Teal had ordered a set course, gossip soon got round the ship. The privateers were greatly cheered by the news of seeing home again. The mate, the bosun and the master gunner discussed it in the galley over mugs of grog and hot water, but scepticism had set in after their initial cheeriness, particularly with the bosun. "Huh, we'll never catch the Frenchie – that ship's as swift as a flea over butter. She's already outsailed us once."

Swilling his mug around, the mate took a sip. "Aye, right enough, but this time she doesn't know we're chasin' her. Who ever heard of a ship pursuin' another from the Caribbean t'the Bay o' Biscay?"

Nodding his grizzled head, the master gunner agreed. "Right, matey, the last thing that froggy will expect t'see is Teal in a big new vessel comin' after him."

The bosun was determined to keep up a gloomy outlook. "An' what'll that give us, a chance to fight an' get killed afore we ever see England an' home again? Take my word, mates, Teal's doin' all this to get hold of the buccaneer's treasure. But what'll we get out of it, eh? Not a penny piece. Look at me, I'd have been better off servin' in the Royal Navy on a ship o' the line instead of on a lousy privateer. At least I'd receive half pension for this broken leg o' mine!"

The mate scoffed. "That ain't a broken leg – 'twas only sprained when that spar fell on it."

Full of self-pity, the bosun moved his leg and winced. "Well, it feels as if it's still broke! Wouldn't it be nice if a spar fell on Teal or, better still, a full mast? We'd be free men then, an' we could sail to Dover, sink the ship an' split the treasure atween us!"

Nudging him sharply, the master gunner murmured, "Stow that talk. If Teal hears ye've been fermentin' a mutiny, you're a dead man. Hush now, here comes Cookie!"

The Irish cook bustled into the galley, muttering aloud. "Goin' home to dear old England, is it? Nobody's mentioned dear old Ireland! I'd sooner see the darlin' Liffey flowin' through Dublin than London an' the River Thames. An' have ye heard the man givin' out his orders like a Wexford washerwoman with tuppence t'spend on a Monday . . ."

He went into an imitation of Teal's foppish accent, which brought smiles to the faces of his shipmates. "You there, cook, demn yer eyes! Where's me Madeira, eh? An' y'call this a fresh fish, sirrah? 'Twas fresh when the Bible was written. Take the confounded thing out o' me sight! I'll have ye flogged an' keelhauled if ye look at me like that again. Out o' me sight, ye insolent cockroach, be off!"

Ludon sat on the deck beneath the galley window, listening to all that was said and storing it in his mind for future reference: talk of mutiny, murder and ship scuttling, disrespect of the captain. What was it the cook had likened Teal to? A Wexford washerwoman. Wouldn't Redjack be pleased to hear that when the time came!

Ludon was not quite sure what form his plan would take nor when he would be able to put it into effect. But all he saw and heard was of value to him. After all, was he not but one lowly prisoner in the midst of enemies?

12

DAWN'S WELCOMING LIGHT FLOODED THROUGH the cabin as fresh ocean breezes ruffled the edges of charts on the captain's table. Ben and Ned sat on the bed anxiously watching the Frenchman, to whom Ben had related the whole tale.

Thuron pondered the fantastic narrative, stroking his rough beard for quite a while before speaking. "If any man had told me all this, I would have had him locked up as a mad person. But I know you are telling me the truth, Ben. From the first time I looked into those strange eyes of yours, I knew you were different from anyone I had ever met. Who can tell, maybe some odd fate has brought us together. I am not sufficiently educated to question it – I believe you."

Ben sighed with relief, feeling as if an enormous weight had been lifted from his heart.

Ned sent him a thought. "Thank goodness our captain is a man we can trust, eh, mate?"

Unthinkingly, the boy answered aloud. "He certainly is, Ned!"

Thuron smiled, gazing into the dog's trustful eyes. "This fellow can understand everything I say, I'm sure of it. I could tell you were just talking together – what was he saying to you, lad?"

Ben told the captain, who seemed immensely pleased. "I wish I could speak with Ned. He looks a handsome and intelligent fellow. Hahaha! Look at him, he heard me!"

The black Labrador stood up on the bed and struck a pose, which he hoped looked both handsome and intelligent. Ben laughed along with the Frenchman. "I'm afraid you can't hold conversations with Ned, sir, but he can nod yes or no to anything you need to ask him. Right, Ned?" The dog nodded to affirm this.

Thuron's eyes lit up. "That's a very valuable thing to know. Thank you, my friends. I am a fortunate fellow to have such wonderful companions. But we'll keep it our secret. The crew wouldn't understand."

Ben agreed. "Except maybe Pierre. He's a good man, too, Cap'n."

Thuron nodded. "They're all good men in their own ways, but Anaconda was the best of them. I can't tell you how I miss that giant of a man, may his soul find peace. He was a slave, you know – we ran away together, deserted from a corsair galley many years ago in the Indian Ocean, just off the coast of Madagascar. We were together for a long time. When I got my first ship, I wanted to make him the mate. But Anaconda wouldn't hear of it. All he wanted was to be steersman. I remember him saying, 'I will command your ship's wheel and take you wherever you want to go. You are my captain, and my friend for life!' And that's the way it was until yesterday. Ah, my poor friend, my poor friend, my heart grieves for him."

Ben had to turn his face away as the French buccaneer captain wept openly. Ned whined and laid his head in Thuron's lap.

"Sail ho, to the southeast. Sail ho!"

Brushing a sleeve roughly across his eyes, Thuron quickly

straightened up to the lookout's call. "Sail! Let's hope 'tis not an enemy."

All hands were crowded to the rail as the Frenchman sighted through his telescope at the distant vessel. He nodded knowingly and spoke to Pierre. "Good job I saw him before he hauled up a decoy flag. I'd know that one anywhere. 'Tis the Barbary corsair, *Flame of Tripoli.* Only one captain, Al-Kurkuman, flies a flag with a red scimitar on a gold background. Hoho, look, he's striking his colours and running up a Portuguese merchant flag, the rascal. Who does he think he's fooling?"

As the *Flame of Tripoli* altered course to intercept the *Marie,* Ben could see that its sails were blood red. He tugged on Thuron's sleeve. "Cap'n, does he mean to do us harm?"

Thuron put away the telescope. "Only if he gets the chance, lad. Al-Kurkuman's a slaver. He's bound for the Isle of Cuba with a cargo of misery purchased from the coasts of Mozambique. I can't abide traffickers in human flesh, Ben, but we've got to be diplomatic with Al-Kurkuman. He's dangerous to any he thinks are weaker than himself. Leave this to me – I can handle him. Pierre, run out all cannon and arm all hands! Stand ready and wait on my word!"

As the *Flame of Tripoli* hove nearer, Ben saw the captain known as Al-Kurkuman. He was everything a Barbary corsair should be, an Arabian Indian of mixed blood. He glittered in the sunlight, draped in chains, necklaces, beads, rings and bangles, all of pure gold. Clad in light-green silk, wearing a black turban mounted with a ruby, he stood boldly out on the prow and grinned – even his teeth were plated with beaten gold.

Ned passed Ben a thought. "If he fell in the water, he'd go straight to the bottom, carrying all that weight. I'll never dress like that. When I'm captain, a simple, thin gold collar will be enough for me!"

Ben patted his dog. "That's very sensible of you!"

They both started as a loud bang issued from the *Marie.* Thuron had touched off a cannon, sending a shot roaring across the other ship's bows as a sign that the *Marie* stood armed and ready for trouble if need be.

Al-Kurkuman did not even flinch as the cannonball whizzed by overhead. He grinned even wider, bowing and touching his chest, lips and forehead with an open hand.

Thuron returned a short courteous bow, smiling as he called out, "The fair winds and calm waters be always at your back, Captain Kurkuman. The Indian Ocean is far off. Have you lost your way, my friend?"

The *Flame of Tripoli* came almost alongside as she backed water. Looking as if he had found a long lost brother, Al-Kurkuman replied, "Thuron, old comrade, I took you for a fat little French merchantman – accept my humble apologies!"

Captain Thuron nodded at his cannon array and the men crowding the rigging, all fully armed. He continued the game. "I am like yourself, O illustrious one, a dove with sharp teeth. What news have you of this great world?"

Gold jewellery jingled as the Barbary corsair shrugged. "Nothing surprising, it is full of men, both bad and good. Tell me, have you crossed the wake of a Greek Navy vessel? She has been trailing me ever since I put into Accra for supplies. Why would the Greek captain want to detain an honest merchant like Al-Kurkuman, I ask you, old friend?"

It was Thuron's turn to shrug. "Life is a mystery. How would I know? The Greeks are a suspicious people. Where are you bound?"

"To Belém in the South Americas," Al-Kurkuman lied. "I carry farming implements to the settlers there. And you?"

"To the Isle of Malta with a cargo of wax to make candles." Thuron returned the lie with a straight face. "It was good to cross your path and meet an old friend again. I must go. May the spirits of the seas guide you on your way, Al-Kurkuman!"

The Barbary corsair smiled like a shark with gold teeth. "Peace be unto you, Raphael Thuron, and may the djinns of paradise attend you. A moment, friend. That boy, the puny whelp you have there, will you sell him to me? Fattened up a bit, he would fetch a coin or two in the markets of Marrakech."

Thuron gave Ben a playful cuff. "Who, this wretch? Alas, friend, how could I sell my own son, though he eats more than he is worth and he suffers the sickness of the brain."

Al-Kurkuman looked sourly at the boy, then laughed. "Then starve him, beat him well and educate him. Maybe next time we meet I will trade you another for him!"

Without another word from their captains, both ships went their ways. Thuron kept his men armed and all cannon still loaded and showing until they were out of range.

Thuron watched Ben and Ned. He could tell they were conversing. "Well, lad, what did you make of all that?"

The boy came near and whispered to the Frenchman, "Ned's a bit put out that Al-Kurkuman didn't notice him. He thought the least he could do was to offer a bid for the handsome, intelligent dog. What do you think, Cap'n?"

Thuron replied in a whisper, "Tell Ned that if Al-Kurkuman had bought him, he'd be on the dinner table tonight."

The boy watched Ned stalk off with his tail in the air. "He's very offended, Cap'n. You shouldn't have said that – his feelings are hurt now."

The Frenchman chuckled. "I'll get the cook to make it up to poor Ned. Meanwhile, let's run up the French flag and get our *Marie* looking like a peaceful merchantman."

Ben looked at him, puzzled. "But why, sir?"

Thuron ruffled the lad's hair. "I've got a feeling we might meet the Greek Navy ship. Don't want her thinking we're buccaneers, do we? Lend a hand disguising our cannon ports, then take a turn on lookout for our Greek friends."

That afternoon Ben stood in the crow's nest armed with the captain's telescope, sweeping the empty leagues of ocean for'ard and aft. All that could be seen was a tiny dot off to the northwest, which was the receding Barbary corsair. Ben liked the lookout post. He had learned to enjoy its giddy motion, the boundless azure arch of sky above, cloudless now, broken by the odd sight of a winging albatross or predatory skua. Below him the deck shifted alarmingly, always rolling from side to side. He saw Thuron emerge from the galley and present Ned with a scraggy mutton bone. Good old Ned, his faithful friend.

Ben was taken by surprise as the head of a crewman called Mallon appeared over the edge of his perch. The buccaneer winked at him. "Cap'n sent me up to relieve you for a spell, lad." He climbed up alongside the boy. "No sign of sail yet?"

Ben handed him the telescope. "None at all, except the slaveship, but she's nearly over the horizon now."

Mallon shook his head. "That 'un's a bad vessel, an' Al-Kurkuman's an evil captain. Real pirates, that lot!"

Ben stared out over the waves. "Cap'n said he was a Barbary corsair. We're called buccaneers, aren't we?"

Mallon shrugged. "Pirates is what we're all called, lad. There's buccaneers, filibusters, freebooters, ladrones, pickaroons, corsairs an' sea dogs, most bad an' a few good. But 'tis the likes of Al-Kurkuman who gets us all tarred with the same brush. One pirate's the same as another to a privateer or navy cap'n – they'd hang us all!"

Ben looked askance at Mallon. "Surely they wouldn't hang us?"

The buccaneer laughed grimly. "Of course they would, the law's the law. There's no such thing as a good pirate. We're all gallows bait. Those privateers are the worst – they're naught but pirates like us, with a letter o' marque to make their crimes legal. Have ye ever seen a pirate hanged, lad?"

Ben shook his head hastily. "Never, have you?"

Mallon nodded. "Aye, one time I was ashore in the Bahamas without a ship. I saw a pirate, man named Firejon, executed by order of the governor. 'Twas a fancy affair. All the ladies an' gentry turned out in their coaches to witness it. I stood in the crowd. Firejon was a bad 'un – there was a big price on his head.

"British Royal Navy had sunk his ship an' brought him ashore in chains. Some said hangin' was too good for Firejon, 'cos of his terrible crimes. So they flogged him first, then sat him in a cell for two days on bread and water. There they gave him a rope, so he could make a noose for his own neck. I tell ye, the hanging 'twas an awful sight to see. The governor refused to let Firejon wear chains or manacles."

Ben was fascinated and horrified at the same time. "Why was that?"

Mallon pursed his lips. "So he wouldn't hang quickly with the weight of 'em to pull him down. A local preacher wrote out a poem that they made Firejon read aloud from the scaffold afore they turned him off. I can still remember that poem word for word. Would ye like to hear me say it, Ben?"

Without waiting for a reply, Mallon launched into the verse.

"Come all ye mothers' sons who sail the sea,
Attend to this last tale that I will tell.
Embark not on a life of piracy,
'Tis but a dreadful trip which ends in hell.
Those honest ships you plunder, loot and sink,
Good vessels at your mercy, which you wreck,
For gold to waste, in taverns where ye drink,
Will one day drop the noose about your neck.
For once I was a wicked buccaneer,
I scorned the laws of man and God on high,
But now, with none to weep or mourn me here,
Upon this gallows I am bound to die.
Take warning now by my untimely end,
A judgement day must come to everyone.
Too late for me my evil ways to mend,
O Lord have mercy now my days are done!"

Mallon paused for effect, then continued. "Then the soldiers set up a roll upon their drums . . ."

Suddenly Ben felt queasy. Grasping a ratline, he swung out of the crow's nest and began climbing down. "I think I've heard enough, thanks!"

Mallon brought the telescope up to his eye and peered aft. "Sail abaft, Cap'n. I think 'tis a Greek man-o'-war!"

Ben felt far more frightened than he had at sighting the Barbary corsair. Suddenly he knew why Raphael Thuron wanted to give up being a pirate and live peacefully ashore.

Ned looked up from the remains of his mutton bone. "I thought you were used to shipboard life, mate. You look seasick to me. Here, Cap'n, come and take a peep at this boy!"

Thuron had not heard Ned, but he saw that Ben was pale and unsteady. The Frenchman threw an arm about the boy's shoulders. "What ails ye, shipmate?"

Ben tried to straighten himself up. "I'll be all right, sir."

Thuron glanced up at the man in the crow's nest and back to Ben. "Hah, you've been listening to that sack of woe and misery. I'll wager he told ye all about a pirate hanging. Did he recite his favourite poem, too?"

Ben wiped a forearm across his sweat-beaded forehead. "Aye, Cap'n, he did, it was a dreadful thing –"

"Rubbish!" Thuron interrupted the boy. "He made it all up from gossip that he's heard. Take no notice of Misery Mallon. How he ever got to be a buccaneer I'll never know. They say he was a preacher once, but the congregation banished him for stealing money from the offertory box. I'd have flung him overboard long ago, but he'd frighten the fishes with his tales of horrible pirate executions!"

Ben managed a smile. "But what about the Greek Navy vessel?"

Ned was standing with his paws on the rail, watching the approaching ship. Thuron scratched fondly behind the dog's ears. "You leave that to me an' Ned. We'll take care of it, won't we, fellow?"

The dog nodded his head as he contacted Ben by thought. "Aye, don't worry, Ben, I'll take off my cutlass, hide my brass earrings and cover up all these tattoos. They'll think I'm just a harmless old cabin hound!"

Ben tugged at his dog's wagging tail. "Good idea. No one will ever know you're Naughty Ned, terror of the high seas!"

The Greek ship was named the *Achilles.* Smart as a new pin, it was rigged out with even more guns than a privateer and carried archers as well as musketeers. They lined the decks, all hands fit and ready for action. The *Achilles* stood off, broadside to the *Marie,* cannon loaded and pointing right at her.

Thuron hailed the captain in a world-weary voice. "What d'you want, bothering honest merchants? Aren't there enough pirates and rascals to chase?"

The Greek captain, who wore a white linen kilt and a long blue stocking cap, replied in excellent French, "A merchantman, eh? What cargo do you carry, sir?"

Thuron threw him a disgusted glance. "None. We were boarded and robbed by a Spanish pirate. Woven cane chairs, that's what the villain took, a full cargo of them. May his bottom get splinters in it every time he sits down, curse him!"

The Greek captain laughed. "Pirates will steal anything, sir. You were lucky to escape alive. So you have nothing aboard?"

The Frenchman gave an eloquent shrug. "Nothing, Captain, you can come and see for yourself."

The Greek stared hard at Thuron for a moment, as if making up his mind whether or not to search the *Marie.* Ben could feel his legs trembling. Then Ned began barking and showing his teeth ferociously.

The *Achilles'* captain shook his head. "No, no, you have had enough trouble already. But what are you doing in these waters, sir?"

Thuron put on a hopeful expression. "I have heard there is good work to be picked up coastin' the Mediterranean!"

The Greek made a deprecatory gesture. "You would do better cruising my home waters, the Aegean Sea. There are more islands there, and the trade is good. Tell me, though, in your travels, have you seen a red-sailed ship, the *Flame of Tripoli*? She's somewhere in these waters, I'm sure. Have you caught sight of her?"

Thuron answered truthfully. "We encountered that vessel early this morning, Captain. She's a slaver, taking a cargo of slaves to the Americas. Her master even wanted to purchase my son here, didn't he, Ben?"

The boy nodded dumbly and allowed Thuron to continue. "Luckily we were unladen and gave her the slip. By now that slaver will be gone over the horizon, sailing due northwest.

"You could run him down in two days' hard sailing, Captain. Slavers are evil men. I hope you catch him and string him up, aye, and all his crew!"

The Greek captain saluted. "Be sure I will, sir. Any man who trades in human beings needs hanging. Good day to you!"

Thuron saluted back. "Good day to you and good hunting, sir!"

The *Achilles* waited until the *Marie* had gone by. Then she altered course and began piling on sail to chase the slaver.

Thuron let out a sigh of relief. "I wonder why he didn't board and search us?"

Ben exchanged thoughts with Ned, then explained to the captain in a murmur that the rest of the crew could not hear. "Ned could tell by his eyes that he was afraid of dogs. That's why Ned barked and showed his teeth. 'Twas just a simple thing, Cap'n, but it changed the Greek's mind – he was scared of being bitten if he came aboard."

Thuron picked the black Labrador up bodily and kissed him. "You clever lucky dog, what are you, eh?"

Ned wriggled furiously, sending outraged thoughts to Ben. "Uuurgh! Tell this great whiskery lump t'put me down. I'll never kiss any of my crew when I'm captain. Most undignified!"

13

THERE ARE few diversions or amusements for seamen under sail across an entire ocean – other than hard, monotonous routine. Gossip and talk, known as scuttlebutt, provided the main release of feelings for the crew of the *Diablo Del Mar,* now renamed the *Royal Champion.* The usual run of conversation centred on the injustices all hands were forced to endure under a captain such as Redjack Teal. This fitted in quite nicely with Ludon's scheme, giving him leeway to widen the gap of disaffection between the crew and their captain.

Though Ludon was not an educated man, he knew that the policy of divide and conquer was a workable idea. He looked and listened constantly, finding opportunities to carry tales back and forth in secret. There was nowhere a prisoner at sea could escape to. Accordingly, the mate, who would not tolerate idle hands aboard, had given Ludon the job of cook's assistant. He served meals to the common seamen on the mess deck and, much to the cook's relief, was employed to fetch and carry meals to the captain – a heaven-sent gift to the lone conspirator.

Life aboard the *Royal Champion* became increasingly difficult, owing to Ludon's scheming. If a man grumbled about his victuals, suddenly Teal was made aware of it. Being a disciplinarian, Teal would mete out harsh punishment on the offender. This made the crew resentful and surly, particularly when Ludon would let slip that the captain regarded his crew as ignorant, wayward oafs. Amidst a welter of truths, half-truths and downright lies, every man aboard became suspicious of his own shipmates.

One evening, Ludon was serving the day's meal out on the mess deck. He studiously avoided putting out food wherever there was an empty seat. The bosun growled, "Ahoy there, Frenchie, fill those plates for the gun crew!"

Ludon paused. "But they are not here."

Bad-temperedly, the bosun slammed his knife down on the tabletop. "I said fill those plates! Who are you to say who'll eat an' who won't? Here comes the gun crew now."

Sitting down to the table, the master gunner held up his hands, all swollen, red and scratched. "Lookit that, we've had t'boil an' scrape out every gun barrel aboard, musket an' cannon. Been hard at it since dawn! See Taffy's hand there, all bandaged up. He got it jammed in a culverin bore. Wonder he never lost it!"

The bosun inspected the grimy, blood-soaked bandage. "I'd keep a fresh wrappin' on that hand every day if'n I was you, Taffy. Save it goin' poison on ye. Ah well, that'll learn ye t'keep your gun barrels clean, Gunny."

With his spoon halfway to his mouth, the grizzled old master gunner exploded with indignation. "My guns have always been clean. I've served twenty years as master gunner an' no cap'n has ever accused me of havin' a dirty gun aboard!"

Almost apologetically, the bosun replied, "Then why did Redjack punish you an' your men?"

The one called Taffy gestured with his bandaged hand. " 'Cos someone tipped a pail o' rubbish over the cannon nearest to Teal's cabin door!"

Cramming the loaded spoon into his mouth, the master gunner chewed furiously with his few remaining teeth, speaking through a full mouth. "Just let me get my hands on the scum who did it!" He spat out a lump of half-chewed meat. "Garrgh! Is this supposed t'be salt pork? Tastes more like a dead horse out of a glue boiler!"

He glared at Ludon. "Have ye got nothin' better'n this to feed hungry men, eh?"

The French prisoner shrugged. "Cook says 'tis all he has, but your captain, he dines well enough on fresh fish. He is not short of fancy biscuits or Madeira to go with it."

Pushing his plate away, the bosun spoke sneeringly. "When was it ever different? The crew gets the slops while the cap'n dines like a lord. Here, Frenchie, take this garbage an' toss it over the side."

Pointing a finger in Ludon's face, the master gunner snarled, "An' keep it clear o' my cannon, or else . . ."

Ludon scraped the leftovers into a pot and stalked out of the mess-deck cabin.

When he had gone, the bosun's eyes narrowed, and he nodded towards the door, muttering low, "I don't trust that 'un. I been noticin' lately, the Frenchie's ears wiggle like a little pig whenever we're talkin'. Take it from me, mates, guard your tongues while he's about!"

The mate stared oddly at the bosun. "D'ye think that Frenchie's carryin' tales back to Redjack?"

Taffy answered for the mate. " 'Twouldn't surprise me – he's got the looks of a rat. What more could ye expect of a buccaneer deserter who sold out to that Spanish pirate?"

Stabbing his knife into the tabletop, the bosun looked around at all hands. "So, what're we goin' to do about it, mates?"

Being a fair-minded fellow, the master gunner replied, "Nothin' without proof. Ye can't condemn a man just because of his looks. There's been many a mistake made like that."

Joby, the dead carpenter's mate, picked up the fiddle that had once belonged to his former friend and twiddled a few chords on the instrument. It seemed to break the tense atmosphere.

The old master gunner cracked a gap-toothed grin. "Come on, Joby, sing us a song. I'm fed up o' sittin' here lissenin' to talk of mutiny an' murder. Cheer us up, mate!"

Joby smiled brightly. "Shall I play 'The Jolly Cap'n'?" He ducked swiftly as several chunks of ship's biscuit were hurled at him, then twiddled another chord or two. "I've put new words to it, listen."

Off he went, singing an insulting imitation of the original.

"Ho the wind will never blow, me lads,
So we've got to row the boat,
An' as for Cap'n Teal, the pig,
I'd like to slit his throat.
He wears a fine red jacket
An' drinks Madeira wine,
Why should we call him captain
When we could call him swine!

Hurrah hurrah hurrah, me boys,
He feeds us naught but swill,
An' makes us taste the rope's end,
That's why all hands look ill!

His father was a pig, me lads,
An' his mother was a sow,
They sent him off a sailin',
We're lumbered with him now . . ."

Joby's voice trailed away, and the fiddle gave a discordant screech as the bow trailed over its strings.

Captain Teal stood in the open doorway. His buckled shoes clacked against the deck as he strode up to the table. Teal's voice shook with barely controlled rage as he faced the unfortunate Joby. "Greatly amusin', I'm sure. Well, carry on playin', man!"

Placing the instrument on the table, Joby swallowed hard. " 'Twas only by way of a little joke, sir."

Teal picked up the fiddle, weighing it in one hand. The crewmen watched him in dumb silence as he suddenly flung it at the bulkhead. When it hit the floor, he jumped on it with both feet, stamping and kicking savagely at the dead carpenter's favourite instrument. It shattered and smashed, chips of wood, pegs and bow strings scattering over the mess-deck floor.

Redjack Teal stood amid the wreckage, his eyes narrowed to mean slits. "A little joke, eh? Demn your insolence, fellow!"

Teal's accusing gaze fixed both the bosun and the master gunner. Spittle sprayed the air as he yelled at them, "Anythin' to say about the victuals, eh, eh? Meat's like a dead horse! Crew eatin' slops! What's the matter, gentlemen, cat got your tongues? Nothin' t'say about how I dine like a lord? Speak up, demn your eyes!"

Both the bosun and the gunner held their horrified silence.

Redjack suddenly went calm. He smiled slyly at them. "Next thing ye'll be talkin' mutiny behind me back."

Shaking his head, the master gunner called out hoarsely, "Beg your pardon, Cap'n, but we've never said a mutinous word agin ye –"

Teal interrupted by drawing his silver-mounted pistol and cocking the hammer. "Have ye not indeed? Well, me brave boys, I'm goin' t'make sure ye don't get the chance. Mr Mate, attend me here!"

The mate sprang upright and saluted. "Aye, sir!"

The captain pointed to Joby, the bosun and the master gunner with his pistol barrel. "Take these men in charge. They are to be put aboard the *Devon Belle,* one at each masthead. Half ration of ship's biscuit'n'water for a week. That'll cure 'em of any mutinous mutterin's against me!"

The men picked up the pieces of sailcloth that they used as cloaks in rough weather, but Teal shook his head. "Go as y'are, barefoot, too. Hard lessons must be learned the hard way. Mr Mate, see them to their posts, if y'please!"

Obediently the mate touched his forelock. "Aye aye, Cap'n."

"No, wait!" Teal tapped his chin thoughtfully with the pistol sight. "Bring our froggy prisoner here, will ye?"

Two crewmen escorted the puzzled-looking Ludon into the cabin. Redjack smiled benevolently at him. "Ah, there y'are, monsieur. I've decided you shall go along an' spend a week aboard the *Devon Belle* with these three rascals, on half rations of hardtack biscuit'n'water."

Ludon took one glance at the grim-faced trio, then fell on

his knees, grabbing Teal's red jacket hem. "But, Cap'n, sir, what wrong have I done ye?"

Teal dragged himself free, sending Ludon sprawling with a kick. "Tellin' tales an' causin' disaffection among me crew, sirrah, that's what you're guilty of. Take 'em away!"

The three crewmen were marched out by the mate, followed by two other sailors dragging Ludon, who was sobbing pitifully, "No, no, Cap'n, sir, you cannot do this to me!"

Teal uncocked his pistol, chuckling at his cruel scheme. "Ye mealy-mouthed toad, I'll show ye what I can't an' can do aboard me own ship!"

Aboard *La Petite Marie*, Ben was putting the finishing touches to the repairs he had made to the window in the captain's cabin. Canvas sheet was not as good for letting in light as the original glass windows, but it kept spray and wind out. Using the hilt of a heavy dagger, he knocked the final nail into the pleated canvas edge. Ned entered the cabin and looked around, sending a thought to his friend. "Bit dark in here, isn't it?"

Ben put aside the dagger. "Aye, but 'twill do well enough. At least we won't see the *Flying Dutchman* through it."

Ned remembered what he had come for. "Oh, I think the cap'n wants to see you, Ben. He's up in the bows."

As they made their way along the deck, Ben looked back over his shoulder. He passed a mental message to Ned. "See that fellow Gascon? He crossed himself and spat over the side after we'd passed. I wonder what's wrong with him?"

The black Labrador waved his tail airily. "Oh, him, he's my least favourite man aboard this ship. He glares at me a lot, I don't know why. I've never done him any harm."

Thuron was shouting from his position in the bows, "Ben, come here, there's something I want you to see!" The boy mounted the bowsprit and locked his legs around it.

The Frenchman gave him the telescope, pointing. "Dead ahead, you can just make it out – land, lad. That's the islands of the Azores. Now point your glass downwards and take a look into the ocean. What d'you see, Ben?"

Scanning the surface on either side of the bow wave, Ben tried his best to see something distinctive. "Nothing really, sir, just a sort of white blotch now and then, but it's pretty far below us. Is that what you mean?"

Ned was frantically passing messages to Ben. "White blot, what kind of white blot, tell me?"

Thuron provided the answer. "Remember, I told you there was a whole world beneath the ocean. What you see are the tips of mountains, huge tall peaks. We're sailing over the great ridge, a sunken range of mountains that runs from Greenland almost to the earth's southern tip. Wait until you see the Azores – I think they're part of those mountains. Just higher peaks than the rest, sticking up out of the sea to form islands."

Ben lifted the telescope until he sighted on the rocky peaks of the Azores in the distance. "This world is a marvellous thing, Cap'n. It's so vast!"

La Petite Marie dropped anchor that afternoon in a deep lagoon of the main island. Ben and Ned marvelled at the lush tropical greenery that clung to the mountainous rocks around them.

Pierre lowered the jolly boat and invited them aboard with the party that was going ashore. "Come on, you two, we'll get some fruit and fresh water."

Ben and Ned sat either side of Pierre in the stern. The boy

noticed Gascon crouching in the bows and flashed a quick thought to his dog. "I wonder what he's up to? He's looking pretty furtive."

Ned wrinkled his forehead. "Huh, hope he falls overboard and drowns!"

Ben frowned at the black Labrador. "Ned! That's not a very charitable thought."

Ned sniffed. "I don't care, I don't like that fellow and he doesn't like me, or you. I can sense it."

Pierre was unaware of the conversation and chatted away happily. "Lots of good fruit and vegetables growin' on these islands, Ben. They're long-dead volcanoes, and the soil is rich."

They spent the remainder of the afternoon foraging on the slopes, gathering quantities of the island's produce, some familiar, some new to them, but all wonderful. Some of the crewmen found a little waterfall that cascaded down into a pond on the mossy ledges. Ben and Ned joined them in the crystal-clear water, bathing and splashing each other, laughing like a band of children. For the boy and his dog it was a golden day to remember, far from the rigours of seafaring and the fear of the *Flying Dutchman* haunting their dreams.

They returned to the *Marie* in the late evening to find a grim-faced Thuron awaiting their arrival. He nodded as he checked the boat's crew. "Gascon isn't with you. I suspected as much!"

Pierre looked bewildered. "I hadn't noticed he was missing!"

The captain slung a musket across his shoulder and picked up his cutlass. "Oh, Gascon has jumped ship all right. Ben, you stay here with Ned. Pierre, take four men to row the boat. I'm going to hunt that rascal down!"

Ben could not understand the captain's reasoning. "But why not just let him go, sir? He's not much use."

Thuron explained, "If 'twere just that Gascon is a surly and idle man, he could go for all I care. But while you were on the island, I checked my gold and found that someone has helped himself to it. That can only be one man – Gascon! He can't run far on the Azores. Pierre and I will have him back here, ready to sail at dawn tomorrow."

Ned stood with his paws on the rail, watching the departing jolly boat as he imparted a thought. "You see, I told you I didn't like that Gascon!"

Ben fondled the dog's silky ears. "What a good judge of men you are, sir. I'll wager that when you become captain, you won't have crew like him aboard your ship."

Ned regarded the boy huffily. "Your humour is misplaced, sir!"

Later they sat together on the afterdeck with the crew. A pale moon was reflected in the calm waters of the lagoon, and not a breeze stirred anywhere. It was warm from the day's heat. A crewman was singing softly.

"Come, my love, gentle one, hearken to me,
For I'll bring you a fortune someday.
I'm naught but a man who must follow the sea,
Let me tell you ere I sail away.

When the wind stirs the rigging,
And the white sail's on high,
My heart is as sad as the lone seagull's cry.
Wait for me, pray for me, 'til once again,
I sail back to you o'er the wide ocean's main.

And what will I bring for you, ma belle amour?
A bracelet of jewels so fine,
Some silk from Cathay, that I know you'll adore
And a ring on your finger to shine.

So be true to your sailor,
Wipe the tears from your eye,
For when I return you will nevermore cry.
With my feet on the land, and my love by my side,
'Tis farewell to sailing, I'll make you my bride."

Ben gazed up at the star-strewn skies, passing Ned a thought. "That's a pretty little melody, eh, mate?"

Ned panted as though he were chuckling. "Aye, but just look at the singer. He's a whiskery old doormat with an eye patch and only one tooth in his head. I think any poor girl would run a mile at the sight of him returning!"

The boy threw a playful headlock on his dog. "Shame on you, sir, criticizing others, just because you're a handsome dog!"

Ned cocked an eye towards Ben. "Cruel but beautiful, that's me!"

It was not on the next dawn but three days later that an anxious Ben saw the jolly boat's return. Gascon's hands were bound behind him, and the crew had to haul him aboard. Thuron looked tired and worn out. All hands gathered to see what he would do.

Pierre whispered to Ben, "Slippery as an eel, that Gascon, but we caught him in the end. Cap'n ain't too pleased at losing three days."

Ben experienced a moment of horror as Thuron drew his dagger. He faced the deserter and shouted to the crew.

"Look!" With a few slashes he sliced through the felon's pockets and coat lining. Gold coins glinted in the late-afternoon sun as they clinked upon the deck. Taking Gascon by one ear, Thuron shook him roughly. "Couldn't wait for the share-out, could you, rat? I should have let you run off with the other three at Puerto Rico. At least they never thieved from the captain and shipmates! Take this scum out of my sight. Put him in the anchor-chain locker until I decide what to do with him!"

As he was dragged off by the bosun and several others, Gascon began shouting, "Throw me in the sea an' let me swim ashore. I know all about you an' your lucky friends, Thuron. I ain't stayin' aboard this ship. She's cursed, I tell ye, cursed!"

Pierre silenced Gascon with a hefty blow to the jaw. He bundled the half-conscious deserter into the chain locker. Barring the door, Pierre growled a warning. "Shut your lyin' mouth an' be thankful you're still alive, thief. Cap'n should've run ye through with that dagger!"

Thuron glanced at the sky, judging the breeze. "We'll haul anchor an' sail at tomorrow's dawn."

It was warm that night, and Ben and Ned settled down to sleep on the open deck. The black Labrador gave thoughtful voice to his opinion. "Pierre was right, the cap'n should've slain that villain!"

Ben replied, "That sounds a bit ruthless, mate."

Ned closed his eyes, adding a final comment. "I've got a bad feeling about Gascon. I think there's going to be big trouble for us while he's aboard this ship."

14

CAPTAIN REDJACK TEAL HAD NOT PUT IN AT the Azores. Sailing under fair weather and favourable winds, he set a course straight for the Bay of Biscay and the coast of France. Unknowingly, the *Royal Champion*, with the *Devon Belle* still in tow, had passed up the chance of catching *La Petite Marie* unawares, lying as she was in a single-exit lagoon with her captain absent ashore. As usual, Teal was seated in his cabin being attended upon hand and foot. He had just finished a breakfast of fresh fish, biscuits and Madeira. A crewman was busily polishing his captain's buckled shoes, whilst another brushed vigorously at the red hunting jacket, which Teal had donned. Redjack had just placed his white-stockinged feet into the shoes when a knock sounded. He primped at the crisp white stock overlying his shirt. "Come!"

The mate entered and saluted respectfully. "Come to report a man missin', Cap'n, the French prisoner."

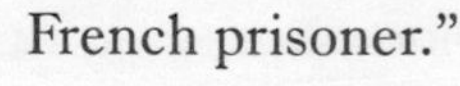

Teal held his arms wide as a crewman belted the Spanish sword and scabbard about his waist. "Really? I'm surprised he lasted this long, eh!"

The mate looked at him questioningly. "Sir?"

Looking away from the cheval glass, the privateer captain shook his head pityingly. "Oh, use your head, sirrah! A demned froggy informer, alone on a ship with three English lads he'd been tellin' tales about. I'd have wagered a side of gammon to a pig's snout that he'd have had a fatal mishap long since, eh! How do I look?"

The mate tried to sound enthusiastic at Teal's attire. "Ye cut a good dash, sir, all shipshape an' Bristol fashion!"

Teal sniffed. "Confound Bristol, London's the place t'be seen. Faith! Are ye goin' to leave your captain standin' here all day, or will ye attend the door an' let me out on me own deck? Move y'self, man!"

Once on deck, Teal swept the starboard horizon with his telescope. Highly satisfied with what he saw, the privateer smiled brightly at his steersman. "Hah, just as I thought, Cape Ortegal on the Spanish coast. Admirable navigation, even though I do say it meself! Keep her out from the coast 'twixt Gijón an' Santander. We'll skirt the Gulf o' Gascony, then up to the Arcachon Basin, eh! Mr Mate, ye can fetch those three ruffians here from the *Devon Belle*. Have 'em report t'me."

There was a definite spring to Teal's step as he strode the deck. He felt pleased with himself.

The three miscreants – the bosun, Joby and the master gunner – had murdered Ludon some time during the previous night. They had climbed down from their masthead perches and cornered the informer. It was all done swiftly, a quick rap over the head with a belaying pin, and the unconscious Ludon was hurled overboard with a necklace of holystones to hasten him underwater. Now they stood ashen-faced and resigned in front of their captain, who, they were certain, would inflict extreme punishments on them.

Redjack circled the trio, looking them up and down. Much to their amazement, he winked at them and laughed. "Frenchie went missin' durin' the night when 'twas nice an' dark, eh? Strange fellow . . . Did any of ye see him takin' his midnight dip?"

The bosun acted as spokesman for his mates. "No, sir, we was too busy keepin' life'n'limb together atop the masts, sir. None of us seen nothin', Cap'n."

Teal nodded approvingly. "Well said, true blue an' never betray one's shipmates, eh? That's the British way, m'lads! Methinks ye've had enough of mastheads an' half rations. A happy ship's what's needed, so I'm returnin' ye to duties aboard the *Royal Champion.* Be good men, behave yourselves, an' serve king an' captain loyally. Well, what have ye got to say for yourselves, eh?"

The trio could scarce believe Teal's change of heart. They tugged furiously at their forelocks, chanting, "Aye aye, Cap'n! Thankee, sir!"

But Teal had stridden off towards his cabin.

Joby stood openmouthed – he had fully expected to be hanged for murder. "Well blow me down, Cap'n's changed tack for the better!"

The master gunner nodded his grizzled head. "Aye, an' so would I if'n I was sailin' in these waters. Spain an' France ain't friendly to English vessels, especially privateers. Old Redjack's goin' to need every man jack of us in case of attack, that's what I say!"

The bosun agreed wholeheartedly. "Redjack wouldn't look too happy with a Spanish or French man-o'-war comin' at him. Not with a bosun an' a master gunner out o' commission. What say you, Joby?"

The former carpenter's mate grinned. "Let's go an' see what Cookie's got in the pot. My stomach's stickin' to me spine with 'unger!"

The bosun threw an arm around Joby's shoulder. "Good idea. There should be plenty o' vittles in the galley. There's one mouth less to feed – the Frenchie's!"

They hurried off to the galley, laughing like children.

By nightfall the *Royal Champion* had passed Gijón and was halfway to Santander, running at full sail, with the *Devon Belle* tagging behind like a puppy dog.

Redjack pored over the charts in his cabin, humming the melody of "The Jolly Captain". He felt that now, more than at any other time in his life, luck and good fortune were at last smiling down on him. What a tale would be told around the taverns and fashionable coffeehouses of London! Redjack Teal arriving home with a fine Spanish galleon and two others in tow, carrying with him a fortune in gold coins, the weight of a man!

He would become a legend in his own lifetime.

Morning sunlight glittered over the ocean as *La Petite Marie* weighed anchor and sailed. Raphael Thuron stood at the wheel, grinning at the antics of Ben, who, with his dog's assistance, was taking a turn at steering the vessel.

The Frenchman encouraged his lucky friends. "Hold her steady, that's the way! Now take her a point east. Not too far, Ben! Watch Ned, he's got the hang of it!"

The black Labrador stood on his hind legs, both forepaws resting on the wheel, chiding Ben. "You heard the cap'n – hold her steady, mate, like I'm doing. If I weren't going t'be a cap'n one day, I think I'd make a first-class steersdog!"

Ben tried to keep from laughing as he steadied the wheel. "Sorry, Ned, I can't help it if I'm only a clumsy human!"

Mallon and another buccaneer named Corday were hauling up pails of seawater and swilling the midships decks. Hearing Thuron's laughter, they turned to watch the boy and his dog at the wheel. Mallon shook his head. "Just look at that, mate. It ain't right. I never heard of a lad an' a hound at the wheel of a ship, have you?"

Corday lowered his voice. "I'm beginnin' to think there's some truth in what Gascon's been saying."

Mallon eyed his shipmate. "Tell me."

Corday emptied his pail, watching the water run off through the scuppers. "Gascon says those two are Jonahs, an' bad luck to all hands aboard. He says that –"

Pierre's hand descended hard on Corday's shoulder. "Who says what? Come on, man, spit it out!"

Both Mallon and Corday went silent. Pierre folded his brawny arms, staring sternly at them. "Only fools listen to the scuttlebutt of a thief an' a deserter. Better not let the cap'n hear you say a word agin Ben an' his dog. Now get on with your work an' stop tittle-tattlin'. If ye've got anythin' bad to say about anybody, then say it about me. But say it to my face!"

The loyal Pierre strode off, leaving the subdued pair to continue their chore in silence.

Ben and Ned were still having fun at the wheel when Pierre called the captain to one side and whispered in his ear, "I think 'twould be a good idea if you or I steered the *Marie,* Cap'n. Either that or let the crew take their turn at the helm."

Thuron raised his eyebrows quizzically. "What? Don't ye like my lucky friends guiding our vessel? Look at them, Pierre, those two will be as good as Anaconda was someday. What's the matter with ye, man?"

The bosun of the *Marie* averted his eyes. "There's a bit o' talk goin' around, Cap'n. Some of the crew don't like it."

Any good humour the Frenchman felt suddenly evaporated. "They don't like it, eh? Then they'll just have to endure it. I'm master aboard the *Marie,* and 'tis I who gives the orders! But what don't they like, Pierre? What's all the talk about?"

Pierre shifted his feet awkwardly. "I know it sounds foolish, Cap'n, but the rumour is that Ben and Ned are a pair of Jonahs – bad luck to all hands."

Thuron immediately relieved his two friends at the helm, taking the wheel himself. "That's enough for one day, mates. Go to the cabin and tidy my charts away, will ye? We need to look shipshape for our homecoming to France."

Ben saluted smartly. "Aye aye, Cap'n. When we've cleaned the cabin up, I'll get you something to eat from the galley."

A frown creased Thuron's brow. "No, don't do that, lad. Stay in the cabin with Ned. Stay away from the crew for a bit. Don't ask questions, Ben, just do as I say."

A bewildered glance passed between the boy and his dog, but Ben obeyed without comment. The Frenchman watched the pair wander off to his cabin. An uneasy feeling crept over him. Had someone found out about Ben and Ned? It was a worrying problem to contemplate. Most seamen were not very well educated, but practically all of them were superstitious, particularly buccaneers. If a crew began believing rumours about having a Jonah aboard, there would be no question of reasoning with them. No matter how well a captain treated his men, there would be no stopping them once their superstitions took hold. Both he and his two lucky friends would be in grave danger.

The black Labrador peered through the partially open cabin door as he communicated with Ben. "Here comes the cap'n. I wonder what's wrong. He looks worried."

The Frenchman entered and sat down on the bed, then beckoned to them both. "Close that door. I must speak to you."

Ned pushed the door shut with his forepaws. Ben stared anxiously at the captain. "What's the matter, sir?"

Thuron spoke earnestly. "What you told me, Ben, about your past life. Have you repeated anything to the crew?"

Ben shook his head vigorously. "No, sir, not even to Pierre. I wouldn't breathe a word to anyone, except you!"

The captain sighed heavily. "I believe you, lad. But the men are talking among themselves. They say that you and Ned are two Jonahs, bad luck for the *Marie* and all aboard her."

Ned connected a thought to Ben. "I knew it! Didn't I tell you that Gascon would cause trouble for us?"

Ben turned to Thuron. "Ned thinks that it's Gascon who's been putting the word about."

The Frenchman patted the black Labrador's back. "Aye, and I think he's right. Do ye remember Gascon shouting out when Pierre was locking him up? He said this ship was cursed."

Ben agreed. "Yes, but he couldn't possibly know about me

and Ned. What are we going to do about it, sir?"

Thuron thought a moment before he answered. "There's not a great deal we can do. Ben, I want you and Ned to keep yourselves away from all hands – stay in this cabin. With a bit of luck things may just die down naturally. We're not too far from France now. Perhaps they'll forget all this silly talk. With the prospect of seeing home again, and with having some gold in their pockets, all hands may forget about cursed ships and Jonahs. Will you do that for me, lad?"

Ben grasped his friend's big strong hand. "Of course I will, and so will Ned. We won't let you down, Cap'n!"

Thuron stood up and made for the door. "Well said, Ben. I knew I could trust you. I'll have Pierre bring your food from the galley. Remember now, with the exception of Pierre and me, you must talk to nobody."

Lying with his chin on the floor, Ned watched the door close. "Just when I was learning to be a steersdog!"

Ben scratched behind the dog's ear soothingly. "Cheer up, mate, we'll be in the Bay of Biscay by this time tomorrow, and in a day or two more we'll be on dry land."

Over the next few days, the boy and his dog remained confined within the captain's cabin. It was not a pleasant time for either one. Ben had a strong feeling of impending doom, reinforced by constant nightmares of Captain Vanderdecken and his accursed ship, the *Flying Dutchman.* Both Ben and Ned became afraid to sleep – every time they dropped into a slumber, the visions came pouring in. Nightmares of being back aboard that hellish craft, of the icy, mountainous seas off Cape Horn battering and pounding away at the ship. Ice-crusted ropes keening an eerie dirge as hurricane-force winds ripped and tattered sails into shreds. Faces, leering, scarred, cruel and merciless, of dead men walking the decks like zombies. An angry sky, with black and purple storm-bruised clouds boiling out of it. And Vanderdecken! His tortured mind giving voice to the curses and oaths he was bellowing aloud at the heavens.

"Ben! Ben, lad! Are ye all right? What ails ye?"

The boy opened his eyes to see the homely face of Pierre hovering above him as he received Ned's thought. "Thank goodness for Pierre. I was so trapped by that awful dream, I couldn't move a muscle to wake you!"

Ben sat up, rubbing his eyes. "I'm all right, thank you, Pierre. It was nothing but a horrible dream."

The bosun placed fresh water and two bowls of hot stew beside the bed. "Don't worry, mate, everything will be all right. Don't pay any attention to crew's gossip. They're only simple, ignorant men who know no better. A bit like myself, I suppose."

The boy felt a real kinship, and pity, for Thuron's bosun. "You're not an ignorant man, Pierre. You've always been good to me and Ned – Cap'n Thuron and you are the only real friends we have."

Pierre poured water for them both to drink. "You lie back now, mate. Try an' get some sleep. Me an' the cap'n won't let ye down. Only one more night after this an' you two will set foot on French soil. I'll wager you'll both make lots o' new friends there. I've got to go now. Don't open the door to anyone except me or the cap'n."

When they had eaten, Ben and Ned felt more relaxed. They fell asleep on the big cabin bed, the dog with his paws across the boy's legs. Ben felt himself floating in his dreams. Up and away he went, with Ned at his side, high into the soft night skies. Below he could see *La Petite Marie,* lying like a toy amid the shifting, moon-silvered waves. A euphoric calm descended upon Ben, and he felt almost like an infant, basking in the cradle of heaven, surrounded by pale glimmering stars, one of which was drifting slowly towards him. As it drew closer, he saw that it was an angel, the same one who had delivered him and Ned from the *Dutchman*! Like soft peals of bells across distant meadows, the beautiful vision's voice caressed his mind.

"Take not the gold of lawless men,
And heed now what I say:
When thy feet touch land, 'tis then
That thou must haste away.
Leave behind that life and walk,
Look not back at the sea,
Whilst retribution brings the Hawk,
New times unfold for thee."

Morning brought with it a misty drizzle and a light fog, but there was no wind to speak of. Ben woke to see Captain Thuron laying out columns of gold coins on the table.

Ned passed a thought as he, too, came awake. "Aye aye, mate, what's going on here?"

Ben repeated the Labrador's question to the Frenchman.

Thuron left off arranging the golden coins, his expression grave. "We've got trouble aboard, lad! I'm a trusting fool not to have believed 'twould come to this. The crew have released Gascon. I think there's about to be a mutiny!"

Ben bit his lip. "It's all about me and Ned, isn't it, sir?"

The captain straightened a stack of gold with his thumb. "Aye, though I don't know how they found out about you an' the *Flying Dutchman*. Leave this to me, though. The closeness of France and their shares of the booty might soften them up a bit."

There was a light rap on the cabin door, and Pierre entered, carrying a cutlass and a primed musket. "The crew want words with ye, Cap'n. All hands are out on deck. Gascon an' Mallon are the ringleaders."

Thuron rose, sweeping two of the coin stacks into either pocket. "Ben, you an' Ned stay here. Come on, Pierre, we'll see what this is all about!"

The crew of *La Petite Marie* seemed reluctant to meet their captain's eye. They huddled on the midships deck, sheepish and sullen. Thuron grasped the rail of the afterdeck, staring down at them. "Well, lads, what is it, eh? I've never harmed a man for speaking his mind."

Gascon and Mallon held a brief whispered conference, then Gascon stepped forward, pointing up at the captain's cabin. "That lad an' his dog, we want 'em both off this ship. They're bad luck, you know they are!"

Thuron shrugged and smiled. "Now don't talk foolish. How would I know a thing like that?"

Mallon nodded towards Gascon. "He was at the helm when the boy started yellin' out in his sleep, ain't that right, mate?"

Gascon folded his arms, looking very smug. "Aye, you can't fool me, Thuron. I saw ye go into the cabin, so I listened at the door. Hah, ye didn't know that, did ye? I heard every word that accursed brat told ye. All about how he escaped from the *Flying Dutchman* many years ago, an' here he is today, large as life an' not a day older. The curse o' Satan's upon both the boy an' his dog. They're Jonahs! If they stay aboard all we'll see of France is the bottom o' the Bay o' Biscay. Ye can't deny the fact – every man jack here is with me an' Mallon, an' I warn ye, we're all armed!"

The captain descended to the middle of the stairs leading to the deck. Emptying his pockets, he set out two stacks of gold coins and beckoned to both ringleaders. "Ned an' Ben have been with us since Cartagena. They've been lucky for me – you've all heard me say so, many times. Before you do something you'll regret, take a look at this gold. There's your share, Gascon, even though ye were a thief an' a deserter. That other share is yours, Mallon. Go on, take it!"

Both men scurried forward and claimed their shares. Thuron watched them filling their pockets. "Every man aboard will get the same. By tomorrow morn ye'll all be on French soil, headed wherever the fancy takes ye – home, or the nearest tavern. Now, is that bad luck? Did a Jonah do that to ye?"

Gascon drew his musket and pointed it at the captain. "Aye, 'tis bad luck for us, I'm a wanted man in France, an' so are most of this crew. We're taking over the ship an' sailing her to Spanish waters. We'll scuttle her off the coast of Guernica. That way we can take our own chances, either to stop in Spain or to cross the border into France."

Thuron appealed to the men in a reasonable voice. "Why did ye not tell me this before? I would have scuttled the *Marie* off the coast of Arcachon. I know of some quiet spots around there. But if ye want to sail for Spain an' sink her there, so be it. I'll come with ye an' not begrudge any hard feelings that've passed between us, eh?"

Mallon set his lips in a stubborn line. "Not with that boy an' the dog aboard, we ain't takin' no chances!"

All this time Pierre had been at the helm. Now he suddenly spun the wheel and called out aloud, "We're headed for Spain, sure enough. Hoist all sail! The French Navy is comin', four men-o'-war under full sail!"

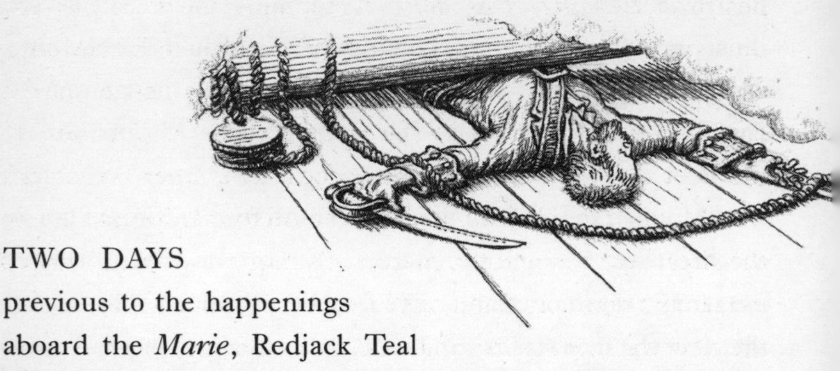

15

TWO DAYS previous to the happenings aboard the *Marie*, Redjack Teal had arrived off the coast of Arcachon. The privateer sailed close to the shore so he could check on his bearings.

Teal stood on deck, tapping the chart as he viewed the coastline. "Demn me if that ain't a piece o' first-class navigatin', eh! There's the port of Arcachon with its inlet, an' that great harbour which lies in the basin beyond. Bassin d'Arcachon, just like it says on me chart here. Remarkable!"

He waggled an imperious finger at the mate. "You there, take her offshore an' a few points south. 'Tis quieter on that stretch of coast. Can't dawdle here, eh, don't want the locals gogglin' from the town at us. Haw haw haw!"

The mate touched his forelock. "Aye aye, Cap'n. Helmsman, take 'er about an' watch your stern on *Devon Belle*'s forepeak. Two points south. Move yourselves afore this mist clears an' we're spotted. Jump to it!"

Unfortunately, the *Royal Champion* and the *Devon Belle* had been seen: blocked from Teal's view by the harbour entrance, four French Navy ships lay close to the quay. The biggest and most fearsome of these vessels was a newly constructed destroyer, *Le Falcon Des Monts*, its captain none other than the illustrious fleet maréchal Guy Falcon Saint Jean Des Monts, victor of many sea battles. The naming of his new ship, the largest gunboat yet built by the French Navy, was in tribute to the fleet maréchal's impressive record. The other three craft were ships of the line, all men-o'-war. All four ships had lain in the Arcachon Basin at the maréchal's request. Now he wished to take his new command out to sea on a naval exercise to test the new warship's performance. That morning, together with his three other captains, the maréchal had sat in his stateroom, discussing plans and strategies for the forthcoming manoeuvres. Charts were spread across the table. The captains listened respectfully to their maréchal, under whose command they were proud to serve. He was a tall, sombre man, prematurely grey, with a stern countenance, his keen dark eyes, weather-lined face, tight lips and aquiline features denoting a strong air of authority.

The conference was about over when there was a knock upon the door. A naval lieutenant entered, shepherding two of the local townsmen in front of him. He beckoned towards the fleet commander. "Tell the maréchal what you saw. Speak up, you have nothing to fear."

The elder of the two jerked a thumb back over his shoulder. "Sir, we were out on the hills this morning, on the point by the harbour entrance, looking for gull eggs. I chanced to look seaward. It was misty, but I saw a ship out there."

The maréchal's eyebrows rose. "What was this ship like, sir?"

Impressed at being addressed as "sir", the townsman answered as accurately as he could. "It looked like a Spanish galleon, a big one, sir. But it was flying English colours. Even though it was misty, I could see it had more deck guns than a merchant would carry."

The maréchal nodded, his interest quickening. "Well done, sir. This ship, which way was it bound?"

The townsman pointed. "To the right, er, south, sir, down towards the Gulf of Gascony. About just over an hour ago, sir."

Clapping the man's shoulder, the maréchal gave him a smile. "My thanks. You did well, sir! Lieutenant, see that these fellows get a ham apiece and a basket of eggs between them."

The moment the door closed behind the men, the maréchal turned to his captains. "It seems as though we have either a pirate or an English privateer in our territorial waters, gentlemen. Forget the manoeuvre plans we discussed. The best baptism for my new ship should be one of blood and fire! You will make way under full sail. I will lead the flotilla. Stand by for my commands as we go. Action is the order of the day, gentlemen!"

Less than an hour later, the four French warships cleared the point with *Le Falcon Des Monts* in the lead, guns at the ready, white sails billowing, the fleur-de-lis flag streaming from her stern. Smiling with satisfaction, the maréchal noted his own personal banner waving out from the foremast peak: a falcon with wings outspread upon a field of green, the symbol of his family name. None of the sailors called it a falcon, though. It was known by the title their maréchal had earned in many sea battles, and the name by which they referred to him . . . the Hawk!

• • •

Ben felt the *Marie* list sideways as she slid into a sharp southerly turn, then heard the shout from Pierre. Ned pushed past him as he opened the cabin door. Dashing out on deck, he passed a message to Ben. "Four men-o'-war, eh? Come on, mate. Let's see what's going on!"

All animosity between the crew and Thuron was momentarily forgotten. The Frenchman was roaring orders for extra sail and sighting anxiously through his telescope at the four warships astern of them. He handed Ben the glass, shaking his head and furrowing his brows. "Look, lad, 'tis the French Navy, an' they're comin' on fast!"

As Ben peered at the lead vessel, he felt icy fear clamp its cold hand in sudden shock on top of his head. The feeling was transmitted to Ned, who communicated urgently: "What is it, Ben, what d'you see?"

The four last lines of the angel's poem pounded through the black Labrador's brain, like hammers striking an anvil.

> "Leave behind that life and walk,
> Look not back at the sea,
> Whilst retribution brings the Hawk,
> New times unfold for thee!"

This thought was reinforced by Ben's message. "That big ship in front, it's flying a hawk upon its flag!"

Thuron grabbed Ben's hand. "Come with me, lad. Bring Ned too!"

• • •

Hurrying them both into his cabin, Thuron slammed the door. He knelt by the bed and hauled out two heavy-packed canvas bags, tied together by their necks. Ben watched as the captain wrapped the bags in a sailcloth. He could tell by the dull clink that they were filled with gold coins.

"What do you need those for, Cap'n?"

The Frenchman placed the bags on the bed. "This is my share o' the gold, Ben. Some of it is for you and Ned!"

The boy stared dubiously at the bags. "But we don't need gold, Cap'n. Besides, Ned and I never earned it."

Ben was surprised at the force with which Thuron seized him by both arms and shook him. "Listen, lad, this gold is ours – mine an' yours. I've got to get you both ashore somehow!"

Ben saw the desperation in his friend's eyes. "Is it that bad, Cap'n? Can't we outsail them? We've done it before."

The Frenchman relaxed his grip. "Not this time, lucky lad, we've got no chance at all. They'd chase us, surround our *Marie* an' sink us all, ship an' crew!"

Ben clenched his fists resolutely. "Then let's stand and fight them – you know a few tricks. Remember the Trinidad Shuffle?"

Thuron smiled sadly and ruffled Ben's hair. "Ben, Ben, 'tis no use, lad. You know as well as I that we've played out our string. That's why I want you an' Ned off the *Marie*, before she goes down. Now here's what you must do. As soon as I can, I'll try an' slip ye ashore in the longboat with that gold. Wherever you come ashore, Ben, wait for me. They'll probably engage us long before we reach Spain, but I'll note where ye go ashore. If the *Marie* goes down, I'll try to keep her offshore, just far enough for me an' Pierre to swim for land. Now I must go back on deck, lad. Remember what I said."

• • •

Further down the coast, just off a small town called Mimizan-Plage, the *Royal Champion* and the *Devon Belle* lay at anchor.

Redjack Teal was taking Madeira in his cabin when the look-out banged urgently on the door and shouted from outside, "Cap'n, 'tis *La Petite Marie*! She's just crossed the horizon behind us to the north."

Teal swiftly donned his red jacket, calling back, "Good man, which way's she headed?"

The reply came without delay. "South, sir, about a point off where we're lyin', headed this way, though!"

Without waiting for assistance, the privateer buckled on his own sword and hurried out, muttering to himself, "South, eh? Me luck's holdin' well. Come t'me, Thuron, I'll stretch your neck an' empty your pockets for ye!"

The mate and the bosun were swinging ropes' ends and bellowing out orders, galvanizing the crew into life. "Open ports, roll out all cannon!" "Make sail, step lively now, buckoes. Full sail!"

The crew of the *Marie* were more intent on what lay in their wake than what lay ahead of them. Thuron took the opportunity to smuggle the gold from his cabin and drop it in the ship's jolly boat. He called out an order to his helmsman. "Pierre, take the *Marie* in closer to shore! I'll fetch the boy an' his dog."

Ben and the black Labrador emerged from the cabin as Thuron began loosing the jolly-boat stays. Just then Gascon and Mallon came running, with loaded muskets brandished. Whilst Mallon covered Pierre, Gascon pointed his weapon at the captain, snarling, "What's goin' on here, what're ye up to, Thuron?"

The captain gave Ned and Ben a broad wink before turning to answer Gascon. "I'm putting the lad an' his hound ashore – maybe then our luck'll change. Ye said yourself that they were Jonahs. Now put that pistol away an' keep your eye on the navy ships, see if they're closing in on us. Go on!"

Gascon slunk off at the sound of his captain's voice being raised in anger. Before Ben could resist, the Frenchman lifted him up and dumped him into the boat. Ned leapt in beside his master.

Thuron let go the ropes, and the jolly boat splashed down into the sea. The captain leaned over the side, instructing Ben in a hoarse, urgent whisper, "Our gold is under the stern seat, wrapped with some sailcloth. Ye can see the coast from here, lad. Don't waste time, row for it fast as ye can. Set a course for yonder hill on the shore – see, the one with the trees growin' atop it."

He blinked a few times, then managed a broad smile. "Ben an' Ned, my two lucky friends, may your luck go with ye. Remember now, wait for me, until this time tomorrow at least. Go now!"

Ben took one last look at Raphael Thuron, the buccaneer captain. Then, turning his back on the *Marie*, he gripped the oars and began plying them. He was lost for any words to say as tears sprang unbidden to his clouded eyes. The boy felt a great leaden weight in his chest. Ned sat in the prow, facing the coast and not looking back. The black Labrador shared every thought and feeling with Ben. They had both seen the mark of fate stamped upon Thuron's face and knew they would never see him again.

Gascon came dashing out of the captain's cabin, pointing at the jolly boat and bellowing to all hands, "The gold's gone, 'tis in the boat. Stop them!"

Ben threw himself flat, and Ned crouched low. A rattle of musket shot peppered the water around them. Thuron slew Gascon with a mighty cutlass slash as he roared aloud, "Get away, Ben! Row for your life, lad!"

Out of the blue came a great whoosh and a bang, followed by a splintering crash. The guns of *Le Falcon Des Monts* had shot the *Marie*'s stern away. With cannon blazing, the French Navy vessels sailed in on their target. Fanning out, the three men-o'-war pounded the buccaneer vessel broadsides, whilst their flagship sailed straight in, raking the decks from astern with chain shot and musket fire from the sharpshooters in the rigging. Pierre's body was draped across the wheel, his dead hand still clutching it. Masts crashed amid blazing sails and smouldering cordage. *La Petite Marie* began settling in the water as salvo after salvo of cannon blasted holes in her from port and starboard. Trapped beneath a fallen jib spar, Captain Thuron's sightless eyes stared up at the sun through the black smoke of destruction that surrounded his ship. Settling back like a crippled seabird, the *Marie* began to sink stern first.

Navy cannon continued to batter her as her prow rose clear of the waves. She hovered for a moment, then with a monstrous hissing and gurgling slid backwards into the depths and was gone forever.

Aboard his flagship, the Hawk held up a hand. "Cease fire!" He turned to a lookout who had climbed down from the topmast to report. "Well, what is it?"

The man saluted. "Maréchal, there is another ship, a gunboat flying English colours!"

The Hawk's aquiline nose quivered, and his eyes lit up. "So, an Englishman, eh, where away?"

The lookout replied, "To the south, Maréchal. She was hugging the coast, waiting on the other ship, I think. When she spied us, she veered off and began sailing further south, sir."

The Hawk drew his telescope and scanned the seas ahead. "Ah yes, there it is, a Spanish galleon sailing under English colours – she has a smaller vessel in tow."

He strode to the forepeak, acknowledging with curt nods the crew, who were cheering his first victory in the new ship. On the forecastle, the Hawk gave orders to his officers. "Well, gentlemen, I know my ship's firepower. There is one less enemy in French waters now. Let us see how we sail under speed. I intend to capture the English ships before they can make it into Spanish waters. We will not sink them – they will be taken as prizes. Inform the other captains that I will go under full sail in the vanguard. Tell them to follow with all speed and await my commands!"

Ben had not turned his head to look back. He was not just heeding the angel's warning; other demons were closing in on him, too. He lay in the bottom of the jolly boat, oblivious of his surroundings. The roar and boom of French Navy cannon blended with those far-off noises of Cape Horn – crashing seas, tearing rigging and howling storm. Vanderdecken laughing madly, bound to the helm for eternity and being swept off into the maelstrom of oceans at the world's end. Spine-chilling recollections, mixed with the demise of the *Marie*, mingled in the boy's mind until he lost all sense of reality.

It was Ned's blunt, rough claws that brought him to his

senses. The faithful dog was scratching at his back, sending out frantic, urgent warnings. "Ben, wake up! Move, Ben, move. We're sinking!"

The boy spluttered as his face struck the bottom of the jolly boat. Coughing and spitting seawater, he sat up. Ned seized his shirtsleeve and tugged at it with his teeth. "Come on, mate, we'll have to swim for it. This boat's full of musket holes – we're lucky we weren't hit!"

Recovering himself, Ben realized the predicament they were in. He grabbed the dog's collar, heaved him overboard and leapt into the sea alongside him. Taking a bearing on the shore, which was only a few hundred yards off, he kicked out. "Straight ahead, Ned, it's not so far!"

For the first time in his life, Captain Redjack Teal knew the meaning of fear: four French Navy warships were bearing down on him. The master gunner came hurrying up, carrying a stick topped by a smouldering mixture of tar and rope. He looked hopefully to Teal.

"I could load the stern culverins with chain shot, Cap'n. May'ap we could clip the big feller's foremast. That'd slow him down a touch, sir."

Teal snatched the stick and flung it into the sea. "Ye demned idiot, yonder's the French Navy! Can't y'see the guns they're sportin', man? Hah, that scoundrel's just longin' t'see a puff o' smoke from even a musket an' he'll blow us to doll rags! Get the mud out of your eyes, man. Did ye see what they did to Thuron?"

He watched miserably as the new ship tacked, circling out to come round in a curve ahead of him. The other three vessels manoeuvred to close the trap, one to port, the other to starboard, whilst the remaining one stayed close behind in his wake. The privateer stamped his elegantly shod foot in temper. Life was so unjust! After pursuing a fortune in gold from the Caribbean, right across an ocean, his dreams of wealth and glory had been cruelly snatched away in just a few short hours. Add to this the indignity of being taken by the French without a single shot being fired. The entire episode was an utter debacle! He sprinted to the stern at the sight of the bosun and mate loosing the stern ropes. "What'n the name of jackasses are ye about there?"

The mate saluted, trying to sound helpful. "Er, we were castin' the *Devon Belle* adrift, sir. She might make that Frenchie behind us run afoul of her, sir – that'd give us a chance of escape."

Teal was nearly out of his mind. He became quite petulant. Kicking the mate on his shin, he sprayed him with spittle as he ranted and shouted into the man's face, "That ship is mine, mine, d'ye hear?"

He rounded on the unsuspecting bosun and kicked him also. "I'm the captain of these ships, or haven't ye noticed, eh? Demned ass of a gunner, wantin' to fire on four battleships, this other buffoon thinkin' we can turn an' run away. Has everybody aboard lost their confounded minds –"

"Englishman, strike your colours and slack sail!" An officer was hailing him with a megaphone from the ship behind. Teal's shoulders sagged. It was all over.

He turned to the mate, who was rubbing his shin. "Strike y'colours, take in all sail. I'll be in me cabin."

• • •

The Hawk sat in his stateroom, the crimsoning twilight giving its new woodwork a rosy hue. He listened carefully to the information his officers had gathered from the crew of the *Royal Champion.* It was always best talking to the men before interviewing the master. They had less reason to lie than their captain did.

He sat back and mulled over what he had heard, his fingers tapping a tattoo upon the tabletop. Then he signalled to a waiting lieutenant. "I will see the Englishman now."

Trying feebly to resist two burly gunners, Teal was swiftly frog-marched into the maréchal's presence. The privateer looked indignant and dishevelled; the gunners held his arms tightly, preventing him from tidying himself up.

He immediately began to protest. "Sirrah, is this any way to treat the captain of one of His Britannic Majesty's vessels? Tell these ruffians to release me instantly. I'll not be laid hands upon in such a demned rough manner!"

The maréchal glanced up from some papers he was studying. His unblinking gaze, coupled with the haughty way he looked a man up and down, had Teal feeling both unnerved and embarrassed.

The privateer attempted to pull himself free, but the two gunners held him easily. He tried to sound reasonable. "Sir, I appeal to you, order these rogues to unhand me. I, sir, am like you, an officer and a gentleman!"

The maréchal reduced him to silence with a baleful glare. "You dare compare yourself with me, you scum?"

He waved Teal's own parchmented credentials at him and spat out the word vindictively. "Privateer! A filthy mercenary, carrying a letter of marque or reprisal. There is no lower form of life on land or sea. You are a prisoner of war and will be treated as such!"

Captain Redjack Teal suddenly wilted beneath his captor's scorn. He whined like a bully who had just had the tables turned on him. "I was only carryin' out my king's orders, sir. You cannot punish an innocent man for that!"

The maréchal snorted. "I do not intend punishing you – that is for a military tribunal to decide. Whether you hang or go to the guillotine is immaterial to me. Stop weeping, man! They may spare your life and assign you with your crew to the convict working parties at Marseilles. There you can do a lifetime's penance rebuilding the harbour walls under the lash of your jailers. Take him away!"

A short time later, Teal found himself below decks in the Hawk's new vessel, chained by the ankle to the rest of his crew. They chuckled wickedly as the bosun tugged the chain and sent him flat on the deck. "Well, look who's here, mates, 'tis the Jolly Cap'n. Up on your feet, Redjack, an' dance a hornpipe for us!"

Teal cowered, trying to pull himself off into a corner, but the mate dragged him out by his manacled foot. "Ye powdered popinjay, didn't ye hear the man? He said dance, so come on, step lively now, let's see ye dance!"

Two marines, pacing the grating overhead of the prisoners' accommodation, winced at the sounds of Teal's sobs and screams for mercy. One of them shrugged casually. "I think that crew did not love their captain very much."

For full two days, that boy and dog
Did sit upon the shore bereaved,
No food nor drink would pass their lips,
As for lost friends they grieved.
Sad tears which fell like April rain
Were soaked into the earth and lost,
And only two from all that crew
Were left to count the cost.
Pursued by foes, both live and dead,
From Caribbean to Biscay's Bay,
Commanded by an angel's word
To turn and walk away.
What trials and perils lie ahead,
Decreed by heaven and the fates?
The *Flying Dutchman* haunts the seas,
As her accursed captain waits . . . and waits!

Book Two

THE RAZAN

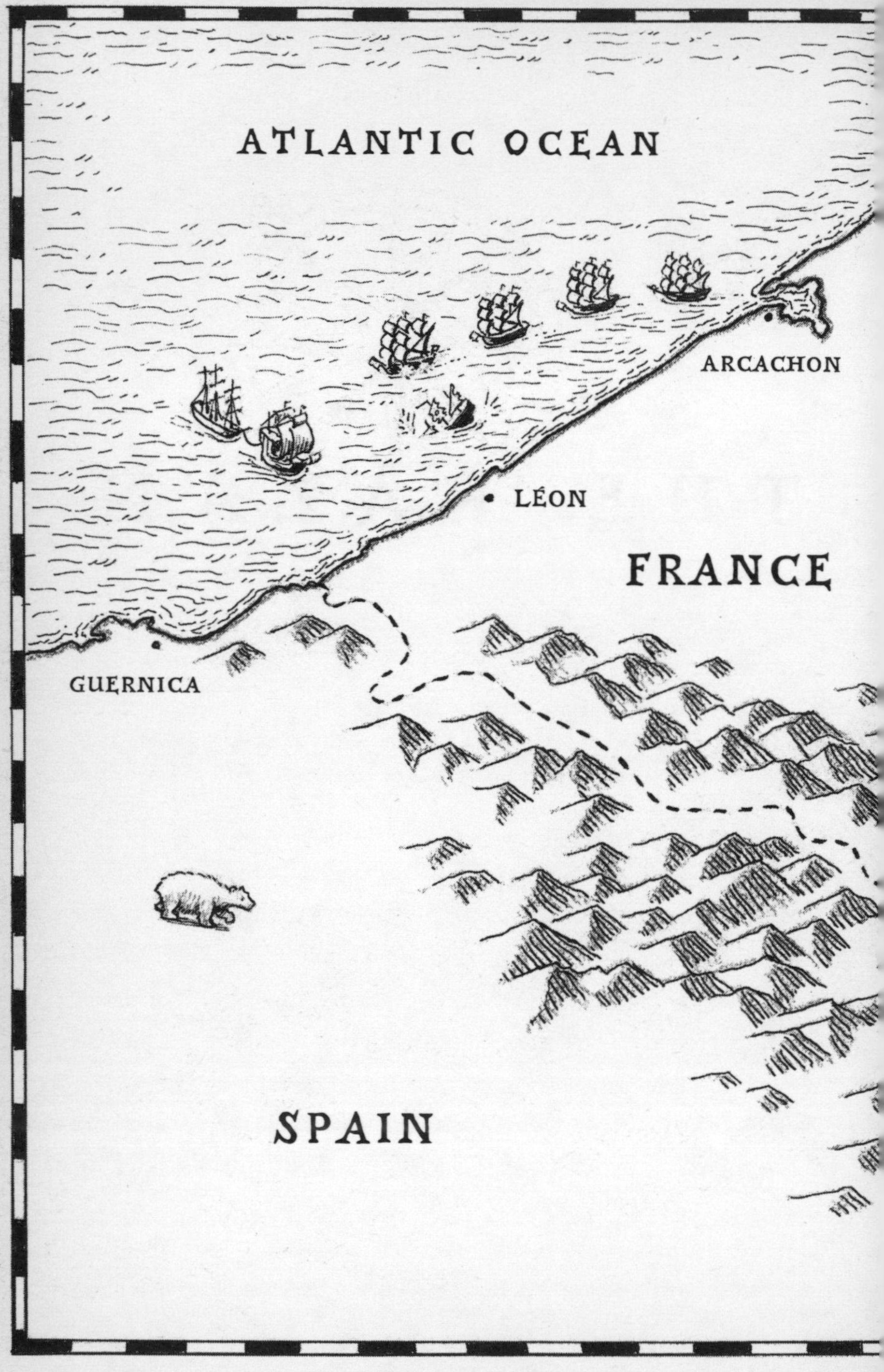

ATLANTIC OCEAN

ARCACHON

LÉON

FRANCE

GUERNICA

SPAIN

VERON
RAZAN
CAVES
ANDORRA

16

IT WAS A GREY DAY. THE WEATHER WAS NEIther cold nor warm, but windless and dull. Drizzle fell in swathing curtains from a sky the hue of much-watered milk. Ben and Ned had been walking inland for several days, avoiding villages and any place where people lived. They crouched in the lee of a rock jutting out of a field, huddling together, unable to escape the enveloping wetness. Ben imparted a thought to Ned. "D'you think they'll still be searching for survivors from the *Marie*?"

The black Labrador shook his head. "Well, there's been no sign of anybody since dawn. We're alone out here. Those villagers will be back home now and the sailors back aboard their ships. We must get something to eat, Ben – a couple of sour apples and two turnips are all we've had since we left the coast."

Blowing rainwater from the tip of his nose, Ben agreed. "Aye, my stomach's been growling worse than you, mate. See up ahead there, top of that slope a few fields away? It looks like woodland to me. Shall we give it a try?"

Ned raised his head and squinted into the rain. "Why not? At least we'll get some decent shelter under the trees. I'm not fond of this country, it's too quiet altogether. Come on, all we're doing is getting wetter sitting here."

The sound of water squelching and splashing from the grass and earth beneath their feet was muffled by the downfall as they ran across the eerily silent landscape. It was tough going for tired limbs as they made their way uphill. Breathless and saturated, Ben and Ned finally arrived beneath the shelter of the trees on a thickly wooded hilltop. A variety of whitebeam, juneberry, elm, beech and various conifers grew in profusion to provide a fairly dry covering overhead. The two friends sat with their backs against a broad elm on the fringe, gazing out over the dismal countryside.

A shudder passed through Ben as he rubbed his hands up and down both arms. "Huh, what I wouldn't give for a cheery old fire, that rain has chilled my bones!"

Ned settled down, chin on paws. "A good old fire, eh? I'll let you know if I come across one. Maybe it'll brighten up by mid-noon and we'll take a proper look around. Meanwhile, I'm tired. Let's take a nap for an hour or two."

Ben lay down by the dog's side. As they watched the rain drifting down out in the open, weariness overcame the pair, and, eyelids drooping, they dropped into slumber.

Ben was not aware of how long he had slept. He woke shivering to the feel of Ned's rough tongue licking his hand. It was almost dark.

The boy complained, rubbing his eyes. "What did you wake

me for, mate? I was having a nice sleep there. Nice but cold. Brrrr!"

The Labrador's mental message reached him. "That good old fire you were going on about, it's not too far from here."

Ben stood up, peering into the thick, darkening woodlands. "Where? I can't see it."

Ned pointed with his nose, like a hunting dog. "Over that way somewhere. I can't see it either, but I can smell it. Let's go easy now, we don't know what sort of person lit the fire. Follow me, but quietly, Ben, quietly."

Ben trailed in his dog's path, through bush and foliage and round the gnarled trunks of big, ancient trees. Ned halted after a while, sheltering himself behind an oak. "There it is – told you I could smell fire."

Ben stood on tiptoe to get a clear view of the distant light. He could make out a small pedlar's cart, its shafts resting on the ground in a small clearing. The two friends crept forward until both could see properly. A man was sleeping by the fire, and there was no sign of a horse or donkey to pull the cart. A girl in her midteens was sitting chained to a cartwheel, a scarf bound round her mouth as a gag.

Unwittingly, Ben trod on a dry twig. It snapped underfoot. The man, a big fat fellow, grunted in his sleep and rolled over onto his back. He began snoring loudly, but the girl saw them. She locked eyes with Ben.

The boy held a finger to his lips, hearing Ned's thought. "Not much use telling her to be quiet – she's got no choice with that gag on. Look, her eyes are moving up and down. She's nodding towards something. Let's get a bit closer!"

A wooden club with a leather-bound handle lay close by the

sleeping man. Ben knew immediately that the girl's eyes were signalling him to use the club on the man. He looked at Ned. "What shall we do?"

The dog's thoughts were not in the least hesitant. "That's a pretty girl the fat rogue's keeping prisoner. Wallop him with the club, Ben. That way we'll be able to free her, and he'll get a sound night's sleep. Go on!"

Bent almost double, the boy inched forward into the firelight. The girl was urging him on, nodding her head furiously. Ben was unsure what force it would take to stun the big fat man, but he lifted the club and gave the fellow's head a sharp rap. The man sat bolt upright, one hand rubbing his head, the other shooting out to grab the boy's leg as he roared angrily, "You little murderer, what the h–"

Ben swung the club overarm, closing his eyes as he heard the loud *bonk* it made on the man's skull. Ned trotted into the firelight, nodding his approval. "That's more like it, mate. Get that gag out of the maid's mouth!"

Throwing down the club, Ben swiftly knelt and undid the scarf. The girl was indeed pretty – almond-skinned, doe-eyed and slender with a mass of black curls framing her face. Ben was taken aback by the vehemence in her voice.

"That lard barrel has the key to these shackles on a string around his neck. Get them here before he wakes up. Quick!"

Lifting the man's head, Ben pulled the string over it and took the key, then undid the lock that held her wrists chained to the metal wheel rim. No sooner was she free than the girl bounded over, grabbed the club and whacked it down hard twice on the unconscious man's ankle. He moaned softly. She raised the club high, her voice harsh.

"Here, I'll give you something to whine about!"

Ben caught her arm and wrenched the club from her. "What are you trying to do, kill him?"

Taking several long, burning branches from the fire, the girl bound them together like a torch. "Hah! That'd be no bad thing, he deserves killin'. Let's get out of here!"

Grabbing a small bag from the cart, she tossed it to Ben. "Here, you carry the food!"

Ned ran hard on her heels, exchanging thoughts. "She's a fierce one, mate, I wouldn't like to get on the wrong side of her. See the way she swung that club!"

"Maybe she did it with good reason, Ned. Anyhow, at least we've got food and the means to make a fire. I wish she'd slow down. Whew! That girl can certainly run!"

It was quite a while before the girl stopped running. She chose a spot deep in the woods, surrounded by trees and backed by an outcropping of several tall rocks. "Get wood for a fire before this torch burns down to nothing!"

Wordlessly, Ben and Ned foraged around for dry wood. As she built the fire, the girl took the branches of dead pine that Ned was carrying in his mouth.

She beckoned Ben to sit beside her and stroked Ned. "This is a good clever dog, I like him. What's his name?"

The boy began opening the bag she had taken from the cart. "I'm Ben, and he's called Ned. What's your name?"

She snatched the bag from him. "Karayna, but they call me Karay." She took a small stale loaf of wheat bread from the bag. Breaking it into three equal pieces, she handed one to Ben, threw the other to Ned, and began tearing at her own portion.

Ben watched her face in the firelight – she was indeed very nice-looking. "You were pretty hard on the man, Karay. Why?"

She rubbed at her wrist where the chain had chafed it.

"Huh, that miserable gutbucket! We were in prison together, at Léon, but we broke out and stole the cart. Since then he's used me like a horse, making me pull the cart and get his food for him. He chained me to the cart every night, said he was going to sell me in the mountains on the Spanish border. Don't worry about that fat worm any more – he won't find it so easy to get along with a broken ankle. Nobody treats me like that and gets away with it!"

Ben chewed on the hard bread thoughtfully. "What were you both doing in prison?"

Karay elbowed him smartly in the ribs. "That's no business of yours. But, if y'must know, I was a singer and he was a clown. We went from town to town, entertaining on market days. He'd mingle with the crowd while I sang, and I'd do the same when he was doing his act."

Ben frowned. "Mingle with the crowd. What for?"

She smiled scornfully at him. "To pick pockets and purses, of course. I'm good at it, you see. 'Twas that fat greasy ass who got us caught, not me. Anyhow, what are you and your dog doing wandering this forest?"

Ben stared into the fire. "Oh, nothing really, just wandering."

Karay laughed. "Hahaha, who d'ye think you're tryin' to fool? I bet you two are the ones those sailors and townsfolk were searching for. Came off that pirate ship the Navy sunk. I heard them talking in the jailhouse."

Ben felt a flash of resentment towards the outspoken girl. "No, we didn't, and anyhow, I don't want to talk about it!"

Karay pouted her lips and tossed her hair. "And I don't want to hear about it, so there!"

Her gesture so amused Ben that he mimicked it. "Huh, and

I'm not so sure I should be keeping company with a thief. So there!"

Instinctively they both burst out laughing. After that the atmosphere was a lot more friendly. Ned joined them both by the fire. Stroking the dog's silky ears, Karay watched him blink appreciatively. "I wish I had a dog like good old Neddy," the girl mused.

Ned immediately bristled, contacting Ben. "Tell her!"

He stalked off to the opposite side of the fire and lay in the shadows while Ben explained to Karay. "He doesn't like being called Neddy, it makes him sound like a worn-out old nag. He much prefers Ned."

The girl stared into Ben's clouded blue eyes. "How d'you know?"

Ben shrugged. "He told me."

She chuckled. "I suppose you two talk together a lot, eh?"

The boy stirred the fire with a branch. "When friends are together for a long time, they get to know each other."

Karay stared into the flickering flames. "It must be nice to be like that. I've never known anybody long enough to be really friendly with – parents, family or companions. D'you suppose we'll get to know each other in that sort of way?"

Suddenly Ben felt a pang of pity, both for himself and for Karay. He could see her out of the corner of his eye, staring into the fire. A barefoot girl clad in a long, tattered red dress with an old black shawl thrown about her shoulders. Ben knew that someday he and Ned would have to walk away and leave, never again to see her. Or to let her see him, an eternal boy, never growing old.

He was about to concoct an answer that would not hurt her

feelings when Ned's voice entered his mind. "Stay still, Ben, don't look around or bat an eyelid. We're being watched!"

Ben did as the dog bid him, though his mind was racing. "Who is it, Ned? Is there more than one of them? I've still got this branch in my hand to poke the fire. Are they armed? Can you see them?"

Ned's mental reply came back. "I think there's only one. He's just peeping round the corner of the rocks behind you both. I've shuffled back into the bushes, so he doesn't know I'm here. Now, I'm going to circle behind him. The moment he makes a move I'll jump on his back and knock him down. Be ready with that branch, Ben, and lay him out if he gets rough. Here goes!"

Unaware of what was going on, Karay sat back against the rock. Pulling her shawl close, she began drifting into a doze. Ben's grip tightened on the branch as he tried not to look alert. Slight crackling from the fire was the only sound in the still night as seconds passed like hours. Ben tried letting his eyelids droop, acting as a decoy, though his whole body was tensed like a steel spring.

Suddenly a slender-built young fellow, carrying a battered leather satchel over one shoulder, stepped from behind the rocks. He started to speak.

"I saw your fire – *oof*!"

Springing pantherlike from the top of a rock, Ned landed on the intruder, knocking him face down. Ben leapt up but was pushed aside as Karay bounded past him. The girl jumped with both feet on the newcomer's back, forcing the breath from him in a whoosh as Ned nipped to one side, avoiding her feet.

She knelt on her victim's shoulderblades, grabbed a knife from the back of his belt and seized him by the hair. Tugging his head back savagely, the girl pressed the knife blade against his throat, growling like a tigress.

"Be still or I'll cut your throat!"

Ben guessed the intruder was about his own age. His eyes were wide with fear, staring straight at Ben, who hurried over and grabbed Karay's wrist. "Stop, don't hurt him!"

The girl frowned at him. "Why not? He was carrying a knife – maybe he was goin' to rob or murder us!"

Ben forced her hand to the ground and placed his foot on the knife blade. "He doesn't look in a position to rob or murder anyone at the moment, thanks to you. Now then, you robbing murderer, what's your name?"

"Dominic," the captive managed to gasp as he tried to regain his breath. "I mean you no harm, honest – *uurrgh*!"

Karay dragged his head further back, hissing viciously into his ear. "Then why were you sneaking around, spyin' on us an' carryin' a knife, eh?"

Ben had put up with enough of the girl's barbaric behaviour. He passed a swift thought to Ned. "Settle her, mate, before she breaks that poor fellow's neck!"

The black Labrador rushed her, pushing Karay off the young man with a powerful thrust of his forepaws. Ben retrieved the knife and stowed it in his belt, then held out his hand to the stranger named Dominic. "Up you come, mate!"

He held out his other hand to the girl. "You too, Karay. I hardly think Dominic is a murderer or a thief – he looks friendly enough to me."

Karay gave Ned a frosty glare as she dusted herself down. "Pushing me over like that, and I thought you were my friend!"

• • •

They went back to the fire and sat down together, though it took some time for Karay to regain both temper and dignity. Dominic was not one whom anybody could take a dislike to, for he had a gentle manner, a soft voice and a winning smile. Ned sat with his head on Dominic's knee, gazing up at him as he communicated with Ben. "I like Dominic, he looks like a real pal!"

Karay was still doubtful. She questioned him closely. "What brings you to this part of the woods? Where are you bound?"

He pointed east. "I was going to the fair at Veron to see if I could earn some money."

"I can always make money at country fairs," bragged Karay.

Ben's voice carried a note of sternness. "Not by stealing, I hope. You'd end up in prison, probably we would, too."

The girl began to get huffy again. "I've no need to steal, if it's a good fair – people will pay to hear me sing. I'm a great singer." She changed the subject by turning back to Dominic. "How d'you earn your living? By selling things?"

For answer, Dominic opened his worn leather satchel. He produced charcoals, chalks, a slender steel file with a broken tip and some pieces of slate. "I make faces."

Ben's interest quickened. "You mean you're an artist? I've never met an artist. Who taught you, did you attend a school?"

Dominic was already at work, glancing up and down at Ned as he scraped away at a piece of slate with the broken file. He talked as he sketched. "Nobody ever taught me, I was born with the skill to draw. I come from Sabada in Spain, but I was banished from there when I was very young. Hmm, this is an interesting dog."

Ned's thought reached Ben. "I'll say I'm interesting –

noble and handsome, too. Told you I liked Dominic –"

Ben interrupted the dog's thought. "Why were you banished?"

Dominic concentrated on his portrait as he answered. "They were ignorant people, but sooner or later I am driven from any place I go. People think I am a magician, and they get scared – I don't blame them. My pictures are like no others. When I draw the likeness of anybody, man, woman or child, the truth is in my picture. I cannot help it – good, evil, deceit, envy, love, tenderness or cruelty. All of these things show up in my work, it is as if I can see into the very heart and soul of those whom I sketch. Ah, here you are, Ned, this is you, honest, noble, handsome and above all, faithful. Though there is something else behind those wonderful eyes that I cannot quite capture. Look!"

Ben, Ned and Karay all gazed at the finished sketch. It was everything Dominic said it would be. Ned placed a paw on the artist's knee as he communicated with Ben. "This is absolutely brilliant! It's as if I'm looking at myself in a still pool. It's me to the life!"

Ben agreed, speaking out loud to the others. "This is truly remarkable! You have a great talent, Dominic!"

Karay chimed in, "Aye, you're pretty good. Will you draw me?"

Dominic took out a piece of flat, dried aspen bark and began sketching on it with a charcoal stick, shading and shadowing with deft flicks of his thumb to give depth. When he came to the eyes, he chuckled. "You are quick and clever, Karay, with a swift temper. Everything you see that you want must become yours. You are a rogue and a thief, but a pretty one."

The girl snatched the knife from Ben's belt and pointed it. "Who do you think you are, talking about me like that?"

The artist held up the picture, with the eyes completed. "See!"

Karay gasped with shock – it was all there. Her beauty and wildness were captured perfectly, along with the furtive slyness of a thief shining from her eyes. Her cheeks reddened as she grabbed the bark portrait and hid it beneath her shawl.

"This is mine now. I'll pay you for it when I make some money. Now 'tis your turn, Ben. Go on, draw him, Dominic!"

For a moment Dominic locked eyes with Ben, gazing hard. Then he shook his head and began putting his materials back into the satchel. "No, no, I cannot draw Ben!"

Karay teased him. "What's the matter, haven't you got the skill? Or are you just scared to, eh?"

Ben looked away from Dominic, for he knew what the artist had seen. Over half a century in a boy's eyes, the wild seas, Vanderdecken and the *Flying Dutchman,* roaring oceans, thundering cannon, Captain Thuron lying dead beneath deep fathoms in a sunken ship. That and a thousand other things, things not of this earth. Like the terrifying beauty of an angel damning a ship and its crew to eternity.

Ben took the knife gently from the girl. "Let him be, Karay. How can he draw bad dreams and nightmares – there have been enough of those in my life, eh, Dominic?"

The artist agreed. "Too many for a simple facemaker."

Karay snapped her fingers together. "You're the Facemaker of Sabada! I've heard of you before. Hah, I expected you to look like some kind of terrifying wizard. Weren't you the one who was locked in the pillory in the town of Somador for the picture you made of the magistrate's wife?"

Dominic nodded. "Aye, that was me, though I didn't want to sketch the woman in the first place. Her husband, the magistrate, he insisted on my doing the portrait – he said that I was to make her look beautiful and gracious."

Ben handed the facemaker's knife back to him. "And did you?"

Dominic chuckled. "I tried to, but she came out looking as she really was, a glutton and a miser." His face hardened. "For that, the magistrate had me beaten and locked by my head and arms in the pillory for three days and nights. So, you see, this talent of mine can sometimes be a millstone about my neck."

They sat in silence for a while. Karay began to feel sorry about her treatment of Dominic. She saw him cast a brief glance at the crust of bread in her hand. "Do you have any food in your satchel, Facemaker?"

He smiled ruefully. "Alas, no, just drawing materials and an empty flagon I use for drinking water."

The girl peered into the darkness. "If there were a stream or a lake near here, I could have got us some fish."

Ned's ears perked up as he sent a message to Ben. "Tell her I'll find water. There's always some about in woodlands. Hope there's fish, too. I'm starving!"

Ben answered the thought. "Right, then, we'll have to start playing silly little games for our friends' benefit." He took the flagon from Dominic's satchel and let the dog sniff it as he spoke to Karay. "Watch this. Here Ned, good dog! Water, where's the water, boy?"

The black Labrador chuckled inwardly. "As if I didn't know, eh? The things I have to do to impress folk!" He wandered off slowly, sniffing the ground and the air.

Ben turned to Karay. "Go with him, he'll find water for you."

The girl was delighted. "Good old Neddy . . . I mean Ned. Sorry."

Together they took off into the night.

Ben looked across the fire at Dominic. "I'm glad you didn't try to sketch me. What did you really see?"

The Facemaker of Sabada averted his eyes. "Too much, my friend, far too much. I have enough problems of my own without adding your burden to my mind. How has one of your age lived through such perils? I saw things in your eyes I have never seen, even in dreams. Somebody my own age who has had the experiences of so many years. No, Ben, it is too much for me to understand, let's not talk about it. Your secret shall remain with you, and Ned, too, I think. Trust me, I will be a true friend to you both."

Ben shook the artist's outstretched hand gratefully. "Thank you, Dominic, I know you'll be a rare and good pal. There, that's that! I hope Karay and Ned find water soon. Tomorrow we'll travel together, all four of us, to the fair at Veron. But, for now, let's enjoy a bit of peace and quiet without our fierce girlfriend."

Dominic smiled. "Oh, she's fierce and quick-tempered all right, but Karay has a good heart, I know it."

Still feeling the odd drops of rain, they sat back and relaxed, the fireglow creating a small cavern of light and warmth in a dark forest night.

Both the lads had dozed off for the better part of an hour when they were roused by Karay and Ned returning. Boisterously the dog and the girl romped in, emptying their spoils onto a flat chunk of rock. Karay was wet but triumphant, and Ned shook water from his coat, woofing softly as he gave out thoughts to

Ben. "Fish! Look at those beauties, I caught one of 'em!"

Karay busied herself with the four fat rudd, strung through their gills on a thick reed. "Pass me your knife, Facemaker. Your Ned's a good fisherdog, Ben, he caught this big one!"

She chattered away animatedly whilst cleaning the fish. "Ned found a stream, quite slow runnin' and clear. I tickled the rudd out from under the bank, an' Ned trapped one in the shallows. Found watercress too, see? Got some wood sorrel, dandelion roots an' raspberries. You just watch me, I'll make a meal for us, fit for a king . . ."

While Karay rattled on, Ned communicated with Ben. "You should've seen her, mate, she let those fish swim into her hand, tickled them a bit, then slung 'em out onto the bank. A body would never be hungry long with Karay as a pal!"

The girl was as good as her word. They dined on roast fish with chopped herbs and toasted bread. The raspberries provided a dessert.

Karay sucked on a fish bone. "That's the last of the bread – how far is it to Veron?"

"About six hours' steady walking," Dominic replied.

Karay piled more wood on the fire. "Good! If we set off at dawn we should make it about midday. Get some sleep now."

Ben saluted her. "Aye aye, ma'am, right away!"

Ned stretched out and sighed. "Bit bossy, but a good cook!" Ben was surprised when Karay lay back and began singing. Her voice had the husky sweetness of a Spanish lady he had heard singing on the quay at Cartagena, soothing and melodic.

"I will search the wide world over,
By the sea or by land,
Like a dove I'll soar the seasons,
'Til I touch his hand.
Through the towns where folk gather,
O'er lone windswept hills,
I will never cease roaming 'til
My dreams he fulfils.

And I'll cry to the moon above,
Where oh where bides my true love?

Will I see his face at dawning,
Like a poor maiden's prayer?
In some purple-shaded valley,
Will he be waiting there?
In the still silent waters,
Will his fond face I see?
Ever smiling, eyes beguiling,
And he'll love only me.

Then I'll cry to the moon above
Here oh here is my true love."

Ben slept more peacefully than he had in many a long night, with the embers warming him and Ned stretched by his side, surrounded by the tranquillity and silence of enveloping woodland darkness. No nightmares of Vanderdecken steering the heaven-cursed *Flying Dutchman* across storm-torn seas of eternal damnation marred his dreams. Rose-hued mists tinted the boy's slumber. From afar the angel spoke, soft, clear, but insistent.

> "A man who has not children
> Will name you as his son.
> In that hour, you must be gone!
> Turn your face back to the sea,
> You will meet another one,
> A father with no children,
> Before you travel on.
> Help him to help his children,
> As his kinsman would have done."

All night the words echoed through Ben's mind. He did not puzzle over them, knowing that he was unable to resist any destiny that heaven had already planned.

A FINE SUNNY MORNING reigned over all as they left the woodlands, emerging onto a hilltop. Ben stopped a moment to take in the pleasant panorama. Dominic explained where they were and whither they were bound. "We're travelling south – those mountains you see ahead are the Pyrenees. It's up hill and down dale from here. That third hilltop, 'twixt here and the mountains, that's Veron. Perhaps we can save a bit of climbing by following that stream around the hills and through the valleys."

Karay set off, calling back to them as she ran alongside Ned, "Come on then, we'll race you there!"

Ben watched them dashing downhill. "Let them go. She'll get tired of running before Ned does. Come on, mate, we'll walk like ordinary, sensible folk."

He and Dominic set out at a leisurely pace. They found the girl sitting panting on a stream bank at the foot of the next hill. Ned was tugging at the hem of her dress. He looked up at Ben approaching and sent him a message. "Weak, fickle things human beings are. Look, she's out of breath already – a puppy'd have more stamina than this girl!"

Dominic winked at Ben, remarking to Karay as they strolled past her, "Good morning, ma'am. If you sit there all day you'll miss the fair at Veron. I'm told 'tis a good one!"

Both boys ducked as the girl splashed stream water at them. "Wait for me, you villains!" She had to run to catch up with them.

Veron was classed as a town, albeit a rather small one. It sat atop a gently sloping hill, with a meandering path leading up to its gates. Veron must once have been a fortress, for it was enclosed by stone walls, ancient but thick and solid. The fair was little more than a weekend market held once each month from a Friday midday to a Monday late noon.

Ben and his friends arrived early, taking their place behind a line of country folk waiting to be allowed through the town gates by the wall guards. They shuffled along with the motley crowd, their eyes roving with interest over the colourful scene. Carts piled high with fruit, vegetables and rural produce jostled behind rustic smocked drovers herding cattle, sheep, goats and horses. Wagons bearing disassembled stalls of painted wood and dyed canvas trundled uphill, hauled and pushed by entire families. Geese and ducks flapped between the wheels, honking and quacking, adding to the noisy cavalcade as the fairgoers, chiding youngsters and discussing prospects, all shuffled forward, eager to be inside the gates.

As they got closer to the entrance, Ned sent a thought to Ben. "Look, people are having to pay a toll to get in."

Ben turned to Karay and Dominic. "Looks like it's been a waste of time coming here. We've got to pay the guards to get in. I don't have any money – do either of you?"

Dominic's face fell. "I didn't know you had to pay admission. I haven't got a single centime on me!"

Karay shook her head, stifling a scornful giggle. "What a pair of bumpkins! Money, huh! Who needs money to get past those gates? Leave this to me. You two just hang about and look as you do now, a real pair of yokels. I'll do all the talking."

Ben shrugged. "As you say, ma'am, we'll follow the leader!"

The two wall guards were only ordinary town watchmen, each sporting a crested armband and a helmet that had seen better days. They carried long, antiquated pikes and barred the gates after each entrant in an overblown manner of importance.

Ben communicated an uneasy thought to his dog. "I hope she knows what she's doing – that's a long hill to be kicked down."

The black Labrador nuzzled his hand. "Trust Karay, m'boy, she looks as if she's done this before a few times!"

As the four of them approached, both guards lowered their pikes, barring the entrance. The bigger of the two held out his hand. "Two centimes each, an' one for the dog. That's, er . . ."

"Seven centimes," the smaller guard said.

Karay looked puzzled. She directed her attention to the big guard, letting her hand rest on his arm. "But, Captain, didn't our mother or father pay you?"

Being addressed as captain made the guard puff out his chest. He gazed down officiously into the pretty girl's eyes. "I don't know your parents, miss, and no one's paid me extra to allow others in today!"

Karay fluttered her eyes and grasped the guard's arm. "Oh, Captain, you surely must know them. Emile and Agnes? Our family has the pancake and honey stall. They left home hours before we did."

The guard saw Karay's lip quiver. He patted her hand gently. "Well, they mustn't have arrived yet, miss. You an' your brothers stand to one side now an' wait for them, eh."

Ben was amazed to see a tear spring unbidden to the girl's eye. Karay was clinging to the guard's arm now, gazing imploringly up at him, her voice all atremble. "Oh please, Captain, you must let us in. If our parents are not there, our stall space will be taken by someone else. I think the wheel must have come off the cart again. Father will be fixing it – they'll be along any minute now, expecting to find us watching their stall space. We're a poor family, Captain, but we're honest. I'll bring the money straight out to you, as soon as the stall is set up and we're selling our wares."

The guard began to soften. He murmured to his partner, "What d'you think?"

The smaller guard shrugged. " 'Tis up to you, Giles," he whispered.

Karay suddenly brightened up. "Giles – that's him, isn't it?" Ben and Dominic nodded eagerly as the girl pressed her point. "Mother said she'd pay you, Captain, she told us to ask for the tall, good-looking one. Giles, she said!"

Most of the people behind them were getting impatient and calling out for Karay to move aside so they could get in. Giles shook his pike and bellowed, "Silence, or none of you will enter the fair. I'll say who gets in!"

Karay continued with her pleading. "I promise, Captain, I'll bring the money out as soon as possible. I'll bring you a pancake each, too, with butter and honey on it, piping hot!"

That settled the matter. Giles lowered his pike. "In you go, quick now! Oh, and could you manage a squeeze of lemon juice on those pancakes?"

Karay pushed Ben and Dominic in front of her through the gateway. Ned stood by her side as she replied, "I'll make them myself, with plenty of lemon juice. See you later, Captain. Come on, boy, before our space gets taken!"

The guard watched them hurry inside and winked at his companion. "Good manners, that girl – pretty, too!"

Inside Veron's main square there was a real bustle of festive atmosphere. Stalls were packed together so tightly that folk had to push and jostle to negotiate the narrow aisle spaces. The friends sat together on a broad flight of steps that fronted a grand manor house with a southern exposure.

Dominic chided Karay humorously. "No sign of Emile or Agnes yet. Oh dear, I wonder where Mother and Father have got to. You're a great liar, Karay!"

The girl slapped his arm lightly. "Well, at least I got us into the fair, didn't I, my slow-witted yokel brother."

Ben chuckled as he ruffled Ned's ears. "Don't forget now, you owe those guards seven centimes and two hot pancakes."

Ned's thought chimed in on Ben. "Mmm, thick with butter and honey. No lemon for me, thanks."

Karay's eyes twinkled. "Pancakes, that's what we need, I'm famished!"

She rose swiftly and cut off towards the stalls.

Ned pawed at Ben's leg. "We'd best go after her. There's no telling what that young madam will be up to next!"

"You're right, mate." Ben returned Ned's thought. He

pulled Dominic up from the step. "Come on, Dom, it's a bit risky letting that little thief wander off alone."

Karay had found herself a pancake stall where there was only a middle-aged lady attending to it. The girl stood back, watching everything closely.

"Thinking of stealing pancakes now, are we?"

She turned to see Ben, Dominic and Ned behind her. Karay hissed at them angrily, "I'm not stealing anything – she'll give me some pancakes gladly. Now be quiet and let me study that stall. I'll get us some food!"

Ned nudged his head against Ben's leg. "I'd do as Karay says if I were you. Give her a chance."

After a while Karay sauntered over to the stall, where she waited until the woman was not busy serving. Passing a forearm across her brow, the woman sighed. "Pancakes are two centimes each, three with butter, four with honey and butter, three with just salt and lemon juice. Do you want one, miss?"

The girl stared hard at the woman, letting a silence pass before she spoke. "You work very hard for a widowed lady."

The woman wiped her butter ladle on a clean cloth. "I've not met you before, how d'you know I'm a widow?"

Karay closed her eyes and held up a finger. Her voice was slow and confidential, as if sharing a secret. "I know many things, madame. The eye of my mind sees the past as well as the present and the future. That is my gift, given to me by the good Saint Veronique, whom I am named after."

The woman crossed herself and kissed her thumbnail. "Saint Veronique! Tell me more!"

Karay's eyes opened. She smiled sadly and shook her head. "It tires me greatly to use my skills. I have just come from Spain, where I was given five gold coins for seeing into the fortunes of a noble lady of Burgos."

The woman's mouth set in a tight line as she mixed pancake batter. "You're a fortuneteller! My money is too hard-earned to spend upon such fancies and lies!"

Karay looked proudly down her nose at the pancake seller. "I already have gold coins. What do I need with your few centimes, Madame Gilbert?"

Batter slopped from the bowl as the woman stopped stirring. "How do you know my husband's name?"

Karay replied offhandedly, "It was never the name of the children you did not have. Shall I see into your future?"

The woman's face fell. "You're right, we never had children. If you don't want money for telling my fortune, then why did you come here? What do you want from me, miss?"

The girl smiled, sniffing dreamily at the aroma from the stall. "My grandmother used to make pancakes for me exactly like the ones you make – proper country style, eh?"

The pancake seller smiled fondly. "Ah, yes, proper country style . . . You could tell my fortune and I'd give you one."

Karay turned her head away as if offended. "Only one?"

Shooing off a wasp and covering the honey pail, the woman spread her arms wide. "How many then, tell me."

Karay played with her dark ringlets a moment. "Eight – no, better make it a dozen. I have a long way to travel, and the food they serve at some inns is not to my taste."

The woman looked a bit shocked. "Twelve pancakes is a lot!"

Karay shrugged airily. "I could eat them easily, with enough honey and butter spread on them. It is a small price to pay for knowing what life and fate will bring to you, madame."

The woman wiped both hands on her apron. "I will pay!"

Karay came behind the planks that served as a counter. "Let me see the palm of your right hand."

The woman proffered her outspread palm. Karay pored over it, whispering prayers for guidance from Saint Veronique loudly enough for her customer to hear. Then she began.

"Ah yes, I see Gilbert, your husband, he was a good baker. Since he has gone you have worked hard and long to set up your business. But fear not, you aren't alone. Who is this good man who helps you?"

The woman looked up from her own palm. "You mean Monsieur Frane, the farmer?"

The girl nodded. "He is a good man, even though he has lost a partner, his wife. He comes to help you often, yes?"

The woman smiled. "From dawn to dusk, if I ask him."

Karay smiled back at her. "He thinks a lot of you. So does his daughter."

The pancake seller agreed. "Jeanette is a good girl, almost like a daughter to me – she visits a lot, too. Tell me more."

Karay made a few signs over the woman's palm. "Now for the future. Listen carefully to what I tell you. Do not go home tonight – take a room at a local inn. Stay a few days longer after the fair. Sit by the window each day and watch out for Monsieur Frane and Jeanette, they will come. You must tell him that your work is tiring you, that you no longer want to continue with it. Tell him you are thinking of selling your house and bakery and moving."

The woman looked mystified. "But why would I do that?"

The girl silenced the woman with a wave of her hand. "Do you want me to see further into your future, madame?"

The woman nodded, and Karay continued. "I see you happily married, a farmer's wife, with a dear devoted daughter. The only baking you will bother with is their daily bread and cakes to eat in the evening around your farmhouse fire. Trust me, madame, your fate will be aided by your own efforts. Saint Veronique sees you as a good person, I know this."

Suddenly the woman threw her arms about the girl and kissed her. "Are you sure twelve pancakes will be enough, my dear?"

Back on the steps outside the manor house, two boys, a girl and a dog feasted on hot pancakes spread thick with country butter and comb honey. Ben licked his fingers, gazing at Karay in awe. "Tell us how you managed to do it. Widow, farmer, daughter, husband's name, and who, pray, is Saint Veronique?"

Karay's explanation made it all sound simple. "Veron is the name of this place, so I thought Veronique made it sound nice and local. I don't know who Saint Veronique is, but she certainly helped us. The cart was a good clue. It had been painted over but I could still see the words, the name in white, beneath the last coat: 'S. Gilbert. Baker'. He was nowhere to be seen, the woman was working alone and she'd had the name on the cart painted over. So I guessed she was a widow, without children, too. That woman's middle-aged; if she had children, they'd probably be about our age. If that was so, they'd be helping their mother to run the business. She leaves her house alone to travel here: someone must watch it for her – the farmer Frane. A single woman could not handle it all, so he helps her. If his wife were alive, she would not hear of such a thing. He would not be allowed to spend most of his day at a widow's house and neglect his own. The woman was wearing a bracelet, a cheap pretty thing, not the sort she would spend money on. I guessed that a young girl had bought it for her. I was right. So, the farmer has a young daughter. They both like the pancake lady. Two people, a widow and a widower, living close to each other. The girl Jeanette likes the widow; to the widow, Jeanette is the daughter she never had. As for the rest, I was only telling that woman what the future could hold if she played her cards right. What's wrong with her becoming a farmer's wife and having a daughter? That's what she wants, isn't it? I was only telling her the best way to do it. Monsieur Frane and Jeanette would be very sad if she sold up and moved away. It'll happen, and they'll be happy together. Mark my words!"

Ben shook his head admiringly. "Don't you ever guess wrongly?"

The girl licked honey from her fingers. "Sometimes, but I can always manage to talk my way out of mistakes. The whole thing is just luck, guesswork, a bit of shrewd watching, and telling the customer things they like to hear. Right, let's set up stall here on these steps. Dominic, get your sketching stuff out. Ben, you and Ned sit here by me, try to look poor but honest. I'll start singing to attract the customers. Come on, now, we can save some of the pancakes for later. Dominic, do another sketch of Ned."

The dog sat by Karay's side and winked at Ben. "You look poor, I'll look honest!"

Karay folded her shawl in two and spread it out at her feet to catch any coins that were thrown. Dominic took up a piece of slate and his chalks. Ben sat on the other side of the girl, listening as she sang sweetly.

"Oh kind sir and madam, you good children too,
Pray stop here awhile, and I'll sing just for you
Of mysterious places, across the wide sea,
Of distant Cathay and of old Araby,
Where caravans trail, like bright streamers of silk
To far misted mountains, with peaks white as milk,
And ships tall as temples, spread sails wide and bold,
All laden with spices, fine rubies and gold,
Fine harbours where garlanded flowers deck piers,
In the lands of great mandarins, lords and emirs,
Where beautiful maidens, with priests old and wise,
Sing songs or chant prayers 'neath forgotten blue skies.
Have your eyes not beheld them, then hark to my song,
And your heart will be there, in sweet dreams before long."

Gradually a few people gathered. One of them was an old fellow pushing a cart on which he had a churn of buttermilk, a ladle and some earthenware bowls. When Karay finished her song, he applauded loudly, calling out, "What a fine voice! Sing some more, young maid!"

The girl held out her hand to him. "Let me get my breath, sir. Come on up here and get your likeness sketched by a real artist. We won't charge you much!"

The old fellow chuckled, shaking his head. "No thank ye, miss, I haven't got money to spend on pictures. Besides, who'd want to sketch a battered old relic like me, eh?"

Ben coaxed the old man up and sat him on the top step, facing Dominic, and reassured the reluctant sitter. "We're not talking money, sir. A bowl apiece of your buttermilk to quench our thirst would be enough. My friend is a good artist, you'll like his picture, I'm sure. Don't be shy. Here, I'll let my dog sit with you, he's a good companion."

Some of the watchers called out encouragement to the old fellow, and he finally agreed to be sketched. "Go on then, it'll give my wife something to throw mud at when she's angry with me!"

Dominic captured the spirit of the old buttermilk vendor amazingly. More folk had gathered to watch, and they viewed the likeness with astonishment.

"Oh, it's wonderful, what a nice picture!"

"Aye, very lifelike. He's even drawn that black dog, with its paw on his knee, see!"

"Doesn't the old man's face look kind and jolly!"

Ned watched them admiring the picture as he contacted Ben. "A true artist, eh? He's made me look even nobler on that sketch, and see the old man's eyes. Every crinkle and crease is perfect. You can see by looking at them that he's a cheery old codger with a good nature. Right, who's next to have their picture sketched – with the noble Ned, of course. I'm getting used to being famous!"

Ben tugged his dog's tail. "Stop boasting and drink your buttermilk, the man's waiting on his bowls. Though he'll have to wash that one before he serves buttermilk in it again."

The black Labrador sniffed. "I should think so too. Peasants using the personal bowl of Ned the Noble!"

Men and women began clamouring to have their pictures sketched next, even holding out coins in their hands. Karay nudged Ben. "Haha, we're in business now!"

Dominic looked around before choosing his next subject. He guided a young woman carrying a baby boy up to the step. She was obviously poor – her clothing was worn and frayed – but her baby looked clean and healthy.

The woman tried to avoid Dominic, her cheeks red with embarrassment as she pleaded with him. "Please, sir, I have barely enough money to feed my baby. I cannot afford your cost!"

The Facemaker of Sabada spoke gently to her. "There will be no cost, lady. For the privilege of sketching you both, I cannot pay you. But I will give you two pancakes, one for you and one for the babe. Hold him on your lap now, sit still and face me please."

Slumping down on the steps beside Ben, Karay heaved a sigh of resignation. "Two customers, no, three, if you count the baby, and what have we earned so far? A bowl of buttermilk apiece! Why don't we go and seek out some beggars, perhaps this facemaker'd like to sketch them free! Maybe we could give them the clothes off our backs for allowing us to do them the favour. Fools, that's what we are!"

Ben was not pleased with the girl's callous attitude. "Oh, stop grizzling, there's nothing wrong in helping people a little. There are other things in this life besides money. Where would you be if I hadn't helped you when you were chained to a cartwheel?"

Karay was about to make a sharp retort when they were interrupted by a richly clad lady, mounted sidesaddle on a chestnut mare. Her voice was loud and imperious. "Tell that boy he can sketch me next!"

Ned growled menacingly as she spurred the horse forward. The chestnut reared, but the lady brought it forcefully under control. She wagged her quirt at Ben. "Tie that dog up, or I'll have it destroyed!"

The boy took hold of the Labrador's collar. "I'm sorry, ma'am, Ned thought your horse was going to trample us."

He ignored Ned's indignant thoughts. "Pompous baggage. Both she and her horse could do with a lesson in manners!"

The lady was pointing at Dominic with her leather quirt. "Finish that picture quickly, I don't have all day to sit here waiting whilst you mess about with peasants!"

The facemaker continued sketching, though his eyes were hot and angry as he flicked them up at the mounted lady. "Then be on your way, ma'am, because I don't intend making a likeness of you!"

The young woman with the baby started to rise, but Dominic beckoned her to stay put. "Sit still, I'm almost done."

The onlookers had to scatter as the lady wheeled her horse about and rode off, glaring hatred at Dominic.

Ned broke free of Ben's hold and chased after the horse, barking furiously, causing the animal to break into a gallop. The lady was forced to hold on to her ornate hat as she bounced up and down awkwardly. Stall holders laughed and jeered at her ungracious exit, some even cheering Ned as he made his way back to Ben's side.

Dominic held up the slate containing the picture of the young woman and her baby, amid gasps of admiration from everyone around. There was beauty and honesty in the woman's face, and love for her child. Happy innocence and trust shone from the babe's eyes – it was a perfectly beautiful likeness. He passed it over to the blushing mother, together with the food he had promised her. She curtsied deeply, stammering her thanks.

"My husband will be pleased to see this hanging over our fireplace. Thank you, thank you very much, sir!"

Dominic bowed and smiled at her. "Tell him that I said he's a lucky man to have such a pretty wife and baby."

Shortly after the mother and child's departure, Dominic had just started to portray a fat, jolly housewife when a commotion arose between the stalls. He looked up from his work. "What's all the noise about?"

Karay climbed one of the gateposts of the big manor house. "I think we're about to find out. Here comes trouble! It's the guards and that toffee-nosed lady you turned away."

Dominic began gathering his materials. Ben stayed seated. "No use running, mate, let's stick together and see what they've got to say. We haven't harmed anybody or stolen anything." He looked pointedly at Karay. "Have we?"

Climbing down from the gatepost, she joined him. "What are you lookin' at me like that for? I haven't lifted anything. You're right, we'll stick together!"

Ned looked imploringly at Ben. "I wish you'd said we should run for it. I'm guilty of disturbing a horse!"

The mounted lady, both guards from the gate and a guard captain strode up the steps, dispersing any curious onlookers before them. Dominic forestalled the captain by addressing him. "My friends and I haven't done any wrong. I refused to sketch this lady because I am free to choose whom I draw!"

Ned's thought crossed Ben's mind. "I don't blame Dominic. Just look at the frosty-faced fishwife – the behind of her horse would have made a more handsome picture to draw!" Unwittingly, Ben laughed aloud at his dog's comical observation.

The guard captain, a neat-uniformed and stern-faced man, glared at him. "So you think it's funny, eh?" He indicated the group with a wave of his gauntleted hand. "Are these the ones?"

The smaller guard from the gate answered. "Aye, Captain, that's them. They slipped by us without paying, both boys, the girl and the dog. We couldn't leave our post an' give chase."

The woman pointed her quirt at Dominic. "That's the one who insulted me, impudent young wretch. I demand that you do something about it, Captain. My husband is the prefect of Toulouse, he wouldn't allow that sort of behaviour in our town, I'm certain of that!"

Hands clasped behind his back, the captain circled Ben and his friends, lecturing them severely. "This is no laughing matter, as you'll soon find out!"

Karay smiled sweetly at him. "Oh come now, sir, we aren't really guilty of anyth–"

"Silence!" The captain's face reddened as he shouted. "Defrauding the guards by entry without payment! Setting up business without licence, fees or permission! Trading on the very steps of Comte Bregon's residence, where none are allowed to set up stall! Insulting a lady visitor to Veron and setting a dog upon her horse! And you have the effrontery to stand there and tell me that you've done no wrong? Arrest them and take them away immediately! The dog, too!"

Ned bared his teeth and growled ferociously. Ben slipped his hand through the dog's collar, warning him mentally. "Hush now, mate, no use making things worse. It looks like we're in real trouble with the authorities."

Village folk watched in silence as the four miscreants were marched off towards a barred entrance in the wall at the far side of the big house.

A LONG BRICK TUNNEL LED THEM OUT INTO A sunny walled garden. With the captain in the lead and the two guards at the rear, the four friends emerged, blinking from the

darkness of the passage. It was obviously the carefully tended garden of somebody wealthy. Rose and rhododendron bushes skirted the walls, fronted by all manner of border flowers. A circular red gravel path surrounded an area of rockeries, with streamlets gurgling about them. At its centre was an ancient gazebo with stunted pear trees growing on either side. Inside the gazebo, an old man with a wispy beard sat upon a woven-cane divan. He was clad in a nightshirt, over which he wore a quilted silk jacket.

Comte Vincente Bregon did not sleep well at night, thus he passed the warm summer days in his garden, catching small catnaps to while away the hours. His eyes opened slowly at the sound of feet crunching upon gravel. As the captain passed, he saluted his master. Bregon stopped him with a slow gesture of his parchment-skinned hand. He looked at the three raggedly dressed young people and the dog.

The captain had to crane his head forward to hear the old man's voice. "Where are you taking those children and their dog?"

Standing stiffly to attention, the captain spoke officiously. "Unlicensed traders, sir, young lawbreakers. A week or two in the dungeons will teach them some discipline and manners!"

The old comte's eyes twinkled briefly as he addressed Ben. "Are you a very desperate criminal?"

Ben immediately liked the comte – he looked wise and kind. "No, sir, apart from not paying my two centimes entrance fee to your village fair – oh, and one centime for Ned here."

The comte nodded slowly and smiled. "Ah, I see. And this Ned, will he bite my head off if I try to stroke him?"

Ben chuckled. "Hardly, sir, he's a well-behaved dog. Go on, Ned, let the gentleman stroke you. Go on, boy!"

The black Labrador trotted over to the comte, passing a thought to Ben. "I do wish you'd stop talking to me as if I were still a bumble-headed puppy. This looks like a nice old buffer. I'll charm him a bit, watch!"

Ned gazed soulfully at the comte and offered his paw. The old nobleman was delighted – he accepted the paw and stroked Ned's head gently.

"Oh, he's a fine fellow, aren't you, Ned?"

Ben heard his dog's comment. "Aye, sir, and you're not a bad old soul yourself. Mmmm, this fellow's an expert stroker!"

The comte nodded dismissively at the captain. "You may go, leave these young ones with me."

Blusteringly the captain protested, "But, sir, they were trading on your own front steps, and they insulted the prefect of Toulouse's wife –"

Cutting him short with an upraised hand, the comte replied, "Huh, that hard-faced harridan, it's about time somebody took her down a peg. Go now, take your guards back to the fair and continue with your duties. I'll take care of these vagabonds!"

Looking like an indignant beetroot, the captain marched his men off, back through the tunnel.

With open palms, the old man beckoned them forward. "Come here, my children, sit on the carpet by my chair. Pay no heed to my captain, he's a good man, but sometimes a bit too diligent for his office."

Seating themselves at his feet, they repeated their names one by one. The comte patted the big black Labrador. "And this is Ned, I already know him. My name is Vincente Bregon, comte of Veron, an ancient and useless title these days. I like pears, do go and pick us some, Karay."

The girl picked five huge soft yellow pears from the nearby branches, which grew right into the gazebo window spaces. The fruit was delicious, and the old man wiped juice from his chin with a linen kerchief as he questioned them.

"So then, tell me about yourselves. You, Karay, what do you do?"

Wiping her mouth upon her sleeve, the girl replied, "I am a singer, sir, the best in all the country!"

The old fellow chuckled. "I'll wager you are. Come on, girl, sing me a song, a happy one. I love to hear a good voice giving out a jolly air. Sing for me!"

Karay stood up, clasping her fingers at midriff height. She gave forth with a happy melody.

"Oh what care I for faces long,
Or folk so melancholy,
If they cannot enjoy my song,
Then fie upon their folly.
Small birds trill happy in the sky,
They never stop to reason why,

And as for me, well nor do I,
It costs naught to be jolly.
Sing lero lero lero lay,
Come smile with me, we'll sing today
A merry tune or roundelay,
All of our cares will float away,
With no need to sound sorry!"

As the last sweet notes hung on the noontide air, the comte wiped his kerchief across his eyes and sniffed. "Pay me no heed, child. Your song and fine voice gladden my heart, though my eyes have a will of their own. Now, Ben, what particular talent have you to display, eh?"

From where he was sitting, Ben looked up into the kindly old man's face. "Me, sir? I don't do anything in particular, Ned and I are just friends of these two. We don't sing like Karay, or sketch like Dominic."

The comte patted Ben's head affectionately. "They're very lucky to have friends like you and Ned. Friendship is the greatest gift one person can give to another. Tell me, Dominic, what sort of things do you sketch?"

"The features of people, sir," Dominic replied. "I am known as a facemaker."

Patting his wispy hair and smoothing his beard, the comte held his chin up. "Do you think you could picture my likeness?"

Dominic took a piece of parchment, charcoal and chalks from his satchel, and looked up from where he sat cross-legged on the carpet. "You have an interesting face, sir, I've been saving this parchment for a good subject. Lower your chin and look down at me, sir."

• • •

A golden afternoon rolled slowly by while Dominic sketched leisurely, taking his time not to miss any detail in the comte's lined features. Ned stretched out and took a comfortable nap. Karay wandered off around the garden, admiring the flowers and the mullioned windows of the stately manor. Ben sat on one of the open windowsills, breathing the fragrant air cooled by running water and laden with the heady scent of blossoms. Somewhere nearby, a mistle thrush warbled a hymn to the cloudless blue sky. Bees hummed a muted accompaniment to the bird's song, while a butterfly, all iridescent blue and purple, landed on his shirtfront and perched there with wings spread wide. A calm serenity pervaded Ben's mind. This was a world away from storm-torn seas, the *Flying Dutchman* and Captain Vanderdecken. Memories of his buccaneering days and of poor Raphael Thuron seemed to be a dream of the distant past. His eyes were slowly closing when Dominic announced, "There! I think I've captured your likeness pretty well, sir."

Karay came in from the garden, Ned woke up and Ben went across to see the result of the facemaker's art. All five gazed at the picture, which the old nobleman held in his trembling hands – it was Vincente Bregon, Comte of Veron, to the very life, and far beyond that. Every line and crow's-foot wrinkle, every time-silvered hair of beard and head were startlingly lifelike.

The old man's voice quivered as he spoke. "The eyes! Tell me, young one, what did you see in my eyes?"

Dominic pondered his answer before replying. "I saw wisdom, sir, but also the loss and grief of a man who once was happy, now turned to loneliness and resignation. Do you wish me to continue, sir?"

The comte shook his head wearily. "I know the rest, what need to tell an old man of the anguish he has lived with so long."

Ben reached out and touched the comte's cheek. "Then why don't you tell us, sir? Maybe 'twould do you good to talk. We'll listen, we're your friends."

The comte blinked. He stared at them like a man awakening from a dream. "Yes, you are my friends! I feel as if you were sent here, to listen and to help me!"

Carefully, he rolled the parchment up and offered it to Ned. "Take this, but go lightly with it. I will have this picture framed and hung in my house." Ned took the scrolled sketch gently in his mouth.

As he held out both hands, the old fellow's voice took on a new briskness. "Now, my young friends, help me up, let me lean on your strong arms. We will go indoors. There's good food inside – I never knew children that couldn't eat well. You shall hear my story after you have dined."

It was a house of great splendour, with silk hangings, suits of armour and ancient weapons decorating the walls. The comte disregarded their curiosity and took his newfound friends straight into the kitchen. There he bade them sit at a large, well-scrubbed pine table amid the surroundings of cookery and serving equipment. Shelves loaded with plates, drinking vessels and tureens ranged all around; copper pans, pots and cauldrons hung from the oak-beamed rafters. Their host sat with them. Rapping on the tabletop, he called querulously,

"Mathilde, is there nobody here to serve a hungry man a bite of food, eh?"

An enormously fat old lady, bursting with energy, came bustling in, wiping chubby hands on a huge apron. She retorted sharply to his request, "Hah, hungry, are we? Can't take meals at proper times like civilized folk. Oh no, just wait until 'tis poor Mathilde's time for a nap, then march in here shouting your orders!"

Her master's eyes twinkled as he argued back at her. "Cease cackling like a market goose, you old relic. Bring food for me and my young friends here, and be quick about it!"

Ben hid a smile – he could tell that the pair were lifelong friends, that this was just a game they were playing with each other.

Mathilde the cook folded her arms and glared fiercely at the young people, curling her lip. "Friends, you say? They look like the rakings and scrapings of some robber gypsy band. I'd lock up my silverware if they entered my house. Is that a black wolf you've got sitting on my nice clean chair? Wait while I go and get a musket to shoot it with!"

Ned looked at Ben and passed a message. "I hope she's only joking. That old lady looks dangerous to me!"

The comte returned her glare and shouted in a mock rough tone, "I'll fetch a musket and shoot you if food doesn't get here soon, you turkey-wattled torment!"

Mathilde managed to stifle a grin as she shot back at him, "Torment yourself, you dry old grasshopper carcass. I suppose I'd better get that food, before the wind snaps you in two and blows you away!"

When Mathilde had departed, Karay took a fit of the giggles. "Oh, sir, d'you always shout at each other in that dreadful way?"

The old man smiled. "Always. She's the dearest lady in all the world, though she rules my household as if I were a naughty child. I don't know what I'd do without my Mathilde."

The food, when it arrived, was excellent: a basin of the local cream cheese, some onion soup, a jug of fresh milk, peasant bread and a raisin cake with almonds on it. Mathilde served them, muttering under her breath about being murdered in her bed by beggars and vagabonds. She recoiled in mock horror when Ned licked her cheek, fleeing the kitchen before being, as she put it, torn to pieces by the wolf in her own kitchen.

After an extremely satisfying meal, the friends sat back and listened to their host unfolding his narrative. Drawing a heavy gold seal ring from his finger, the comte placed it on the table. "This seal carries the crest of my family – it is carved with a lion for strength, a dove for peace, and a knotted rope for union, or togetherness. The family of Bregon have always tried to live by these principles. We have held these lands for countless ages, trying to live right and taking care of all under our protection. I was the elder son of two born to my parents, but I had the misfortune of never being married. I was the scholar – once I had ambitions to enter a monastery and become a monk, though nothing ever came of it. My younger brother was far more popular than I. Edouard was a big man, very strong, and skilful with all manner of weapons. When our parents passed on, we ruled Veron together. But Edouard left all the affairs of the village and the management of this house to me. He would go off on adventures, sometimes not coming home for long periods of time. One day he rode off south, alone. Edouard loved adventuring. He went towards the Spanish border, into the Pyrenees, intending to hunt. Whilst he was in the mountains, he suffered an accident, a fall from his horse, which left him unconscious, with a head wound. My brother was found, though, and was taken in by a powerful family called the Razan."

Dominic leaned forward, his voice incredulous. "The Razan!"

The old man's eyebrows raised. "Ah, my young friend, so you have heard of the Razan?"

Dominic nodded vigorously. "Over the mountains, in the Spanish town of Sabada, where I come from, folk talked of little else. Honest men would make the sign of the cross at the very mention of their name. When horses or cattle went missing, sometimes even people, everyone would whisper that it was the work of the Razan. Mothers would use their name to frighten naughty children. 'The Razan will get you!' Yet nobody really knew who they were. Our priest said that they were evil magicians from Algiers who knew the dark ways of wizards and witches. But I'm sorry for interrupting you, sir, please carry on with your story."

Stroking his wispy beard, the comte continued. "One hears all manner of tales about the Razan; some say they are from Africa, others, from the mountains of Carpathia. I think a lot of these things are fables, put about by the Razan themselves to instil fear in ignorant peasants. I myself have had reports of them putting spells on folk, turning men, women and children into fishes, beasts or birds. They prey on superstition and rule simple minds by terror of the unknown."

Returning the signet ring to his index finger, the aged nobleman sighed. "My brother, Edouard, was frightened of nothing. Whilst he was being nursed by the Razan – who must have known who he was, or they would have slain him just for his horse and weapons – Edouard was smitten with love for a Razan girl. She was the only daughter of the Razan, and very beautiful. Ruzlina, for that was her name, would have none attending Edouard but herself. Her mother, Maguda, must have seen the possibilities of allowing them to be together. It would be an easy, and legal, way for the Razan to gain a foothold in Veron, a village they had long coveted. Together, Ruzlina and Edouard went through a form of ceremony that passes for marriage among the Razan. He brought his new bride back here when he was fully recovered. How that girl had lived among such a wicked brood as the Razan, I'll never know. She was honest, true and gentle-natured – I could readily understand why my brother had fallen in love with her. They both lived happily in this place for nigh on two years.

"Then tragedy struck the house of Bregon." Here the comte paused, as if finding it difficult to continue.

Ned went to him, laying his head on the old man's lap and gazing up at him with soft, sympathetic eyes as he contacted Ben. "The poor fellow, see the sorrow in his face?"

Ben nodded and placed a gentle hand on their host's shoulder. "Tragedy, sir?"

Dabbing his eyes with a kerchief, the comte explained. "Ruzlina died giving birth to her first child. It was a son. Edouard was so stricken with grief that he could not bear to look upon the child. He locked himself away in his chambers. Mathilde and I cared for the newborn baby, christened Adamo. It was a sad household, my young friends, full of sorrow and mourning, as if a light had gone from all our lives. Then, not more than three days after Ruzlina's death, her kin, Maguda the mother and four of her brothers, appeared as if by magic on the steps of this house. I have never beheld a more sinister or barbaric-looking woman than Maguda Razan – she was the very picture of a witch. Dressed in black weeds of mourning, with her face painted in strange symbols, she pounded upon my door with her staff. Edouard would not leave his rooms to talk or even look upon her. She claimed the body of her daughter to take back to the mountains for burial in the Razan family vault. I could not refuse her this request. But it was her other demand that I could not bring myself to grant. She wanted little Adamo!"

Dominic stared at the old man anxiously. "You didn't let her have him, did you, sir?"

A defiant glimmer entered the comte's eyes. "No! I would not give up a newborn infant to murderous robbers, never! Maguda and her brothers departed with Ruzlina's body in a casket. The brothers were silent, but Maguda Razan screamed like a wounded tigress. She called down all manner of curses upon Edouard, me and the house of Bregon. The villagers were so frightened that they ran away and hid. She made smoke and fire appear from the air, yelling vengeance and death, blaming my brother for the loss of her daughter. Then the Razan were gone – they vanished, leaving behind only smoke clouds and burning ashes."

Karay could not help but ask, "So was that the end of it, sir?"

Shaking his head, the aged nobleman answered her. "No, child, that was only the start. Bregon was plagued by thefts and fires and all kinds of wicked doings. No matter how I barred the gates or stationed guards on the walls, the Razan would find their way in. However, I surrounded this house with armed men – I would not give up my nephew, Adamo."

Ben smiled. "I wager you were very fond of him, sir."

The comte resorted to wiping his eyes; his voice went husky. "Fond? The child meant more to me than life itself. He was raven-haired and dark of eye. Even as a baby, Adamo had a huge physique, strong and big-boned. But he was a calm child, very very silent. He never cried, or laughed out loud, or even chuckled. Doctors looked at him and assured me that he had the power of speech, that he was not born mute. Yet he never made a sound – well, hardly. Sometimes he would call Mathilde ' 'Tilde', poor little fellow. My brother Edouard could not bear to be in his own son's presence, can you imagine that?"

Ben felt he had to ask the question. "What became of Edouard?"

The comte turned the ring on his finger. "This ring belonged to Edouard. He wore it on his little finger, yet it is far too large for my index finger. This will give you an indication of his size. However, he was brought down by a single sip of wine. It was the work of the Razan, I'm sure of it. Somehow, one of them entered this house, got into his rooms and poisoned the wine. This took place two years to the day after his wife died. Now, let me tell you the final, and most awful, part of this sad story. On the day we buried him, Mathilde was preparing food whilst I was at the funeral. It was a bright warm afternoon, and she let little Adamo play on a rug out in the garden, where she could see him from the kitchen window. But the moment she looked away, he was gone!"

Ben spoke as the thought from Ned crossed his mind. "The Razan!"

The comte nodded, then leaned forward, resting his forehead on both hands. "That was eighteen years ago this summer. I have not seen the boy since, nor heard news of him."

Ben felt enormous pity for the Comte de Veron, but he was slightly puzzled. "Did you not go out and search for him, sir?"

Closing his eyes wearily, the old fellow replied, "The Razan sent me a message – it appeared on an arrow, shot over the walls. If I tried to leave Bregon, they would invade it and take my village for themselves. A lock of the boy's hair was with the note, to prove they had him. I sent out two pairs of brave men. They never returned. So, now you see my dilemma. I am a prisoner in my own village, and I don't know, after all these long years, whether Adamo is even alive!"

They sat in silence, feeling enormous sympathy for the aged nobleman's predicament. The comte remained immobile, still with his eyes closed and both hands supporting his forehead as he leaned on the table. Faint sounds of the market fair drifted in on the sun-warmed noontide air. Outside in the garden, the thrush had been joined in song by a blackbird.

Ben communicated with Ned. "Well, now we know what the angel guided us here for. We must help this good man to get his nephew back. What d'you think, mate?"

The dog lifted his head from the old man's lap as he answered. "Just show me a Razan and I'll put a spell on the seat of his breeches. I like this old gentleman, Ben – we must help him. I'm with you, and I'll bet that Karay and Dom are too!"

It was Ben who broke the silence. "Do you know where the Razan make their home in the mountains, sir?"

Opening his eyes, the comte sat up straight. "The only one of our family who knew that was my brother, and he would not have found the place had not the Razan carried him there when he was injured. Edouard said that it was high in the Pyrenees, somewhere 'twixt Viella and Monte Maladeta, not far over the Spanish border."

Ben looked to Dominic. "Are you familiar with that area?"

Shaking his head, the facemaker replied, "Sabada, where I

come from, is southwest of that region. I never travelled over that way, I'm afraid –"

The comte interrupted him. "Wait! Garath, our old family ostler and blacksmith, might know something. He and Edouard were great friends, they often talked together. Garath is one of the few I can really trust. I'll get him."

Ben helped the comte up. "We'll come with you, sir, no need to tire yourself. Lend a hand here, you two!"

The facemaker and the girl were assisting the old man through the door when he halted. "Wait," he said. Opening a heavy stone jar that stood on a shelf, he took out several rough lumps of pale brown sugar. The comte winked at Ned and whispered, "For the horses, they know me." He thrust the sugar lumps into his dressing-gown pocket.

Garath was no longer a young man, but Ben could see that he was a fellow of great strength. He wore no shirt beneath his leather apron, and thick, corded muscle and sinew stood out on his grey-haired forearms. He had the hind leg of a roan mare locked between his knees, while he cleaned out the frog of her hoof with a small knife.

Garath looked up as they entered the sweet-horsy-smelling stall. "Come to have your bones jolted, sire? 'Tis a fine day for it."

"No, no, my friend, these old bones would have to spend a week in bed if I tried to sit a horse, let alone ride it." The comte laughed. "Meet my young friends, they have a question to ask you."

As they were introducing themselves and chatting to Garath, the mare dipped her muzzle into the old man's pocket and snorted. The comte chuckled. "Are you stealing my sugar, madame? Come out of there and I'll give you some, eh, and a bit for my good friend Ned also. There you are!"

As the horse and the dog crunched sugar happily, the comte explained his visit to Garath. "My young friends want to know whether my brother ever told you anything about the location where the Razan have their den."

Patting the mare's well-brushed flank, the blacksmith nodded. "Monsieur Edouard said something of it once. High up in the border peaks, he said. In Spain, someplace 'twixt Viella and Maladeta – wild country!"

Ben flicked the mop of tow-coloured hair from his brow. "We already know that, sir. Was there nothing else you can recall – any small detail that might help?"

Garath went over to pat the withers of a hefty grey, which the comte was feeding sugar to. "Hmm, let me see. Oh, aye, there was something he said, it comes back to me now. The men hunting wild boar. He said that was the last thing that he saw before he passed out from his accident. Men hunting wild boar. Then he said that he would know the spot where the Razan stronghold was if he could only find the place where the men were hunting the boar. Then he seemed to forget what he was talking about and wandered off. 'Twas the injury to Monsieur Edouard's head, you know. He was never quite the same after that fall from his horse."

Karay looked disappointed. "That is all you can remember?"

The blacksmith shrugged. "Ma'am, 'twas all he said, he never spoke of it again after that day, and I never asked him."

Dominic stepped in and presented the blacksmith with a sketch he had made whilst the man was talking to them. The facemaker had done it with charcoal, on an old cask lid he had found lying about.

Garath looked at his own likeness on the wooden lid and

bowed slightly. "My thanks to ye, sir, though I think you made me a bit too handsome in this picture. Do I really look like that?"

Dominic nodded emphatically. "Indeed you do, Garath, but that's not good looks I portrayed, it's honesty and hard work."

The comte inspected the likeness, commenting as Garath turned away, his cheeks reddening at the old man's compliment: "An honest man is hard to find. This is a true picture of you, Garath. See the eyes, they reflect truth and the long, faithful service you have given my family."

The blacksmith bowed. "I'm sorry I couldn't help you and your friends more, sire."

Evening shades were starting to fall as they sat in the comte's parlour, sipping cold fruit juice. The old man was giving orders to Mathilde. "There will be five for dinner tonight – make sure there is plenty for these young ones at the table. Oh, and tell Hector to air out the beds in the guest rooms."

Mathilde gave Ned a wide berth as she trundled out, muttering under her breath about being eaten out of house and home by gypsies and savages.

Karay wriggled with excitement as she addressed the comte. "D'you mean we can sleep in real beds in this big house? That's very kind of you, sir. I've never slept in a real bed before!"

The old man's eyes twinkled briefly. "You'll soon get used to it, child, and the boys also. I like good company around my gloomy old house, so stay as long as you wish."

Ben shook his head regretfully. "I wish we could, sir, but if we are to find Adamo, we'd best leave tomorrow."

The aged nobleman's face was suddenly serious. "Thank you for your offer, lad, but it is far too dangerous. Besides, what makes you think that you could find my nephew?"

Ben explained. "We are strangers to Veron, everyone saw us arrested by your guards, sir. My friends and I don't look exactly like visiting royalty, do we? Look at us, four poor travellers. Even Mathilde said we look like thieves and gypsies. What better cover could we have? Nobody would suspect us of being your agents. We could wander anywhere at will – who'd pay much attention to us?"

The comte stared into Ben's haunting blue eyes. "I don't know what it is, but the moment I saw you and Ned, Karay and Dominic being brought into my garden today, I had a strange feeling that things were about to happen."

Dominic spoke earnestly. "We will help you, sir, I'm sure of it. Put your trust in us and we'll prove our friendship."

The old man looked from one to the other. "You have a plan?"

Ben was about to say that they had no plan, but they would think one up, when Ned's thoughts claimed his attention. "Listen to me, mate. Repeat what I'm thinking to the old fellow, here's my plan . . ."

Ben repeated Ned's thoughts aloud to the comte. "Let everyone think we've been thrown in prison over the business on the steps. We'll stay here until Monday, when the fair's over. Though we'll have to keep our heads down, it wouldn't be wise to let word get about that we're houseguests and not prisoners. When the fair ends, have your guards drive us from Veron with lots of loud warnings that we're lucky to be set free from the lockup."

The comte scratched his beard. "But why such an elaborate charade? Wouldn't you be better merely slipping away at dawn?"

Ben continued translating his dog's thoughts. "No, no, sir, we want people to think that we're a bunch of no-goods. If, as you say, the Razan can appear in secret, then I'll wager there're some of them among the fair's visitors. We'll be in a much better position if they think we are villains like them!"

Karay gave Ben a sly nudge and winked at him. "Very good! You're not such a bumpkin as I thought you were, Ben. How did you think of a plan like that?"

The strange boy shrugged. "Oh, it wasn't my idea, it was Ned's!"

The black Labrador huffed indignantly at their laughter. "Huh! What's so funny? My brain's as good as any human's. Better than some, I'm certain!"

Dominic tugged Ned's tail playfully. "Good thinking, fellow, you'd make a fine robber's dog!"

The comte grew serious once more. "Are you sure you want to do this, my friends? You'll be putting yourselves in great peril."

Ben took their host's hand. "What sort of folk would we be if we couldn't help a friend like you, sir? Don't worry, we'll find Adamo and bring him back safely to you."

The old man was forced to resort to wiping his eyes again. "My children, if you could do this, you would earn my eternal gratitude!"

19

MAGUDA RAZAN and her followers lived in caves high in the Pyrenees on the Spanish side of the border. Maguda trusted no man and considered the women of the caves to be inferior beings, senseless baggages who lusted after silks and jewellery. Maguda Razan had eyes that held mysterious powers and was feared by those who served her, any of whom she could bend to her will. An awesome array of potions, scents, powders and spells, coupled with her hypnotic gaze, made her absolute ruler of her rocky domain. Widowed in her younger days, she relied on her four brothers for knowledge of the outside world. They were sombre, close-mouthed men and proficient assassins.

Lesser caves and tortuous passages ran into the mountains, all terminating at the main cavern where Maguda held court deep in the heart of her stone world. It was a vast cavern, furnished to strike terror into the very soul of ignorant thieves and impressionable peasants. Silent as the grave, it had the likenesses of many sinister idols carved into the walls: men with the bodies of reptiles and ferocious beasts, women with multiple limbs and cruel staring eyes, each image with a different-coloured fire burning at its base. Sulphurous yellow, blood red, oily black and many other hues of hellfire. Together they created a noxious cloud that hung beneath the cavern ceiling like a pall. Amid a welter of long-dead and stuffed creatures, Maguda Razan sat on a fabulous throne, which was said to have come from the palace of an emir. It was draped in skins of all manner and decorated with beads. Maguda Razan could barely reach its arms with her hands outstretched. She sat like a venomous spider at the centre of a web. Small, and clad in wispy wraps of black, blue and puce, she had hair that stood out from her head in a crown of dyed orange, streaked with steely grey roots. Between the deep-etched lines of her face, dark, cabalistic tattoos overlaid her bloodless skin. But it was the eyes of Maguda Razan that fascinated the onlooker – restless pinpoints of deep light shining out of muddy yellowed pupils, never still, always restlessly searching back and forth like a questing cobra.

A man knelt before her, backed by a Razan brother. He was weeping helplessly. Maguda's head never moved as her eyes slanted down towards him. Her voice a sibilant whisper, questioning, probing.

"Why did ye hold back the necklace which was with the loot from Port Vendres? Tell me, Luiz."

Always keeping his eyes averted from her, Luiz sobbed. "Madame Razan, it was naught but a cheap trinket. I knew my woman liked such things, it was worthless!"

Maguda Razan's voice sounded reasonable. "Worthless or not, it belonged to the Razan. Where is this necklace now?"

Her brother held it up. It was indeed a cheap thing: small beads woven on several strands to represent a snake.

One of Maguda's incredibly long-nailed fingers moved, pointing. "Put it on his neck, hold up his head, so I can see him."

Fastening the necklace on Luiz, the brother seized a handful of the man's hair and pulled his head back. Luiz found himself staring directly into the eyes of Maguda.

Her voice was like a sliver of ice sliding across oiled silk. "Look at me, gaze long at my eyes . . . long . . . long . . . long! I will not hurt thee, Luiz. The snake which ye stole from me is brightly coloured. Did ye know that such snakes are always deadly? Was it not one such snake that took the life of Egypt's queen long long ago? Can ye feel it, thief, pulling its coils tight around thy worthless neck? Seeking out a vein. A place to sink small fangs into . . ."

Both of Maguda's hands rose, fingers curved like claws, her voice rising to a shriek. "Thou art dead! Dead!"

Blood suffused the man's face as he clapped a hand to the side of his throat, gurgled horribly and fell over sideways. His legs kicked convulsively, and his back arched. Then he went limp. Lifeless.

Maguda's voice rang out, flat and callous. "Take yon necklace off him, give it to his woman!"

The brother reached out, then hesitated. Her tone turned to one of contempt. "It won't bite thee, 'tis only a cheap necklace. Take it off!"

Gingerly the brother obeyed. Maguda watched him scathingly. "See his neck, there's not a mark on it. Imagination, 'tis all it was, yon fool died because of his own stupid imagination!"

Her brother took the necklace and slunk off, murmuring under his breath, "Imagination, and those eyes of yours, sister, that's what the man died from!"

Much to his surprise, her voice followed him, echoing around the cavern and its surrounding passages. "Aye, thou art right, brother, but beware, mine ears are as sharp as mine eyes. Nothing escapes Maguda Razan!" He broke into a run, dashing past the eldest of his brothers, who was on his way to see Maguda.

She watched the man enter her cavern, noting the flicker of fear in his eyes as he skirted the spot where the dead thief lay. Her voice halted the eldest brother even before he reached the throne. "Tell me of thy visit to Veron market fair. What news of Comte Bregon? Think hard and speak true, Rawth!"

The eldest brother of the Razan, Rawth, made his report. "I never saw the old man, they say he never leaves the house."

Maguda let out a hiss of exasperation. "I know that, but did any come or go from there, new faces, strangers?"

Rawth shook his head. "Only some young 'uns, who were arrested for not paying their toll and for unlicensed trading."

Maguda's fingernails rattled as she smote the throne arm. "Tell me of them! Didst thou not hear me say I want to hear all?"

Rawth had not heard his sister say any such thing, but he was not prepared to argue – he had seen what happened to any who contradicted Maguda. "I saw three of them being led off by the guards. They are probably in the dungeons now. Two of them were boys, one about fourteen summers, light-haired, blue-eyed, the other about the same age, handsome, Spanish-looking. The girl looked older than the boys, but not by much – she was of gypsy blood, I think. A pleasant singer she was, I heard her sing. She was on the house steps, drumming up trade for the Spanish boy to make likenesses of folk."

He stood silent as Maguda mused aloud. "A facemaker, eh? What of the other boy, the blue-eyed one?"

Rawth shrugged. "Oh, him, he did little but stand around with his dog –"

Maguda interrupted her brother. "Dog? Ye said nothing of a dog. What manner of animal was it, tell me!"

Rawth described Ned. "Of the breed they call Labrador. A big creature, black 'twas. Why do ye ask?"

She silenced him with a wave of her hand. "A black dog, that could be an omen. Send watchers to wait outside the wall of Veron until these young ones are released. I need to know more about them, which direction they go in. Leave me now, I need to be alone, to think."

When Rawth had departed, Maguda took up a staff and rose from her throne. Leaning heavily on the staff, she visited each of the stone idols around the cavern's edge, throwing coloured incense upon the fires at the feet of the statues and muttering to herself as the smoke billowed up to thicken beneath the high ceiling. After a while she went back to the throne. Using a human skull on the seat beside her as a centrepiece, Maguda Razan cast bones, pebbles and striped stone fragments over the grisly crown of the skull. Watching which way they fell, she chanted in a high, singsong voice.

"Earth and water, wind and fire,
Speak to me as I desire.
Take mine eyes beyond this place,
Show to me each stranger's face.
Spirits of the deep and dark,
This Razan hath served thee true,
Open up their hearts to me,
Say what secrets I may see,
I who bind my life to you!"

She sat awhile, contemplating the skull and its surrounding jumble of rocks and bone, her eyes closed, swaying slightly. Then Maguda Razan emitted a low moan, building up into a shriek like that of a stricken animal. It echoed round the bowels of the mountain and its caves, bringing Razan tribal members, both male and female. They halted at the cavern entrance, watching fearfully as Maguda arose from the steps where she had fallen from her throne. There was vexation and rage in her voice as she screeched at them.

"Go, all of ye! Seek out those who were imprisoned at Veron. Capture them, the two boys, one dark, one fair, the girl and the black dog. Bring them back here to me, I command ye!"

Staggering back up to the throne, she seated herself, waiting until the clatter of departing feet retreated into silence. Petulance and ill temper showed in her sneer. Unable to bear looking upon her equipment of sorcery, Maguda swept it away. Skull, stones and bones tumbled down the stairs. Landing upright, the skull lay grinning sightlessly up at her. Maguda spat at it. Her vision had been thwarted. She had been granted a glimpse of the *Flying Dutchman* – but only a glimpse. The sight of evil she delighted revelling in had been cut short. The fair-skinned boy, he who owned the black dog – she would see all of the *Dutchman* in his eyes. Maguda Razan quivered with anticipation. She would bring the boy under her power when she had him alone, and then . . . *then.*

Rain began falling from an overcast sky on the afternoon of the fair's end. Folk began packing up stalls and wares to leave early before a downpour set in. Hidden beneath hooded cloaks and equipped with packs of food, Ben and his friends stood at the grilled gate by the tunnel door.

Comte Vincente Bregon gave Ned a final pat, and kissed Karay's cheek and embraced the two boys. "Go now, young friends, this rain will provide cover for you. Garath, take them as far as the gates – you know what to do. Nobody must know you were my guests and not prisoners. Let us hope when we meet again the sun will be shining and we will be smiling. May the Lord protect and keep you from harm!"

Not many people lingered to see them marched to the gates by the good blacksmith, though the few who were witness to the scene saw Garath crack his whip over the heads of the freed prisoners and warn them sternly, "Gypsies, thieves, be off with you! Thank your lucky stars my master was in a lenient mood. Go on, get out of Veron! If you are ever seen within the walls again, you will be tied to a cart and whipped all the way to the Spanish border!"

Ned barked as Garath cracked the whip several times, then the big black dog hurried out of the village in the wake of his companions.

Ben squinted his eyes against the increasing rain as he looked towards the mountains. "We'd best cut off southeast through the forested slopes. It'll give us some protection from this weather!"

Thunder rumbled in the distance as they squelched off across the grassy slopes outside the walls of Veron. Dominic looked back at the remainder of the market traders setting off in other ways to go to their homes.

Karay called out to him, "Come on, Facemaker, keep up! Don't be lagging behind!"

As he caught up with the others, the girl gave him a scathing glance. "What were you gaping at those bumpkins for – fresh faces to sketch? You might as well draw pictures of turnips as of those tight-fisted clods!"

Dominic noticed that Ned was watching the departing traders, too. "You'd do well to take a lesson from Ned and me. Take a peek at those folk yourself, see how many are watching us, and then tell me: how many of them are ordinary people, and how many are Razan spies, watching which way we're headed?"

Ned passed Ben a thought. "Wide awake, mate, that's me and Dominic. Bet you never thought of that!"

Ben answered his friend's message aloud. "Good thinking, Dominic. Perhaps we'd best go another way, just to mislead them."

On Ben's advice, they cut off at a tangent that led away from the forested mountain foothills. It was late afternoon before the coast was clear. Lightning flashes lit the gloomy landscape, and thunder boomed closer, as Karay halted at a swollen stream that threaded its way out of the woods and the high country.

"I don't know if we'd leave much trail in the rain, but no one would be able to track us through running water. Let's wade through this stream, up into the woods."

The three friends went knee-deep in the icy cold waters, holding hands to stay upright.

Ned followed, grumbling thoughtfully. "Huh, rained on from above and soaked from below. I've seen better days for trekking. At least the rain forests in South America were warm. What d'you say, mate?"

Ben gripped the black Labrador's collar, assisting him. "Aye, nice muddy rivers full of snakes, with all manner of insects biting and stinging and tickling. Piranha fish, too. Oh for the good old days. Would you trade them for this?"

Ned looked mournfully up at his friend. "Point taken!"

At twilight, hauling themselves gratefully out of the stream, they entered the trees. Karay sat down and examined her feet. "Just look at these toes, they're blue and numb from the cold, and wrinkled like raisins!"

Dominic chuckled. "Well, it was your idea. Up you come, m'lady, let's find somewhere warm and dry. Steady on, Ned, d'you have to shake yourself all over us?"

Ned actually winked at Ben. "Bet you wish you could dry yourself like this. Us hairy old dogs have an advantage over you pale, thin-skinned humans. Superior breeding, y'know."

Ben tweaked his dog's ear. "Oh, I see, then I don't suppose a superior creature like you will bother sitting around a warm fire – built by us measly humans of course?"

Apart from the constant spatter of rainfall on the treetop canopy, the forest was silent and depressingly gloomy, thickly carpeted in loam and pine needles. Hardly any rain penetrated the arboreal thickness. It was Ned who found a good spot to make camp for the night. He bounded off through the trees and returned with his tongue lolling as he passed on the message to Ben. "Haha, at least we'll be dry until morning, I've found a great place! Follow me, O weakly fellow, I'll show you. Oh, and if you humans make a fire, I may do you the honour of sitting by it."

It was a deep cleft in a big rocky outcrop. Ben patted his dog affectionately. "Well done, mate. It's practically a cave!"

Dominic found some dry, dead pine needles, and setting

flint to the steel of his knife, he coaxed a fire into life by blowing gently on the tinder. He peered at the rock walls. "Artists were here long before us. Look!"

Crude representations of dancing people were drawn upon the rough rock walls in black, red and ochre, stick-legged men, women and children dancing around what appeared to be a fire.

Karay piled dead wood on the flames, commenting, "I saw a cave like this once, in the D'Aubrac Mountains. A gypsy woman said the drawings were more than a thousand years old, done by tribes who were shepherds and charcoal burners. They used to live in places like these."

As evidence they found a heap of charcoal at the cave's narrow end. Ben and Karay piled it on the fire. It gave out a good heat and glow once it began burning. Dominic spread their cloaks on nearby rocks to dry out. Warmth seeped through their bodies, steam rising from their hair. Ben opened one of the sacks and doled out bread, smoked ham and cheese, and also a flask of pale wine laced with water.

As they ate, Dominic pointed to the wall drawings in the flickering glow. "See how the shadows play across those pictures – you'd think the people were actually dancing!"

A noise at the entrance caused Ned to stiffen, and his hackles rose as he growled. Ben passed him an urgent thought. "What is it, Ned, what's out there?"

Glowering towards the entrance and baring his teeth, Ned replied, "A wild boar. The scent of our food must have attracted it. Maybe it lives here now, who knows? I'll chase it!"

Karay whispered to Ben, "Something's upsetting Ned!"

Ben caught a glimpse of narrow, savage eyes at the entrance. "I think it's a wild boar, Ned'll send him on his way."

"No, keep hold of him!" Dominic hissed. "Have you seen the tusks on those things? That boar would injure a dog badly. Better leave it to me."

He chose a thick burning pine branch from the fire and dashed towards the entrance, shouting, "Yaaaah! Gerroutofit!"

The boar grunted and snorted, half turning. When Dominic was quite close to the beast, he lashed out, striking it several hard blows with the flaming brand. The boar squealed and ran off, leaving behind an acrid smell of burnt hair. Dominic flung the blazing wood after it, still shouting, "Yaaaah! That'll give you a hot bottom! Go on, leave us alone!"

Karay looked at him with a new respect. "That was a brave thing to do. I'd run a mile from a wild boar!"

The facemaker shrugged. "What I did was what the villagers used to do when the old boar wandered into our settlement in Sabada."

Ned remained awake on watch that night, wary that the boar would return. Sometime after midnight, the rain ceased. Inside the cave, the fire sank to glowing embers. Ben was awakened by his dog's quiet whimpers in the oppressive silence. He stroked the Labrador's flank. "Are you all right, mate?"

Ned licked the boy's hand. "I must have dozed off for a while, Ben. I could swear I saw the faces of Vanderdecken and his crew out there among the trees, watching us."

The boy scratched the soft fur under his dog's chin. "It's just tiredness, Ned. Have a sleep. I'll keep watch. Though I'm sure Vanderdecken couldn't follow us here – he's bound to the seas by heaven's curse. But I know what you mean, I was having a few dreams like that myself before you woke me. Go on, take a nap, try to dream of more pleasant things."

Ned settled his chin on his front paws, letting his eyes

close. "Just as you say, Ben, but I don't like this area, and I feel there's more to come before we find the Razan. Oh, there's no use trying to think different, mate. Don't forget, I can read your thoughts, and they tell me you're thinking the same thing. You're scared – me too! We both are. These forests and mountains – there's an eerie feel about them. It's like something we've never come across."

Ben watched the black Labrador as sleep overcame him. He knew, with an awful sense of foreboding, that Ned was right.

20

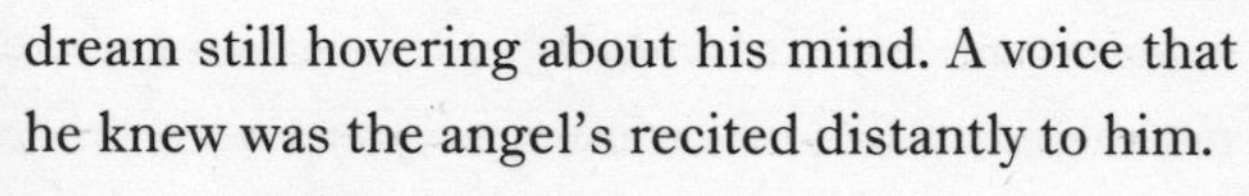

DAWN'S FIRST FEEBLE LIGHT CREPT INTO THE cave as Ned lay on guard near the entrance. The black Labrador was in a peculiar state of semiwakefulness, with snatches of dream still hovering about his mind. A voice that he knew was the angel's recited distantly to him.

> " 'Tis thou who must show the way,
> when visions of evil arise.
> Others may see what ye cannot,
> So be guided by thine own eyes."

Another voice chimed in. "Who's that? Come forward and be recognized!"

Ned woke immediately, knowing that the second voice was no dream. Thankfully, it was far enough away for only a dog to hear. Ben, Karay and Dominic were still asleep. Ned slipped out to investigate as yet another voice reached his ears.

"Put up your club, 'tis only me – Cutpurse the clown!"

Shuffling through the undergrowth on his stomach, Ned moved noiselessly forward until he found the source of the voices.

A group of ten men, clad in gypsy rags, all well armed with clubs, knives and muskets, were watching a man emerge from the trees. With the group were a ferocious-looking mastiff dog and a brown bear, both wearing spiked collars and long iron-chain leashes to restrain them. Ned's gaze settled on the fellow who was joining them. It was the fat rogue who had imprisoned Karay. He limped miserably out of the tree cover, leaning heavily on a home-made crutch. The leader of the band, a mean-faced villain with a marked squint, sneered mockingly at the newcomer. "Hah, what happened to you, Cutpurse?"

Wincing as he laid aside his crutch, he leaned against a tree and related his tale bitterly. "I thought I'd struck lucky last week. I captured a young girl – a singer she was, with a good voice. But she had us both taken by the constables, for stealin'. We broke out o' prison together an' stole a cart. Then d'ye know what the young hussy did? She stole the cart an' ran away from me!"

Ligran Razan, the group's leader and the second eldest brother of Maguda, sniggered scornfully at Cutpurse's plight. "Broke your leg, too, did she, ye fat greasy fool!"

Cutpurse pouted sulkily. " 'Twas my ankle, not the leg. I fell and broke it when I was chasin' her."

Ligran eyed Cutpurse with disgust. "How you ever came to be part of the Razan, I'll never know. Pick up that crutch an' let's get going. Better shift yourself, we aren't stoppin' for any who don't keep up. Stop pullin' faces and whining! Come on, blubbernose!"

Ligran headed off, leaning backwards against the iron chain he was grasping as the dog pulled on it, straining forward.

Three others flung more chains around the bear. They dragged the wretched creature along with them, striking it with long sticks as it made piteous, muted noises of distress.

Ned waited until the coast was clear, then dashed back to the cave and nosed Ben into wakefulness. The dog imparted his mental message of all he had witnessed. Ben thought about it for a moment before answering. "Don't wake Karay or Dominic. Let's go outside, I've got an idea. Don't worry, mate, I'll give you full credit."

Karay and Dominic sat up rubbing their eyes as Ned and Ben dashed back into the cave and roused them.

Dominic looked bewildered. "Where have you two been?"

Ben cautioned the facemaker, "Keep your voice down. Ned heard noises a short while ago, so I went with him to see who it could be. We saw a gang of men – I think they're probably from the Razan tribe, rough-looking and all well armed. They had a dog and a bear with them. Oh, and guess who joined them, Karay? That fat greasy one whose ankle you whacked with his own club – he was limping heavily."

The girl gritted her teeth angrily. "I should've killed him when I had the chance. It was you who stopped me!"

Ben held up his hand. "Don't shout, sound can carry from here. What's done is done. I'm glad you never slew the villain."

Karay stuck out her lip defiantly. "He deserved to die, the slimy rat. Why should you be glad he's alive?"

Ben explained. "Because he's travelling with the others now. He's injured and bound to slow them down a bit. That'll make it easier for us to follow them. Where else would they be headed for but the Razan hideout?"

Dominic agreed. "Right! I'll wager they can lead us to Adamo. As soon as we've had breakfast, we'll pick up their trail."

It was too dangerous to light a new fire. They broke their fast with some fruit and cheese before leaving the cave.

The previous night's heavy rain had ceased, and the sun came out, turning the forested slopes into a dense area of steamy mist as it heated the saturated ground and trees. The friends went in single file, with Ned leading. It was not a difficult trail to follow. A dog, a bear and eleven men left plenty of tracks. It was not more than an hour before Ned heard the band up ahead. He halted and passed Ben the information. "We'd best slow down, I can hear them. Let's not get too close, mate."

Ben pointed to the dog. "Look at Ned's ears – he must be able to hear them!"

Karay's voice dropped to a whisper. "Mist and fog can deaden sound. We must be very close to them. Let's stop awhile."

Ned passed another message to Ben. "Stay here, I'll go ahead and see what they're up to. Be back soon."

Before the boy had a chance to argue, his dog had vanished into the mist. Ned moved through the trees like a dark, silent shadow. When he saw the men, he cut off left and crept along on the same course as the band, watching and listening.

Ligran Razan looked back over his shoulder. "Where's that useless bag of blubber Cutpurse, lagging behind, is he? Bring him up front here, I'll move him!"

Two of the men dragged Cutpurse forward, stumbling and pleading. "Ow-ow-ow! Be careful of my poor ankle, will you? Ligran, leave me here to rest a bit, I'll catch up with you later."

A thin, cruel smile hovered about the villain's face. "I ain't leavin' you anywhere, fatty. If anybody found you they'd soon have you blabberin' where our hideout is. This'll stop ye dawdlin' – Gurz can help you to keep in front."

Ligran took the end of the chain on which he was holding the mastiff. Grabbing Cutpurse roughly, he hooked the chain through the fat man's belt and secured it. "Hahaha, just try stoppin' Gurz, an' he'll have ye for lunch. Hup, Gurz, hup, go on, boy, off with ye!"

Cutpurse only had time to grab the chain when he was hauled forward, hopskipping, limping and staggering as the big mastiff dragged him along in its wake. "Howwoooh! No, please, let me go, let me go, I'll keep up!"

Ligran nodded. "Oh, you'll keep up all right – Gurz'll make sure o' that! Come on, you lot. Let's go, see if ye can't make that thing move faster!"

The three men who were holding the bear's chains jogged forward, tugging the animal along. Its collar had spikes both inside and out, and the bear made choking noises as the spikes dug into its neck. Others followed behind, striking out with whippy branches at the pitiful creature, forcing it into a fast shamble.

Ned had seen enough. He ran off, not daring to try and make mental contact with the bear, lest it unwittingly betray his presence to the men.

By midday the mists had cleared, and the sun was beating down on the mountain slopes. There was a slight dip at the woodland edge, giving way to a small valley. Behind this, the snow-capped peaks stood like massive sentinels. Ben and his friends hid in the tree fringes, watching the Razan band below in the valley. They had camped by a clear mountain lake and lit a fire. Two of the men were cooking up oatmeal and maize porridge in a cauldron over the flames. It was served out to the members of the robber band as they sat about, eating and calling out to one another. Ben could hear them clearly from where he lay hidden.

The fat Cutpurse lay exhausted near the lake shallows, his injured foot immersed in the water. He was still chained to Gurz, the big mastiff, evidently terrified of the ferocious brute, which sat growling by his side. Ligran took a ladle of the steaming mush from the cauldron. He slopped half of it on the ground and watched Gurz lap it up.

Stirring Cutpurse with a light kick, Ligran grinned. "I'd better feed him or he'll eat that ankle o' yours. What's the matter, Cutpurse, got no bowl with ye? Oh, well, you'll just have to eat yours the way it comes."

He poured the other half of the porridge from the ladle straight onto the fat man's jerkin. The rest of the robbers guffawed at the look on Cutpurse's face. Ligran smiled. "Stop moanin' and eat it up before it gets cold!"

Cutpurse was about to dip his fingers in the warm porridge when Gurz snarled at him. He pulled his hand back and lay terror-stricken. Having finished his own portion, the mastiff stood over the frightened man and began lapping up the porridge that lay in a glutinous puddle on the thief's stomach.

Ligran was laughing uproariously at the spectacle, when one of the bear's handlers called out, "Ligran, d'ye want me to feed this thing?"

The leader went and refilled the ladle from the cauldron.

"He's supposed to be a dancin' bear, let's see him dance for his supper. Come on, bear, dance! Up off your hunkers an' dance!"

Ben turned away from the scene below. "I can't watch any more of this. What makes those people so cruel and callous?"

Dominic turned to face him. "They're Razan. Murder, thieving, cruelty and wickedness is a way of life to them. That's how they've become so strong and feared by ordinary folk."

Karay watched for a moment, then she, too, turned away, brushing a hand across her moist eyes. Her voice quivered as she spoke. "Oh, that poor bear! If I get even the slightest chance I'm going to free him. I promise I will!"

Listening to the bear's muted sounds of anguish, Ned looked at Ben. "I'll free him, too, if I can, the poor old thing!"

It was noon before the Razan broke camp and moved on. Ben and his friends had to stay where they were hidden until the Razan left the valley and circled away out of sight around the mountain's base. On reaching the lake, they stood at its edge, looking up at the mighty rocks ahead of them.

Dominic shaded his eyes against the sun. "They went off around that jagged bit up there – we'd best follow right now. If we lose sight of them, it'll be difficult tracking over bare rock."

It was not too hard mounting the side of the valley. By mid-afternoon they had reached the jagged rock that Dominic had pointed out. Loose rock scree dotted with growths of avens and horseshoe vetch seemed to spread all over the area.

Karay shrugged as she looked around. "Which way now?"

Ned took a good sniff around, then passed Ben a thought. "Follow me, I could smell that big stinky mastiff a mile off!"

The black Labrador trotted off into the larger shale, which

looked like the up-jutting teeth of some dead primeval monster. The others followed him, leaping from crag to crag. Ned paused, his ears rising.

Ben heard the dog's thought. "Aye, that's them, up a bit and to the right!"

Night fell swiftly in the high places as late afternoon, twilight, then dusk followed one another in fast succession. The scree and shale gave way to smooth, unyielding rock. Laboriously, they trekked up a winding path, feeling carefully for safe places to set their feet. A wind sprang up, harsh and chilling.

Cupping her hands, Karay blew warmth into them and sniffed. "We'd better look for somewhere to shelter. I'll bet that lot of villains ahead of us have made camp by now."

The best they could find was a dry bracken bed beneath an overhanging rock. It was not at all comfortable, being open to the winds on both sides. Karay sat down dejectedly. "This'll have to do, I suppose. There're no caves round about."

Dominic took out his knife and began cutting bracken. "I'll show you what hunters do up in the high places. Gather as much bracken as you can, and pile it up against the rock here." By the time they had gathered enough bracken, their hands were numb with cold. Dominic lit the bracken, directing them to sit facing the blaze, close together, with their cloaks around them forming a shelter. Ned squidged in between Ben and Karay as the facemaker explained: "With the rock overhanging us and our cloaks acting as a shield, the firelight glow will be hidden."

Ben warmed his hands gratefully. "I shouldn't think even the Razan would be out on a night like this. We're pretty safe here. Wait while I dig some food out."

They ate cheese and some of the ham with a loaf of bread. Dominic broke open the loaf, then toasted it over the fire and divided it into four. It tasted very good.

Night closed in around the four figures crouched around their fire on the bleak mountainside. The bracken did not last long, as it was brittle and burned quickly.

Dominic tossed his toasting twig into the embers. "We're in for a cold night. 'Tis a pity there isn't any wood hereabouts – all the forestland's far below us now."

Karay shivered. "My back is freezing. That wind seems to go right through these cloaks!"

Ben rose and trampled the fire embers flat, until the spot was just a warm patch of ground. "There's nothing more to burn, mates, so let's sit on the ground with our backs against the rock. It might help a bit."

When they had settled themselves and huddled together, Ned climbed over Ben and lay in front of Karay. "There! That'll keep her warm. Ben, I can hear somebody coming this way. Quick, tell our pals to duck under the cloaks and keep very still!"

Ben whispered to the other two, "Someone's coming. Let's throw the cloaks over our heads and keep quiet!"

Ned shuffled back and got under the front of Karay's cloak. A moment later, the tap of a staff end hitting the rock became audible. Ned had been right – someone was coming. Ben peeked through an open fold of his cloak, covering his mouth so that his breath would not mist out into the open.

It was an old woman, bent almost double – whether it was from old age or the heavy jumble of tattered shawls, scarves and blankets draped across her back, Ben could only guess. She leaned for support on a tall pole from which the bark had been peeled, making the wood appear stark white. She halted not far from where the travellers lay hidden, then slowly she turned until she was facing them.

Ben caught his breath, then immediately relaxed. The old crone was blind. She wore a dark strip of cloth bound about her eyes. He caught Ned's thought. "She can't see us, mate, though I've never seen a woman who looked more like a witch in my life!"

Ben stared at the old one. He had to agree with the dog: her face was like a bundled-up and creased parchment with hairs sprouting from odd bumps all over it. Above her shrunken, toothless mouth a hooked nose practically touched an uptilted chin. Truly the image of a witch. When she spoke, her voice was wheezy and shrill. "Are ye friend or enemy?"

They kept silent, scarcely daring to breathe. She swung the staff. Ben felt the whoosh of air as it whipped by, inches from his face.

The hag took a pace forward, calling out, "I am Gizal, friend of the Razan. I know ye are there. Speak."

The friends held their silence. Gizal cackled nastily. "A touch of my staff can turn folk into bats, toads or worms. So, my children, if ye speak not, I will cast a great spell on thee. 'Tis the last chance I'll give you. Now speak!"

Dominic felt Karay's hand grasp his beneath the cloaks. The hag took another pace forward and grasped the staff tight in both her clawlike hands, swinging out as hard as she could. *Thock!* The wooden pole struck the rock, sending a shock through the hag's body and stinging her hands into numbness. She fell backwards, letting go of the staff and wailing with pain. "*Nnnnnyyyaaahhh! Yeeeeeeehhh!*"

Ben clasped his hand over those of Dominic and Karay, urging them to remain quiet.

Gizal rolled about, clutching her clenched fists to her mouth in agony and making a noise as if she were humming. "*Mmmmmmmm!*"

After a while she pulled herself up onto her knees and started crawling about, arms outstretched as she searched for her fallen staff. It had dropped between Ben and Karay, one end up against the rock, the other end on the ground. Gizal blundered forward, her hands grasping the air as she came closer to them. Ned took a chance. Poking his head from the cloak, he butted the pole outward. It toppled, striking the old woman's shoulder. Instinctively she grabbed it. Slowly she hauled herself upright, hissing viciously through her shrivelled lips.

"I curse thee to the pit of Eblis and the fires of the damned! Ravens shall pick over thy bones and maggots devour thy flesh whilst thou art still alive and praying for death!"

She shuffled laboriously off into the night, still muttering the direst of curses and predicting unthinkable ends for the four companions.

They waited quite a while before anyone ventured to speak. It was Ben who finally broke the silence. "Whew! She's got a very nasty mouth on her for an old lady."

Karay sounded nervous. "She looked just like a witch – maybe she can really curse folk."

Dominic laughed. "You don't believe in all that old rubbish, do you? Huh, I wish we had some of those hellfires she was raving about here right now. At least we could get warm from them, eh, Ben?"

The boy stood up, stamping life back into his cold feet. "Aye, right, Dom. Don't worry about some old biddy's curses, Karay.

I've been cursed at much worse than that, and look, I'm still here. Ned, too!"

The dog's thoughts cut in on Ben. "We may be here, but I think we'd be better off somewhere else. That old Gizal is bound to run into the Razan gang up ahead. No matter how quiet we kept, she knew we were here. If she tells the Razan, I'll bet they'll send men to search us out. I don't think they take kindly to being followed."

Ben mentally thanked Ned and suggested to his friends that they needed to find somewhere else for the remainder of the night. They broke camp hurriedly.

Further up the mountain, Ligran Razan sat beneath a canvas awning, cooking goat meat over a fire and listening to Gizal's story. He gave her wine and a few of the roasted goat ribs to pick on as he weighed the situation. Gizal was respected among the Razan hierarchy – it was not considered wise to ignore her words. Ligran kicked out at a man lounging nearby. "Rouge, you an' Domba take Gurz. Track back down the mountain an' see if ye can capture whoever 'twas hidin' out there."

Gizal butted in. "There'd be two, mayhap three, and a dog. I'm sure I could smell dog. Look ye for young ones, their breathing was gentle, not noisy like grown folk."

Rouge, a big redheaded ruffian, clasped the chain to the mastiff's collar. "Gurz'll sniff 'em out, never fret, Gizal. Me an' Domba will give the brats a good slappin' before we drag 'em back here. If they've got a dog, so much the better, look at Gurz there. Eh, boy, 'tis a long time since you had a whole dog to yerself for dinner, eh?"

Domba jerked the lead, coaxing a snarl from the big ugly mastiff. Both men picked up their long knives and set off, with Gurz sniffing noisily at the ground as he tugged them along.

Gizal gulped wine greedily, falling into a fit of coughing before she turned her face to Ligran. "So then, how is thy bear behaving himself on his way home?"

Ligran took a burning piece of pinewood from the fire. He threw it at the bear, who was bound to a rock by iron chains. The animal gave a frightened moan as the burning wood bounced off its paw.

Ligran chuckled. "I've a feeling ye took all the runnin' out o' that one. I'm teaching him to dance now. Maguda will enjoy that – she's never had a dancin' bear to amuse her."

21

BEN KNEW HE HAD PICKED THE WRONG direction to search for a camp. The path he had chosen narrowed as it rose. Now they were on a high ledge. Above them was only the cold night sky. At their backs was smooth rock towering upwards. With his back against the rock, Ben saw only space and a stomach-churning drop to the forest below if they missed a single footing. Spreading his arms wide against the rock face, he touched Dominic's fingers. "Maybe we'd better go back and look in a different direction?"

The facemaker inched forward until he was clasping Ben's hand. "No, press on. I think we'll find someplace up ahead, maybe a cave or a deep rift. Don't look down, though, just keep your face level with the side of these rocks, and don't try to walk. Shuffle sideways – not too fast, nice and easy does it."

Obediently, Ben kept his gaze level, though every now and again his eyes would stray to the sickening drop from the ledge. He called out, "Are you all right, Karay? Can you manage?"

The girl answered, trying not to show the fear she felt, "I'm fine, I'm holding on to Dominic's other hand and Ned's ear!"

The dog's thoughts entered Ben's mind. "I'm not complaining, but she's got a grip like a vice for such a pretty, slim girl. You just push on ahead, Ben. I think there must be a touch of mountain goat in my family, I'm doing rather well. Go easy and look after yourself!"

Ben returned the Labrador's thoughts. "Thanks, Ned, I will. I don't suppose there's any indication of those Razan following us, is there?"

Ned's reply was not a cheerful one. "I was hoping you wouldn't ask that, mate. Now don't go telling Karay or Dominic, no sense in frightening them into a wrong move, but I've just this moment heard that big slobbering mastiff. He's got a bark like a bull with colic. There're two men with him, and they're just debating whether or not to follow us out onto this ledge."

The one named Domba made the mastiff's chain fast to a low spur of rock. He peered apprehensively up the narrow winding ledge, then chanced a glance below. Looking away swiftly, he threw a hand over his eyes. "No use clamberin' about here, they wouldn't dare take this route, I'm sure of it!"

Rouge, the big redheaded robber, snorted scornfully. "This is the trail Gurz has sniffed out, we go this way."

Domba tried another excuse. "It could be just a decoy trail.

Take Gurz an' have a look. I'll wait here an' keep my eyes open for them in case they've gone another way."

Rouge shook his head in disgust. "You're scared, Domba. That's the true reason y'don't want to go – you've got no stomach for it. Look, your legs are shakin', you gutless worm!"

Domba tried to push past Rouge, desperate to be back on safer ground. "Call me what ye like, I'm not goin'!"

Rouge grabbed Domba's collar and whipped out his knife. "Oh yes ye are. Now get goin', or I'll slay ye myself. Come on, loose that chain from the rocks an' follow Gurz. I'll be right behind, don't even think of turnin' back!"

Domba undid the chain and wound it about his wrist. Gurz took a sniff at the path and gave a gruff bark. Then he was away, straining at the chain lead as he dragged the terrified man out along the narrow mountain ledge.

Ben and his party heard the mastiff's bark. Karay gave a sob of dismay. "It's the Razan, they've found us! What do we do now?"

Dominic squeezed her hand reassuringly. "Don't be afraid, keep going at a steady pace, don't try to hurry. They can only go at the same rate as us. See anything up ahead, Ben?"

Dawn was beginning to streak the sky as Ben peered ahead. His reply carried a note of hope. "Aye, there's a slight bend, let's get round it. There may be some place better there, perhaps a crack to hide in!"

Suddenly, Ben's feet skidded on the rock. As Dominic pulled him back from the brink, he half slipped, then steadied himself. "Whooh! Thanks, Dom. Be very careful, there's ice on the ledge. Water from high up has trickled down and frozen in the night." With painstaking care the four travellers shuffled hand in hand around the icy bend, which shone dully in day's first pale light.

Ben's heart sank when he saw where they were. The narrow ledge gave way to a broad, sloping slide of bare rock dotted with pockets of shale. There was no further path between the snow-clad peaks above and the ground far, far below. Dominic sized up the situation. Behind them the mastiff set up a series of deep, baying barks. The hunters were hot on their trail now.

The facemaker came to a swift decision. "Let me get in front of you, Ben. There's a crack in the rock face, I can reach it! We'll go upwards, I can see a deep pocket of shale there. The rock must have fallen down and filled a big crevasse. If we can make it onto the shale we're safe!"

Ben glanced up at the route his friend had indicated. It was an extremely slim chance and very risky, but he knew they had to take it. He spoke his thoughts aloud. "There's no guarantee that shale won't slide if we get to it. As for going up there, I'll do that. I've had some experience at climbing ships' rigging. Right, take your cloaks off and give them to me. Don't ask questions, there's no time!"

Ben took Dominic's knife and slit the three wide-skirted cloaks through their back seams from top to bottom. Knotted together, the six pieces made a makeshift rope. Taking one end between his teeth, Ben had Dominic hold the other. With a small skip and a jump, he launched himself out above the crack in the rock's sheer face.

For one heart-stopping moment, Ben's cold hands slid down the icy surface. Then he caught the crack and hung there. Ned's thoughts were crowding in on him as he did – the dog praying, "Oh please, lovely angel, don't let my Ben fall. Keep him safe, let him live, and I promise to be a much better Ned in the future. Honest I will!"

Hand over hand, Ben moved along the fissure until it became broader and deeper, then levered himself up and found that he could wedge his feet in and stand upright. The mastiff's snuffling and baying seemed quite close now – and he could hear Rouge urging and threatening Domba along.

"Don't stand still, fool, you'll freeze with fright. Keep goin', they can't be far ahead!"

Dominic tied the cloak end around Karay's waist, instructing her, "Try to climb. Ben'll pull you up if you slip."

The girl ventured gingerly out. She had not gone more than a few feet when she slipped. Ben braced himself. "Hang on, mate. Wait until you've stopped swinging, then climb!"

Karay shut her eyes tight. She swung to and fro like a pendulum, then caught her foot on a rough spot and began attempting to climb. Ben heaved stoutly on the rope, pulling her up until he reached her with his hands. Perching in the rocky crack, she undid the cloak rope. Ben knotted a piece of rock into the end and swung it back to Dominic.

Ben called out Ned's thoughts, instructing Dominic on what to do. "Tie it round Ned, under his front legs. Give him a bit to hold on to with his teeth, then swing him out."

Dominic complied with the orders. Ned went swinging out into space, still mentally beseeching the angel, "Oooooh! Listen, good angel, do the same for me as you did for Ben, and I promise to make a better boy of him. Just don't let Dominic's hands slip, dear sweet nice angel!"

A moment later, Ben and Karay had hauled Ned up into the crack. Dominic's shout reached them, loud and urgent. "Throw the rope back, quick, they're here!"

The mastiff's ugly head poked around the bend of the ledge, followed by a white-faced Domba, then the triumphant Rouge, who snarled at his companion, "Hand that chain to me!

I'll watch Gurz, you get past the dog an' grab the lad. The others'll climb back here when they see what I do to him. Go on, move yourself, slowcoach!"

Flattening himself against the ledge wall, Domba inched past the mastiff. Dominic reached out to the swinging rope and missed it. He caught it on the second swing, at the same moment that Domba grabbed his shoulder with one hand. Seizing the rope with both hands and his teeth, Dominic swung out with Domba clinging to him. Ben and Karay, with the help of Ned's jaws, leaned back and took the strain of both bodies. The cloak made a ragged, tearing sound as Dominic spun. Domba was still clinging behind him as they hit the rock face. His head cracked against it and he let go.

"*Yeeeeeaaaaarrrrr!*"

Dominic tried not to look at the robber's body sailing through empty space. As he felt the cloak rope ripping, he babbled out a stream of entreaties. "Pull me up, Ben, pull me up pull me up don't let me fall, Ben, please please please!"

Next thing he knew, Dominic was clutching both of Ben's hands as Karay and Ned clung grimly to the shredding rope. "It's all right, Dom, I've got you, safe and sound. Up ye come!"

Rouge looked across to where the four escapees perched in the crack on the mountain face. He wagged a finger at them, as if reproving naughty children. "Done it now, ain't ye. Gone an' killed my poor friend Domba!"

Karay shouted back at the robber, "Rubbish, it was his own stupid fault, you'll get the same if you try anything!"

Rouge shook his head and laughed. "Hoho, brave words, little maid. But I ain't tryin' anything. You an' your pals are stuck there with no place to go . . . Come on, climb back over here, I won't hurt ye!"

Ben had seen the robber's type before – quite a few times. He threw back his head and laughed at Rouge. "Haha, who d'you think you're trying to fool? We know you're a Razan. We'll stay right here, thankee!"

Rouge wound the mastiff's chain around his hand as he replied, "Right then, you stay there. As for me, I'll go back to camp an' get some others. We'll be back, carryin' muskets!"

He noted the stunned silence and the anxious looks the young people exchanged. "Ain't so cheeky now, are ye?"

Ben caught Ned's thoughts in the pause which followed. "Dear angel, remember those promises I made to you? Well, er, I'm sorry, but I'm going to have to break them a bit. But it's all in a good cause, to save my friends' lives. So forgive me!"

Ned teetered on the edge of the crack, tail straight out, hackles rising and teeth bared. The black Labrador began barking, growling and snarling thunderously at Gurz. Ben took hold of his dog's collar. "Ned, what's wrong, boy?"

But Ned ignored him, rearing up on his hind legs, straining against the hand holding his collar. Foam flecked from the Labrador's mouth as he howled like a wild animal at the mastiff.

Gurz howled back and set up a series of short angry barks.

Rouge tugged on the dog's chain. "Quit that row, ye great idiot!"

Ned barked in return, roaring furiously. The rock face resounded with the noise of both dogs, then without warning Gurz took off, dragging Rouge with him. The robber's feet skidded on the ice as the huge mastiff pulled him forward. Gurz made a massive leap out into space, as though he were trying to reach the crack with a mighty bound. But he never made it. Both man and mastiff plummeted into the valley, howling the last sounds they would make on this earth. It was a long way down – they looked like two black spots crumpled on the rocky foothills.

Dominic could only shake his head in bewilderment. "What happened there?"

Ned explained mentally to Ben. "I made some nasty remarks about his parents, his mother the donkey and his father the pig. Then I challenged him to a fight, but I said that he could never jump this far, like I had!"

Ben stroked his dog's head, staring into the liquid brown eyes. "But we swung you on the rope from the ledge to here."

Ned managed a doggy look of innocence. "Aye, but he hadn't arrived to see that part. Mastiffs aren't too bright, y'know. I'm sorry I had to do it, but that redheaded rogue didn't leave us too much choice. 'Twas either that or get shot."

Ben ruffled his friend's ears. "I'm sure the angel will forgive you. I certainly do, it was a very clever idea!"

Bright morning sun began driving away the clouds and warming the air. Dominic flexed his stiff legs. "Well, friends, where to now?"

As if in answer to the question, there was a piteous call. "*Maaaahaaah!*"

Ben pointed back to the narrow ledge. "Goats!"

Two of the creatures stood staring at them across the void, shaggy-coated, cloven-hoofed and with expressions of curiosity in their odd eyes. By the difference in their sizes, they looked like a nanny goat and her little kid. The mother nuzzled her little one as it stood bleating, "*Maaah maaaaahaaah!*"

A voice from around the bend called to them. "Sissy, Paris,

what've I told you about running off like that? If I've told you once, I've told you a hundred times!"

A large, strong-looking woman clad in man's attire came around the bend. Over the rough cloak she wore was a coil of rope with an ice axe tucked into its loops. She tended to the goats, shooing them back off along the ledge, before turning her homely, weather-beaten face to the four friends. "What are ye doing out there, children? You don't look like Razan, but who can tell these days?"

Instinctively Ben knew she was friendly. He smiled at her. "No, ma'am, we're not Razan, we were just trying to escape from them. But we're stuck out here, I'm afraid."

The goatherd lady returned Ben's smile. She peered over the ledge at the three tiny figures crumpled below on the rocks. "The only good Razan's a dead 'un, you did away with them well."

Karay retorted, a little indignantly, "No, we didn't, it was their own fault. And anyway, they'd have killed us if they could have!"

The woman shrugged the rope from her shoulders. "No matter. If you stay there much longer, you'll freeze. Let's get you back to safety. Huh, you're worse than some of my goats for getting y'selves stuck in awkward places!"

She tied one end of the rope to her axe handle and began whirling the device expertly. Hurling it high over their heads, she landed the axe in a rock fissure above them. Tugging to make sure the rope would not drop, she threw it to Ben. "Tie the dog on. Give him a good hard push, away from me. I'll catch him on the backswing."

Ben heard Ned thinking as he was hurled off across the rock face, "Whoooooo! Hope the good lady has strong hands!"

He had no need to worry. The big woman caught him lightly and set him on the ledge. He sent Ben a relieved thought. "Ha-haha, she's twice as strong as Anaconda!"

Karay went next, then Dominic and finally Ben. When they were all safe, Ben held his hand out and introduced himself and his companions.

The woman shook his hand cheerily – she had a grip like a vice. Ben winced. "Thank you very much, ma'am, we're sorry to put you to any bother."

She flicked the axe from its fissure. Catching it skilfully, she wound the rope back over her shoulder.

"My name's Arnela. 'Tis no bother, lad. I've swung crevasses on the rope many a time. Aye, and with a pair of goats slung across my back. Come on, you'll want feeding. Young 'uns always do, goats or humans."

When they got off the ledge, Arnela led them on a switchback of a route through secret paths and over jumbles of rock. She gathered goats along the way, chiding each as she herded them ahead of her. "Achilles, where've you been, you badly behaved fellow! Clovis, tell that kid of yours to stay with the rest! Shame on you, Pantyro, stop acting the goat and lead the herd like I taught you to!"

Arnela stroked Ned's head absently. "Hmm, nice dog, aren't ye? I'll wager you've more sense than all these creatures."

Ben was not at all surprised when Arnela's dwelling turned out to be a cave, though it was so well concealed that nobody noticed it until she pointed it out. "There you go, straight in behind that little waterfall. See if you can do it without getting wet – I can, watch!" She rounded the corner of a rift covered with wet moss and mountain plants and vanished behind a small cataract that flowed into a pool and overspilt into a stream. Arnela patted each one's back as they came through into the cave, checking to see how wet they had got. "Ah well, you'll learn. Ned's the only dry one among ye."

She ducked outside again. They could hear her calling to the goats. "No, don't stray too far or there'll be no fodder for ye. Atlas, stop nibbling those plants, d'ye hear me?" A moment later she was back inside, waving her hand at immense piles of dried grass heaped everywhere. "Sit ye down on the goats' dinner while I get a fire going."

In a deep crevice at the back of the cave, Arnela kindled a fire from the ashes of a previous one, chatting away animatedly. "Always use charcoal, nice red glow, no smoke. This is my summer and autumn home. Winter and spring I take the herd down to the forest, got my other place there, hidden, like this one. Here, Karay, do somethin' for your living, girl, bring me that basket of eggs. You boys fetch the flour an' milk, you'll find some fresh herbs there, too, on that shelf."

The eggs were those of mountain birds, some big and speckled, others plain white. Karay handed Arnela the basket. "I thought you'd be making a stew of goat meat," the girl said.

The big woman fixed her with an icy glare. "Goat? People in their right mind don't eat goat, it makes them silly. I wouldn't dream of eating my goats, they're my children. I'll make you a special treat of mine. Mountain bread and herbs with good goat cheese, 'tis my secret recipe, you'll like it."

• • •

Arnela was right, they did like her secret recipe. The food was homely and delicious. As they ate, Dominic related their story, from the day of their arrival at the village fair up to their encounter the previous night with Gizal, the blind woman. Arnela listened intently, showing great interest whenever Adamo's name was mentioned.

When Dominic finished, the goatherd lady sat staring into the fire. "So, you have taken on a mission to save the comte's nephew. 'Tis a brave and courageous thing you do. But let me warn you, the perils and dangers of going up against the Razan could cost you your lives – they are an evil brood!"

Ben could not help remarking, "You live in these mountains, ma'am, but they don't seem to bother you. How is that?"

A baby goat wandered into the cavern, bleating piteously. The big woman took it on her lap and stroked it gently until it fell silent and dozed off in the warmth. Then she began telling the friends her own history.

"I come from Andorra, high in these mountains, between France and Spain. I knew neither mother nor father, the only life I had was that of a tavern drudge, even as a very young girl. The owner said that gypsies left me on his doorstep one night. The townsfolk were scared of me, they said I was a mountain giant. I was big, you see. Though I was only young, I was taller, broader and stronger than anybody. By the time I was ten, all the local boys had given up teasing me, because I had beaten most of them soundly for their cruel taunts and jibes. My life was not a happy one. I slept in the stables, with donkeys and mules for company. Then the day came – I must have been nearly twenty years of age. One evening in the tavern, the mayor's brother, a fat pompous lout who had been drinking overmuch, began making sport of me. I ignored him, which made his mood turn nasty. As I passed by with a trayful of food and drink he stuck out his foot, and I tripped and fell heavily – meat, ale, dishes and tankards were everywhere. The owner came running across the room and started beating me for my clumsiness. Well, I got up and laid them both out with a blow apiece, the tavern owner and the mayor's brother. The guards and constables were sent for. I fought them, but they were too many for me, and I was dragged off and thrown in prison. It was more a kind of outhouse than a real dungeon. While the mayor and the citizens' committee were meeting to plan some dreadful punishment for my crimes, I broke through the roof, which was only thatch and old timber, and escaped!"

Dominic, his parchment and charcoals before him, was drawing Arnela as she sat talking to them. He chuckled. "You've certainly led an adventurous life, my friend. What happened after that?"

Arnela stared at her strong, weather-tanned hands. "I ran away and went to live among these mountains and the forests below, knowing the townsfolk wouldn't dare follow me into Razan territory. Nobody except outlaws dwell in this region."

Karay sat with her chin cupped in both hands, her eyes shining with admiration for the brave goatherd. "But weren't you afraid of the Razan?"

The big woman scoffed. "They knew I was a fugitive from the law. Their menfolk didn't bother me, but several of the Razan women tried to intimidate me. Hah! I sent them on their way nursing bruises and broken limbs, I can tell you. Especially the ones who tried to steal my goats. The Razan tend to leave me alone these days, and that's the way I like it!"

Picking the baby goat up tenderly, Arnela laid it gently on a stack of dried grass. "I think I'll call that one Morpheus, he's done little else but sleep since he was born. Dominic, you mentioned Adamo before. Let me tell you, I know him."

Ben was immediately curious. "Tell us about him, please."

The big woman nodded her head and sighed. "Several times over the years I saw the boy, always being hauled back to the Razan caves after trying to escape. My heart warmed to him at first sight, because he was big like me, and strong, too. You only had to look at him and you knew even from behind that it was Adamo, a mountain of a young man!

"Anyhow, let me tell you. One night, about a month ago, it began to storm and rain. So, I went out to the cliffs to gather my goats in here, out of the weather. That was when I saw him – he was hiding in the rocks like a hunted animal, hungry and soaked to the skin. I brought him into this very cave, dried him and gave him food. At first I thought he was a mute because he sat by my fire half the night without saying a single word, just gazing at me with those beautiful brown eyes of his. But gradually I got him to talk. Adamo did not know who his mother or father were, but he could remember a big house where he thought he may once have lived or stayed. He could recall a kindly old gentleman and a nice old lady, but that was all. One thing he was sure of, though, he didn't belong with the Razan – their mountain caves were a prison to him. The old one, Maguda Razan, kept telling Adamo that she was his grandmother and the only kin he had living in the world. Poor Adamo, he begged her to let him go free, but Maguda refused. His hatred of being made to live in the company of robbers and murderers drove him to try to escape. He never got far – Razan men hunted him down and brought him back to the caves. Adamo was normally a quiet, lonely boy, but after he was first recaptured he refused to speak with any Razan, particularly Maguda. Many times as he grew he tried to escape and break away over the years. Each time he was brought back. Maguda threatened him with all manner of horrible things, but this did not stop Adamo.

"He told me all this that night I hid him in my cave. Came the dawn, I awoke to find he had gone. Soon after, a band of Razan came here and searched the area. Ligran Razan was their leader. He's worse than all his brothers put together, that one. A big mastiff dog he brought with him picked up Adamo's scent, and away they went, a pack of wild animals led by a wild animal! I haven't seen Adamo since, pray heaven and all the saints that the poor boy escaped this time. I haven't seen them dragging him back either, so at least that's something to keep my hopes up. Though you can never tell with the Razan – maybe they captured him and took him back by another route."

Ben felt enormous sympathy for Arnela. "Don't worry, ma'am, when we get to their hideout we'll find him, if he's there. If not, we'll scour all of France and Spain until we can return Adamo to his uncle in Veron."

Dominic presented her with his finished picture. "Thanks for your help, Arnela. I hope you like this, I did it for you in thanks for your help and hospitality."

The facemaker had portrayed Arnela in profile, sitting with the baby goat on her lap by the fire. Beauty and simplicity of heart radiated from the parchment. Every line and weather mark on the big goatherd's ruddy features caught her kindliness and strength of humanity.

Her voice was husky with reverence for the artist's skill. "Dominic, I have never seen anything like this, 'tis a wondrous thing. I will keep it on my driest wall. It will always remind me of you, my good friends. Now, is there anything I can do to help you? Just ask. Anything?"

Ned leaned his chin on Arnela's knee and gazed up at her. "This wonderful person would come with us, I know she would. But the goats are her children – what would become of them if she left the herd to go off adventuring with us?"

Ben caught Ned's thought and spoke his answer aloud. "Oh, don't trouble yourself, ma'am, we'll be all right. Though I'd like you to keep watch for us on our return. We may need to get out of these mountains pretty fast."

Arnela stroked behind Ned's ears. "I'll watch night and day for a sign of you. Now you must rest, it's safer to travel by night if you want to avoid discovery. Lie down now, children."

They lay warm and cosy on the dried grass, Ned with his eyes half closed, watching Arnela mending their torn cloaks with goat-hair twine and a large bone needle.

Just before the Labrador dropped off, he heard her gathering grass and murmuring to the goats who had strayed inside. "Hush now, Ajax, and you too, Pantyro, let the young 'uns sleep. They've got enough to contend with, or they will have soon. Come on, now, outside, all of you, have dinner out in the fresh air. Clovis, can't you do something about that kid of yours, I've never seen such bad manners. Out with you!"

Lulled by the safety of the cave and its flickering firelit shadows, Ned sent Ben a message. "I wouldn't mind being one of Arnela's goats, they certainly get the best of treatment and care from her. Hmm, maybe not, though. Goats are a pretty thick lot,

I'd never be able to put up with all that maaahing and baaaing, would you, mate?"

But his thoughts fell on deaf ears. Ben, Dominic and Karay were already soundly slumbering.

Ben had the feeling that it was evening outside when Arnela wakened them. She had bowls of vegetable soup and some bread and honey prepared for them.

"Eat plenty now, young 'uns, it might be some time before you get another good meal. Here, I've fixed up your cloaks as best as I could – needlework was never my strong point. I've packed a little food for you, and I've thrown in one of my extra ropes and an ice axe, you'll need them."

Having eaten, the four companions went outside to take their farewells of their newfound friend. It was cold. Frost glittered on the rocks, and the sky above was a vault of dark velvet, pierced by a million pinpoints of bright starlight and a pale lemon-rind slice of moon.

Arnela's formidable arms encircled their shoulders. "Go now, and take all my fondest wishes with you. Stay to the right winding paths – avoid the left ones, or you'll finish up stranded on some ledge. Lead them off, Ned, you good dog. Go on, don't look back, and tread carefully."

They trudged away with Arnela's voice fading behind them. "Come out of that water, Theseus, d'you want your hair to freeze? Narcissus, stop looking at yourself in the pool. Clovis, don't act silly, I've got your kid here with me. Come on, all inside now, that means you, too, Pantyro!"

22

NIGHT IN THE high mountains was like being stranded on some strange planet. Silence reigned. In the clear air, every sound was magnified and echoed. The travellers walked gingerly onward, keeping their voices to hushed whispers lest they betray their position to anyone in the vicinity. It was hard going, all upwards, and each pace had to be made carefully across the eerie expanses of white snow and ice and black pockets of shadow.

They had been going for two hours or more when Karay's breath plumed out like steam as she whispered to Dominic, "Hadn't we better rest awhile and catch our breath?"

Ben heard her and called a halt. He chose a spot in the deep shadows of a crag to one side of the path. No sooner had they installed themselves there than voices were heard.

Ned's ears rose as he contacted Ben. "Sounds like two men. Good job we got in here out of the way."

It was the fat rogue Cutpurse and a weaselly looking older fellow called Abrit. They shuffled by within twenty feet of where the friends were hiding. Cutpurse stopped, leaning on a staff he was using as a crutch, and scanned the ground suspiciously. "Look, there's tracks here!" There was obviously no love lost between the two men, for Abrit treated Cutpurse as if he were a half-wit. It showed in his voice. "Of course there's tracks, lard gut, they're the tracks we made on the way up. Look, there's the dog's paw prints out in front. Come on, stop slowin' me down or we'll never find Rouge an' Domba, or the dog. Now what's the matter?"

Cutpurse lowered himself painfully and sat down on the snow. "My ankle's killin' me, it's agony to walk any further. Listen, why don't we find some place where we can lay up for the night? Then tomorrow we can catch up with the rest an' tell 'em there was no sign of Rouge, Domba or Gurz. We're just killin' ourselves, blunderin' round in the dark!"

Abrit scoffed at the idea. "Hah! All right, we'll do that. But when we get back, I ain't sayin' nothin'. You tell Ligran Razan you couldn't find 'em. How does that sound to ye, eh?"

Cutpurse pouted childishly and nursed his injured ankle. "That Ligran's got it in for me – he'd slay me as soon as look at me. Cruel, that's what it is. Sendin' a man out on a search with a broken foot. Huh, just wants t'be rid of me, Ligran does!"

Abrit nodded. "Me too. I've never got on well with Ligran. So, all the more reason for findin' Rouge an' Domba. We'll be savin' our own lives by doin' the job. On your feet, fatty!"

Cutpurse began to rise. Then a thought occurred to him. "I think we're goin' the wrong way. Look, there's only tracks goin' upwards. Where's the tracks Rouge an' Domba left when they came down? I can't see any."

Abrit scratched his head. "Y'could be right there. They must've been searchin' on another path. Maybe over the side of the icefield yonder. We'd best go an' take a look!"

Ben breathed a silent sigh of relief as they watched the two robbers hobbling off over the wide, lumpy icefield, which sloped away to their left. Karay whispered, "Thank goodness our trail was mixed up with the tracks of the others."

The two robbers were about a third of the way into the icefield when Ben turned to Karay. "Do you feel rested enough to carry on now?"

The girl began making her way forward indignantly, muttering to herself, "Of course I am! It wasn't just me who needed a rest, you two were panting worse than Ned!"

To prove her point she dashed out of cover, accidentally stepping on an ice-covered bit of rock. Her feet left the ground, and she thudded backwards. An involuntary cry came from her as she fell flat on her back. "Yeek!"

The sound echoed sharply out into the surrounding peaks.

Out on the icefield, Cutpurse and Abrit halted abruptly. Cutpurse waved his staff triumphantly. "They're the ones Ligran wants – come on, let's get 'em!"

Abrit shouldered his companion to one side. "Out o' my way, ye fool, I'll stop 'em!" Pulling a musket from his belt he fired a shot across the cliffside at the girl lying on the ground. The report echoed like thunder.

Ben blinked as the musket ball pinged off the rock behind him. The two robbers were scrambling across the icefield towards them, shouting at them to halt. Then the noise started: a dull muffled sound from above, building up into one massive rumble, growing louder by the second.

Krrrraaaaaawwwwwk!

Dominic dived out and dragged Karay by her feet back under the shelter of the rock. Then he pulled Ben as deep into the shadow as possible. Ned galloped to his master's side.

Dominic's voice was almost lost in the unearthly roar. "Avalanche! Avalanche!"

Powdered snow, hard snow, sheets and columns of ice mixed with rocks, scree, shale and boulders came thundering down as a huge wedge of the mountain, disturbed by the gunshot, toppled down onto the icefield.

Cutpurse and Abrit died where they stood and were swept away by nature's irresistible force.

Ben, Ned, Karay and Dominic, bundled together in the rock's shadow, hugged one another tightly. A monstrous single wall of ice scrunched by, halting with an immense grating crack between the overhanging rock top and the path they had intended to follow. Everything went black, dark as an underground dungeon. Their eardrums reverberated with the thudding, solid waterfall of snow that pounded outside against rock and ice.

This was followed by a silence so complete that it made a ringing sound inside their heads. As rapidly as it had started, the avalanche was over.

Ben's voice sounded muffled as he spoke the words that came to him from Ned. "Is anyone hurt, are we all here?"

Their arms were still around one another as Karay and Dominic replied out of the stygian darkness.

"I bruised my shoulder when I slipped, but I'm still alive."

"More than we can say for those Razan villains, I suppose."

Ben shuddered at the thought of the two men's fate. "Nothing can have lived out there. 'Twas like the end of the world. Ned feels nice and warm, though."

The black Labrador licked Ben's hand. "That's the sweat of pure panic. I think they call it the heat of the moment."

The boy hugged his dog closer. "All we can do now is wait for daylight. Maybe the sun will reflect through all this, and we'll be able to judge our position."

Surprisingly, it was not as cold as they had expected. Their breath and body heat combined to keep the temperature above freezing in the dungeon of snow and ice.

Throughout the remainder of the night, the four friends slept fitfully. Ben was half in and half out of sleep when the dog's thoughts cut in on him. "Phew, it's getting a bit muggy in here, but I can see your face now, mate. Can you see me?"

Ben open his eyes to a blurred grey gloom. "Aye, I can see you, mate, though it's getting a bit difficult to breathe. It must be near dawn outside."

Dominic opened his eyes. "Any food? I'm famished!"

Karay's voice came from over Ned's shoulder. "Me too!"

Ned, with the limited room allowed to him, dug in the snow, which was almost knee high. Ben heard his thoughts. "I've found Dominic's facemaker satchel, anything in here?"

Dominic pulled the satchel free of the snow. "Thank you, Ned. Let's see what's left in here."

They watched as he loosed the straps and rummaged about. "A hard piece of cheese, stale heel of a loaf . . . Aha, what's this? Wine, nearly a flask of it. I'd forgotten about that!"

Karay sat up as best as she could. "I'm glad you did! Now share it out, quick, before I die of hunger!"

Dominic smiled. "Oh, what's your hurry, you'll live. Now eat slowly and don't talk for a while, or we may use up all the air in here. Proper daylight can't be too far off."

Nibbling and sipping, they bided their time. Gradually

the greyness was replaced with a golden glow that began permeating their snowy prison. Ned wagged his tail. "Looks like a nice sunny day!"

Ben pushed the offending tail away. "It might if I could see properly. Keep your tail still, mate!"

He felt around until he unearthed Arnela's ice axe. Ben poked it forward and tapped gently. "Feels like a solid block of ice trapping us in here. What d'you think, Dom?"

The facemaker took the axe from Ben, reversing it until he was holding the metal head. He probed over his shoulder with the butt of the shaft, pushing at a space above him. Loose snow showered down on them.

Karay encouraged him. "That's the way, give it a good hard shove!"

Dominic shook his head, murmuring as he probed, "Gently does it, don't want to bring the whole lot down on us." He pushed further with the haft until it slid forward easily, then withdrew it.

A golden circle of light shone down, centring between Ned's ears. The air began freshening immediately. Ben laughed. "Well done, sir. You've saved our lives!"

They took turns. Working carefully, each one widened the hole, waggling the ice axe and pulling down chunks of ice and frozen snow. As water droplets came down, Ned held out his tongue and caught a few.

Karay knotted the rope about her waist and stood in a crouch. "I'm the slimmest and lightest, so I'll go first. You men, take one of my feet each and give me a good boost."

Ben and Dominic cupped their hands, making stirrups for her feet, then lifted. Her head rose into the hole above. She called back to them. "Right, one, two, three. Hup!" Their heads banged the ice wall as they jerked her upwards.

Karay fell out and forward at the same time, enlarging the hole; then she disappeared. A moment later, her head appeared in the hole. "Ned can come next! Pass him up. Here, boy, give me your paws, good dog, come on!"

The Labrador rose into the sunlight, dispensing cheery thoughts. "Hey, hup! This is good fun!"

Ben did not exactly return the sentiment. "Huh, it should be, you're sitting on my head, you great broad-beamed hound!"

Soon all four were standing out in the fresh, sunlit mountain morning air. Dominic swelled out his chest and thumped it cheerfully with both fists. "Well, friends, onward and upwards, eh?"

A strange voice answered him. "Aye, lad, that's the way we're goin' too. Let's all go together!"

Ligran Razan and five of his followers strolled out from behind the rock that the friends had been trapped against.

Ben was stunned. He shot Ned a swift thought. "Don't move, mate, they're too well armed. Don't try anything!"

The black Labrador speedily replied, "Watch out for me, Ben, I'll be around!" He streaked off down the mountain.

One of Ligran's men unslung a rifle and grabbed a powder flask from his belt.

Ligran stuck out a foot and tripped him. "D'you want to start another avalanche, idiot? Let the dog go, it ain't important. Well, now, what've we got here? Two handsome boys an' a pretty girl." He drew his sword and placed the point against Ben's chest. "What are ye doin' this high up in our mountains, lad?"

Ben tried to look simple and friendly at the same time. "We're travellers, crossing over into Spain, sir."

Ligran's sword flashed in the sunlight. Ben felt the sharp sting as the flat of the blade slapped him across the cheek.

The Razan leader snarled viciously at him. "Liar! Travellers go through the pass, south of here in Andorra. Now tell me the truth or I'll slice the nose off you!"

Karay stepped boldly in front of Ben. She faced Ligran. "He told you, we're going to Spain. Now I'm telling you. Go on, cut my nose off, you coward. I'm not armed like you!"

Ligran raised the sword and struck. It sheared off a dark ringlet of the girl's hair. Karay did not flinch. Ligran let his sword fall and laughed. "I like a maid who has spirit. We'll see how much you have left when Maguda's finished questioning you. You've heard of Maguda Razan – she's my sister."

Karay laughed in Ligran's face. "If all her brothers are as ugly as you, I feel sorry for her!"

The blade quivered a moment in Ligran's grip; his eyes narrowed savagely. Then he turned away and rapped out orders. "Take their rope an' tie them together, hands an' necks! If we hurry we'll arrive back just after the two I sent ahead with the bear. Use your clubs an' beat them if they try to lag behind!"

Tied together with Arnela's rope looping their hands to their necks, the three friends shuffled forward. Ben spoke out of the side of his mouth to Dominic, who was behind him. "Well, at least we won't get lost on our way to the Razan hideout."

A cudgel cracked sharply against his shin. A lanky, scar-faced villain waggled the weapon in Ben's face. "Shut your mouth, boy, or I'll break your leg. That goes for you other two. You're prisoners now, so march!"

23

HUDDLED forlornly on the floor of the big cave, the bear uttered a piteous moan. Razan men and women formed a circle around the animal, watching it curiously. The two who had been sent ahead with it held the neck chains slackly, averting their eyes when Maguda spoke. The matriarch of all the Razan leaned forward slightly. Her huge hypnotic eyes pinpointing on the wretched animal, she croaked venomously, "Ye'll dance before I'm through with ye. Guards, take this thing out of my sight. Away to the dungeons with it!"

Men hauled on the chains, forcing the bear into an upright position. It made a mournful noise as the spikes inside its iron collar dug into its neck fur. They were dragging the bear away, when Rawth, the eldest of Maguda's brothers, entered the cavern and approached his sister.

The hypnotic eyes swivelled in his direction. "Thou hast come to tell me that our brother Ligran approaches, this I already know."

Rawth shrugged uneasily. "He brings captives, two boys and a girl, but no black dog is with them."

Maguda hissed like an angry snake. "Ssssstupid men! Would that I had the strength in my limbs that mine eyes possess. It is I who would have captured all four. Bad omens portend misfortune if the dog is not in my grasp. Bring the prisoners straight here to me when they arrive. Go now, help thy brother!"

Ben stumbled in deep snow, and a guard poked him in the back with the butt of Arnela's ice axe. The boy straightened and struggled on uphill, his mind worried by lack of communication with Ned.

Dominic whispered furtively, as if privileged to his friend's thoughts, "Wonder where Ned is. Not like him to run off."

Karay overheard him and replied shortly, "If I was as fast as a dog, I'd have made a run for it, too. What was he supposed to do – wait around to be captured, or shot?"

One of the guards pushed the girl roughly. "Shut your mouth!"

Ben spoke aloud to distract the robber's attention from her. "Ned's more use to us running free. He'll help us – mark my word, he's no ordinary dog."

Ligran Razan turned and pointed his sword at Ben. "One more word from you, lad, an' I'll chop your tongue off!"

Ben decided it was wiser to keep silent from then on. The Razan leader looked like a villain who would take delight in carrying out his threats. Cruelty and a volatile temper were stamped all over Ligran's coarse features. So Ben held his silence, even as the mouth of the cave came in view. He wanted to shout out to his companions about the red and black figures he could see, scrawled in primitive fashion on the wall outside the cave entrance: men hunting boar, just as Edouard had seen before passing out after his accident. Edouard had said that he would know where the Razan stronghold was if he could find the place where the men were hunting wild boar. Ben was puzzled, but he noted the position of the ancient artwork as he was shoved into the passages branching into the caves.

Lanterns guttered feebly in the dank rock tunnels, which seemed to twist and turn endlessly. Sometimes they would pass side chambers – Razan clan members stared out at them across fires that had blackened and sooted the walls of these miserable hovels where they lived like animals. Water seeped down the rocks of the passages, and a foul odour of communal living, damp, and leftover garbage hung on the still air. Karay noted that nowhere was there sight or presence of children. Then they were in a longer passage, more straight and broad than the ones they had travelled. It even had rush mats and animal skins laid on its smooth floor.

Without warning they were thrust into the lair of Maguda Razan. The friends were startled by the horrific sight: a vast natural cavern with a ceiling so high that it was lost amidst the thick clouds of noxious smoke that snaked upwards in spiralling columns of all hues, from sulphurous yellow and oily green to muddy crimson and acrid blue, mingling in a turgid browny-black mass overall. The smoke columns issued from fires at the bases of monolithic figures, some free-standing but most carved into the living rock of the cavern walls – strange monsters and forgotten deities frightening to look upon, some animal, some human; many half animal and half human with extra limbs. Monstrous forms with horns, fangs and evil leering faces. And there, seated on her throne at the top of a circular-stepped rostrum, was the spider at the centre of this web of unholiness. Maguda Razan!

Her eyes swept over them briefly, then settled on Ligran. Ben saw his throat bob nervously as he swallowed.

Maguda spat out a single word at him. "Fool!"

Ligran stared at his feet, not daring to look her in the eyes. He tried to sound commanding yet respectful. "A harsh word, sister. I lost four good men taking these prisoners for you. The dog was just an ordinary dog that ran off like a frightened rabbit. We couldn't risk a shot at it, for fear of starting an avalanche, so we just . . . brought these three . . ." His voice trailed off into silence.

Maguda snarled at him, "I wanted that dog – the omens told me it was a bad thing for us to let it live. Thou art a fool, brother Ligran. Look at me!"

Ligran reluctantly let his gaze rise. His legs were trembling. A long, curved and blackened fingernail pointed at him.

Maguda spoke. "Thou art a fool. Say it!"

Ligran's lips moved automatically as he repeated the words: "I am a fool."

Maguda sat back, and her hand waved at Ligran dismissively. "Count thyself lucky thou art my brother. Begone to thy cave." Ligran slunk away wordlessly.

Ben felt Karay, who was standing close to him, give an involuntary shudder. Maguda was pointing at her. "Pretty girl, what were ye doing up in my mountains?"

Ben whispered fiercely, "Don't look at her eyes, Karay!"

"Silence!" Maguda shouted. "Rawth, I do not want yonder boy looking at me, attend to him!"

The eldest brother moved swiftly, dealing the boy a blow that laid him senseless upon the floor. Dominic and Karay were overpowered by Maguda's guards as they leapt forward to help Ben.

An evil chuckle came from the throne. "I'm told thou art a sweet singer. Sing for me, girl."

Karay's voice dripped loathing as she struggled between two burly Razan robbers. "I'd never dream of singing for a wicked old hag like you. Never!"

Maguda Razan's smile was a hideous thing to see. "Sooner or later thou wilt sing for me, just like a little bird. Aye, a songbird. I'll have a cage made for thee. 'Twill hang in this cave – ye shall wear a gown of feathers and sing for me each day. A song of why ye came here. Ah, do not think I don't know. Ye came on a wasted journey, though, for the one ye seek is no longer here. Oh, don't look shocked, child, Maguda Razan knows and sees all."

Dominic could contain himself no longer. Straining against the guards who held him, he shouted out, "You lie! Deceit and evil are in your eyes! Truth and honesty are strangers to you. Your world is built on wickedness and lies!"

Maguda turned her baleful glare on him. "Facemaker of Sabada, I know thee. Look at me! For one so young, thou hast a lot to say."

Dominic's gaze was unwavering. He stared straight at Maguda. "I'm not weak and ignorant, you cannot frighten me. My eyes see the truth – your spells and trickeries have no power over me!"

It was like a struggle of wills, one will trying to overpower the other. Maguda's pupils shrank to pinpoints, and her head trembled as she intensified her gaze on the boy in front of her. Dominic's gaze was calm and steady.

Karay had only looked into Maguda's eyes for a few seconds before the power of them made her feel dizzy, and she turned her attention to the floor. Now she watched Dominic, amazed that he could look into the Razan woman's eyes for so long. Ben moved slightly and groaned. Karay edged over to his side and placed her hand on his brow. The contest of wills continued until, much to Karay's surprise, Maguda's withered hand rose to shield her gaze.

Dominic still stood staring. His face did not register the horrors he had envisioned, though he had to control his voice to keep it level. "Death and decay are all I see in your soul, old one. You cannot hypnotize me – I have gifts of my own!"

Maguda Razan's answer sent a chill through Karay's heart. "There are other ways of bringing ye under my power, ways that bold young fools such as ye do not realize. This pretty girl, and the boy from the sea, they are thy friends, I believe . . ."

From between her clawlike fingernails Maguda cast a sly glance at Ben and Karay. Dominic tried to leap forward, but another Razan man tugged him back by the rope looped about his neck, and two more jumped in to assist the pair already hanging on to his arms.

Dominic felt helpless as the realization of Maguda's words swept over him. "Witch! Rotten hag! Leave my friends alone!"

Maguda's triumphant cackling echoed around the vast vault. She pulled a grotesque face at Dominic. "Not so confident now, little boy, eh? Take them away, lock them in the deep dungeons. Let them ponder on what delights I have in store for insolent trespassers!"

After the three friends had been marched off, Maguda beckoned to a dark figure who had been crouching in a shadowy corner close to the cave walls.

"Thy senses did not fail thee, eh, Gizal? Thou wert the first to note the presence of those three young ones."

Maguda's staff tapped upon the floor as Gizal shuffled to the throne. "Have I ever failed thee, mistress? Touch, scent an' hearing serve me better than the eyes of most folk!"

Maguda drew Gizal forward until she could whisper in the blind one's ear, "What think ye of my prisoners?"

Gizal thought carefully before she answered. "The girl is naught, she can be bent to thy will in time. But the one they call the facemaker, he sounds like a problem to me. He is gifted. Thine eyes have no power over him. As to the other boy, the one whom Rawth laid senseless, I cannot say, I have no knowledge of him."

Maguda stared at the ragged cloth that bound her aide's eyes, as if trying to penetrate it. "But the dog, you sensed a dog. It remains uncaptured!"

Gizal sniggered. "What does it matter, mistress? Who cares about a stupid dumb animal?"

Maguda was silent for a moment, then she laughed. "Aye, thou are right, the beast is likely still running. Why fret about a dog? Gizal, ye did a fine job with our other beast, the bear. Little chance of that one running again. Here, my good friend, take this as a reward, and this also."

The blind woman felt the five gold coins Maguda pressed into her hand. She also felt the little glass phial.

"My thanks to thee, mistress. Gold is respected by all, no matter whose hand it comes from. But what is this bottle?"

Maguda whispered confidentially, "I require thy services. I need thee to act as warden to the captives. They need to know the meaning of fear. Use the potion sparingly."

Gizal cocked her head quizzically. "Even on the boy thy brother struck down?"

Maguda's eyes widened. "Especially on him!"

Gizal nodded knowingly. "Ye fear him, mistress?"

Maguda's nails sank into the blind crone's arm as she hissed, "I fear no living thing! Cease thy foolish talk! As queen of the Razan, I have to be cautious. The omens have warned me against yon lad. But even he cannot resist my potions. Now go!"

The dungeons were little more than side caves deep down in the mountain's lower tunnels, each one with an iron barred door fitted across its entrance. Karay and Dominic assisted Ben as the guards shoved them inside and locked the door. They lay on the floor until the sound of their captors' footsteps faded. Dominic helped Ben to his feet, watching anxiously as his friend massaged the back of his neck. "Ben, are you all right?"

Smiling ruefully, Ben continued rubbing. "Oh, I think I'll live, mate. That ruffian had a very heavy hand, though."

Karay stood gripping the bars, peering back along the way they had been brought. "Did you see the poor old bear? I caught a glimpse of him as they marched us along here. They've got him locked up a couple of cells back, three I think."

Dominic placed a sympathetic hand on the girl's shoulder. "I'm sorry for the bear, too, but wouldn't it be wiser to look at our own situation first? We're hardly in a position to help ourselves at the moment."

Karay sat down on the floor and sighed. "You're right, Dom. So, what do we do now?"

Ben found himself a dark corner and snuggled down into his cloak. "Right now all I want is a bit of sleep. That was a cold, hard march up the mountain."

Within a few minutes the other two had joined him, both of them wrapped tightly in their own cloaks and huddling together for warmth in the dank underground cave.

Ben immediately shut his eyes and concentrated on making contact with Ned. No matter how hard he tried, however, there was not a single trace of the black Labrador's thoughts drifting anywhere in his mind. Ben hid his disappointment by reassuring himself that the dog would reach him when the moment was right. He drifted into a dreamless sleep.

Arnela watched the black Labrador as he wandered into her cave, limping and looking weary. Surrounded by her goats, the big woman had been dozing by the fire. At first she thought it was a dream, until one of the nanny goats bleated at the sight of the dog. Arnela came fully awake then. She began pushing goats out of her way. "Ned, is that you? What's happened?"

The dog replied mentally, knowing she could not hear him. "I wish I could tell you, my dear lady, but first I must get this paw seen to. Look!"

Whining softly, Ned offered Arnela the sore paw. She inspected it gently. "You've sliced that on some sharp rock, poor boy – there's a flap of skin hanging from the pad. Let me fix it."

Ned bumped a big goat aside. "It's my paw she's fixing, not yours. Anyhow, you've got little hooves, bet they never get cut on the rocks. Listen, mate, if I give you a message, could you communicate it to Arnela?"

The goat's jaws were working furiously around a mouthful of dried grass. It bleated dumbly at the dog: *"Maaaahahaaa!"*

Ned sniffed disdainfully. "If that's the best you can do, then don't bother. Oh, and mind your manners, keep your mouth closed when you're eating, disgusting beast!"

Arnela cleaned grit out of the wound with warm water, talking in a comforting voice to Ned as she worked. "Don't worry, boy, I won't hurt ye. Stand still now. There, it's nice and clean now. I'll put some balm on it. This is good stuff for healing wounds. I make it myself with herbs and white ashes from the pinewood I've burned. Feels good and soothing, doesn't it?"

The goatherd did not expect an answer, though Ned replied thoughtfully, "It feels wonderful, you kind, clever lady!"

Arnela caught hold of a young billy goat with long, silken hair as he tried to skip by her. "Hold still a moment, Narcissus, I need to borrow a tuft or two from your coat."

With a small pair of shears she clipped a portion from where the goat hair grew longest. Narcissus bleated pitifully. The goatherd sent him on his way with a pat. "Go on, you great baby. That didn't hurt you a bit, stop whinging!"

As Ned watched her separating the hair, he thought, "What are you going to do with that, my friend?"

Arnela continued talking as she ministered to him. "Hair from a young billy is better than any bandage. I wind it around your paw like this, and it protects the wound nicely. By the time your paw's better, it'll have dropped off!"

Ned gazed trustingly at the goatherd. "It feels very good, thank you, ma'am. I'll trust your word as to its dropping off eventually. I mean, it'd look a bit foolish, wouldn't it – a black dog with a white goat-hair paw? Pretty odd, I'd say."

Arnela fed him a bowl of soup and one of fresh goat milk. Ned took them gratefully. She watched until he was finished, then took his front paws in her lap. "Now, where are the children?"

Ned could only gaze at her beseechingly.

She continued, "Have they found Adamo?"

A sudden brainwave struck the dog. He shook his head slowly.

Arnela was astonished. "You shook your head! Does that mean you can understand me, Ned?" The dog nodded solemnly.

Arnela's eyes lit up with wonderment. "You can! You can understand me. Oh, you clever dog!"

Ned licked her hand, thinking to himself, "I could listen to your compliments all night, my friend, but there isn't time. Go on, ask me another question!"

Arnela stared deep into Ned's eyes. "So, what's happened to our friends? Sorry, let me put it another way. Did you get lost from them? Are they still searching?"

Ned shook his head emphatically.

Arnela looked anxious. "Are they lying injured somewhere? I heard the avalanche."

Ned shook his head, waiting on her next words.

"Have they been taken by the Razan?"

The dog nodded vigorously several times.

"They're prisoners – do you know where they are?"

Ned held his head still a moment, then nodded twice.

Arnela shooed away an inquisitive goat before she spoke. "Ned, can you lead me to them?"

Again he nodded in the affirmative.

• • •

Arnela arose, put on her heavy cloak and picked up her rope and ice axe. Then, from a hiding place among the goat fodder, she drew out a pistol that she had captured from the robber clan. It was loaded and primed. Thrusting it into her belt, she patted the dog's head. "Come on then, Ned!"

The big woman halted at the cave entrance. She spoke to her goats as though they were children. "Now there's no need for you lot to go wandering willy-nilly around the mountains. There's food in here, 'tis nice and dry, and water up to our very doorstep. I shouldn't be too long away. Pantyro, I'm leaving you in charge, be firm with them, but no bullying. Clovis, you'd better keep an eye on Pantyro. You're all on your best behaviour, so don't let me down!"

Ned cast an eye over the goats as he and Arnela left the cave. They gazed dumbly at him as he left them with the thought, "I'd hate to be you lot if the place isn't neat and tidy when your mistress gets back!"

A little billy goat bleated at the dog: *"Maaaah!"*

Ned eyed him frostily. "Don't argue with your elders and betters, young fellow!"

With the black Labrador leading the way, Arnela began the long uphill trudge.

Now that he had set his rescue mission under way, Ned concentrated his thoughts upon Ben, sending out messages of hope and comfort. "Ben, can you hear me, mate? It's your old pal Ned. I've got Arnela with me, we're coming to help you, wherever you are. Speak to me, Ben, let me know you're all right!"

As they pressed onward and upwards, the faithful dog began to feel anxious and worried. Ben was not responding.

A TAPPING NOISE WAKENED KARAY. SHE LAY quite still, watching the barred entrance through half-closed eyes. It was Gizal, the blind crone. Behind her came a man carrying a pail and a cauldron with a ladle protruding from it. He placed them where Gizal indicated with her stick, close to the bars. The hag held a finger to her lips, cautioning the man to be quiet. After a moment they both crept silently off. Steam was emanating from the cauldron, a not unpleasant aroma.

The movement of Karay rising woke Ben and Dominic. Dominic yawned cavernously. "Can't you keep still, Karay? I was in a nice sleep there."

Ben sniffed the air. "Smells like food, who brought it?"

The girl reached through the bars and dipped a ladleful. "It's porridge of some sort. The old blind woman and a guard left it here not a moment ago. Hmmm, I'm starving!"

Ben leapt upright. "Don't touch it, Karay! There may be something wrong with the stuff!"

However, Karay was hungry and tasted some on her fingertip. "It is porridge – oatmeal with milk and honey in it. Tastes pretty good to me. If they wanted to poison us, they could have done that long since. We're prisoners, aren't we? Even prisoners have to be fed. There's fresh water in the pail, too!"

Ben hesitated, then consulted the facemaker. "What d'you think, Dom, is it safe?"

Dominic smiled mischievously. "Well, let Karay eat some. If she doesn't scream and keel over, it should be all right."

His remark did not seem to disconcert the girl. Blowing on the porridge to cool it, she ate with relish, wrinkling her nose at the two watchers. "It's delicious. I'll finish the pot if you two are afraid of porridge. Mmm, great stuff!"

Dominic hurried to her side. "You little hog, give me some!"

Forgetting his earlier doubts, Ben joined him. "Steady on there, mates, I'm famished too!"

It was good food, hot and sweet. Between them they devoured three ladles each. Licking the ladle clean, Karay rinsed it in the pail. The friends drank some water to quench their thirst.

All three felt much better with food and drink inside them. They seated themselves against the rock walls, staring at the glow of the lanterns outside.

Ben thrust his hands inside his cloak to keep them warm. "What d'you suppose they're planning to do with us?"

Karay giggled. "Send us some more nice porridge when we get hungry, I suppose."

Ben did not know why he suddenly started laughing. "Hahaha, tell 'em to bring three pans next time, one each!"

Dominic smiled foolishly. "Aye, and we'd like a table, too, with some nice napkins, like the ones the comte has in his big house. Hahaha, lots of napkins, hoho . . . Oh, hahahaaaar!" The three of them held their sides and laughed uproariously, not knowing or caring about the cause of such merriment. After a while their laughter subsided into amused chuckles. Then they fell silent, eyelids drooping. Ben yawned and stretched flat out on the floor, Karay and Dominic listed crazily towards each other as they sat with their backs against the rock. In an incredibly short time they were sleeping deeply. Then the effects of Maguda's potion really took over their minds.

Karay felt she was once again chained to the wheel of Cutpurse's wagon, unable to move her wrists. The fat clown-thief crouched in front of her, grinning maliciously. She was helpless in his presence. At his side he had the steaming porridge cauldron. Cutpurse tipped it gently, allowing her to view the contents. It was not porridge, it was spiders! The one thing in life of which Karay had an unreasoning terror – spiders! Big ones, small ones, hairy ones, smooth ones, some red, others golden, but most of them an iridescent purply black. Scrambling and wriggling over one another, the mass of arachnids strove to get out of the pail. Karay was overcome with frozen horror, her mouth forming an anguished scream that stuck in her throat. Cutpurse dipped the ladle into the pail, and spiders began crawling into it. He lifted the ladle clear, and some of the spiders clinging to the sides of the handle fell to the floor.

Sniggering with delight, the fat robber winked ominously at Karay and teased her wickedly. "Look, pretty one, spiders. Lots of spiders, and all for you!"

Dominic could not abide even the thought of snakes. Loathsome slippery reptiles, cold and slimy, with questing forked tongues and fangs that dripped poison. He had once seen a rabbit that had been bitten by an adder. It lay quivering, eyes glazed, but still alive as the snake coiled about its legs, the blunt nose questing at its victim's neck as its scales slithered over the victim's warm body. Dominic looked up and from his distorted angle of view saw Maguda Razan.

She was standing just outside the cell bars, glaring hatefully at him. Slowly her clawed hands reached for the opening of the voluminous cloak that enveloped her, and she croaked at him, "Am I so hideous that you would not make a picture of my face?" Then she opened the cloak a fraction, and snakes began sliding sinuously out onto the floor. Lots of snakes! One with a dirty grey body and barred yellow markings on its underside wrapped itself around the bars. A hooded cobra with spectacle signs reared up and hissed viciously. Pythons, pit vipers and banded coral snakes coiled and uncoiled around Maguda's feet, swaying, hissing, baring their fangs and constantly being joined by others tumbling out from the cloak. Dominic stared in dread fascination at the jumble of writhing bodies, which had begun moving towards him. He could not close his eyes to block out the awful sight. He sat there leaning askew against the rock, aware of every beady set of eyes centred on him, too petrified to make a single move or sound.

The snakes were coming for him!

Ben's breath caught in his throat suddenly. The entire crew of the *Flying Dutchman*, both the living and the dead, came shuffling up to the bars and stared through them at him. Pale, bloated faces of those who had drowned mingled with the fierce, scarred and coarse-whiskered features of those whom he had known and detested for their greed and cruelty. They leered and grinned knowingly at the former crew lad. Suddenly they were wrenched aside, and he found himself looking into the face of Captain Vanderdecken, leader of them all.

His face was as white as parchment, the thin lips blue from the cold, bared over yellowed teeth like crooked gravestones. His salt-bleached hair, crusted with ice, stood out from his head like an unholy halo. From under their black-pouched lids, Vanderdecken's wild eyes shone insanely, boring into the boy's very heart.

The Dutchman poked a frostbitten, black-nailed finger at Ben. "So this is where ye've been hiding, wretch! I'll always find ye, no matter where you hide! I'll soon have ye back aboard my ship, and we'll spend eternity together, lad. Eternity!"

A litter drew up in front of the cell, borne by six burly Razan robbers, who stood stoically with it on their shoulders. Maguda sat on the litter, watching the faces of the three drugged captives. She took satisfaction at the sight. Each one's eyes were wide open, but unconscious to anybody outside of their potion-induced nightmares. They stared straight ahead, seeing everything that was locked into their personal fears and loathings.

Gizal came hobbling along, her stick tap-tapping the rock walls. She halted by the litter. "Is thy magic working, O mother of spells and charms?"

Maguda nodded. "Aye, 'tis indeed, they are like butterflies pinned on thorns, seeing naught else but that which they cannot stand. Methinks a few weeks of keeping them thus will bend them to my will. They will sing, dance, sketch and plead to please me, 'tis always so."

Gizal bowed. "Truly thou art the greatest of all the Razan!"

Maguda tapped the litter with her foot. "Take me back to my throne, then go, tell others what thou hast seen here today.

Let it serve as a warning to all who would oppose me!"

The party moved off, with Gizal shuffling behind.

Arnela muttered to herself as she gazed up at what seemed to be a sheer wall of snow rearing overhead. "Avalanche must've done this, 'tis not as I remember it. But never mind, Ned, I know we're on the right track. That high crag near the peak is my marker – the Razan's lair is up there. We'll have to go carefully, there might be hidden pitfalls in this sort of snow. Avalanches can do that, y'know."

But the black Labrador was not listening. He was sprawled flat with both front paws covering his eyes. A piteous whimper emanated from his trembling body, building up suddenly into a mournful howl.

The big goatherd woman fell on her knees beside the dog, shaking him gently. "Ned, what is it, boy? What's the matter with ye?"

Her words fell on deaf ears. Ben had somehow transmitted the anguish of his tortured mind to the dog. All the horror and fear of the boy's nightmare were so powerful that Ned became a captive to them. Vanderdecken and his ghastly crew were reaching out to him from behind a grille of iron bars. He was in a cave, a prisoner, helpless to resist the captain and all hands, living and dead, of the *Flying Dutchman*!

Arnela got her strong hands under Ned and lifted him, then cuddled him like a baby, shushing him, lest his howls betray them to the foe.

"There there now, good boy. This isn't like you, Ned. What is it? What's upsetting you? Only little puppies cry and yowl like that. You're supposed to be a big, sensible dog."

In his fevered vision, Ned saw Vanderdecken make a grab for him. Instinctively he bared his teeth and bit at the phantom captain's hand.

Arnela was stroking the dog's muzzle when she felt the sudden change from cowering cur to wild animal. The goatherd pulled her hand away just in time. Ned's teeth ripped through the sleeve of her goat-hair tunic. Shock and anger overcame the big woman. She flung the dog forcefully to the ground. "Ooh! You bad, ungrateful dog!"

Ned felt the heavy impact as he struck the patch of snow, which Arnela's feet had hardened. It broke the spell for a short moment. In that instant he heard the angel's voice ringing out like a peal of thunder.

> " 'Tis thou who must show the way
> When visions of evil arise.
> Others may see what ye cannot,
> So be guided by thine own eyes!"

Ned called out from his bewildered mind to the angel, "I don't understand, tell me what I should do. Please!"

Once more the heavenly being's voice spoke forth.

> "Trust only what thine eyes can see,
> When things are not as they seem.
> Break free to the world of reality,
> Escape thy master's false dream!"

The black Labrador's eyes snapped open. He understood the whole thing in a flash. Somehow, some way, an evildoer had taken possession of Ben's mind. The force was so strong that Ben could not avoid passing it on to him. Ned realized that he had to block the nightmare by concentrating his thoughts upon other things. But first he had to make amends to his friend Arnela. He nuzzled at her foot until she had to lift it slightly, then he thrust his chin under it until she was standing with her foot upon his head. Ned's tail brushed a fan in the snow as he wagged it back and forth.

Arnela sniffed, then a reluctant smile crossed her weather-beaten features. "Well, well, sorry already, are we?"

Ned withdrew his head and nodded sheepishly. She raised him up until his front paws rested on her waist. Taking the dog's face in both hands, she looked into his soft dark eyes. "I don't know what's going on in that doggy brain of yours, friend, but I'm sure you had a good reason for what you did."

Ned nodded solemnly. He pawed at his friend and whined softly.

Arnela ruffled his ears fondly. "Then I'll say no more about it, Ned. You're a good dog! Mayhap you were thinking of Ben and our other young friends. You were fretting and worried about them, that's probably it."

Ned licked her hand and nodded again. She set his paws back down onto the snow. "Right, then, we won't get them free by standing around here all night. Come on, let me go first, I can probe the snow with my axe handle to make sure it's solid to walk on. Keep close behind, boy, walk in my tracks."

Following Arnela up into the high mountainous regions, Ned kept his mind busy by sending out messages to his master. He thought of inconsequential, cheery things, which he hoped might snap Ben out of his frightening dream. "Aye aye, matey, it's me – your old pal Ned. Remember that picnic we had in the jungle a few years back? Haha, that was a good one, we were scoffing away when you suddenly noticed you were sitting on an anthill. Hohoho! I never knew you were such a good dancer, jumping and leaping and smacking your own behind. What a sight! Come on now, admit it, Ben, you didn't sit down for a week after that. Never mind those bad old dreams, mate. Wake up, open your eyes! Talk to Karay and Dominic, think of other things – anything! Hahaha, like me chasing that snobbish lady through the fair on her horse. Hoho, the horse's big fat bottom wobbling all over the place and her hanging on to her hat. What a dreadful hat that was, one of those creations with a dead stuffed lark and a pile of wax cherries on it. You wouldn't want to be seen dead in it on a dark night, eh? Come on, Ben, try and remember the good times, the funny bits."

Whether wading chest deep in powdery snow, scrambling over loose shale and protruding rocks or avoiding patches of sheet ice, the faithful dog never once ceased trying to break the spell pervading Ben's mind.

25

LIGRAN RAZAN AND HIS ELDER BROTHER Rawth unlocked the long, barred cell door and entered. They stared at the three young people, all locked in their own blood-chilling trances, unable to speak, move or communicate with one another.

Ligran chuckled at the sight. "Sweet dreams, eh? I wouldn't like t'be in the middle of a nap like the one they're takin', not for ten bags o' gold!" He kicked Dominic's foot lightly.

Rawth cautioned him, "Careful, ye might break their spell!"

Ligran scoffed at his brother. "Our wicked old sister's the only one who can do that. Look at this." Kneeling, he popped one of Dominic's eyes open wider. The facemaker was still staring straight ahead in a trance. Ligran shrugged. "See, he doesn't even know we're here." He let the lid drop.

Rawth grabbed one of Ben's arms. "Stop playin' around an' let's get this one to Maguda."

Ligran helped his brother to lift the drugged boy; they bore him out of the cell and relocked it. Draping

Ben's arms about their shoulders, they towed him off down the corridor, his feet limply scraping the ground.

The bear gave a low moan as they passed its cell. Ligran stopped briefly. He kicked the bars and snarled in at the wretched animal, "D'ye want me to go an' get my whip? I'll give ye somethin' to moan about!"

The creature fell silent, its sad, dark eyes dull and moist.

The brothers halted at a cave that had a wooden door. It was unlocked. Rawth kicked it twice. The voice that came from within was that of their sister.

"Bring him in."

The cave served as the armoury to the robber clan. Maguda Razan was seated on her litter, this balanced on four small kegs of gunpowder. There were other kegs stacked there, plus an array of flintlock muskets and rifles, pikes, spears and various odd-looking weapons piled against the walls.

Maguda indicated a length of cord lying nearby. "Bind his hands behind and sit him on the floor."

Rawth performed the task, lowering Ben into a sitting position with his back propped against two casks of gunpowder. He and Ligran stood awaiting further orders.

Maguda's long nails rattled together as she shook a hand dismissively. "Begone now, both of ye. Come back with my litter bearers in an hour. Wait! Ligran, pour some of this into the lad."

Ligran took the goblet from his sister. He tilted Ben's head back and trickled some of the potion between the boy's lips. Ben swallowed and coughed.

Maguda held up her hand. "Enough, that should bring him to his senses."

Rawth tried to sound helpful. "Do ye want us to stay around, in case he tries anything –"

He wilted under Maguda's scornful glance. "What need have I of fools? Get out, both o' ye!"

They retreated, closing the door behind them. Maguda peered closely at Ben. His head was lolling from side to side, and his lips were moving slightly. Slowly his eyes opened. He stared wildly around, a note of panic in his voice. "Where are my two friends – what have you done with them?"

Maguda closed her eyes until they were mere slits. "Thy friends are still alive and locked up safe . . ." – she paused for effect – ". . . for the moment."

Ben attempted to sound reasonable, knowing he was in the presence of a wicked and vengeful enemy. "We mean you no harm . . . why are you keeping us prisoner like this? Please release my friends at least, let them go."

The old crone shook with silent mirth. "Brave young liar. Ye came here to rescue my grandson, but, alas, the Adamo that folk knew is gone. He is dead to me forever."

Ben sat up straighter. "He is dead?"

Maguda pointed at herself. "Not by my hand, but by his own stubborn choosing. I will speak no more of him. Ye want me to grant freedom to thee and thy friends. I can do that, but on one condition that only ye can fulfil, boy."

Ben leaned forward eagerly, hope rising with him. "Tell me, what do you want me to do?"

Maguda paused awhile, her fingernails tapping the litter. "I know thou art a strange boy, my omens told me so. Many things has thou seen in a great period of years, far longer than thy appearance can tell to ordinary folk. But I am Maguda

Razan, no ordinary person. The thing is this: if I gazed deep into thine eyes, what would I behold, tell me?"

Ben answered as truthfully as he could without giving away too much. "Ma'am, I have little control over what others see in my eyes. Maybe people see in them just what they wish to."

Maguda scoffed. "Fortune-tellers and charlatans say such things to stupid peasants. Thy words do not fool me. I wish to see what thine eyes really hold. Fate, future, knowledge . . . whatever 'tis, I must know. But beware, if I see sights not unto my liking, 'twill go badly for thee, boy!"

Ben knew it was a chance he had to take. All he could do was go along with Maguda's request. He was afraid for himself, but more so for his two friends, and it was painfully obvious that Maguda was not one to make idle threats. He cast a swift glance at the evil old woman as she sat awaiting his decision. Some inner instinct told him that she was apprehensive. Usually she would be in her great cavern surrounded by guards. Why had she chosen to see him in private? Was she scared of what she would see in his eyes? Did she not want others to see her weakness? Was Maguda Razan really so powerful and invincible?

Ben decided to take the chance and find out. "I hope what you see in my eyes is to your liking, ma'am. I'm ready for you to look into them."

Maguda faced him, closed her own eyes tightly and began muttering incantations in a weird ancient language. Her hands caressed a skull that was on the litter at her side.

Ben sat, resigned to his fate, waiting for her to finish the strange ritual. Without any prior warning, images began invading his mind. He knew it could be nobody but Ned – the dog's communication was so strong, it cut through everything. Ben could not push the images to the back of his mind.

The eyes of Maguda Razan suddenly opened wide, staring at him, boring into his consciousness. She hissed as her hands rose like two long-taloned claws above her head. "Now we shall see. Look deep into mine eyes, boy, give thyself up to my powers!"

Ben met her hypnotic gaze but was surprised to find that he felt nothing. It was merely like staring at an unpleasant old hag.

He smiled at the recollections Ned was sending him.

Maguda Razan blinked then, and her hands dropped slightly. "What is this foolishness? I see thee dancing about in some far forest, smiting thyself and leaping like a mad child. No, wait! I see the fair at Veron now . . . a stupid woman on a prancing horse, chased by a dog! Art thou making mock of me, boy? Dost thou think Maguda Razan is to be made fun of?"

Ben had difficulty keeping a straight face, but he intoned dully, as if hypnotized, "Look deeper and you shall see."

He concentrated his thoughts upon the *Flying Dutchman.* In the teeth of a roaring hurricane off the coast of Tierra del Fuego, amid icy waves and tattered rigging, the face of Captain Vanderdecken appeared. Lank, salt-crusted hair framed the Dutchman's accursed visage, bloodless lips bared from stained tombstone-like teeth, his eyes glittered insanely. Laughing madly, he paced the deck of the doomed vessel, hurling oaths and threats at all about him.

Ben saw Maguda's attitude change at the sight – she was enjoying it, extracting pleasure from the dreadful scene. Her tongue, snakelike, licked withered lips as she cackled, "He is truly the spawn of hellfire!"

Ben hated calling up the visions, but if it would gain freedom for him and his friends, there was no alternative. Pain pounded his temples, lancing like a blade into his mind. He gave no rein to his thoughts, pouring the whole horrific experience out into Maguda's ruthless, staring orbs. Mutiny, murder, quarrels, fights, all that had taken place on the high seas aboard the *Flying Dutchman* on that unspeakable voyage!

Maguda Razan shuddered with delight – she was like a wayward child, giggling, simpering, her wrinkled tattooed face twitching as she received new sights. Wickedness, evil, strife and suffering were her very life's blood – she revelled in unspeakable vileness. Now Ben had lost control of his thoughts, his brain felt as if it were at bursting point. The cave seemed to sway and rock around him as the wild kaleidoscope of that long-ago, ill-fated voyage spewed forth unchecked.

Maguda's laughter echoed and re-echoed, building in its intensity.

Then . . .

Thunder and lightning crashed through the maelstrom of sound, silencing everything! Through the green light of St Elmo's fire, exactly as it had happened all those years before, the angel of heaven descended! Maguda Razan went rigid. She gave out one unearthly shriek and fell stone-dead upon the litter. The sight of a being who radiated so much purity and beauty had stopped the heart of one who represented darkness and evil!

Ben's head slumped forward to rest upon his drawn-up knees. He felt drained but cleansed by the peacefulness and calm that surrounded him. Footsteps came pounding up the corridor outside, and the door burst open. Ligran and Rawth, with a crowd of henchmen, rushed in, followed by Gizal, the blind crone.

Unable to restrain himself, Ligran strode to the litter and prodded at the stiff form stretched upon it. He recoiled instantly, his voice shrill with disbelief. "She's dead . . . Maguda's dead?"

Rawth grabbed his sword and turned upon Ben, shouting, "You killed her!"

He swung the blade at the boy, but Gizal's staff struck his wrist, deflecting the swing. "Fools! Stay still until I find out what happened here!"

The henchmen stepped aside as Gizal tap-tapped her way to the litter. She ran her hands over the body of Maguda, placing her fingers over the nose and mouth to check for breath. Taking a long pin from her hair, Gizal touched it to the pupil of Maguda's eye – there was no feeling of movement. Gizal nodded. "She is dead!"

The men in the cave gave a simultaneous gasp of shock. The blind woman pushed her way through to Ben, laying about at the dumbfounded men with her stick. "Make way, move!" Ben sat quite still and closed his eyes, trying to hide the revulsion he felt at being pawed over by the witchlike hag. Forcing wide his jaws, she sniffed at his open mouth. He winced as she tugged his hair, searching through it, her fingernails scratching as she probed around his ears. Then Gizal leaned upon his shoulder, bending him forward. Ben tried to hold his breath when her rancid-smelling garments enveloped his face whilst she inspected the cords that bound his hands behind his back.

Satisfied, the blind woman stood up. "There be no marks or blood upon Maguda, yet she lies dead. This boy could not have slain her by mortal means – he is bound tight and could not have undone or retied the cord."

Ligran struck his fist against a powder keg. "But how –?"

Gizal silenced him by holding up a hand. "Hearken to me. Only in two ways could yon lad have taken Maguda's life: with his mouth or with his eyes. Either he could have spat poison at her or uttered some powerful spell, though I think not. Rawth, do ye recall when this one and his friends were first brought in front of thy sister? She had thee knock him down, saying she did not want him looking at her, eh?"

Rawth stroked his beard. "Aye, that was as you say!"

Gizal placed a hand upon Rawth's arm. "Bind his eyes. Ye can gag him, too, for safety's sake. Have him taken back to the cells."

Before Ben could protest, his mouth and eyes were bound with filthy strips of rag; then the henchmen picked him up and carried him off, leaving Gizal alone with the two Razan brothers.

Ligran, the more hot-tempered of the pair, paced the cave, shaking his head angrily. "That lad's a danger to us all, Gizal. You should've let Rawth slay him. Here, I'll go and do the job myself!"

The blind woman's staff blocked Ligran's way as she lowered her voice, warning him, "Don't let anger rule thy thinking, Ligran. If the lad did kill Maguda with his eyes, he must be even more powerful than she was. Thy sister ruled through fear. Without one as strong as she, our people would soon leave here and go their own ways, am I not right, Rawth?"

The elder Razan nodded. "True, old one, but if the lad is as powerful as you think, how can we bend him to our service?"

Ligran began warming to the idea. He smiled wickedly.

"Through his two young friends – they are as close as brothers and sister. The boy would not wish them hurt, would he?"

Gizal's staff touched Ligran's shoulder. "Now thou art showing good sense. Leave me to think now. First we will have a great ceremony to impress our people. Maguda must be installed in a suitable tomb before our new leader is made known to the Razan. That will be after the spirit of Maguda appears to us three and names the boy as her successor."

Rawth was puzzled for a moment. "Will she?"

Ligran grinned. "She already has. Brother, did you hear her?"

Rawth caught on then and laughed. "Oh, aye, I heard her. Pity all the Razan couldn't, eh?"

Gizal squeezed Rawth's arm reassuringly. "Fear not, they will! At the right time. There be plenty of hidden places, and the great cavern carries lots of echoes. Leave it to old Gizal!"

Having hatched their plan, the three departed from the armoury cave, leaving behind them the rigid corpse of the once all-powerful Maguda Razan. What Gizal, Ligran and Rawth had missed was the lesson their former leader had learned at the cost of her life: a surety that Good will triumph over Evil, always!

26

IT WAS LATE AFTERNOON OF THE FOLLOWING day. Arnela and Ned crouched behind a jumble of ice-sheened rocks. The ground in front of them was solidified soil, shale and patches of snow in a small escarpment, backed by the pristine white mountain peak.

Arnela pointed, whispering to the dog, "See there, Ned, that's the one and only entrance to the Razan caves. Just inside the rift, straight ahead." The black Labrador focused his gaze on the shadowed hole in the solid rock face, listening to the big goatherd woman. "Those red marks by the entrance, they look like old bloodstains from this distance. But they're ancient pictures of cave dwellers hunting wild boar. I saw them once, some years ago, when I tracked some Razan villains here. Our friends will be imprisoned somewhere inside. Where, I'm not sure. I'll wager there are many caves and passages inside. We'll worry about that when we come to it. Our first job is to get inside. I'm sure

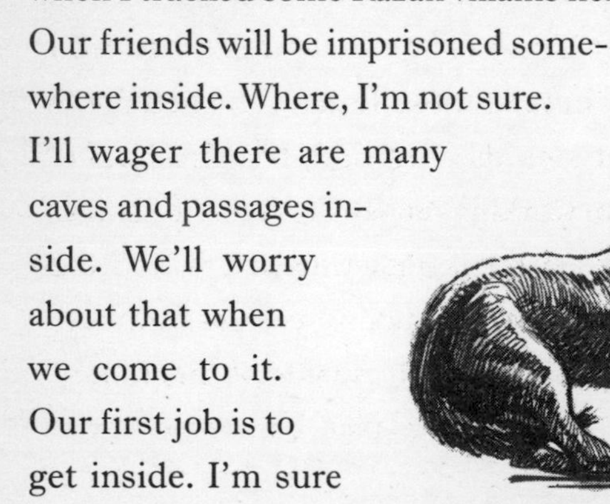

there must be guards at the entrance. Let's hide here and watch until we get a chance. Right?"

Ned snuggled down, nodding his head to show he understood.

After Ben was bundled roughly back into the cell, he lay still, listening to the henchmen locking the barred door and pacing off down the passage. Then he went to work. Still bound, his eyes taped, the boy rolled about until he bumped the rough, rocky wall. Backing onto it, he wriggled along until his tightly bound hands encountered a small ridge. Then he began sawing at the cord, rubbing it back and forth along the stone protuberance. It was slow, painful work, and his hands were cold, swollen and numb from the tightly lashed cord.

"Ben, are you there, mate? It's me, Ned! I'm with Arnela, watching the main entrance. As soon as we can sneak in we'll try to rescue you. How are Karay and Dominic? Are they with you?"

Relief flooded through Ben as he replied, "Good old Ned. I knew you'd come. And you've brought help, too! Great! Listen, pal, I'm a bit tied up at the moment, so I'll make it brief. I'm locked in a cell, somewhere below the big main cavern. I think our friends might be here, if those Razan returned me to the same cell. I know that sounds a bit odd, but I'm bound, gagged and blindfolded. I'm working on getting free. As soon as I know where I am for sure, I'll keep contacting you. So you and Arnela be extra careful, you'll be no use to us if you get captured. These Razan are no fools – they know the inside of this mountain very well. I'll speak to you later, take care now, d'you hear me?"

Ned's answer came through to Ben. "I hear you, mate. Let's hope we can get to you before too long!"

Ben had been sawing continuously whilst sending thoughts to the dog. Finally, he pulled, and the frayed cord snapped in two pieces. Using both thumbs, Ben pushed the gag up beneath his nose and levered the blindfold up until he could see a little. Then, with his teeth, the boy tore off the pieces of cord that were knotted tight about both his wrists. His numbed hands were useless for several minutes. He squeezed back tears, gasping as the blood flowed agonizingly back into his fingers. Finally, reaching behind his head, he untied both the gag and the blindfold.

Dominic and Karay were there, sitting, leaning askew at opposite angles, their eyes wide open. Ben saw their twitching limbs and ashen faces. He knew they were still trapped within the realm of nightmare. Drugged! Ben decided to use Ned's methods of getting through to them, combined with a little addition of his own. Both the porridge and the water were still there outside the cell's bars. He filled the ladle with water, splashed it straight into Dominic's face and began slapping the boy's cheeks hard, shouting in his ear, "Come on, lazybones, rise and shine! Up you come!"

Grabbing his friend beneath both armpits, Ben hauled him upright and gave his shin a smart kick.

The facemaker winced sharply, his hands scrabbling at Ben's face as he whimpered, "Yeeeegh! Get these snakes off me, I can't stand sn– Ben?"

Hugging his friend close, Ben whispered soothingly, "There there now, hush, Dom. It was all a bad dream, the snakes are gone. Keep your mind on good and happy things. They won't bother you any more then."

Dominic blinked tears from his eyes and rubbed his leg. "One of them bit me, Ben, a green cobra, right here by my knee. I think I'm going to die – it stings and pains. Oooohhhh!"

Ben wiped the tears from Dominic's eyes. "That wasn't a snake, Dom, 'twas me. I gave you a good kick to wake you. Sorry about that, mate. We'd better get Karay back into the land of the living. Come on, lend a hand!"

Dominic splashed water in the girl's face. Ben slapped her cheeks and tugged sharply at her hair as he shouted, "Up and about, miss! Let's see you dancing and singing, pal!"

Karay screamed. She scratched and batted at Ben's hands as they pulled her hair. "Eeeeee! Get away, you filthy crawly things! Ugh, spiders! Uuuuggghhh!"

Ben's face was a fraction from hers. The girl's eyes were wide and pleading as she sobbed to him, "Kill the spiders, Ben. Don't let them get me. Kill them!"

It took an hour or more before Karay and Dominic were completely themselves, though they both complained of roaring headaches and some dizziness. Ben explained to them what had taken place. He told them about Maguda Razan's death but had to lie about the visions she had seen in his eyes – he attributed her death to the fact that she was very ancient and must have had a weak heart.

Karay was only half listening at that stage. She was gazing longingly at the ladle in the water pail. "Ooh, my mouth is so dry, I'd give anything for a sip of water!"

Dominic was in complete agreement with her. Ben shrugged. "Touch that water, either of you, and within an hour you'll both be fighting off snakes and spiders again, I warn you!"

Karay massaged her temples moodily. "Well, what are we supposed to do now, just sit here?"

Ben nodded. "There's little else we can do. Don't worry, though, I've got a feeling Ned might come to the rescue soon."

Dominic stared curiously at Ben. "Is that a thought, or just a feeling, friend? Tell me."

Ben's mysterious, clouded blue eyes met those of the face-maker, and he was smiling oddly. "A bit of both, I think."

Two Razan guards who had been posted inside the tunnel entrance stepped outside to enjoy the late-afternoon sunlight. Leaning their flintlock rifles against the rock wall, they stood idly basking in the warmth. They had not been there long when a tall cloaked figure came into view, tugging a black dog on an improvised rope lead. The guards shaded their eyes against the lowering sun, but they could not see the newcomer's face, which was hidden by the overhang of the cloak's hood. The dog dug its paws in, trying to resist being led. But the big, strong-looking figure hauled it along easily and waved a friendly hand at the two guards.

One of them nudged the other. "Look, there's the black dog Maguda ordered everyone to search for."

The other guard viewed the animal sourly. "Huh, lot of good that'll do now that Maguda's dead. They're placing her in a tomb about now – maybe they'll bury it with her, eh?"

As the figure came closer, however, he challenged the person. "Halt, who goes there, an' what d'ye want here?"

The big person spoke confidently. "Naught to worry about, friends, I am of the Razan. I thought Maguda might like a little gift. I found this beast wandering the lower slopes."

The figure continued coming forward. The first guard broke the news. "You've come a bit late, brother, Maguda Razan died last night."

The newcomer pointed to the inside of the tunnel. "Maguda Razan dead? She can't be. There she is!"

Both guards turned to look into the tunnel. Arnela – for it was she – let go of Ned. Seizing both men from behind with her powerful hands, she banged their heads hard against the rock face. They dropped like two logs.

Ned winced at the sight of the two unconscious guards. "Oof! I'm glad I'm on her side!"

Arnela bound both men back to back with her long climbing rope and gagged them securely with their own bandannas. Grabbing a foot of each man, she towed them away easily and stowed them in their own former hiding place. Shouldering both firearms, she pointed to the tunnel. "You go first, Ned. Maybe you can sniff our friends out."

The black Labrador trotted inside, accustoming himself to the flickering torchlit walls as he relayed a message to Ben. "We're inside, Ben. Arnela's just flattened the entrance guards. Where are you, mate, can you give me any help?"

The boy's thoughts answered him. "Ned, I'm sorry, but we haven't a clue about this place. I can't direct you, pal. But if you hear a bear whining and moaning, you'll know we're somewhere nearby. They've got the poor animal in a cell about three doors down from us. Listen out for him."

The dog stopped, thought about Ben's suggestion, then came up with a solution of his own. "The bear might fall silent – he doesn't know we're coming. Tell Karay to start singing and to keep it up. Her voice is higher pitched, so I'll be able to hear it more easily."

Ben turned to the girl with his request. "Sing something, Karay, a nice long song with lots of high notes."

She remained seated and replied moodily, "Who d'you

think you're giving orders to, eh? My mouth's too dry to sing. Besides, I've still got a splitting headache and I don't want to sing. Huh, you can sing to yourself if you like!"

Dominic looked at Ben. "Why d'you want her to sing all of a sudden? Is there a special reason for it?"

Ben made an awkward explanation to the facemaker. "I can feel that Ned's somewhere in these caves, looking for us. I'll bet he's brought help, too. If he hears Karay's voice, it should help in guiding him to us."

Karay stood up and hurried to the bars. "Well, why didn't you say so, Ben? How long shall I sing?"

Ben shrugged. "For as long as it takes, I suppose. Anyhow, it'll save having to listen to our pal Mr Bear – the poor old fellow's moaning and whining is making me sad."

Karay began to sing.

"Don't love a soldier, my fair maid,
You'll have to follow his brigade,
Through the cold and muddy streams you'll wade,
Away across far countries.

Rub a dum dum dum, rub a dum dum dum,
That sound shall be your whole life's sum,
The fife and regimental drum,
Will rob you of your homeland.

And what will you be marching for,
When he leaves you to fight a war?
You'll sit about and grieve full sore,
To pray for his returning.

Rub a dum dum dum, rub a dum dum dum,
You'll grow to hate the beating drum,
When feet are bleeding cracked and numb,
Its sound will keep you marching.

Go choose a cook, a clerk or groom,
Or weaver who toils at the loom,
For he'll not tramp you to your doom,
Like that brave reckless soldier.

Rub a dum dum dum, rub a dum dum dum,
Why even army mules so dumb,
Would sooner hear a guitar's strum,
At home inside his stable!"

Karay stopped singing. She held up a finger for silence.

"What've you stopped for?" Ben queried.

Dominic edged up to the bars. "I hear it, some sort of chant. Sounds like a lot of people coming this way!"

Ben joined his friends at the grille as the chant grew louder. The two brothers Rawth and Ligran passed the junction at the corridor's end. By squinching his face sideways against the bars, Ben could just see them from the corner of his eye. They were followed by a host of Razan men and women. Gizal led the eerie chant, between beats from four gongs.

"Maguda . . . Maguda!
The underworld rings to thy name.
Maguda . . . Maguda!
Widespread thy fear and fame.
Razan, Razan, Razaaaaaan!"

This was repeated over and over in the same monotone as the entire clan marched by, in lines three abreast. At the rear of the procession, twelve sturdy robbers bore a long trestle with the body of Maguda set on her throne on top of it.

Karay watched in silent dread as the macabre cavalcade passed. "They must be taking Maguda down to her tomb. Best place for the evil old hag, that's what I say!"

A message from Ned came to Ben. "Ahoy, mate, we're in a great big cavern, horrible place, filled with coloured smoke and lots of huge strange statues. But there isn't a living soul to be seen anywhere!"

Ben interrupted the dog's thoughts. "Good! You've come at just the right time. The Razan are attending a funeral ceremony on the floor below this one. If you can get to us, we can break free while the Razan are attending the ceremony in the lower caves. Hurry up, pal!"

The bear, who had been whining and moaning continually, now began howling and rattling its neck chains.

Ned's thought winged its way to Ben. "Is someone blowing a horn down there? What's all that racket I can hear?"

Ben answered with frantic speed, "It's the bear, he's started kicking up a right old row. His cell is only three doors from ours. If you can find him, we're only yards away, mate!"

Ben clearly discerned the determination in his dog's reply. "Hang on, pal . . . We're coming!"

Ned tugged at Arnela's sleeve. Without a word she followed him at a run – around the empty throne dais, through the noxious clouds of multi-coloured smoke and into a downward-sloping tunnel. She paused a moment, frowning. "Are those villains making a human sacrifice? What're all those dreadful noises, Ned?"

The black Labrador tugged the goatherd's sleeve so hard that it ripped. She nodded furiously. "All right, all right! Lead on, boy, I'm following you!"

Together they pelted along the narrow, downsloping tunnel, taking a sharp left turn into the prison corridor. Ben's voice rang out joyfully, as he heard their footsteps. "Ned, Ned. I knew you'd find us!"

Arnela arrived at the cell's entrance, panting alongside the dog. "Hah, there ye are!"

Karay sobbed. "Oh, you made it, you're here at last!"

Ever the practical soul, Arnela silenced them. "Time for that later! Let's get you out of there!"

Dominic shook the bars frantically. "They took everything from us except our clothes. We have nothing to work on the padlock with. And we vowed to free the bear if we got out. Just listen to the poor beast howling!"

Arnela pushed him away from the bars. "Step back, young 'uns, leave this to me!"

Taking a musket from her shoulder, she bashed at the old padlock with great force – once, twice! The tumblers of the ancient mechanism fractured under the impact, and the big padlock fell open.

The bear had fallen silent; still chained to the wall, it was at the bars of its cell. Karay hurried to it. Before anyone could shout out to warn her, she put her hand between the bars and stroked its huge face. "Poor old fellow, we'll get you out." The big beast laid its head sorrowfully against the girl's hand.

Arnela gasped in amazement. "Well, will ye look at that, a tame bear. Stay clear of this lock, girl – and you, too, bear!" Again she raised the musket and crashed it down on the side of the antiquated padlock. Once, twice . . . *bang*! – accidentally the rifle discharged, although the lock broke open.

Dominic ran to the end of the corridor, calling back, "Hurry up! That shot will've given the game away – they'll be after us in a moment!"

Ben spotted the wooden door on the opposite wall. It was the armoury cave where Maguda had interviewed him. "Arnela, look, this cave is full of gunpowder kegs!"

The big goatherd shook her head. "Don't even think about exploding gunpowder around here, Ben. We'd bring the mountain down upon us all. Here, take my ice pick and loosen those staples holding the bear's chains to the wall. I've got an idea."

The wooden armoury door was held to the rock by thick leather hinges. These were attached to timber wedges, which formed the doorposts. Arnela whipped out a small hook-bladed knife. It was so sharp that it sheared through the leather as if it were butter. She caught the door as it collapsed outwards. Carrying it into the passage, she walked downwards until she found a place where the rough-hewn tunnel narrowed. That was where Arnela wedged the door. She listened for a moment before hastening back to her friends.

"You were right, Dominic. I can hear them coming. We'd best move fast. Have you loosed those staples, Ben?"

The boy had already extracted one. He shoved the pointed end of the ice pick through the eye of the other one and levered. It popped out and the bear stood free. Karay took the big beast's paw and led it outside. It followed meekly.

Ben could not resist smiling at the sight. "Well, you've certainly found a friend there, Karay. Let's get out of this place, pals!"

They followed the passage upwards, emerging into the main cavern. Arnela handed them each a pistol, which she had taken from the armoury. "These may come in handy. Careful now, they're primed and loaded. I can hear them hammering at that door, listen!"

Sounds of the Razan battering against the door that was wedged across the passage below echoed out clearly.

Crossing the cavern, the friends made their way up to the exit tunnel. Ned ran ahead. He was waiting at the entrance as Ben reached it. The dog shot him a thought. "Look, another door. I hadn't noticed that. Tell Arnela to shut it after us and wedge it tight – that might buy us a bit of time."

Ben immediately passed on the dog's idea to the big goatherd. She looked at the door thoughtfully. It was obviously a stronghold door which opened inwards, standing flat against the wall. Its timbers had been painted and hung with grey cloth, disguised skilfully to resemble the surrounding rock. An enemy would have difficulty finding the cave entrance with the door closed.

Ned's thoughts became urgent. "Is she going to stand there all day thinking about it, Ben? I can hear the Razan, they've freed the tunnel of the armoury door. There's a lot of 'em, and they're coming fast. We'd better do something quickly, mate!"

Arnela produced her knife again. "Right, here's what we do!" She slashed through the leather hinges – there were four of them. The leather was extra thick and well greased but was no match for the big woman's keen blade. Leaping forward, she held the large door, taking the weight of it on her back. Arnela gasped, "Help me get this outside!" The two boys gripped either side of the thick timbers. Ben was surprised when the bear joined Arnela to share the weight.

Now the pursuing Razan could be heard coming into the main cavern. Ligran Razan was shouting, "Get to the entrance! Don't let anyone leave this place alive!"

With a loud *whump!* the door fell flat on the ground. Arnela looked at the slope down the mountainside. It was covered with ice and snow, dotted with shale and scrub grass. "Well, friends, this'll either kill us all or get us away free. Jump aboard, a sleigh ride is our only hope!"

Ned peered back into the Razan stronghold – the robbers were dashing through the main cavern like a huge pack of wolves.

An arrow zipped by him. Ben seized his friend's collar. "Onto the door, Ned, quick!"

Karay was already seated on the grey-cloth-covered door and was hugging the bear, which crouched beside her. Arnela, Ben and Dominic, bent double, pushed the heavy door. It inched forward as they bent their backs, grunting with exertion. Slowly, the entire door began moving on its own as it came onto the slope. Arnela thrust Ben and Dominic on, and with a bound she, too, landed on the door.

Then they were off – just as Ligran emerged from the cave with a crowd of henchmen. One of the men unslung a musket. Ligran grabbed it from him savagely. "Idiot, d'you want to kill us all? Use your bows, fire arrows!"

The big door was still moving rather sluggishly when Dominic felt an arrow whip by, close to his cheek. "Archers! Get down!" The four fell flat, and the bear lay down behind Karay, protecting her. It roared with rage as an arrow clipped it through the thick fur of its shoulder. Arrows rained downwards, thudding into the wooden door.

Just as Arnela felt the sledging door begin to pick up

speed, a shaft pinned her cloak to the timbers. She sat up and unslung her rifle, gritting her teeth together. "Right, let's finish this. Out with those pistols. Fire when I give the order, and let's hope we can outrun what follows!"

Scrabbling around to face the Razan contingent uphill, Ben, Karay and Dominic drew their pistols.

Arnela shouted, "No need to aim. Just fire. Now!"

Four shots sounded out simultaneously. The sound was deafening – it sent echoes rebounding for miles in the high, clear mountain atmosphere. It was like the end of the world! The gunfire was followed by an immense rumble which shook the very slopes. There was a noise like a great *kraaaaawwwkkk!* An entire section of the mountain peak fell away. Ligran Razan and the henchmen standing outside the cave vanished in a heavy white curtain, as did the entire mouth of the Razan stronghold, everyone inside it entombed in countless thousands of tons of ice, rock and snow.

Whipping wind and snow particles stung Ben's face as he lay flat, clinging to his faithful dog. The huge sledge was skimming down the mountainside faster than any arrow from a bow. Ben's and Ned's thoughts were blended in one almighty yell that would not issue from their mouths. "*Yeeeeeeeoooooo-wwwwwww!*"

Dominic's fingernails felt as if they were cracking as he clung to the door like a leech. The bear had both front paws flat across Karay, its claws clamped into the wood as it held itself and the girl down. Ben had Ned's collar between his teeth, and the dog lay with him, both trapped beneath Arnela's back. They hit a bank, ploughing through it like lightning; then, covered in snow, the massive toboggan crested a small ice-clad outcrop and left the ground, sailing out into midair like a bird. The only sound was the wind. All of them, with their eyes tightly shut, knew they were no longer on solid ground. Whirling snowflakes and shrieking wind engulfed them for what seemed an age.

Then came a sickening bump that ripped the breath from their lungs. A bang! They were still rushing onward, though now touching the earth. A crash! Always moving down, hurtling forward. A ripping sound! A *thud!* A loud *swoosh!* A grating noise, followed by a final earsplitting . . . *bang!* Then there was blackness and enveloping silence.

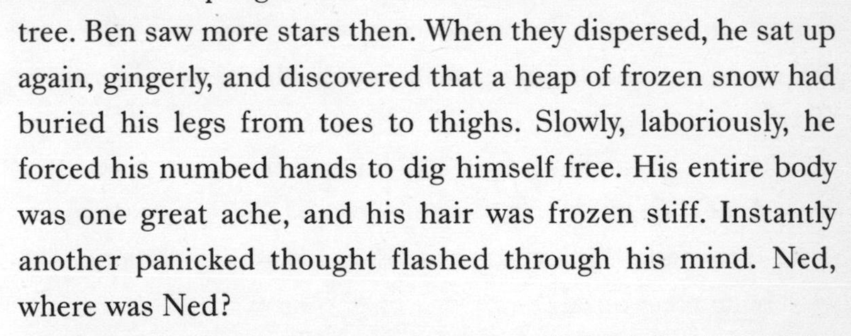

27

IT WAS NIGHT. BEN knew this as his eyes opened – he was facing a star-strewn sky and a half-moon of pure beaten silver. But his legs would not move. Panic overcame him. He sat up rigid and knocked the back of his head on a tree. Ben saw more stars then. When they dispersed, he sat up again, gingerly, and discovered that a heap of frozen snow had buried his legs from toes to thighs. Slowly, laboriously, he forced his numbed hands to dig himself free. His entire body was one great ache, and his hair was frozen stiff. Instantly another panicked thought flashed through his mind. Ned, where was Ned?

A reply came back promptly to Ben. "I think I've joined the angels, mate. Try not to grieve too much."

Ben pulled his legs free. "Ned, where are you?"

"Right above your head, you great frosted lump. Look up!"

There was the faithful hound, draped over a fir branch three feet above his master's head. He wagged his tail carefully. "I'm coming down, get ready to catch me. One, two . . ."

The black Labrador landed in Ben's outstretched arms,

knocking them both flat in the snow. They lay for a moment, exhausted.

"*Maaaaah!*" A bleat rang out, followed by Arnela's voice.

"Ajax the Less, stop nibbling my sleeves, they're ragged enough as it is. Be still!"

Ben and Ned struggled upright as the big goatherd woman came scrunching through the deep-packed snow with a young goat tucked under one arm. She waved to Ben and Ned. "Good evening! Have ye seen the other two and that old bear?"

Ben shook his head. "Not so far. We haven't even checked to see if we're in one piece yet, have we, Ned?"

The dog shook his head no. Arnela chuckled. "You've got the cleverest dog in the world there, Ben, he's worth all my goats put together. Well, here we are, still alive, no thanks to my foolishness. Just look at this mountain – it'll never be the same again. It's a good job the avalanche fell mainly to the left and we shot off to the right. I must've been mad, flying you all down the mountain and telling you to fire all the pistols like that. 'Twas sheer insanity!"

Ben ran to his big friend and hugged her. "You saved our lives, Arnela. Trouble like we were in calls for desperate measures. I dread to think what those Razan might've done to us if we'd been recaptured."

Arnela ruffled Ben's hair, loosening the ice from it. The little goat, Ajax the Less, maaaaahed piteously as the goatherd spoke to him like a spoiled child. "Huh, don't think I'm going to carry you around, stroking ye all night. Go on, off home, young rip, tell your mamma I won't be long."

She turned to Ben and Ned. "You two go with him, the cave's just below this ridge. I had to dig my way into it. The stream and pool have gone, vanished somewhere, but my goats all survived by staying inside. Nothing's the same since we brought the mountain peak down. I'll search for the others, don't worry. Well, go on, you pair! Do something useful, light a fire, put some water on to boil, search about and find something to cook – that's if those goats haven't eaten everything. Ooh, that Pantyro, I'm going to have a word or two with him when I get time!"

Ben stood shivering in the cold, reluctant to desert Arnela. "Are you sure you'll be all right?"

She lifted him bodily until they were face to face. "Why shouldn't I be? Nobody knows this mountain the way I do. You'd only be in the way. I'll find them, go on, off with you!"

Without the pool and the pretty little waterfall, the cave was just a black hole in the snow. Ned ambled in, shouldering goats aside as he passed Ben a thought. "Arnela's already lit the lanterns, thank goodness. Whew, this place smells a bit goaty, though. What a mess!"

Ben took dry pine branches, moss and charcoal, stacking them in the rift that served as a fireplace. He listened to his dog complaining.

"Ahoy there, mate, that's my tail, not a midnight snack! Hmph! You goats, you've been living here like, like . . . animals!"

Ben lit the fire from a lantern, then winked at Ned. "At least animals are more civilized than the Razan. Chase some of the bigger goats out, Ned. It'll make a bit more room in here, and the fresh air will do them good!"

Behind the slate slabs that served as a larder, Ben found goat cheese, some eggs and a few hard barley cakes. He boiled six eggs in the water cauldron. Spreading the cheese on the barley cakes, he sat toasting them. Ned sat by his side, enjoying the warmth from the fire. After all they had been through, Ben's mind was like his body, numbed and exhausted. They ate some of the food, then sat together, eyelids drooping, heads nodding, not attempting to resist the temptation of sleep.

Then a voice roused them instantly. "Here, what's all this? No supper for me?"

Dominic staggered in and fell against Ned. He slumped there. "Never thought I'd see a nice warm fire again 'til I spotted this cave. I saw the light glimmering and made straight for it."

Ben rubbed his eyes and blinked. "Welcome home, Dom, where did you get to? Arnela's out looking for you. Have you seen Karay or our bear in your travels?"

Ice water trickled out of Dominic's hair and ran down his cheeks. "No, Ben, I'm afraid not. First thing I knew when I came around was that I was upside down in a snowdrift. Water dripping up my nose woke me – it took me ages to get free. After that I just blundered about among some tiny trees. Then when I took stock of where I was, I realized I was somewhere in the foothills – the trees were so small because snow and ice from the avalanche had filled the valley. I was actually walking amongst treetops, not tiny trees! Can you believe it? Good job you lit the fire, or I might've wandered about until I collapsed and froze to death!"

Ben watched Dominic tearing ravenously into barley cakes and toasted cheese. "Thank heaven *you're* alive, Dom!"

The facemaker nodded upwards. "More than you can say for those Razan villains. Nobody up there could've survived the avalanche. Though if any did, they'd have been far worse off. Imagine being entombed alive in those caves, a living death!"

Ben stared into the glowing charcoal fire. "Don't forget that the tunnels ran downwards, the debris would have showered into there and filled the caves in a flash. They'd have been slain in the wink of an eye. The Razan are gone forever, I'd bet my life on that."

Dominic covered his eyes with his arm as he murmured, "And Adamo, too, if he was in there."

Ben was forced to agree with his friend. "Aye, our mission failed, even though we rid the comte of the curse of Razan. Though I remember Maguda telling me that Adamo was already dead. She said it in a strange way – I can't recall her exact words. Perhaps tomorrow, when I'm not so tired, it'll come back to me."

Both boys and the dog had fallen asleep in front of the fire. Ben's mind was free of everything. It was like being unconscious, a merciful blackness. Most of the goats curled up around them, wanting to be close to the warmth. It was quiet and peaceful inside the cave. Outside, the night was still, amidst the devastation wrought by the avalanche.

It was in the hour before dawn that Arnela returned. The goats began bleating as the giant figure of their mistress ducked into the cave entrance. Ned leapt up and ran to greet her. His bark wakened Ben and Dominic, and both boys began firing anxious questions at the big woman.

"Where's Karay, did you find her?"

"She's not injured . . . or dead?"

The goats began bleating furiously. They hurried to the back of the cave and continued with their din.

Arnela lifted both arms and roared, "Silence! All of you!"

Everybody, dog, boys and goats, went quiet. Arnela

continued in a normal voice. "No, Karay is not dead or injured. I never found her . . . he did." The bear shambled in on its hind legs carrying the girl. He placed her gently on the ground between the two boys. Bleating aloud with terror, the goats fled the cave.

Arnela warmed her hands at the fire. "I discovered the bear roaming around carrying the girl. He would not let me near her. So I got it to follow me, and here we are. That's all I can tell you."

Ben echoed Ned's thought. "Except to say that we're all alive and together again!"

Morning light filtered into the cave onto a curious scene. The goats huddled in the entrance, fearing to enter lest the bear devour them. Karay, unharmed, sat up drinking herbal tea and gazing affectionately at the sleeping bear. Steam rose from his fur as he lay close to her. The girl stroked him gently. "He stayed with me, carried me and protected me. But why?"

Dominic scratched his head. "Who can say? Perhaps it was because you showed him kindness. It was you who would not leave him in that cell, Karay. You insisted from the first moment you set eyes on him that you would rescue him. He looks like a good creature. Can I stroke him?"

Karay smiled. "Go on, he won't bite you."

Dominic patted the beast's head gingerly. The bear seemed peaceful enough. Encouraged by this, Dominic scratched behind the bear's collar, the way he would with Ned. He was thrown aside as the bear sat bolt upright, pawing at the metal collar that circled his neck.

Karay spoke soothingly to him, placing her cheek against

the bear's huge paw. "Hush now, my poor friend, did he hurt you? Well, I'm sure Dominic didn't mean to, did you, Dom?"

The creature turned his great sad liquid eyes towards Dominic, who stared into them for a moment. He gasped. "Ben, Arnela, get those lanterns and bring them closer to its face – there's something strange about this animal!"

Karay hugged her bear protectively. "Don't hurt him or frighten him. I'll never speak to any of you again if you do!"

Ben reassured her. "I promise we won't. Let Dominic take a look at him – your bear is safe with us, pal."

Plucking up his courage, Dominic sat as close to the bear as he could. Arnela and Ben held the lanterns close while Karay hovered behind the bear, anxiety in her voice.

"What is it, Dominic, what d'you see? Oh, please tell me!"

The Facemaker of Sabada blinked as he gazed deep into the bear's eyes. He blinked again but could not stop the tears that coursed down his face as he sobbed, "It's a man! A man imprisoned in a bear's hide!"

The bear nodded its head, as far as the spiked collar would allow, and gave a long, anguished groan.

Ned was invading Ben's thoughts. "Well, don't sit there gaping, get the poor wretch out!"

Arnela drew her sharp, hook-bladed knife. "I'll free him from that filthy skin!"

Karay held out her hand to the goatherd. "No, friend, I will. Give me the blade. See if you can find soft cloth, or moss, then soak it in warm water. Oh, and have you got anything that'll cut through his collar?"

Karay came around and took the bear's face in both hands. "Be quite still, trust me, I won't harm you."

The bear pressed his nose against her forehead.

"Mmmmmmmm." He lowered his head until it was resting in her lap.

Arnela rummaged about and produced an old file. "I've filed many a misshapen hoof straight with this."

With extreme care, Karay packed the inside of the collar with warm damp moss. Ben could hear her teeth grinding as she muttered with barely controlled rage and fury, "This collar is spiked on both sides. Filthy Razan scum! How could they do this to a human being? I'm glad they're all dead. Glad!"

Arnela slid her hand under the collar and filed away at the green-encrusted copper rivet that held it together. It did not take the sturdy goatherd long. With a single heave of both hands, she bent the iron collar straight and flung it from her. "Go on, Karay, let's see what our bear looks like!"

The girl's nimble fingers felt the row of tough rawhide stitches joining the head to the body. She wiped away with a fresh cloth soaked in semi-hot water. Dried blood and matted fur parted enough for her to see what she was doing properly. Stitch by stitch the sinewy yarn parted until she had worked right around the neck with Arnela's knife. Shielding the head beneath by placing her hand under the hide at the back of the nape, she sliced neatly upwards towards the top of the skull. All this time her patient lay quite still, never uttering a single sound. Arnela had to help her to lift the bear's head skin free – the original bone was still inside the muzzle. It was indeed a real man!

He sat in silence, tears brimming out of his deep brown eyes. His hair – long, greasy and black as a raven's wing – had moulded itself to his head. He had a broken nose, and his skin was like pale wax. A beard of whiskers grew from high on his cheekbones, almost masking his lips. Around his neck were the scratches and scars left by the collar spikes. His teeth were yellowed and stained but in good shape. It was hard to tell, but he looked to be around twenty or so years of age. His eyes never once left Karay's face.

Ned shook his head in amazement. "Well, now I've seen everything!"

Ben agreed with the thought as he turned to Dominic. "Are you thinking what I'm thinking, mate? Look at that face!"

Dominic had studied many faces before, and now his eyes roved over the features. "It's a good face, Ben, a strong one. By the size of it, I'd say there is a very big man inside that bearskin. I've seen faces like that in artwork in great churches and cathedrals – the faces of saints who have suffered greatly."

Karay was hardly aware of Arnela taking the knife from her. The goatherd slit the skin at the wrists, freeing the young man's hands.

Karay whispered to him, "Who are you, can you speak, my friend?"

He touched his throat and made a low noise. " 'Damuuuh!"

Dominic and Ben whooped together. "Adamo!"

A smile like the rising sun lit up Arnela's face. "The little boy from years ago, I knew it! I knew it all along, Adamo, it had to be you!"

Adamo looked at the big woman – he almost smiled. A grunt of recognition passed his lips. Then Karay took charge. "Why don't you all go and see if the road is open through the woodlands. Adamo can't return to his uncle in Veron looking like this. I'll help him to clean up. Arnela, could you put a fresh edge on your blade and leave it with me?"

The big woman understood. She stropped her knife

vigorously on a leather strap, issuing orders. "Ben, you'll find some herbal ointment I made in that little box on the ledge. It's as good as any soap. Dom, heat more water. Here's an old hair slide, Karay, that'll make do for a comb. Come on, Ned, we'll go and scout the path out. You lads can follow us!"

They surveyed the landscape in the bright morning sunshine from the elevated view of a high snowbank created by the enormous landslide. Distant hills appeared fresh and green with the lilac haze of heather patchworking them. Stream water glinted along newly diverted courses. Down in the valleys, larks ascended, trilling in the clear air.

Ben listened to his dog's thoughts. "What a day! It makes life worthwhile. I'm glad our angel saved us from the *Flying Dutchman.* Our friend the old comte and a lot of folk in these regions are going to be very happy, now that we've found Adamo and got rid of the Razan plague!"

Ben agreed mentally. "Aye, Ned, the mission is completed now. It makes me sad to think we'll have to move on, but we could not afford to be seen here years from now, with everyone growing older and us forever the same age."

Dominic looked at his friend's clouded blue eyes. "What's the matter, Ben? You look sad all of a sudden."

Ben had no chance to answer. Ned knocked him flat in the snow. Sprawling on the boy's chest, the black Labrador licked Ben's face furiously as he berated him mentally. "Haha, O mournful moping master, the clever Ned banishes all miseries. I'll soon lick a smile back on your face!"

Arnela and Dominic burst out laughing at the sight of Ben trying to wrestle Ned off and pleading with him. "Yurgh! Gerroff, y'great sloppy hound! Look, I'm smiling, I'm happy! Let me up, please!"

Arnela lifted the dog from her friend. "What's all this about?"

Ben struggled upright, dusting the snow from himself. "Dominic started it, ma'am. Ned was just trying to put a smile on my face. Back, Ned, back! See, I'm happy again!"

The big woman tucked Ned under her arm as though he were a goat, and she set off back to the cave. "Come on, you two. Let's see how our Adamo is looking now."

Karay was sitting outside the cave, enjoying the morning sun with Adamo. She waved as they came scrunching through the snow. "Just take a peep at this handsome fellow!"

The young man's cheeks coloured slightly. He gave a shy smile. Karay had given Adamo a wash, shave and haircut.

Arnela gasped. "Surely this isn't the scraggy old bear we rescued from the Razan? He's got skin like a peach, and look at the length of those eyelashes. Any maiden would give a bag of gold to have eyelashes like that. Karay, I think you'd better hide Adamo from the ladies of Veron when he gets back!"

The girl took Adamo's wide, powerful hand in hers. "I'll fight them if they even glance his way! But he's not quite ready for public appearances yet. We haven't any decent clothing to fit him! He's a big fellow, almost taller than you, Arnela, and broader across the shoulders. Underneath that cloak of yours, which I borrowed for him, Adamo still has on the bearskin. So he's still half man, half bear, eh, friend?"

Ben had only seen Adamo bent and shuffling in his role as a bear. He was taken aback when the young man stood up straight. Karay was right: Adamo was a big fellow. He stayed solemn for a moment, his soft brown eyes looking from one of them to the other. Then he gave an enormous grin and spread both arms wide. The cloak parted, revealing him clad in the bear hide from foot to neck. He danced comically to and fro, kicking up the wide, floppy pads that encased his feet and waving his fur-coated arms round and round. Ned's delighted barks mingled with the helpless laughter of the onlookers. Adamo performed an awkward bow and said a single word, though he had difficulty in getting it out. "F . . . frrr . . . free!"

COMTE VINCENTE BREGON OF VERON SAT IN his gazebo at the centre of his beautiful walled garden. Though it was mid-afternoon, he was still clad in his nightshirt and dressing gown. He looked old and haggard. A small garden beetle trundled slowly over his sandalled foot, a magpie was strutting boldly about on the open windowsill. They were ignored by the old man, who stared unhappily at the fading blooms bordering the gravel path. His mind was elsewhere. The magpie spotted the beetle. It was about to descend on the insect and snatch it, when it was disturbed by footsteps. The bird flew off, giving the beetle an unknowing extension to its short life.

Mathilde, the equally old but energetic cook, bustled into the gazebo, sniffing irately as she placed a tray of food and drink on an ornamental table beside her master. "Still sitting here like a scarecrow, eh?"

Wiping the sleeve of his gown across both eyes, the comte replied wearily, "Go away and leave me alone, woman."

However, Mathilde was not about to go away. She persisted, "Can ye hear the market fair outside? I can. Why don't you put on some decent clothing and get out there? 'Twill do you good. Summer's almost gone, and you sit out here from dawn to dusk, day after day, like some old cracked statue."

He sighed, staring down at the beetle, which was laboriously crawling from his big toenail to the floor. "Give your tongue a rest, Mathilde. 'Tis my own business how I conduct my life. Go back to your kitchens."

Mathilde stubbornly tapped the tray and continued her tirade. "You'll become an old skeleton, eat something! You never touched the nice breakfast I served you this morning, so I've brought you chicken broth with barley and leeks. Look, fresh bread, cream cheese and a glass of milk laced with brandy. Taste it, that's all I ask, just take a little bit."

The comte turned his lined face from her stern gaze. "Take it away, I'm not hungry. Please, give it to one of the servants. I have no appetite for food or drink."

The faithful Mathilde knelt by his side, her voice softening. "What is it, Vincente, what ails you?"

Again he wiped the sleeve across his eyes. "I'm an old fool – worse, an unthinking old fool. On a silly impulse I sent three young people and a dog to their deaths!"

Mathilde stood up brusquely, her attitude hardening. "Oh, 'tis that again, is it? Well, let me tell you, sir, 'twas not your doing – they volunteered themselves to go. Hmph! Gypsies and vagabonds, little wonder they never came back. If you ask me, they've probably joined up with the Razan. They're creatures of a kind, all of them!"

The comte's eyes flared briefly, his voice sharpening as he

pointed a finger towards the big house. "Go, you bad-mouthed old fishwife. Go!"

She bustled off in a huff, muttering aloud, "Well, I've done my duty to the Bregons. Soon we'll have a dead comte on our hands, one who starved himself into his grave. What'll become of Veron then, eh? Those Razan'll march straight in and take over the entire place. Mark my words!"

The comte spoke, not so much to answer her, merely ruminating to himself. "Why does God choose fools to rule? I was deluding myself that Adamo would be still alive after all these years. That pretty young girl, those good young boys and their dog, their lives are lost now, all because of a stupid old man's desires. O Lord, forgive me for what I've done!"

Garath, the comte's blacksmith and stable master, trudged up the three steps into the gazebo. Placing a strong arm under the older man's elbow, he gently eased him into a standing position. "Time for you to go inside now, sir. Shall I send someone out to bring your food in also? That soup still looks hot, you may fancy it later."

Shaking his head, the comte allowed himself to be led off. "Do what you wish with the food. Take me to my bedchamber, Garath, I feel tired."

It was the last day of the market fair, and a few people were leaving early owing to the long journey home they would have to take. Seated in a two-wheeled cart drawn by a lumbering ox, a farmer, together with his wife and teenage daughter, made their way to the gate in Veron's walls. The cart was held up at the gateway. It could not proceed because of an argument that was going on between two fresh-faced, newly appointed guards and five other people. The farmer sat patiently, holding the ox reins, whilst the dispute outside the gate carried on.

Karay's voice rang out. "Five centimes? That's daylight robbery! It was only two centimes apiece and one for the dog last time we came here! Go and get the comte, he'll be glad to let us through for free!"

The tallest of the two guards, who was little more than a runaway farmboy, laughed at the girl's claim. "Hoho, personal friends of the comte, are we? Listen, girl, we may be new t'this job, but we ain't soft in the head. Entrance fees to the fair have risen, how d'you suppose the sergeant can make up our wages, eh?"

Arnela's voice replied with a dangerous edge to it, "You keep a civil tongue in your head, boy, or you'll feel the back of my hand. Where is your sergeant? Go and fetch him – he'll certainly know what to do!"

The smaller guard was even younger than his comrade but was polite and serious. "Ma'am, the sergeant's having his meal in the big house kitchen. You'll have to wait until he comes back here, neither of us is allowed to leave his post. If you pay us the entrance fee, then I'm sure he'll be glad to sort out the difference with you later. Sorry, but 'tis more than our job's worth to let you in free, you understand, ma'am?"

Karay's voice chimed in, "So, then, how much d'you want?"

The taller guard took up the dispute again. "Well, er, five centimes apiece for the two ladies, an' five each for the boys, an' that, er, other person. Let's see, that's twenty centimes all told, if y'please."

Karay's scornful laugh rang out. "Where did you learn to count?"

The guard continued, pretending to ignore her. "We'll call it three for the dog, and, er, say, one centime apiece for those goats, when we've counted 'em!"

Arnela pushed forward, her temper growing short. "Enough of this foolishness, let us in! We've got business with the comte. Stand aside!"

The guards' spears crossed, blocking her path. The big woman pointed a warning finger at the tall guard.

"D'you want me to take those spears and wrap them around your necks and give you both a good spanking, eh?"

The farmer's wife came walking through the gate and entered the dispute. She took coins from her purse, offering them to the guards. "Let these folk through, take these five francs!" She turned to Karay with a smile. "Remember me, Veronique?"

The quick-witted girl recalled everything in a flash. She recognized the lady as the pancake seller whose fortune she had told when they had first come to Veron.

"Oh, Madame Gilbert, what a pleasure to see you again. Thank you so much for paying our toll. I'm, er, with some friends at the moment. We're a bit short of money, until I get a fortune-telling engagement, you understand."

The farmer's wife nodded knowingly. "Of course, my dear Veronique." She winked at Karay. "After what you did for me that day, 'tis the least I can do. I'm no longer Madame Gilbert. I married the farmer. I'm Madame Frane now, and very happy to be so. I acted on the good advice you gave me. That's my husband and our daughter Jeanette in the cart. I sold the pancake business at a handsome profit. My life is so happy now, thanks to you. Well, I must go, we've got a long journey back to the farm. Goodbye, Veronique my dear – that is, if your name really is Veronique?"

Karay whispered in the good woman's ear as she kissed her cheek, "Only when it suits me. Bless you, Madame Frane."

Garath had delivered the comte to his bedchamber. He sat in the kitchen, watching Mathilde crimp the edges of a large plum pie as he worked his way through the tray of food that the comte had left untouched. "Mmmm, that plum pie looks good. Maybe he'll eat a slice for his supper, eh?"

Mathilde made some chevron slits in the centre of the pastry. "I hope he does, Garath. I'm worried sick about the man – he's fading away from lack of good food. That, and the troubles he's created in his mind –"

A timid rap on the kitchen door interrupted Mathilde's woeful musings. She raised her voice irately. "Yes, who is it?"

The smaller of the two guards poked his head around the door, respectfully pulling off his hat and revealing a tousled mop of hair. "Ma'am, I met the sergeant in the square and he told me to bring these people to see the comte."

Mathilde wiped floury hands upon her apron. "People, what people?" A billy goat pushed his way past the guard and wandered into the kitchen. "*Maaaahaah!*"

Mathilde grabbed her rolling pin, shouting, "Yaaah! Get that beast out of my kitchen! Garath, help!"

The guard was brushed aside as, knocking the door wide open, a herd of goats came bleating into the room, followed by Ned and the rest of the party.

Mathilde immediately shouted at Ben, Dominic and Karay, brandishing the rolling pin, "You three, I might have known it! Gypsies, assassins, get out of my kitch– Waaaah!"

She clapped a hand to one cheek. The pie was spoiled as the

rolling pin fell into it. Mathilde swayed, grasping the table edge as she stared at the man clad in bearskin.

Garath saw him too, and his voice trembled as he spoke. "Monsieur Edouard... you're alive?"

Mathilde recovered herself quickly. "Fool! That's not Edouard, 'tis his son, Adamo... but... but... he's a grown man!"

Adamo pushed his way through the goats to the cook, who had been his nursemaid in infancy. "Oh, 'Tilde!" He swept her up in both arms and lifted her onto the tabletop.

Mathilde would not let go of Adamo and rained kisses on him. "See, Garath, he knows me. 'Tilde! That's the name he used to call me when he was little. Adamo! You've come back to me! My Adamo!"

The unbaked plum pie had been swept off onto the floor. Pantyro, Clovis and Ajax the Less began making short work of it, as Arnela watched them ruefully. "I'd have enjoyed a slice of that pie if it had been baked. It's years since I tasted a nice home-baked plum pie."

It was quite a time before order was restored to the kitchen. Arnela herded her goats out into the garden, where they immediately began eating flowers, grass, leaves and anything that resembled food to them. Mathilde seated the five travellers at her table and began producing food like magic. Each time she passed Adamo, she would hug him fondly.

"Here, my love, have some of this almond cake, and a dish of my vanilla custard. The beef stew in the oven won't take long to heat, and the baked carrot and turnip. Garath, bring more ale, and milk, too. Oh, I must pop some of that raisin flan in to warm up. Eat, all of you! Come on, eat, eat!"

• • •

Crimson twilight of early autumn evening flooded through the kitchen windows as Garath lit the lanterns. He kept turning to look at Adamo and shaking his head. "We can't have you walking in on the comte in that state, sir."

Mathilde changed her juice-stained apron for a clean one. "I should think not, 'twould frighten the poor man to death! Garath, tell Hector to get hot water and fill up that big tub you keep in the stables, put lavender water in it, too. I'll sneak up to Monsieur Edouard's old room – there's a whole wardrobe of his clothes still there. He was almost as big as Adamo, they should fit well enough. Then you can take that horrible bear's hide and burn it!"

Ned looked up from beneath the table, where he was munching on an enormous pork chop. "Maybe Adamo would like to burn it, eh, Ben?"

The boy caught his dog's thought and asked Adamo, "Would you like to burn the bearskin, my friend?"

A rare smile lit up the big fellow's face as he pointed to himself. "I . . . burn . . . it . . . Ben . . . my friend!"

The boy's strange blue eyes smiled back. "I wager you will!"

After Garath had left him lying upon his bed, tiredness of both mind and body overcame the old comte. He drifted into a deep sleep, unaware of any activities that were going on downstairs. The few hours he lay there felt as long as a full night's rest. Therefore, he was mildly surprised when he woke to the curtains being drawn open, revealing evening's glorious scarlet sun rays flooding the bedchamber. Confusion set in on the old man. Was he awake, or was it a dream? Shading his eyes, he blinked upwards at the tall, handsome man who was standing by the bed gazing calmly down at him. A strange and limited conversation took place – the visitor spoke only one word. "Pappa?"

Vincente Bregon shook his head. "No, no, our father died many years ago, Edouard, a long time ago. Edouard, is it you?"

Then the strange boy, Ben, this one who had eyes which had looked across seas and oceans, came and sat upon the bed. "No, sir, it isn't Edouard. This is his son, Adamo. We've brought him back to you, just as we vowed we would."

Unsure whether he was still awake or not, the old man nodded. "Of course, Adamo never knew his father. Pappa, that's what he used to call me. Ah, but that was before the Razan stole him."

Before anyone could stop him, Ned bounded up onto the bed and licked the old man's face. Comte Vincente Bregon de Veron sat up straight, fully awake.

Seconds ticked by as he looked into the face of his long-lost nephew, then recognition dawned. Taking the tall man's hands, he pressed his face into them. "Adamo, my dear brother's son, it is you? Adamo! Adamo!"

29

THREE MARKET FAIRS HAD COME AND GONE. Early mists drifted away into a crisp, golden autumn morn. Ben gripped the iron tongs, holding a horseshoe against the front hoof of a placid white mare. Smoke arose from the forged metal in a blue-grey cloud.

From his seat atop a hay bale, Ned winced, passing Ben a thought. "Ooch! Didn't that hurt the poor old nag? It was almost red hot!"

Ben mentally answered his dog's enquiry. "Of course it didn't – horses enjoy having new shoes fitted. Garath's going to show me how to nail the shoe onto her hoof now. Hold still, good girl, this won't take long."

Ned cut in with a horrified thought. "You mean you're going to hammer nails into the poor mare's foot? I'm off, before you and Garath decide to give me a new set of shoes!"

Leaping off the bale, the black Labrador shot outside into the cobbled stable yard. Ned narrowly missed being run down by two more horses that clattered in, with Karay and Adamo on their backs. The girl called out needlessly, "Mind yourself, Ned, or you'll get run down!"

Ned barked his disapproval at the words his mouth could not say. "I'd sooner be run down than have iron shoes nailed to my paws, miss. Have y'seen what those two are doing to a mare in the stables? I'll bet Arnela doesn't do that to her goats!" He dashed off barking to find his goatherd friend.

Karay laughed. "Let's go and see what Mathilde's baking for lunch. Something nice, I hope, I'm starving!"

Adamo helped her down from her horse. Tugging her hair playfully, he remarked in his slow, halting speech, "You are always hungry, Karay!"

She looked up at him fondly. "Huh, look who's talking. Have you noticed how much you can put away?"

Comical innocence shone in Adamo's brown eyes. "I am bigger than you, Adamo needs more food!"

Arnela was sitting in the gazebo with a tiny month-old nanny goat on her knee. Dominic perched against the windowsill, painting them both. He had been given brushes, paints, canvas and an easel, a gift from the comte. Ned came lolloping along. Sitting next to the big goatherd woman, he placed a paw on her knee and gazed faithfully up at her and the goat.

The facemaker chuckled admiringly. "Stay like that, Ned, what a perfect tableau it makes. Well done, boy, good dog!"

The black Labrador held his pose, emitting thoughts that would never reach Arnela or Dominic. "Why d'you think I sat here? Anyone with half an eye could see the picture was off balance. Note the way I present a noble profile in just the right light. If only someone would let me paint, I'd dash off a few masterpieces with my tail. Hidden depths of talent, y'know, quite common among us Labradors!"

The baby goat bleated. "*Maaahaaah!*"

Ned flicked it a glance. "Huh, who asked you?"

Lunch that day was not a snatch-and-bite-in-the-kitchen affair. Mathilde would not even let them enter her domain; she shooed them all out.

"Go and get cleaned up, all of you, put on some fresh clothes, too. Go on!"

Adamo protested, "We are hungry people, feed us, 'Tilde!"

But even his plea did not move the old cook. "The master wants to join you in the dining room, he told me so specially. Lunch will be served in one hour. Go away!"

Ned passed a thought to Ben as they went upstairs. "Maybe the comte wants to speak to us about something in particular."

Ben paused on the stairway. "That's what I was thinking, too. I've been getting an uneasy feeling for the past few days. We've been a long time in Veron, maybe a bit too long."

Ned licked the boy's hand. "Too much to hope that our angel has forgotten about us, I suppose?"

Ben sighed. "I'll wager that angels never forget anything, mate." He shrugged and tried to brighten up. "We're probably worrying over nothing. Come on, let's get dressed!"

He bounded up the rest of the stairs, laughing aloud at the dog's reply. "Dearie me, what shall I wear to lunch?"

• • •

Vincente Bregon looked every inch the Comte de Veron as he entered the dining room – dressed in the finest silks and linens, his hair and beard neatly trimmed, his step vigorous and steady. To the eyes of his guests he seemed many years younger. Seven places were laid for the meal. Ned was underneath the table, already making inroads upon a slab of roasted pork crackling. Ben, Dominic, Arnela, Karay and Adamo sat laughing and chattering with one another, each of them clad in new outfits provided by their host's generosity.

The comte seated himself. Banging the tabletop with mock severity, he raised his voice: "What? My guests sitting here staring at an empty board! Where's that lazy old cook of mine? Dozing in front of the oven fire, I wager. Can't a man get a decent meal in his own house any more?"

Mathilde entered, leading two young maidservants who were pushing a trolley laden with food. Her scornful wit was not lost upon her audience. She wagged a finger in the comte's face. "The lunch has been ready this past quarter hour, waiting on you to dodder downstairs in your bib and tucker. Dozing in front of the oven fire, indeed? The only time I'll do that is when I've got you in the oven, baking some life into those old bones of yours, you crotchety old codger!"

Ben and his friends shook with laughter as the pair exchanged good-humoured insults.

"Be silent, you frowzy old loaf-burner!"

"Yah, go and take a nap, you mumbling old chin-dribbler!"

The comte rose. "I'll not stand for that in my house, madame!"

Mathilde winked at Karay and Adamo as she retorted, "Then sit down!"

The comte chuckled. He patted the empty chair next to him. "No, no, Mathilde, 'tis you who must sit down, here, right beside me. Let the maids serve our lunch today."

Mathilde protested. "Cooks don't sit at table with the master, who ever heard of such a thing?"

But the Comte de Veron would brook no argument. "Madame, I am ordering you to sit and dine with us. When lunch is over, I have things to say which concern us all!"

The meal was delicious. A steaming mushroom soup was followed by salad and a collation of cheeses, ham, brown bread, eggs and a grilled carp. Over a dessert of hot summer pudding and cream they sipped cider, fruit juice and glasses of the local wine mixed with fresh springwater.

Ben nodded and smiled at the amiable banter and conversation of his friends. However, he heard little of it as he and Ned exchanged apprehensive thoughts.

The dog's paw touched his master's foot beneath the table as Ned voiced his opinion. "I don't know why, Ben, but I'm beginning to feel rather uneasy about something or other. I can't think what it is."

The boy reached down and stroked his Labrador's silky ears. He had forgotten the message that the angel had woven into his dreams when he first met Karay. That night in the forest seemed so long ago and faraway.

He answered Ned, trying not to sound perplexed. "I expect our angel will let us know if anything's amiss. Strange, but I can't remember any warning the angel gave me about moving on, can you?"

Ned poked his head out from under the tablecloth hem. "No, I don't recall a thing – that's what's bothering me."

Around the table it had gone suddenly quiet. Dominic

nudged Ben's arm and whispered to him, "Sit up straight, friend. You look half asleep there. The comte has something to say to us!"

Ben suddenly became attentive. "What? Oh, er, sorry!"

The comte drew from his finger the large gold ring that bore his family's crest. It was far too large for him and slipped off easily. He placed it on the little finger of Adamo's right hand, where it fitted snugly.

"This was your father's ring. He was the rightful lord of Veron. The ring carries the Bregon seal: a lion for strength, a dove for peace, and a knotted rope symbolizing union and togetherness. Adamo Bregon, son of Edouard, my brother, you are now to be known as Comte de Veron, as is your birthright!"

The others around the table applauded warmly. Even Ned emerged from beneath the table, his tail wagging furiously. Wiping a joyful tear away with her apron corner, Mathilde turned to the new comte. "Well, sir, are ye not going to say something to us all, a nice speech maybe?"

Adamo stood up. He looked so tall and strong, yet so calm and happy. His broad face broke into a smile, which touched the hearts of everyone present. Then he bowed and kissed Karay's hand, speaking haltingly. "You will be my comtesse, Karay . . . please?"

The girl's answer was inaudible – she merely nodded once.

The old comte took both their hands in his. "I have watched you both. This is what I was hoping for. As for my other friends, Ben, Dominic and our faithful Ned, I have asked myself what I can do to repay you for restoring Adamo to me. You are not servants – it would be churlish and ill-mannered to offer you money. But I know that you have no parents to care for you. In view of this I have reached a decision. In a few days we will go together on a journey. Toulouse will be our destination. There, at the cathedral, I will consult the bishop, and then I will speak with the justices of my wishes, so that all people will know: I intend to give you both my name, adopting you as my sons. Together you will live here as part of our family. As for you, my dearest Mathilde, you shall become a lady companion of our household. No more cooking and working in kitchens . . ."

Neither Ned nor Ben heard the rest of Vincente Bregon's speech. Like lightning at midnight, the angel's message flooded into their minds, blotting out all else.

"A man who has not children
Will name you as his son.
In that hour you must be gone!
Turn your face back to the sea,
You will meet another one,
A father with no children,
Before you travel on.
Help him to help his children,
As his kinsman would have done."

Ben heard Mathilde's voice as the import of the command hit him. She was interrupting the old comte. "No such thing, sir. I'm not going to sit about with nothing to do for the rest of my days. Cook I am, and cook I stay! No silly young girl is going to take charge of my kitchens. Ben, are you all right, boy? You've gone white as a sheet."

The boy stood up, swaying slightly, his mind in a daze as he made up a suitable reply. "I'll be fine in a moment, thanks. A little too much of your good wine, Mathilde, even though there was water in it. Please, don't fuss, I'll go and take a walk in the fresh air. I'll be all right soon. Ned will come with me."

Dominic, the Facemaker of Sabada, stared into his friend's clouded blue eyes. They were distant and sad. "Ben, do you want me to come with you?"

The boy knew that his friend could see the truth of what was about to happen. Ben shifted his gaze fondly from the old comte, to Mathilde, to Arnela, then from Adamo to Karay, and finally back to Dominic. He blinked a few times. "No, mate, you stay here. I only need Ned to go with me."

Then the boy and his dog left the room.

FOUR DAYS LATER, in the late afternoon, Ben and Ned sat on the dunes, staring out to sea at the Gulf of Gascony. All the tears they could cry had been shed. They had travelled fast, both night and day, stopping only to catch a brief hour's rest here and there when weariness got the better of them. Both boy and dog had pushed themselves hard, not wanting to stay amid dear friends who would eventually grow old and die whilst they remained forever young.

Ned snuffled at his master's hand. "Well, mate, we turned our faces back to the sea, and here we are. Ooh, I am hungry, Ben, so hungry!"

Ben nodded absently as he replied, "What I'm wondering is, where's this other one we've got to meet? Remember the second part of the angel's command:

'Turn your face back to the sea,
You will meet another one,
A father with no children,
Before you travel on.
Help him to help his children,
As his kinsman would have done.' "

Ned's ears flopped as he shook his head from side to side. "Sounds like twaddle to me. Another father with no children, yet we've got to help him to help his children. Huh, and who's this kinsman who would've helped the father with no children, to help his children, eh? Even a dog can't make head nor tail of that little lot!"

Ben did not answer right away. He turned his gaze from the sea to the hilltop where they sat and to the trees behind. "Ned, d'you realize where we are?"

The black Labrador was still trying to solve the angel's riddle. "No, should I? Wait, don't tell me, hmmm, sea, hills, small clump of trees . . . Of course! This is the exact spot where we came ashore from *La Petite Marie*'s jolly boat! Well, there's a thing, we've come full circle!"

Ben was standing up, shading his eyes as he turned back to the sea. Ned looked up at him. "What is it now?"

The boy was already descending the sandy dune top. "A little boat, coming to shore this way. Probably a fisherman. Come on, mate, maybe he's got some spare food with him!"

Ned raced after his master. "Food, you've said the magic word!"

They stood in the shallows as the tiny fishing smack nosed towards them. A man appeared at the bow and flung a line in Ben's direction. He shouted a single word. "Hungry?"

Ben's answer was also brief. "Starving!"

The fellow sprang over the side. He was laughing. "How did I guess? Help me get her ashore above the tide line."

Ned gripped the rope end in his teeth as Ben and the man put the line over their shoulders and hauled. With considerable effort they dragged the boat over the ridged wet sand, through some seaweed and debris, then up onto the dry beach above the tide line. The man was poorly clad, barefoot and had a ragged cloak tied about his neck as protection against long hours facing sea breezes. He shook Ben's hand firmly and patted Ned. "Thank ye, friends. See those trees up yonder? Could you gather some wood for a fire? I've got good, fresh mackerel aboard. Got some bread, and milk, too. We can cook a meal!"

Ben smiled. "You caught the fish, sir, we'll get the wood!" He sped off, with Ned outpacing him and thinking happily, "Bread'n'fish, nothing like it when you're hungry, mate!"

The fisherman even had a frying pan. He gutted and headed the mackerel and tossed them into the pan with some herbs and a chopped onion. As he took off his cloak, he jerked a thumb at the waters of the bay.

"High tide's the best time to net fish around here, though you've got to get the job done before the tide turns – it can run out pretty fast and leave you stranded out there." As he loosed the cloak, Ben saw his white collar and well-worn, threadbare black cassock. A priest!

Ned settled down in the warm sand, thinking, "Haha, a priest. So that's the father who has no children. This is him, Ben!"

The priest handed Ben enough bread for him and his dog. "So, what are you doing on this forsaken stretch of shore?"

Ben tossed half the bread to Ned. "We're just travellers, Father, making our way along the coast to Spain. It isn't too far. Do you live hereabouts?"

The priest tested six mackerel he had put on to fry and turned them over with his knife blade. "Just on the outskirts of Arcachon. I have a little parish. Very small and poor . . . we even meet in my house for services, as the church collapsed many years ago. Sandy foundation, cheap materials, the usual story."

Ben noted the large mass of silver- and black-banded fish in the boat. "You missed your trade, Father, you're a good fisherman to land a haul like that."

The priest nodded ruefully. "My flock and I live as a community, helping one another. Chopard, our fisherman, broke his arm last week, so I elected myself to the job until his arm is mended. They're simple people around here, but good. I call them my children, and, as you know, children must be fed."

The fish tasted good. They sat in silence, attending to the needs of their hunger.

Ned was first to finish. He passed Ben a thought. "Look at the father's face – who does he remind you of?"

Ben scrutinized the man's face. Ned was right, there was something rather familiar about the eyes, the strong jaw, the shape of the nose, those sandy brown whiskers. Almost without thinking, Ben found himself saying, "I was at sea once. I had a friend, he came from where you live, Arcachon."

The father licked his fingers, tossing a fish bone into the fire. "From Arcachon, you say? What was his name? I might know the family. We've had a few from the parish run off to sea."

Ben spoke the name of his dead buccaneer captain. "Raphael Thuron."

In the moment the father's eyes went wide with surprise, Ben found his mind invaded by Ned's urgent pleas.

"Easy, mate, go careful. Watch what you say. Lie if you have to!"

The man grabbed Ben's arm with a hand as heavy as the captain's had been. "Raphael Thuron is my brother . . . would your man be about eight years older than me?"

Ben avoided his new friend's gaze. "Aye, about that, Father.

He looked a lot like you, as I remember. Did your brother run off to sea?"

The good father stared into the fire. "Yes, our parents were poor farmers. They wanted Raphael to become a priest one day, but he was too wild. He was forever getting into scrapes." The father smiled. "And getting me into trouble with him. Raphael was a rogue, but a good brother. Please, tell me what you know about him, how is he doing? Raphael said that if ever he got away from these parts, he'd make a fortune in some far country. I wonder if he did."

As he pondered his answer, Ben passed Ned a message. "This is a good man, it would be wrong to tell him lies. If we're to help him and his children, it's best to tell the truth."

Ned replied, "Right, mate, but don't mention the angel."

Ben gently released his arm from the father's grip. "I have news to tell you, both good and sad, Mattieu."

The priest stared deep into Ben's mysterious blue eyes. "You know my name?"

The boy met his gaze. "Your brother told me of you when I first met him. He was one of the finest men I ever knew." Ben's eyes betrayed what he was holding back.

Turning away, Father Mattieu Thuron watched the receding tide. "Something tells me that you're going to say Raphael is dead!"

There was no way to soften the blow. Ben took a deep breath. "That's my sad duty, Father. Captain Raphael Thuron is dead."

A silence followed, in which the priest's lips moved slowly as he offered up prayers for his brother's soul. Ben and Ned sat quietly watching. Wiping a frayed cuff across his eyes, Father Mattieu turned back to Ben and said a single world. "Captain?"

Ben tossed a twig upon the fire. "Aye, a captain. Would it surprise you to know that he was a buccaneer?"

Ben thought for a moment that the priest was weeping again, but he was chuckling and shaking his head.

"It wouldn't surprise me in the least, my friend. Raphael was always a wild one – I'll wager he made a fine buccaneer."

Ben cheered up, remembering his days aboard *La Petite Marie*. "Cap'n Thuron was the terror of the Caribbean, but let me tell you, we – my name's Ben, that's Ned, my dog – we were proud to serve under your brother."

Lit by a full moon, night crept in as Ben sat by the fire on the shore with Ned and Father Mattieu. He related the full tale, from the tavern in Cartagena to the Gulf of Gascony. The priest's eyes shone with excitement, imagining great adventures of palm-fringed islands, Spanish pirates, privateers and a chase across the boundless ocean.

When he had finished the narrative, Ben took a deep drink from the water canteen, listening to Ned's approval.

"Well told, mate, what a great yarn. I'm glad you never mentioned our angel or anything about Veron and the Razan. It was pretty convincing how you said that we'd been hiding and scavenging about the coastline most of the summer. Couldn't have done better myself!"

Father Mattieu shook the boy's hand warmly. "Thank you, Ben, I can tell that you liked Raphael a great deal. I will grieve and pray for him. Thank heaven he was not captured and executed like a common criminal. He died like a true captain, going down with his beloved ship. But what a man my brother was, eh? The places he saw, the adventures he had – I almost wish I'd sailed with him. Raphael packed more into one lifetime than most men do into ten! But I have my little parish to look after, my poor children to attend to . . ." Whilst the good father chatted on aimlessly, Ben noticed an odd change in his view of the bay.

Ned suddenly stood up alert. "Ben, listen, the angel!"

The boy heard the heavenly being speaking a line of the poem: "You must help him help his children. Behold!"

Both Ben and Ned felt their eyes drawn to one spot.

The tide had ebbed fully, leaving a long stretch of beach and shallow offshore water. A cloud floating alone in the clear night sky obscured the moon. However, there was a hole in the centre of the cloud, which allowed the moonlight to shine downwards in one pale shaft of silver light. Right from the skies to the bay's surface it went, spotlighting a small circle of water.

Again the angel spoke: "You must help him to help his children. Behold!"

Ned was tugging the rope at the prow of the fishing boat. Ben sprang to his feet, shouting at the priest, "Come quickly, Father, we need your help with the boat!"

The priest arose and grabbed the rope with Ned and Ben. "What is it, Ben, what do you need the boat for?"

The boy bent his shoulder as he heaved the craft forward. "Save your breath, Father! Just get it to the water and trust me. There's no time to argue!"

It was a long hard haul over the wet beach to the water's edge. Panting and blowing, the two strained at the rope, dragging the fishing smack behind. Ben kept his eyes firmly on the sphere of light, blinking away the sweat that ran smartingly down to blur his gaze. Even when they reached the water, the boat's keel still scraped on the sand. It came free as they waded in knee-deep. Ben heaved Ned aboard as the priest gathered up his sopping cassock and scrambled in amongst the slithering mackerel. "Where to now, Ben?"

The boy pointed at the thin column of moonlight. "Straight ahead, see the patch of light on the water? There!"

Before they actually reached the spot, Ned sighted a nub of timber poking up above the surface. Barking wildly, he threw a thought to Ben. "It's the little mast of the *Marie*'s jolly boat!"

Ben lay in the bow, paddling furiously with both hands until he got hold of the mast. "Father, come here. Hold on to this and don't let go whatever you do!"

Father Mattieu obeyed promptly, seizing the timber as though his life depended on it. Ben took the bow rope and knotted it about his waist, then plunged into the dark waters, gasping with shock as his head struck the jolly boat's keel. It was sitting squarely on the seabed. He felt about swiftly. This pointed bit was the bows. Pulling himself along, he found the stern. His shin barked against the after-end seat. He felt for the sailcloth wrapping and pulled it aside. There it was in a big canvas bag – Captain Raphael Thuron's fortune in gold!

Bubbles started streaming from between Ben's lips, as he desperately tried to hold his breath in. Loosing the rope from his waist, he tied it in a hasty noose. The boy's head pounded unmercifully as he strained to lift the bag of gold. It moved just enough for him to sweep the noose underneath and pull tight. Ben shot to the surface, spluttering and spitting seawater. The priest relinquished his hold on the mast and helped the boy climb awkwardly into the boat.

Ned danced around his master. "You've got it, you've got it! Er, have you, mate?"

Ben burst into laughter, shouting aloud, "I've got it, I've got the gold!"

Between them, Ben and the father heaved the canvas bag up, until it was suspended underwater. Ben lashed the rope securely around the fishing smack's mast. The weight of the gold made the little vessel lean over crazily as they took it into the shallower waters. Ned watched as they both jumped over the side, landing waist-deep in the sea. Father Mattieu sang out as they each gripped an end of the sack: "Up she comes, Ben, right. One . . . two . . . threeeeee!"

A dull clink of wet coins sounded as the bag landed amongst the priest's catch of mackerel.

More wood was added to the fire. Ben drank fresh water to rid his mouth of the acrid salt taste. Ned flicked away a spark with his paw, chuckling mentally.

"Hoho, look at the father. I don't suppose he's ever seen more than two gold coins together in his life. Haha, and I'll bet that those two belonged to somebody else!"

Firelight flickered off the shiny coins as they trickled through the priest's fingers. His eyes were as wide as organ stops. "All this gold, Ben, there's a vast fortune here. D'you realize, we're rich, friend, we're rich!"

Ben shook his head. "No, friend, *you're* rich. That gold is your brother's last gift to you. What'll you do with it?"

Father Mattieu shuddered with delight as he stuffed handfuls of gold coins back into the canvas bag. "A church, I'll build a lovely church, with pews, bells, steeple, altar. I'll call it Saint Raphael's!"

Ben smiled. "I'm sure the Lord won't mind."

The father lay flat on his back, stretching his arms wide. "A farm, too, with cows, pigs, chickens, sheep, fields and crops. Around the farm we'll have cottages for my parishioners, my children. The church will stand in the centre of the farm . . . But listen to me, planning to do this and that. You must share this golden fortune with me, Ben. It would still be lying on the bottom of the sea if it weren't for you!"

The boy refused flatly. "No, Father, Ned and I don't need gold. I won't touch a single piece of it. I told your brother I wouldn't, and I must keep that promise in memory of him."

Ned passed his master a rueful plea. "Couldn't we just keep a few coins, say enough to buy us a week or two of good meals?"

Ben's reply brooked no argument. "The angel never meant us to have any. The answer's no, mate. Father Mattieu can make better use of it than we ever would."

The father took Ben's hand. "If you won't take some gold, then what can I do to help you? Would you like to come and live in my new parish with me? Anything."

Ben clasped his friend's hand warmly. "There are reasons why I can't stay anywhere too long. Besides, I'm a wanted person, a buccaneer, that's why I was planning on escaping to Spain. Now if Ned and I only had a boat . . ."

Father Mattieu cleaned his frying pan in the sand and placed it in the fishing smack along with his other belongings and some bread, herbs and onions. He handed the bow rope to Ned, who took it in his jaws.

"Take this boat. There's food, water and fish to go with it. Take it, both of you, and take my blessing with you!"

With its one small square-rigged sail spread, Ben steered the fishing smack out into the sea when the tide rolled in an hour before dawn. Both he and Ned looked back at Father Mattieu Thuron standing waist-deep in the water, arms spread wide as he called out to them. "May the good Lord bless you for what you have done for me and my children. Go now, my friends, and may the angels watch over you both!"

Ben passed Ned a fleeting thought. "Well, at least one of them will!"

Ben pulled the tiller, sending the little craft towards the Spanish mainland. From out of the east, rosy hues of dawn seeped out into the Bay of Biscay. Looking back, Ben and Ned watched Father Mattieu wading ashore, the bearer of good fortune returning to his parish. The strange boy from the sea and his faithful dog turned their faces to the new day and the perils of the unknown.

Ben felt Ned's thoughts. "Where we are bound, mate, only heaven knows."

The boy pressed his cheek against the black Labrador's soft fur. "I don't care, as long as we're together, Ned."

Soon the fishing smack was naught but a tiny dot on the face of the world's great and mysterious waters.

t is said that in the big house of Adamo Bregon, Comte de Veron, a picture hangs on the wall of the dining hall. This fascinating and beautiful artwork is greatly admired by all who see it. Within a gilt-embossed frame a boy stands with a black Labrador dog sitting by his side. The dog looks gentle and intelligent, its soft dark eyes friendly. An animal that anyone would be proud to own. The boy is poorly clad in the manner of one who follows the sea. Barefoot, with frayed and worn canvas breeches and a tattered calico shirt. His unruly tow-coloured hair is ruffled by the breeze. But it is the lad's clouded blue eyes that draw the onlooker closer. No matter where you stand in that room, those strange eyes are looking straight at you. The boy is leaning on some rocks, with cold mountainous seas heaving behind him. Lightning rips through a storm-battered sky. In one corner, riding the wild waves, is a dim depiction of an unmanned sailing ship, its rigging illuminated by the eerie green light of St Elmo's fire. Many visitors ask why the picture was not painted in a rural landscape with the mountains as a background. After all, Veron is many leagues from the sea. The artist will only say that he saw the picture in the eyes of the boy, who was once as close to him as a brother. If you saw the eyes for yourself, you would readily believe him. In the lower right-hand corner of the picture, the artist has signed his name.

Dominic de la Sabada Bregon